Praise for The Night Stalkers series

"The Night Stalkers series just keeps getting better and better! Buchman might just be at the top of the game in terms of relationship development."

—*RT Book Reviews* on *Light Up the Night*

"A thrilling, passionate story in which love sparks in the midst of helicopter warfare."

—*Barnes and Noble Review* on *Take Over at Midnight*, a Barnes and Noble Best Romance of 2013

"It was delightful to become immersed in this exciting and dangerous world. Exceptional."

—*Night Owl Reviews* on *Wait Until Dark*, a Reviewer Top Pick

"Every scene from this exceptional book had me trying to recapture my breath and afterwards left me craving for more!"

—*Romancing the Book* on *I Own the Dawn*

"Buchman's hard-to-put-down novel, with its nonstop action, surprise villain, and story of forbidden love, will be a real treat for fans of military romantic suspense."

—*Booklist* Starred Review for *The Night Is Mine*

Also by M.L. Buchman

The Night Stalkers

The Night Is Mine
I Own the Dawn
Wait Until Dark
Take Over at Midnight
Light Up the Night

The Firehawks

Pure Heat
Full Blaze

BRING ON THE *Dusk*

THE NIGHT STALKERS

M.L. BUCHMAN

Published by Sourcebooks Casablanca, an imprint of Sourcebooks, Inc.
P.O. Box 4410, Naperville, Illinois 60567-4410
(630) 961-3900
Fax: (630) 961-2168
www.sourcebooks.com

Printed and bound in Canada.
MBP 10 9 8 7 6 5 4 3 2 1

Chapter 1

There were few times that Colonel Michael Gibson of Delta Force appreciated the near-psychotic level of commitment displayed by terrorists, but this was one of those times. If they hadn't been so rigid in even their attire, his disguise would have been much more difficult.

The al-Qaeda terrorist training camp deep in the Yemeni desert required that all of their hundred new trainees dress in white with black headdresses that left only the eyes exposed. The thirty-four trainers were dressed similarly but wholly in black, making them easy to distinguish. They were also the only ones armed, which was a definite advantage.

The camp's dress code made for a perfect cover. The four men of his team wore loose-fitting black robes like the trainers. Lieutenant Bill Bruce used dark contacts to hide his blue eyes, and they all had rubbed a dye onto their hands and wrists, the only other uncovered portion of their bodies.

Michael and his team had parachuted into the deep desert the night before and traveled a quick ten kilometers on foot before burying themselves in the sand along the edges of the main training grounds. Only their faces were exposed, each carefully hidden by a thorn bush.

The midday temperatures had easily blown through 110 degrees. It felt twice that inside the heavy clothing and lying under a foot of hot sand, but uncomfortable was a way of life in "The Unit," as Delta Force called itself, so this was of little concern. They'd dug deep enough so that they weren't simply roasted alive, even if it felt that way by the end of the motionless day.

It was three minutes to sunset, three minutes until the start of Maghrib, the fourth scheduled prayer of the five that were performed daily.

At the instant of sunset, the muezzin began chanting *adhan*, the call to prayer.

Thinking themselves secure in the deep desert of the Abyan province of southern Yemen, every one of the trainees and the trainers knelt and faced northwest toward Mecca.

After fourteen motionless hours—fewer than a dozen steps from a hundred and thirty terrorists—moving smoothly and naturally was a challenge as Michael rose from his hiding place. He shook off the sand and swung his AK-47 into a comfortable position. The four of them approached the prostrate group in staggered formation from the southeast over a small hillock.

The Delta operators interspersed themselves among the other trainers and knelt, blending in perfectly. Of necessity, they all spoke enough Arabic to pass if questioned.

Michael didn't check the others because that might draw attention. If they hadn't made it cleanly into place, an alarm would have been raised and the plan would have changed drastically. All was quiet, so he listened to the muezzin's words and allowed himself to settle into the peace of the prayer.

Bismi-llāhi r-raḥmāni r-raḥīm…

In the name of Allah, the most compassionate, the most merciful…

He sank into the rhythm and meaning of it—not as these terrorists twisted it in the name of murder and warfare, but as it was actually stated. Moments like this one drove home the irony of his long career to become the most senior field operative in Delta while finding an inner quiet in the moment before dealing death.

Perhaps in their religious fervor, the terrorists found the same experience. But what they lacked was flexibility. They wound themselves up to throw away their lives, if necessary, to complete their preprogrammed actions exactly as planned.

For Michael, an essential centering in self allowed perfect adaptability when situations went kinetic—Delta's word for the shit unexpectedly hitting the fan.

That was Delta's absolute specialty.

Starting with zero preconceptions in either energy or strategy allowed for the perfect action that fit each moment in a rapidly changing scenario. Among the team, they'd joke sometimes about how Zen, if not so Buddhist, the moment before battle was.

And, as always, he accepted the irony of that with no more than a brief smile at life's whimsy.

Dealing death was one significant part of what The Unit did.

U.S. SFOD-D, Special Forces Operational Detachment-Delta, went where no other fighting force could go and did what no one else could do.

Today, it was a Yemeni terrorist training camp.

Tomorrow would take care of itself.

They were the U.S. Army's Tier One asset and

no one, except their targets, would ever know they'd been here. One thing for certain, had The Unit been unleashed on bin Laden, not a soul outside the command structure would know who'd been there. SEAL Team Six had done a top-notch job, but talking about it wasn't something a Delta operator did. But Joint Special Operations Command's leader at the time was a former STS member, so the SEALs had gone in instead.

Three more minutes of prayer.

Then seven minutes to help move the trainees into their quarters where they would be locked in under guard for the night, as they were still the unknowns.

Or so the trainers thought.

Three more minutes to move across the compound through the abrupt fall of darkness in the equatorial desert to where the commanders would meet for their evening meal and evaluation of the trainees.

After that the night would get interesting.

Bismi-llāhi r-raḥmāni r-raḥīm…

In the name of Allah, the most compassionate, the most merciful…

Captain Claudia Jean Casperson of the U.S. Army's 160th Special Operations Aviation Regiment—commonly known as the Night Stalkers—finally arrived at the aircraft carrier in the Gulf of Aden after two full days in transit from Fort Campbell, Kentucky.

The Gulf of Aden ran a hundred miles wide and five hundred long between Somalia in Africa and Yemen on the southern edge of the Arabian Peninsula. The Gulf connected the Suez Canal and the Red Sea at one end to the Indian Ocean on the other, making it perhaps the single busiest and most hazardous stretch of water on the planet.

Claudia tried to straighten her spine after she climbed off the C-2 Greyhound twin-engine cargo plane. It was the workhorse of carrier onboard delivery and, from the passenger's point of view, the loudest plane ever designed. If not, it certainly felt that way. Shaking her head didn't clear the buzz of the twin Allison T56 engines from either her ears or the pounding of the two big eight-bladed propellers from her body.

A deckhand clad in green, which identified him as a helicopter specialist, met her before she was three steps off the rear ramp. He took her duffel without a word and started walking away, the Navy's way of saying, "Follow me." She resettled her rucksack across her shoulders and followed like a one-woman jet fighter taxiing along after her own personal ground guidance truck.

Rather than leading her to quarters, the deckhand took her straight to an MH-6M Little Bird helicopter perched on the edge of the carrier's vast deck. That absolutely worked for her. As soon as they had her gear stowed in the tiny back compartment, he turned to her and handed her a slip of paper.

"This is the current location, contact frequency, and today's code word for landing authorization for your ship. They need this bird returned today and you just arrived, so that works out. It's fully fueled. They're expecting you." He rattled off the tower frequency for the carrier's air traffic control tower, saluted, and left her to prep her aircraft before she could salute back.

Thanks for the warm welcome to the theater of operations.

This wasn't a war zone. But it wasn't far from one either, she reminded herself. Would saying, "Hi," have killed him? That almost evoked a laugh; she hadn't exactly been chatty herself. Word count for the day so far: one, saying thanks to the C-2 crewman who'd rousted her from a bare doze just thirty seconds before landing.

The first thing she did was get into her full kit. She pulled her flight suit on over her clothes, tucking her long blond hair down her back inside the suit. Full armor brought the suit to about thirty pounds. She shrugged on a Dragon Skin vest that she'd purchased herself to give double protection over her torso. Over that, her SARVSO survival vest and finally her FN-SCAR rifle across her chest and her helmet on her head. Total gear about fifty pounds. As familiar as a second skin; she always felt a little exposed without it.

Babe in armor.

Who would have thought a girl from nowhere Arizona would be standing on an aircraft carrier off the Arabian Peninsula in full fighter gear?

If anyone were to ask, she'd tell them it totally rocked. Actually, she'd shrug and acknowledge that she was proud to be here...but she'd be busy thinking that it totally rocked.

The Little Bird was the smallest helicopter in any division of the U.S. military, and that made most people underestimate it. Not Claudia. She loved the Little Bird. It was a tough and sassy craft with a surprising amount of power for its small size. The helo also operated far more independently than any other aircraft in the inventory and, to Claudia's way of thinking, that made the Little Bird near perfect.

The tiny helo seated two up front and didn't have any doors, so the wide opening offered the pilot an excellent field of view. The fact that it also offered the enemy a wide field of fire is why Claudia wore the secondary Dragon Skin vest. The helicopter could seat two in back if they were desperate—the space was small enough that Claudia's ruck and duffel filled much of it. On the attack version, the rear space would be filled with cans of ammunition.

In Special Operations Forces, the action teams rode on the outside of Little Birds. This one was rigged with a bench seat along either side that could fold down to transport three combat soldiers on either side.

Claudia wanted an attack bird, not a transport, but she'd fight that fight once she reached her assigned company. For now she was simply glad to be a pilot who'd been deemed "mission ready" for the 160th SOAR.

She went through the preflight, found the bird as clean as every other Night Stalker craft, and powered up for the flight. Less than a hundred miles, so she'd be there in forty minutes. Maybe then she could sleep.

As the rapid onset of full dark in the desert swept over the Yemeni desert, Michael and Bill moved up behind the main building that was used by the terrorist camp's training staff. It was a one-story, six-room structure. Concrete slab, cinder-block walls, metal roof. Doors front and back. The heavy-metal rear one was locked, but they had no intention of using it anyway.

The intel from the MQ-1C Gray Eagle drone that the Night Stalkers' intel staff had kept circling twenty thousand feet overhead for the last three nights had indicated that four command-level personnel met here each night. Most likely position was in the southeast corner room. Four of the other rooms were barrack spaces that wouldn't be used until after the trainers had all eaten together at the chow tent. The sixth room was the armory.

Dry bread and water had been the fare for the trainees. Over the next few months they would be desensitized to physical discomfort much as a Delta operator was. Too little food, too little sleep, and too much exercise, especially early on, to weed out the weak or uncommitted.

He and Bill squatted beneath the southeast window that faced away from the center of the camp; only the vast, dark desert lay beyond. Shifting the AK-47s over their shoulders, they unslung their preferred weapons—Heckler & Koch HK416 carbine rifles with flash suppressors that made them nearly silent.

Bill pulled out a small fiber-optic camera and slipped it up over the windowsill. As they squatted out of sight, the small screen gave them a view of the inside of the target building for the first time.

Not four men but eight were seated on cushions around a low table bearing a large teapot. Michael recognized five from various briefings, three of them Tier One targets. They'd only been expecting one Tier One.

A long table sported a half-dozen laptops, and a pair of file cabinets stood at one end. They hadn't counted on that at all. This was supposed to be a training camp, not an operations center.

They were going to need more help to take advantage of the new situation.

Michael got on the radio.

"USS *Peleliu*. This is Captain Casperson in Little Bird..." She didn't know the name of the bird. She read off the tail number from the small plate on the control panel. "Inbound from eighty miles at two-niner-zero."

You didn't want to sneak up on a ship of war that could shoot you down at this distance if they were in a grouchy mood.

"Roger that, Captain. Status?"

"Flying solo, full fuel."

"In your armor?"

"Roger that." Why in the world would they... Training. They'd want to make sure she wasn't ignoring her training. Kid stuff. She'd flown Cobra attack birds for the U.S. Marines for six years before her transfer and spent two more years training with the Night Stalkers. She wasn't an—

"This is Air Mission Commander Archie Stevens." A different voice came on the air. "Turn immediate heading three-four-zero. Altitude five-zero feet, all speed. You'll be joining a flight ten miles ahead of you for an exfil. We can't afford to slow them down until you make contact, so hustle."

She slammed over the cyclic control in her right hand to shift to the new heading.

Okay, maybe not so much a training test.

Exfil. Exfiltration. A ground team needed to be pulled out and pulled out now. She'd done it in a hundred drills, so she kept calm and hoped that her voice sounded that way. She expected that it didn't.

"Uh, Roger." Claudia had dozed fitfully for six hours in the last three days, and most of that had been in a vibrator seat on the roaring C-2 Greyhound. No rest for the weary.

Once on the right heading, she dove into the night heading for fifty feet above the ocean waves and opened up the throttles to the edge of the never-exceed speed of a hundred and seventy-five miles per hour.

The adrenaline had her wide-awake before she reached her flight level.

Fifteen minutes later, Claudia rolled up behind a flight of three birds moments before they crossed over the beach and into Yemen. The FLIR night-vision gear painted an image across the inside of her helmet's visor of two Little Birds and a Black Hawk.

No, it wasn't a Black Hawk, it was a DAP—a Direct Action Penetrator, the nastiest gunship ever launched into the sky.

Well, weren't they going to have some fun tonight.

One of the Little Birds was the attack version; that's the one she wanted. The other was a transport like the one she was flying.

Odd. Neither the DAP nor the attack Little Bird showed up on her radar as more than signal noise, though the transport Little Bird did. It was as if they weren't there, but she could see them. No time to think about it now.

"Captain Casperson"—a female voice—"take right

flank off *Merchant*. You'll be taking the southeast corner of a one-story building. *Merchant*, you'll take the team from off the northwest. *May*, expect the LZ to be hot, especially near *Merchant*, so be ready to suppress it hard."

Merchant was obviously the other transport Little Bird, so she moved up into formation beside it. The pilot waggled his bird side to side to wave hello. She answered in kind. Nice to be welcome despite being the late arrival to the party.

Whoever was giving the orders was pilot in command, not the remote Air Mission Controller. The only female DAP pilot she knew of was Chief Warrant Lola Maloney. There were only five women in SOAR, but Claudia hadn't tried to keep track of them. Actually, she'd purposely tried not to. They were in combat and she'd been in training, so by ignoring them, she'd felt freer to simply drive herself to be the very best. She was used to making her own way, had been doing it since she was a little kid.

Still, now that she'd made it, it might be nice to have another woman in the same company she was going to.

She hadn't really thought about that.

Claudia was only the sixth woman of SOAR, fifth now that Major Emily Beale had retired. She'd applied for the 5th Battalion, D Company, because even in a regiment as elite as SOAR, the 5D was rumored to be the very best. That was her kind of team. That she'd actually landed the assignment was a little daunting. Well, she'd have to prove she was up to it in the next ten minutes.

They crossed over the beach, dropped down to

twenty-five feet, and began following the ups and downs of the dry, rolling terrain. No need to talk; it was just what you did.

~

The moment that Michael heard the faintest beat of an approaching helicopter, he whispered into his radio the same word he'd spoken twenty-four hours ago when they'd jumped out of an airplane at thirty-five thousand feet.

"Go."

They had less than sixty seconds; it was all they should need.

He and Bill rose.

His first silenced shot punched a hole through the window glass. The second took out the overhead lamp, plunging the southeast room into darkness. They dove through the window in unison as they pulled on their night-vision goggles.

There was the low boom of a breaching charge removing the building's front door—must have been locked. Patrols would have left no time to pick it. The other two operators were tasked with clearing the remaining five rooms and securing the front of the building.

The soft double-spit of suppressed gunfire coming down the hallway said that at least one person had been elsewhere inside the building. They were dead now.

Michael managed to kick six of the rifles aside before the al-Qaeda leaders could react. Bill, who was standing back to give him cover, shot the seventh in the arm and the eighth in the head, twice. Abu Nassir Wafi, a lead trainer, was down. He was the toughest fighter and the least important asset in the room. The double tap to the head was a good choice.

After a brief scuffle, they had the seven remaining men gagged, with zip ties around their wrists and ankles. They lifted and threw each tied man back out through the window. Some grunted through their gags as they landed atop one another.

Bill pulled a short roll of heavily reinforced black garbage bags out of a pouch along his pants' calf—a trick that the SEALs hadn't learned before the bin Laden raid. Word was that they'd wasted valuable time scrounging old gym bags to cart out the intel they'd found inside Osama's fortress. He and Bill began dumping laptops and files into the bags.

The birds were close overhead. He could hear the helicopters' rotor roar drowning out the near-constant fire from the front of the building, the quiet double spit of the Delta operators' HK416s echoing down the hall, and the sharp barks of AK-47s wielded by the terrorist trainers out in the compound.

"All evac on southeast side," he told the helos. He didn't need to tell the other two operators to fall back to join them in the southeast room. They'd know to do that as soon as they were ready.

He emptied the last file drawer and tossed the sack on top of the struggling al-Qaeda leaders.

He and Bill jumped over the sill, not taking much care about who they landed on.

The other two operators followed them out, just moments before a large detonation shook the building and blew fire out the window inches above their heads.

The inside team had left a booby trap in the weapons'

store. The building was now secure—the entire inside was engulfed in flames.

~

The landing zone was a total shit storm, just like a typical training scenario except this time the bad guys were trying to kill the good guys with live rounds.

The air was thick with the hail of small-arms fire as Claudia swung her helo wide to clear the streamers of fire that punched out the windows of the building to all sides. She settled as close as she dared beside the southeast wall of the building.

Merchant threw up a world of dust as it dropped in beside her.

Two men came running toward them, but she could see the small infrared patches on their shoulders that identified them as friendlies so she kept her hands on the controls rather than grabbing for her weapon. They were also each carrying large heavy sacks. The bigger guy—and he was way big and broad-shouldered—headed for *Merchant*.

The smaller man tossed his bag on top of her own gear in the rear and returned to the group of bound men on the ground.

Two more friendlies moved to squat at the corners of the building and were laying down cover fire against anyone who tried to circle around the building to the helicopters. Anyone remaining out in the compound had the two gun platforms circling above to keep them occupied.

There was the harsh roar of a minigun sluicing down five thousand rounds a minute, interrupted by the harsh sizzle of rockets and matching explosions just moments later.

For now, they were in a quiet bubble behind the shield of the building, but it would only last another few seconds.

Claudia let go of the controls and took up her weapon to guard for approaches over the desert.

The big guy-little guy team moved to cut the prisoners' feet loose in pairs. They hustled their prisoners onto *Merchant*'s bench seats, tied them in place, and shot each with a tranquilizer injection into their necks. In moments, they had four tied and slumped bad guys on *Merchant*'s benches. The two friendlies who'd been working guard at the corners of the building clambered onto *Merchant* and the bird dusted off. The two soldiers continued providing cover from their positions aloft.

The other two soldiers started her way, herding the last three prisoners.

On a quick sweep, she spotted a figure running toward them over a low dune beyond the camp.

No "friendly" infrared tags on the man's shoulder, and his weapon was up. She popped the safety and unleashed a three-shot burst. He cried out and fell to the ground.

By the time she turned back, they had the prisoners tied on and drugged out. The big guy sat on an outside bench and the smaller one slipped into her empty copilot seat.

At his nod, she grabbed the controls and was out of there, staying low and racing directly away from the gun battle still roaring across the compound, the two attack helos and the armed terrorists going at one another.

Claudia knew it would be a very one-sided battle. There was a reason that "Death Waits in the Dark" was one of the Night Stalkers' mottoes.

She crested a dune and spotted an outlier guard in her infrared night vision. Someone lying on the back of the dune face, spread-eagled and holding a weapon.

"Shooter!" she called out. She needed both hands on the controls, and this wasn't a gunship; she had no weapon other than the one hanging across her chest.

Even as she spun to give the man in the copilot's seat a better angle, he twisted in his seat and fired downward through the open door—two shots so close together that they almost sounded like one.

The man turned back, not even bothering to watch the results of his effort.

Though they were already moving at over fifty miles per hour, Claudia could see the bad guy on the ground convulse. His shot went wild and a rocket-propelled grenade blew up the face of a dune.

Damn, she didn't know anyone could really shoot like that. She was good, but that shot was insane.

Not wanting to hang around and see who else was lurking in the dunes, she rolled right to cut the shortest route back to the coast and laid down the hammer. Right at redline on the engine RPMs, she was outta there. Behind her she could see the bright flashes of the DAP Hawk and the attack Little Bird tearing up the camp. *Merchant* was just two rotor diameters off her port side.

Ripples of adrenaline raced through her body like shock waves from a bomb blast. Her old Marine SuperCobra was a pure attack helicopter. She'd flown plenty of protection runs during an exfiltration, but she'd never flown transport right down in the thick of it. It was a whole different up-close-and-personal kind of ride that still had her heart pounding and her breath running short.

The man beside her didn't say a word. He simply sat back with his rifle laid across his chest.

He kept his hands lightly on the weapon but closed his eyes as if he was perfectly comfortable and not just thirty seconds from a life-or-death mission. He'd been the one actually in the battle, and she was the one being wound all the way up.

He began tapping the back of his helmet lightly against the back of his seat. It wasn't frantic, like nerves. It was slow, almost gentle; a stark contrast to the shooter of a moment before.

"You okay?"

"Sure." He kept up the tapping.

She found herself echoing the rhythm with one finger tapping against the cyclic control in her right hand.

"IMF," he added softly.

IMF? I am fine. Probably. Everything in the military was an acronym, and some made as little sense as that.

Though the IMF was also the Impossible Missions Force—the secret branch of the military in the *Mission Impossible* movies—and Delta specialized in impossible missions just like the one falling rapidly behind them.

"You and Tom Cruise." She kept her tone neutral. "Just fine."

He stopped his tapping and turned to stare at her.

She ignored his searching attention.

In the exchange, she'd found his quiet rhythm. It was…the way an evening breeze might move through the Sonoran Desert of her youth in Arizona. *Tap. Pause. Tap. Pause. Tap.* Gods, she could feel the harshest layers of the adrenaline draining slowly out of her system. *Tap. Pause. Tap.*

Time, which had been compressed out of all recognition, began to have meaning again.

Her heart rate had returned to normal by the time she crossed a final berm and was once again "feet wet" over the ocean. She climbed back up to fifty feet and trailed *Merchant*. The other two aircraft, finished with the camp, were formed up behind them. Now she could finally spare the attention to look at her companion clearly for the first time.

He'd finally turned back to watch forward. He seemed small only when compared to the big soldier who'd been with him and was perched on one of the outside benches. Sitting next to her, he looked to be her height, perhaps another inch or two taller.

MICH helmet, not a lot of heavy armor like she wore, and enough ammo to suppress a midsized city.

Four guys attacking an entire terrorist camp at sunset. Coming away with seven hostages and what she assumed were large sacks of intel.

Only one group was that bug-shit crazy. She'd never flown with them, only knew them by myth and rumor. In eight years of service, Claudia couldn't be sure if she'd ever even met one of them before.

Delta.

Scary bastards, making her damned glad they were on her side.

Still, Claudia made it a personal policy to steer well clear of scary bastards who were bug-shit crazy.

A policy she had no intention of changing.

Michael registered many things about his pilot.

Female by her voice.

She flew well, with a smoothness that he liked, as if she knew exactly who she was and where she was going. It was a trait they looked for in Delta operators; only the very best had it. And no one but the very best made the Delta grade.

There was nothing to see. Flight suit, armor, and vest. Flight gloves, full helmet with projection visor, and even her lower face covered with a breathing mask and radio mike that let pilots breathe and be heard in even the dustiest and noisiest environments.

But he couldn't stop glancing over.

No one got his jokes. The few who noticed them go by did so only after painfully long pauses. Most wouldn't even get that IMF could be "I'm fine." But to make the jump to *Mission Impossible* and then answer with the next step beyond that he hadn't even seen himself—the name of the character he would be parallel to… Damn! That impressed him almost as much as anything else she'd done in their brief acquaintance.

He'd heard another female pilot was incoming into SOAR's 5th Battalion, D Company, so this must be her. Making it into the 5D said she was already an exceptional pilot. She hadn't harassed him about his tapping thing; just checked in with him and then moved on, which said she knew to trust a soldier's self-assessment. For some reason, his tapping drove a lot of people nuts.

It wasn't like the jittery leg that so many soldiers had, though that was trained out of Deltas. Actually, not all that many guys with those kinds of nerves made it into Delta to begin with.

The gentle tap, tap was how he let the adrenal rush of action run out of him. The gentle rhythm reminded him of climbing trees in his childhood when he'd been seeking somewhere no one else could go. It wasn't escape; it was going higher and farther than anyone before him that charged him up.

Right now he shouldn't be thinking about her; he should be assessing the team's performance. What could they have done differently to capture all eight unfriendlies? How could they have anticipated the arrival at the camp of four Tier One targets or the presence of so much unexpected intel? If there'd been anything to gather in the other rooms, there simply hadn't been time to look. They definitely should have had another bird in deep backup; pure luck they'd gotten this one. The entire camp had erupted in blazes of gunfire from the trainers, answered by the dragon roars from the hovering attack platforms responding with rockets and miniguns.

But that didn't reorient the direction of his thoughts.

This pilot simply allowed him "to be," which he appreciated. Even Emily Beale, as well as they'd gotten along, had never understood his little jokes. Or quite known what to make of him.

Not surprising, Michael. You're not the most accessible dude in the Force.

That he knew for damn sure.

He liked this woman sight unseen.

He also knew that, which was surprising.

The prisoners' knockout shots wore off as they arrived on deck at the USS *Peleliu*, making the unloading a little chaotic. Michael was on the verge of dosing them again when the CIA team arrived from the carrier to take custody. He sighed; they sure did love their debriefings. It would take the next four hours to cover a sixty-second actual engagement. About normal.

Then he'd noticed the new pilot, still sitting in her Little Bird. No, sagging in her seat.

He touched her on the arm and she startled.

"When was the last time you slept?" He slid up her visor and removed her breather mask. She had a nice face that he decided fit her well, even though he knew almost nothing about her.

"Uh"—she blinked at him—"last time I what?"

"Okay." He'd certainly seen this enough times. She'd held it together for the flight but was wholly tapped out now that it was over. It took four, perhaps five, days without a full sleep—depending on the person and the number of catnaps they'd managed to steal—to make them like this.

Michael unbuckled her harness and eased her out of the helo, taking most of her weight by lifting the big D-ring attached at the center of her vest. The D-ring was there in case she crashed in somewhere and needed a rope rescue. Well, this was a type of rescue, and the heavy vest and flight suit blocked most of the feeling of grabbing her right between the breasts.

He leaned her against the side of the helo, tugged on

her rucksack after letting out the straps a bit, and slung her duffel over one arm.

One of the CIA guys was hustling over to drag him off for debriefing.

"I'll be right back."

The guy got all officious. Right until he spotted the look in Michael's eye and scurried back to wherever he'd been.

Michael had thought to coax her along, but she was really past that.

He slipped an arm around her waist and guided her down through the ship. Flight deck…hangar deck… down to second deck. He stopped a Navy orderly who knew where to aim them.

Her bunk was right near the other SOAR women, which made sense.

When he got her there, she simply stood in the middle of her quarters, weaving and staring down at the bunk.

Michael dumped her duffel and pack.

Since she was clearly unable to manage for herself, he undid her helmet and pulled it free. Then the fire-resistant inner hood. A shower of shining blond hair cascaded over his hands, reminding him of silk and water.

Her FN-SCAR rifle, survival vest, and Dragon Skin underneath. Smart woman.

He was not about to undo the front of her flight suit as he had no way of knowing what she did or didn't wear under there, and she was already giving him trouble.

He never had problems concentrating around women. But something about this one…

Even exhausted, travel-worn, and battle weary she smelled of the desert night and—

Cut it, Michael.

So he did. "You okay from here?"

She nodded vaguely, which he'd take as a yes.

He was a step from making good his retreat when her hand rested lightly on his arm.

Turning to face her was the big mistake.

She stepped into his arms and wrapped her arms around his neck for a moment, ignoring all the spare magazines pocketed across his chest, the two rifles over his shoulder, and both of his sidearms. She simply rested her head on his shoulder a moment and whispered, "Thanks."

Then she turned away and, knees buckling, collapsed face-first onto the bed.

When she didn't move, he turned out the light and closed the door—not even pausing to remove her boots, shutting himself away from her.

Then he hurried off to lose himself in the clutching grasp of the CIA debriefing team.

Better that than to face his thoughts about her warmth and the soft hair that had brushed his cheek and the gentle, female scent of the most attractive woman he'd ever held in his arms, no matter how briefly.

Chapter 2

MICHAEL ROLLED OUT OF HIS BUNK AND GAVE "THE man" his morning hundreds. First, through his hundred fingertip push-ups, he listened to the sounds of the ship. All quiet. The USS *Peleliu* flight operations were generally quiet through the day now.

He would not think of last night or the way she—

He did an extra fifty push-ups.

Maybe there'd at least be time to learn the pilot's name.

An extra twenty-five.

It was supposed to be a quiet day after all.

Not so long ago, the *Peleliu* had seen night and day operations. They were stationed off the coast of Somalia watching for pirates. Last summer the schedule had been very hectic with a brutal operational tempo. Every night had been spent doing ocean sweeps to catch the small Somali raider craft heading for the shipping lanes. During the day they seemed to constantly be rushing to the rescue of ships under attack. A half-dozen other warships from various nations plied these waters, but they were spread over two million square miles of ocean along fifteen hundred miles of coast.

Now it was March. Six months after their focused strike retaking all of the northern ships and hostages in a single night, the Somali pirates had mostly folded up shop—at least in the north.

The pirates' four main leaders were dead, two from in-fighting and two killed by Delta Force. Lieutenant Bill Bruce was a D-boy now, so Michael would claim his kill as Delta, even though he'd still been a SEAL at that time. It had taken six more months of cleanup raids and monitoring, but the area was now quiet. Not totally safe, but certainly not the hell of the last decade. Just last night, EU NAVFOR had downgraded the northern region of Operation Atalanta to a maintenance stance. The southern region of the operation was another matter.

Through his hundred sit-ups, Michael began organizing his day, or rather his night, since that's when they flew their missions. The Night Stalkers lived in a flipped-clock world, flying at night, sleeping during the day. The clock on the bulkhead wall told him it was only sixteen hundred—four in the afternoon. That meant he had time for a run on the USS *Peleliu*'s hangar deck before breakfast and the preflight briefing.

Maybe that would help shake the new pilot out of his system. And why was he fooling himself about that? So wasn't going to be that easy.

The mission switchover in the north from fighting pirates to keeping them under reasonable control probably meant reassignment soon anyway, so he really didn't need to worry.

Michael had intentionally embedded himself as Delta liaison with the D Company of Special Operations Aviation Regiment's 5th Battalion. They were the very best, and he enjoyed working with them because they had the highest op-tempo in all of SOAR. They also had the highest mission-success rate. They never stayed in maintenance or sweep positions; the 5D always flew at the very outer edge of the envelope.

If they ever did stagnate, he would have to move on. Part of being Delta was constant training, constant pushing to be ready no matter what came down the pipe. And part of being himself, he knew, was always finding the next impossible thing and conquering the hell out of it.

The 5D, also nicknamed the Black Adders, kept him challenged physically and mentally. Every day. They were the purest edge Michael could find.

How pure edge was the new pilot? She'd been good and steady last night. If that was fresh off training, it was a good sign. But last night's mission had been more noisy than complex.

Something told him that she had plenty of edge, though. Less than thirty seconds past the outer boundary shooter, she was unraveling his jokes in a calm, smooth voice.

And that hair. The soft weight of it as it had spilled over his hands and—

Shit!

After his sit-ups he rolled up off the steel deck and pulled on shorts, T-shirt, and running shoes. One of the advantages of being a colonel was having his own sink in his own room even when visiting on a Navy ship. A quick shave and he was out the door and headed up to the hangar deck. He wore his dark brown hair long but kept his face clean-shaven. Different Special Ops Forces soldiers made different choices, but casual was the keyword. Special Ops weren't about uniforms; they were about blending in on an undercover mission.

The hangar on the *Peleliu* was an open space

immediately below the flight deck of the amphibious assault ship. Essentially a small aircraft carrier, she presently boasted a half-dozen SOAR helicopters on her deck. Her current operations meant no Harrier Jump Jets were needed, which left the hangar space free to use as a running track except when they were rebuilding a shot-up bird or one was undergoing major scheduled maintenance. Even then, the mechanics would take over a bay at the far end of the deck and the track would just be a little shorter for a time.

Climbing the ladder from the bunk deck below, he could tell the hangar was mostly clear. He tried not to run when the fifty Rangers hit the hangar for their two hours of PT. U.S. Rangers were many things, but one of them was not quiet, especially during physical training. They ran in packs and were always teasing and harassing each other. And they sang as they ran, shouting "Ran-gers!" every fifth lap. They could make the hangar-deck run actively painful with the echoes reverberating throughout the space.

At present he could tell there were only two heavy-footed runners and one lighter one by the echoes in the cavernous, gray steel space that towered three stories high. It was a mostly clear space two football fields long and the better part of one wide. He'd seen it packed with thirty aircraft folded and stowed shoulder to shoulder. That was also when a reinforced battalion of Marines was aboard, which none was now.

The *Peleliu* had been slated for retirement and decommissioning. When the Marines were done with her, SOAR had asked to use the old ship as a forward operations platform in Somali waters. In his judgment, which he'd reported to the Pentagon, the repurposing of the ship was an operational asset of the first order. With one quarter of the normal Navy personnel, she also wouldn't be an overly expensive ship to keep in operation. After forty years at sea and almost a year past her planned retirement, the old lady was still going strong.

The heat of the day in the Gulf of Aden was its normal moderately hot and intolerably muggy. The setting sunlight poured in the large opening at the rear of the deck, which meant they were steaming east. By the motion of the ship, they were moving at eight knots, loafing along at one third of her full cruise speed.

That would be changing tonight after he spoke with the commander.

As he started stretching out, he automatically assessed the other three runners on the deck. A pair of SOAR early risers. Five p.m.—seventeen hundred hours—was their rise and shine, eighteen hundred meal, nineteen hundred briefing, and aloft thirty minutes later at full dark if there was an operation.

The third one—newly returned just last week from Delta training and his wedding and honeymoon—was his new assistant, Lieutenant William Bruce.

Michael timed his stretches so that he'd be ready to run when Bill lapped by. He watched Bill approach. Delta training had shifted his stride despite his ten years in the Navy and spending half that time in the SEALs before Michael recruited him. There was an agility to Bill's gait that he had lacked before. The SEAL training had made him a high-endurance mile-eater. The Delta regimen had added flexibility.

Michael did a final stretch on his hamstring and

began to trot in place. Three steps to get up to speed and he fell in close beside Bill without making him shift his stride. He smiled a good morning.

Trisha O'Malley, the SOAR Little Bird pilot who Bill had married, usually ran with him. She'd very vocally refused to besmirch her Irish heritage with his Scottish name, even if she was condescending to marry him to "dilute the ultimate shame of his blood."

A nod to the space between them, where the little redhead would normally fit between them, asked the question.

"New flyer meet-and-greet." Bill's deep voice matched his big frame.

The Little Bird pilot.

He still didn't know her name.

Definitely have to fix that.

He also needed to fix how she was occupying so many of his thoughts despite that lack of a name.

With unspoken consent, he and Bill closed the space between them, then both kicked it up ten percent and began lapping the SOAR runners. Their own feet echoed much more lightly within the cavernous space than those of the flyers, despite their greater speed.

Captain Claudia Jean Casperson had been led to her new quarters last night and pitched facedown into her bunk. Whoever had guided her had been kind enough to turn off the light and close the door.

She only had been awake long enough to wash her face and unpack when there was a knock on the door.

A short redhead stood in the gray steel corridor. The

woman was slight, freckled, pretty, and wearing full flight gear. Was this the woman who'd been on the radio last night from the DAP Hawk?

"Why aren't you in your gear? C'mon. Suit up, newbie!" Different voice than on the radio. That meant there were two women in the 5th Battalion's D Company. No insignia on her flight suit.

Unsure what to do, Claudia saluted.

"Cut that out! Damn it, don't they teach you anything about forward theater of operations?"

A salute was so ingrained, and what did it matter in a pilot? Sure, grunts on the ground didn't salute when in the field because that indicated who was in charge to an unfriendly sniper. But on a Navy ship she—

"No, I can see you thinking it. But no, not even here. You can do that crap all you want on U.S. soil, but that's it from now on. Clear?"

"Uh, yes, sir. Ma'am."

Claudia knew better than to protest about only just arriving or not having received orders to be battle ready. She simply turned to pull on the gear she'd stripped off less than twenty minutes before while the woman waited. In moments they were clambering up through the decks to reach the flight deck.

She knew this ship well. The eight hundred feet of the amphibious assault ship *Peleliu* were a Navy-gray haven afloat in the infinite blue of the ocean off the Horn of Africa—a desert far more barren than the central Arizona hills she'd grown up in.

Yet, it was strangely like coming home. Two years ago she'd departed these decks aboard a massive Sea Stallion helicopter—the largest bird in the U.S.

military—marking the last day of her final two-year tour as a Marine Corps pilot. And now that crazy lady named Fate had returned her to the same ship under a different branch of the service flying the MH-6M Little Bird, the military's smallest helicopter.

All that really mattered was that she'd finally made it. She'd been gunning to join SOAR since the day she saw that the first woman had made it three years before. If a Black Hawk pilot could make the jump, so could a Snake pilot. Only she'd do it better.

Jumping from a Marine Corps AH-1W SuperCobra "Snake" would have been a big step down if she'd just gone standard Army. But to join the Night Stalkers of the 160th SOAR...even hard-core Marines admitted they were exceptional, although SOAR was technically part of the Army and therefore should fall under the umbrella of disdain for "all of the pitiful services who hadn't made it to being Marines." Oorah!

When they arrived on deck, the heat slapped against her. The sun was lowering toward the horizon, but it was still a couple hours until sunset. The steel plating radiated with waves of heat that blurred the far ends of the ship, though it was only a hundred yards in either direction from where they'd emerged amidships.

The redhead called over to a man standing close beside a Little Bird helicopter. "Hey, Dennis, did our mechanics go over the repair on the bird that CC brought in?"

Claudia hated that nickname but wasn't awake enough to try correcting it. Besides, she didn't yet know who she was dealing with here. Correcting your future commanding officer on first meeting was never a good idea.

"All done and certified. The carrier guys fixed it up good, Boss Lady. Max is glad to have his bird back. Let's remind him to crash here rather than on the carrier next time."

"He's just lucky his bird was the only thing shot up," Trisha replied.

"Got that straight. Nice flying last night, Captain Casperson."

"It's Claudia. Thanks." They traded nods. So Dennis flew the Little Bird named *Merchant*. His acknowledgment cheered her up. Despite all of her service, spending two years in training and then being thrown directly back into the fray had been something of a shock.

Now if she only knew who the hell the redheaded "Boss Lady" was. Claudia was still pretty sure she hadn't been the commanding pilot on last night's exfil sortie.

She tried to recall the roster of other women in SOAR but had no better luck than last night.

She also hadn't really expected to be assigned to the Fifth Battalion, D Company straight out of training. The company's reputation was absolutely sterling. More like platinum with gold mixed in. It was an honor to have the chance to fly with the 5D, even if it was an unexpected one. That this woman was here spoke of skill, not gender bias…she hoped.

"If we don't call her 'Boss Lady,'" Dennis told Claudia as they circled close around his helo, "her ego gets all out of control. And let me tell you, that is so not a pretty sight."

Dennis was a handsome Eurasian man with an easygoing manner. His smile appeared simply friendly, not implying anything or trying to check her out despite the flight suit, which was a relief. Actually, few men in SOAR had raked her body with their eyes and leered, a common enough occurrence in the other forces. Or maybe everything would change when she got out of the flight suit.

"She may be boss"—Dennis offered a conspiratorial wink—"but she ain't no lady."

"Hey, I am too. I'm a respectable married lady now." The woman who had yet to say her name or rank fished out her dog tags, which had a pretty ring threaded on the chain, and waved the ring at Dennis.

When he opened his mouth to respond, she shut him right down.

"Careful there, Mr. Dennis Hakawa. Don't be disparaging a D-boy's lady or I'll have him sit on you."

"Yes, sir, Trisha, ma'am." Dennis pretended to be scared but headed off without further argument.

Well, at least now she had a first name.

Trisha was a Delta operator's wife? Wow, was that ever a hard-road choice for a marriage!

Married to the one who'd ridden beside her last night? Why did she feel a small twinge of disappointment at that?

Utterly ridiculous.

They'd said about two words each, but she'd liked the way he sat there so peacefully right after action. A Marine would be boasting and roaring high on adrenaline. The Delta operator last night had simply sat quietly through the flight.

Wait!

Was he the one who'd guided her to her cabin? He

was. She came up with a face. Rugged. Dark eyes and hair. It was a face filled with the man behind it. Even after just a single hazy glimpse through a hammer-load of exhaustion and adrenaline crash, she could picture that face perfectly. It wasn't one that you'd call handsome, not until you saw the man behind the eyes, and then it was…

Claudia was losing it. Totally brain dead. He was just some guy who'd helped her to her cabin. Probably this Trisha's husband.

There was a vague memory of something else about him, but it slipped away when she tried to focus on it.

So Trisha had married a D-boy? She must be even crazier than she acted.

It certainly wouldn't be Claudia's first choice—or second or third. Those guys went way out beyond any place that even hinted of being the front lines. They walked into the most dangerous places on the planet, and no one ever knew if they walked back out, because they never said anything. According to the Pentagon, they'd been formed in 1979 *and* didn't exist. At all. They routinely denied the existence of "The Unit" despite what the little bits of news of it that had slipped out over the years.

The rumors about them were that they were misfits who hated the government and lived for the combat. That it was a troop of men who loved the fight but hated the system. All rebels and chaos and no control.

They were also said to be the absolute, number one counterterrorism team on the entire planet. That they were now even better than the British SAS that they'd been based on. Who knew where the truth lay inside those shadows. She, for one, would be glad to pass on finding out.

"C'mon." Trisha led Claudia across the flight deck to another Little Bird just like the one she'd circled past moments before.

Except it wasn't.

Dennis flew the MH-6M, the same as she had last night. It was an aggressive flier designed to deliver four to six troops into places no other helicopter in the business could fit into. It was a bird that Claudia knew like the back of her hand after two years of SOAR training.

Trisha led her to an AH-6M Mission-Enhanced Little Bird, *A* for attack. These birds had been custom-designed to SOAR specifications. Instead of the two benches running down the exterior sides of the helicopter for the Special Operations Forces soldiers to ride on, she had a pair of M134 miniguns on the inside mounting points of the little side wings, and a pair of seven-rocket pods on the outer points for firing 2.75-inch Hydra 70 rockets. Claudia had really been hoping for an assignment to an attack version.

"Wait a second."

"Girl is sharp."

Claudia ignored the sassy tone and studied the helicopter. Six-blade rotor rather than the standard five, and a highly nonstandard shape to the hull, though still matte black like every other SOAR bird. Even the weapons were encased in odd-shaped carbon fiber housings. The windscreen still had the slightly bulbous shape that always reminded her of a cross-eyed hamster, but that was the only familiar shape on the whole bird.

It had to be a stealth rig, but she'd never heard of such

a thing in a Little Bird helicopter. Everyone knew about the stealth bird that crashed in bin Laden's compound when they took him down back in 2011, but that was all. The evidence of the one that crashed had said that there were at least two stealth rigs on that mission.

She looked about the deck. Two of the helicopters parked here were the normal transport Little Birds—Dennis's bird and the one other that she'd flown. A massive twin-rotor Chinook helicopter, the heavy lifter of SOAR, was parked in the stern-most position of the flight deck.

Forward there were a pair of standard-looking transport Black Hawks and another Black Hawk that might have once been a Direct Action Penetrator weaponized bird but looked like nothing she'd ever seen. It too had an atypical number of rotor blades and the same radar-deceiving stealth shape.

That was why she'd been able to see two of the birds on infrared last night, but not on radar. The 5th Battalion, D Company, in addition to being the best, was clearly the stealth arm of the 160th SOAR.

"Holy crap!" What had she just landed in?

"Pretty cool, huh? We used to have a second stealth DAP but Major Henderson crashed it right before he retired, something about getting its tail shot off on an exercise, which I'm not buying at all. I bet he was into something nasty, but I've never found out the story on that one. All hush-hush. I guess they decided that we didn't need another one and gave us the Chinook and this sweet little stealth bird instead." She patted the helicopter on the nose as if it were a puppy.

Claudia wondered which one she'd eventually fly.

Her specialty was Little Birds and there were only the three of them here. It sounded as if all three already had lead pilots. Maybe she was someone's new copilot.

"Now, let's see you fly one. I already preflighted her."

Claudia wanted nothing more, but she wasn't stupid. She just needed to figure out how to say it to this rankless woman.

Straight out was the only way that came to mind.

"Don't take this wrong, but I don't know who you are..." She left a pause that the woman declined to fill with an answer. "I don't fly a bird I didn't preflight myself."

"Be my guest." The infuriating woman waved for her to proceed.

Trisha stood and watched without comment as Claudia went over the Little Bird herself. As expected, everything was immaculate. SOAR always maintained their birds wonderfully. They had the highest operational availability percentages of any outfit in the U.S. Armed Forces, probably on the planet, and now she could see some of why. Even the Marine mechanics couldn't match this level, not in an operational environment.

This bird had seen some action—small swatches of hundred-mile-per-hour duct tape patched a number of holes like badges of honor. As she popped the engine covers for a visual inspection, she could see by some newer parts just what abuse this bird had taken in battle. She whistled silently. Two of the damage points must have made for ugly flights to get home. The bird also canted slightly to one side. The landing skid on the right was newer than the one on the left. She considered asking why but doubted she'd get an answer.

She turned to face this Trisha. "Good to go."

"You're crazy," Trisha said with a smile that Claudia would give good money to wipe off her face. Maybe the petite redhead had a personal vendetta against blond captains. "Three things you missed."

Claudia reviewed both the physical checklist she'd carried around as well as the matching tally in her head. She hadn't missed a thing.

"You didn't preflight the pilot." Trisha pointed a slender finger at Claudia's chest. "Barely awake is fine; that's why we're going aloft now to see how you're doing when it's the end of a long mission or an early alert. But tell me the last time you one: ate; two: drank water; or three: knocked back some electrolyte in this heat."

Chagrined, Claudia reached for the thigh pouch on her flight suit.

Trisha leaned back against the Hydra rocket launcher on the shady side of the bird and waved for Claudia to sit on the edge of the copilot's door. Again the woman waited with what Claudia suspected was uncharacteristic patience.

She couldn't think of what to say, so she tapped some electrolyte into her water bottle then sat and ate an energy bar. In the late afternoon, the *Peleliu*'s flight deck was unusually quiet; the two of them appeared to be the only life. A glance up and she could see a few shadowed figures behind their windows on the ship's nav bridge.

A lone sailor leaned on a rail and looked down at

them from thirty feet above. For a moment he made her wish she'd chopped her hair back to Marine Corps short so that it wouldn't be so obvious she was a woman. No, she was past that. Now she'd just pull up her Ice Queen cloak, and to hell with him or any man.

When she was done eating and hydrating she felt better and, with a nod for permission, clambered aboard. Trisha circled around to the pilot's side.

"Captain, huh?" Trisha asked as Claudia began powering up the bird.

"Yes, ma'am. And you are..."

"A pain in the ass. At least so our commander keeps telling me."

Claudia wasn't about to argue with that.

Trisha waved for her to take the controls and pointed up and west.

Claudia cleared her flight with the *Peleliu*'s air boss in PriFly—Primary Flight Control jutted from an upper story of the ship's superstructure—and pulled up on the collective with her left hand. The Little Bird sounded different from inside, still loud but smoother somehow. She'd never listened to a stealth helicopter before. She knew the innovation was that the sound was directionless from the ground and the helo was likely to sound as if it was departing right before it landed on you, but she was surprised so little was changed in the cockpit. Trisha nodded that it was sounding right, so Claudia went with it.

Just before they cleared the edge of the assault ship's deck, a pair of men emerged onto the deck.

"Damn," Claudia couldn't help exclaiming over the headset. "They breed them handsome out here." She'd been exposed daily to the men of the nation's best and fittest fighting corps, but these two guys would have stood out in any crew.

"The pretty one's mine," Trisha announced in no uncertain terms.

Claudia inspected the duo through the forward windscreen as she climbed the helo toward, then over them. The pretty one had to be the big guy, at least a head taller than Trisha. And he wore nothing but running shorts and a pair of sneakers. A scar ran down across his big chest. This must be her Delta Force husband. And he was indeed very pretty.

Good.

That meant his companion was not married to Trisha.

The other one had definitely been the man beside Claudia on last night's flight. Her vague memory of his face had been a complete underestimate.

He was totally arresting.

Significantly shorter than the big guy, maybe five-ten, and with a sleek frame that, like a greyhound's, looked to be all muscle. He was perhaps the handsomest man she'd ever seen. His rich brown hair fell past his ears, but even at this distance his eyes were his knockout feature. Not the color, she was too far away to check her memory of darkest brown.

It was the way they tracked her across the sky. She'd never felt so self-conscious before. Even when they were thousands of feet up and still climbing to the west, she could feel him watching her.

That's when the missing piece of last night clicked into place. A memory of being held in his arms. Of feeling for just that instant that she was perfectly safe from all that was changing around her.

She shook it off.

Safe was not real, didn't exist.

On top of that, Claudia reminded herself, he was also scary and bug-shit crazy.

Oddly, those two details didn't push her away as she'd expected. Still, there was no way she was going to be drawn in either.

~

Michael watched them aloft. Trisha wasn't flying. She flew the way she did everything else, flat out. He knew instinctively who was at the controls. That steadiness and smoothness to her flight was as clear as a fingerprint. That her face looked as amazing as she flew…

He wanted to laugh. Well, if the rest of her looked that good, he was totally screwed.

A meet-and-greet, Bill had said. No one dragged a pilot aloft before breakfast, especially after the shape she'd been in last night; that was just plain cruel. No one except Trisha O'Malley. Flat out. The way she flew and the way she made love.

Michael wondered if she'd told her husband that Trisha and he had been lovers briefly, a year before she and Bill met. Even if Trisha hadn't, Bill would have to know. Wouldn't he? Michael still didn't have a clear answer to that, so he once again kept his mouth shut.

They shared a glance and headed into the command tower. Michael had been doing some research while Bill was in the six-month operator training course at Delta. Didn't matter if he'd been a SEAL for half a decade, he'd needed OTC to make sure he met Delta standards and shared the skill set.

Now with Bill back, it was time to go sit with the ship's commander and lay out his idea for the next mission.

~

Trisha was talking about everything except SOAR or who she was. She was laying down this whole story about fighting in the Boston gangs, with a posh Boston accent that Claudia thought had gone out of style with President Kennedy. Street gangs? Not likely. Was she even a pilot? Was this just a way to haze a new team member by conning her into a free ride?

Claudia had a pretty good feel for the helicopter now. When she'd asked for permission, Trisha had simply replied, "Shake her out."

Well, if the woman wasn't real, Claudia could claim ignorance. She'd grab any excuse to see what this bird could really do.

Full power climbs, hammerhead stalls, nosedive descents, near-stall turns, autorotate… They were high enough to safely try all of the maneuvers without risk. Stealth had done nothing to inhibit this bird. It was still incredibly responsive, as all SOAR-specified Little Birds were. This was indeed a dream machine.

Trisha had kept her hands and feet riding on the controls, but her touch was so light that Claudia could barely feel it through their shared controls, even on the more drastic maneuvers she tried. The linked cyclics—the joysticks between their knees that controlled pitch and roll—rode light and responsive in her right hand. The collective along the left side of her seat included the throttle and controlled the amount of the rotor's lift.

Trisha's feet were even light on the rudder pedals that controlled which way they faced. There was just enough contact to give Claudia an intimate connection to the woman sitting beside her.

As Claudia grew accustomed to the bird, she began to be more aware of her surroundings. The Gulf of Aden, two hundred miles wide at this point, stretched clear and blue in every direction. Long white wakes marked the tiny dots of container ships and tankers working through the waters. The sun was an hour, maybe two from the western horizon.

"What's that?" There was a dimness in the south that she couldn't identify.

"Haboob, dust storm." Trisha didn't even bother to glance over. It was as if she already knew what Claudia was thinking. Not a feeling she much liked. "Tower would have warned us if there was any risk out here. That's what took down three of our birds during Operation Eagle Claw back in 1980."

As if Claudia didn't know the history of her new unit. Actually Eagle Claw hadn't been the Night Stalkers, but it was such a part of their history that she'd heard a lot of flyers take ownership of it. Both the good and the bad.

The Night Stalkers were born from one of the worst maintenance disasters of any helicopter mission anywhere, ever. The attempt to extract the hostages from the Iranian embassy had left hardware and bodies scattered across the high desert. From that failure had been born the 160th SOAR, and no one was more conscientious about the condition of their craft.

She could feel herself really not liking this woman much. However, this might be her commanding officer and the pilot who she'd be flying with for the next five years, so she'd better get over it. She wasn't totally unbearab—

Trisha collapsed forward onto the cyclic control. The two joysticks were connected together and Claudia's slammed far forward and left. The helicopter pitched forward and down. She tried fighting the cyclic against the woman's body weight. They did a sickening full roll and began losing altitude fast.

As they entered inverted flight, Trisha's body flopped against her. At least that gave her control of the collective, and she savagely twisted them back upright. This time she was ready as Trisha's weight flopped back against the cyclic.

She dropped the collective and grabbed the cyclic with her left hand. Reaching back with her right hand to the seat belt harness control at the top of Trisha's seat, Claudia toggled it off release mode. Now, just like a seat belt locked up for a car crash, the back of Trisha's harness could only get shorter rather than allowing her to lean forward as necessary.

Using both hands, Claudia jerked back on the cyclic against Trisha's weight, forcing the helo's nose straight into the sky. Trisha's body flopped bonelessly back in her seat, the harness retracting to hold her in place. Whatever the hell had gone wrong with her, Claudia would figure it out once they were safe—massive stroke or coronary failure by the look of it. If there'd been a gunshot, she hadn't heard it.

They were now falling tail-first toward the ocean. Claudia pitched forward, then grabbing the collective, cranked the throttle wide open and yanked up on it to regain altitude. She threw the Little Bird into an evasive maneuver just in case she was being targeted. She'd lost two copilots over her six years in the Corps—one out of the Corps and one all the way into the ground—and she felt sick that she'd just lost another, and on a training fli—

"That will never do." Trisha's clear voice over the headset made Claudia jerk sideways to face her. The woman was inspecting the panel as if nothing had happened. She calmly reached over her shoulder to release her harness.

"You lost over eight hundred feet in that maneuver. When my copilot was shot and collapsed forward, I had to recover in a hundred feet. Made it too, mostly. Hit hard enough that I kinda crunched up one of the skids and my butt was sore for weeks despite the shock seat. I'll take her back. Pilot has controls."

"Roger," was all Claudia could manage. Half of her was screaming about an unfair goddamn test. The other half was trying to figure out how she could have recovered in just a hundred feet.

Trisha rolled the helo into an inverted dive and plummeted toward the ocean in a slowly winding inverted spiral. That in itself was an almost impossible maneuver.

She now knew at least one thing about Trisha; she was an incredible pilot. Claudia struggled to form a coherent thought as she watched their eight thousand feet of altitude unwind at an alarming rate that was making her ears pop every five to ten seconds.

"How did you do that in a hundred feet?"

"Tell you the truth..." Trisha's voice was calm as could be, despite hanging upside down from her harness and continuing their death spiral toward the sparkling waters of the Gulf. "I have no idea. I did it because it was either do it or auger in and make a big crater in central Somalia. Wasn't much of a fan of the latter idea just on general principles."

"What was his name? Or her name?" His name. She'd have heard if one of the five other women in SOAR had died. Four women, now that Major Beale had retired when she got pregnant.

"Chief Warrant 2 Roland Emerson, as fine a copilot as I've ever flown with. Same rank as me. Patricia O'Malley at your service."

Apparently Claudia had done well enough to have earned the honor of learning Trisha's rank and name despite the eight-hundred-foot tumble.

Trisha rolled out of the inverted dive just two hundred feet over the ocean as if it was the most natural maneuver in the world. The flight deck of the *Peleliu* lay a thousand yards dead ahead.

Claudia had flown for the Marine Corps for a full four-year tour plus two more and then two years of training for SOAR. She rather doubted she could do what Trisha had just done without a lot of practice.

That was it! She almost laughed aloud.

"You bloody sneak!"

"What?" Trisha sounded all sweet and innocent.

"How many times did you practice that crazy inverted descent before you used it to make me feel inferior?"

"Well..." Trisha's smile was radiant. "I didn't practice it special for you. I had this amazing commander back in the Screaming Eagles. I liked doing things to keep her on her toes."

"Did it work?"

"Naw. Emily was way too good a pilot. She did some shit at the end of my rollout that almost had me crapping my pants instead."

Emily. That had to be Major Emily Beale, the first woman of SOAR. The one who broke the gender barrier with the Night Stalkers. The reason Claudia knew she could get in.

The comparisons would have been inevitable even if they'd never met. They were both tall and blond and were in the elite pool of female SOAR pilots. Claudia had ignored those side comments as well as she could, but there was no question that even Beale's historical presence had driven Claudia ahead.

Maybe Claudia could like Trisha a little bit. If she'd flown with Beale, Claudia could certainly respect her.

Chapter 3

Michael noticed when Trisha entered the chow line despite the busy room. He and Bill sat at their usual table in the far corner with their backs to the wall and exits to their right and straight ahead. At the nearer tables, the eight men of the two D-boy fire teams sat eating quietly. SOAR and Navy spread about the low-ceilinged, gray wardroom mess of second deck, though rarely mixing. A cluster of Rangers at the far end of the mess was making most of the noise.

Then the new pilot appeared behind Trisha. She was several inches taller and built quite differently. Everything about Trisha was petite, except perhaps her temper and her boundless energy.

The other woman had straight, blond hair that spread over her athletic shoulders despite being up in a sleek ponytail. She'd shed her SARVSO vest and, like Trisha, had stripped her flight suit down to her waist and tied the arms around her middle.

What Michael saw made him damn glad he hadn't tried to help her out of her flight suit last night. He'd have been toast.

She was amazingly shapely, not big, just...right. Her T-shirt indicated that she probably had six-pack abs below her full curves. Even on the ground she exhibited the quiet steadiness that Trisha thoroughly lacked. Clearly this was his new pilot. *The* new pilot, he corrected himself. She walked the way she flew, which was amazing to watch.

He was so screwed.

"Hey, Michael! Hey, Billy!" Trisha plunked her tray down on the table. "This is CC. That's Michael and this sweet piece of soldier is Billy the SEAL."

"I'm Delta now."

"Tough. Your nickname has already been stuck on you—by your loving wife. So don't even consider trying to change it. Sit, CC."

"It's not CC. It's Claudia."

"Not CC?" Trisha shrugged. "Pretty fussy of you, but okay." Trisha sounded as if she was granting royal dispensation in allowing Claudia to retain her own name.

"Thanks."

Trisha didn't even blink at Claudia's dry tone, but Michael couldn't stop the quick laugh that bubbled out from somewhere. Thankfully Trisha missed it, though Bill was looking at him as if he'd suddenly grown a second head.

Claudia arched one perfect eyebrow at him and then set down her tray and sat.

Trisha started simultaneously eating and talking as fast as the rattle of gunfire.

Michael knew better than to attempt any form of interruption and started working on his apple pie.

"Took her up. She done good. I pulled a Roland on her. Took her eight hundred feet to save us, and she almost cut my chest in two ramming the collective home." She grabbed Claudia's bicep and squeezed it as the woman sat down tentatively. "See, she's strong. Hey, you really are."

He'd never really understood Trisha's need to shock. Roland had taken a dud RPG to the head and died instantly. Maybe it was Trisha's—what did she call it—her dealing mechanism.

Then he looked back at Claudia, almost as close as last night but not hidden behind all the gear. He tried not to ever let looks influence him, but she was stunning.

She even ate the way she flew, smooth and powerful. Nothing about her looked practiced; she was just herself. She was also one of those women who have perfect dancer's posture. Trisha always leaned or slouched, as if she'd been made of rubber. Claudia sat with a straight back and her chin up. Even with the inevitable sports-bra lines showing through the tank top she was—

"You're staring, Michael." Trisha spoke around a mouthful of hamburger.

"I was? Sorry. A new face and an attractive one. I—"

"Whoa! A compliment from the colonel. You better watch out, Claudia."

And Trisha constantly wondered why he talked so little.

Bill grabbed the back of Trisha's hand that held her burger and shoved it up and into her mouth, forcing her to take such a large bite that even she couldn't speak around it. Recruiting Bill to Delta really had been a good choice.

"Ignore her," Michael suggested. "Where are you from?"

He paid no attention to the wide eyes and raised eyebrows Trisha aimed in his direction.

Maybe she was choking.

Good.

~~~

Claudia ignored Trisha. Though she appreciated the compliment on her flying. Leave it to Trisha to make a wholly insufficient introduction.

A colonel? Colonel Michael. Of Delta Force? A colonel back in Fort Campbell commanded all five battalions of the Night Stalkers.

Michael's hands could never be mistaken for a flier's. They were too rough, and he had a big callus in the webbing between his thumb and forefinger. Right where her hand hurt after an afternoon on the practice range. Did this guy shoot so much that he had an actual callus from it? It matched the one on Billy...Bill. And Bill was Delta Force.

A Delta Force colonel? And still in field operations rather than flying a desk. Or maybe in Delta it was killing a desk. Whichever, that meant he wasn't merely scary, bug-shit crazy; he was probably at the outermost envelope of them all.

The most extreme Delta operator?

He didn't look old enough to have climbed the ranks yet, which meant he'd done it through an immense amount of skill—too much to keep back. There was a hardness to him, a strength that made him appear both powerful and...she searched for the right word...safe?

Yes, that's what she'd felt last night for a brief moment in his arms, and it was still right.

Safe.

Not something she'd ever found anywhere except deep inside herself. Never expected to either.

"I'm from a little town called Bumble Bee originally,"
~~~

she answered his question. The others had a blank look, but not Michael. He just waited. Of course he'd know that no one had ever heard of it and she'd automatically explain. "Ghost town about sixty miles north of Phoenix. Out in the deep desert. How about you?"

"The redwoods."

Having swallowed at least half of what she was chewing, Trisha scoffed at him around the rest of it. "What? Like up a tree?"

Claudia noticed that Bill was keeping his own counsel. So these were his friends, and they didn't even know where Michael was from.

"Is the wood actually red?" She'd never seen one.

He appeared to like that she'd skipped over all the normal questions and moved right along.

His simple nod, before returning his attention to the big slice of apple pie he'd been working on when they arrived, flustered Trisha no end.

Claudia liked that Michael could do that to the irritating woman. Even if Trisha wasn't intentionally irritating, which Claudia was beginning to think was true, that didn't make her any less annoying. Maybe once you got to know her.

But there was more than that. It was as if Claudia had just passed some test by not saying any of the obvious things. So Michael thought he was a deep and subtle one, did he?

She was on the verge of teasing him with, "Is it nice up there, Colonel Michael?"

No. Even that was too expected.

He was Mr. Strong-and-Silent, dropping his little tidbits to see how others reacted. Wasn't that just too cute for words. D-boy colonel with little mind games, ones that he apparently enjoyed playing on himself.

So why would he say he lived in the redwoods? Beyond the test of her reaction, she could see some truth in his response. That wasn't where he lived; that's what lived inside him.

She lived in Bumble Bee, Arizona. But where she came to life was out in the hard-scrabble hills of the Sonoran Desert as they climbed toward the Bradshaw Mountains. That's where…

Ah.

"Can you hear the world breathe up in your trees, Colonel Gibson?"

Trisha looked at her like she'd gone nuts, and Bill simply looked lost. But she didn't care about them; she kept her attention on Michael.

He was slow in returning that dark-eyed gaze from his apple pie to study her face.

She'd expected his eyes to be penetrating or even icy, something appropriate for a Delta Force colonel. But they weren't. They were the eyes of a man who didn't expect to be noticed and looked surprised that he had been.

He hesitated long enough to show that it was a carefully considered answer. The trees were terribly important to him.

She understood perfectly.

For her, the rolling sagebrush and scrub oak of the steep hills around Bumble Bee were a constant call. She missed that perfect peace, only made all the deeper when a white-tailed deer passed by or one of Mr. Johns's cattle got loose again and dislodged a rock that skittered down the hillside. She tried to imagine the different quiet of tall redwoods. She couldn't quite picture it.

"Yes." His voice was actually rough with the unexpected truth.

"Sounds nice," she offered.

"It is."

Trisha asked what the hell they were talking about.

Bill stayed silent.

Claudia started eating her own meal, feeling as surprised as he looked. For the first time, someone else had understood exactly what she meant about the desert.

~

"You're technically not on duty until tomorrow." Almost without Claudia noticing, Michael had slid up beside her after she'd dumped off her tray.

"But?" There was clearly a "but" in his statement. If this was a pickup line, she was going to be very disappointed.

"If you go to sleep now, you'll sleep through the night and be completely out of sync."

She'd slept most of the day, but coming off a two-day deficit, a mission, and the flight with Tricia, she was ready to sleep another full eight.

Actually, it was more like a five-day deficit. She'd started with the two-day final flight test—which had been brutal with long distances, rugged terrain to follow at impossibly low altitudes, and time constraints to make a grown woman weep, if there'd been a spare second to do so. There hadn't. That had transitioned straight into graduation and being declared mission-qualified, then loaded within hours onto a transport bound for the

Persian Gulf. The changes were almost overwhelming. The all-important test that she'd passed just three days ago was already ancient history—on the far side of a flown mission into the desert of the supposedly friendly country of Yemen.

"Well, I'm in no shape to fly at the moment."

Not a line she'd ever have said intentionally; she must be more tired than she thought. In the military, a woman simply didn't leave an open line like that, not even in as elite an outfit as SOAR. She braced for some joke about her "shape being made to fly" or some such crap.

If the colonel *was* working a pickup line, she'd just walked straight into it.

The question she had to ask herself was how much would she have to take because she was new to the outfit and he was a colonel? Not much, her years in the Marines decided—not in her current state of sleep deprivation, not even from a senior officer.

"No mission tonight." Michael had taken her statement at face value. "But I think you might wish to attend the briefing."

Not her first choice at all. She'd be asleep within thirty seconds of hitting the chair and end up slumped on the floor of the meeting room on her first day with the company. Hell of a first impression.

"I'll try not to be boring."

She laughed. It just burst out of her.

No one had ever been able read her like that.

Claudia had been accused of being an Ice Queen any number of times in her career, just because she liked keeping herself to herself. Of course, the guys said it because she wouldn't sleep with them, which also had made the nickname useful. She'd learned early on the advantages of nurturing the image. She would occasionally let carefully selected men through her barriers, discreet ones who had no association with the Corps, though none of them had stuck for more than a few months.

But some of the women called her that too, which made her wonder. It was exactly the sort of thing Trisha would have said, if she'd thought to.

Claudia was far too tired to try to make sense of Trisha at the moment.

She was about to decline when Michael tipped his head in a gentle "C'mon."

It was charming, and she was tired enough to be charmed a little. She hadn't missed his compliment or how much it had surprised his tablemates. And she'd never met someone who might understand the attraction of her desert. But maybe, just maybe, he did.

Share her desert with Colonel Michael.

She noted that in her head, it wasn't an interrogative but rather a flat statement. Too young to be going senile, perhaps going psychotic? She'd known him for…an embrace, a meal, and a firefight.

Well, that only verified that they were both soldiers to the core. The average couple couldn't point to the obliteration of an al-Qaeda cell as their meet-cute.

Couple? She really was losing it. It was a good thing she wasn't one of those people whose brains connected directly to their mouths with no filter.

With a shrug of acceptance—which she deemed safe enough—she followed him up the steel ladders, through the ringing hangar deck where dozens of SOAR and

Navy people were now scattered along a makeshift track, and on up to the flight deck.

The sun was close to setting off the starboard side. The entire line of the horizon was glowing a soft orange, especially to the south. The particulates thrown into the air by the dust storm were making for a spectacular sky.

She noticed that all the helicopters were still on the deck, tied down with no one working on them. The stealth birds even had loose cloth covers that would mask their shape from aerial observation. Right, only moments ago Michael had said no mission tonight. In her current state she'd be lucky to remember her own name from one minute to the next.

If there was no flight, then what was the briefing about?

He turned for the door into the communications platform, as the above-decks tower was called. She could tell he didn't know the ship as well as he might. He could have saved more than twenty steps from the wardroom mess to here by traveling aft and then climbing the inside ladder.

But Delta operators didn't make mistakes and they always knew their terrain.

Perhaps he'd wanted to spend a longer walk with her. She must really be exhausted to be having thoughts like that one. She told her brain to shut up and turned to study the sunset to buy herself a moment.

Hadn't it been setting astern just an hour before? Yes, she'd been flying out in the Gulf of Aden and the coast had been south. Now they'd rounded the Horn of Africa and were headed south into the open ocean.

Something else had changed. This ship had been her

home for years and she knew it intimately. They were moving at close to full speed, based on the brisk wind sweeping the length of the deck.

She breathed it in deep: ocean air, hot metal, and spent jet fuel. If she moved to the farthest stern extent of the fantail, she'd catch just the slightest whiff of diesel exhaust shot up into the air through the funnels atop the communications platform.

Michael had led her halfway along the platform, past a half-dozen rooms she knew all too well from when this ship had been servicing the Marines.

For most of her history, the *Peleliu* had transported seventeen hundred Marine grunts and could launch enough SuperCobra helicopters and Harrier Jump Jets from the flight deck, and amphibious water craft from her sea-level well deck to get all of those troops on the move fast.

Claudia had spent countless hours attempting to read a book in the squad ready room while on "alert hold" status.

They'd passed the "pee room" where every pilot had to pee in a cup before every flight to prove they were "Marine clean."

Now, beneath the setting sun, the old ship felt new and fresh. No longer a jarhead pilot among thousands, Claudia was a SOAR pilot. A Night Stalker. One of the best helicopter pilots on the planet. And in the 5D besides.

And the man beside her was probably the most senior D-boy in the field, making him pretty much the best warrior on the planet. She could sense his quiet center as surely as she could smell the oncoming darkness.

There was a tiny release inside her, as quiet as a

skittering stone slipping down a sandy hillside. It was a part of her "safe" memory from last night's sleep-blinded embrace.

What more was there in Michael's arms other than "safe"?

She was just dumb enough and brain hazed enough to ask the question.

Claudia had never been a big fan of unanswered questions.

She turned to face him, his quiet, assessing eyes not blinking for a moment.

A half step closer…

Michael thought he'd be shocked. Was sure he would be. They had only met just…

His mind blanked when Claudia brushed her lips over his.

His mind never blanked.

There wasn't heat. There wasn't fire.

No…

There wasn't *only* heat and fire.

Beyond those, there was a moment of impossible perfection as if this sensation, this soft intimate touch of only their lips was indeed the goal he'd been seeking since he'd climbed his first hundred-foot tree seeking the pinnacle that you could never quite reach.

He tasted her. Could almost imagine that he could taste her beloved wild desert, for he'd seen that connection in her as clearly as she'd seen it in him.

Some timeless moment later…

He never lost track of time.

But he just had.

…Claudia shifted back that same half step.

She didn't try to fill the silence with words. No apologies. No false compliments. Nor true ones.

Her blue eyes studied him as intently as his studied her.

There weren't questions either.

There was a simple, stupefying rightness.

He turned and held the door for her to enter the passage to the number two ready room. A door heavy enough to block most of a Harrier jet's noise on takeoff or landing—which was major.

A door that felt as if it was opening to many places at once.

Claudia crossed through the passageway into a room she didn't expect.

Instead of containing the heavy table with bolted-down benches—on which she used to rest her butt until it was so sore it hurt to stand when the "saddle up" or the "stand down" order was finally issued—this was a comfortable office. A small table, a couple of couches, even comfortable chairs. All bolted down in case of rough seas, but still very pleasant.

It was just wrong. She'd come home to… Just wrong.

Lieutenant Commander Boyd Ramis, who'd been First Officer on the vessel when she'd been here as a Marine pilot two years ago, was seated at the desk. He'd made the room his office.

Claudia couldn't help herself. No matter what Trisha had said, she snapped to attention and saluted sharply.

The Lieutenant Commander rose and returned the salute without complaint or equivocation. Then held out his hand and offered a firm handshake. "Welcome back aboard, Captain Casperson. Pleasure to see you again."

Boyd was good at that. He might be only an okay commander, but he surrounded himself with good people and he listened to them. And he kept them loyal by always knowing their names, their wives, even most of their kids.

"Thank you, sir." Sure enough, despite a two-year gap, he asked about her mom but not her dad, recalling that he'd died of cancer during her former service aboard. She considered telling him about her stepfather and how happy he and her mom were in Flagstaff, but she didn't want to start that conversation with everyone around.

She chose the least-comfortable-looking chair to stave off sleep as long as possible and tried to assess the others as they arrived. It wasn't a big crowd.

Boyd and Michael, Trisha and Bill. She remembered Petty Officer Sly Stowell, the head of the ship's amphibious assault craft, managing to dredge up his name a moment before he had to remind her. By his greeting he definitely remembered her. Female Marine pilots were still counted in the dozens rather than the thousands, so he had a distinct advantage. Sly moved off; apparently he and Michael had some mutual respect going as they fetched coffee and stood together, though it was a silent respect because neither man spoke.

But Claudia had little doubt where their attention was

focused. Michael was working a little too hard at not looking at her.

Fine, Mr. Crazy Delta Colonel.

But she wasn't having much luck ignoring him. Didn't want to.

A kiss chaste enough for a brother, if she'd had one… Okay, it hadn't been that chaste. Still. A kiss like that shouldn't be changing her view of anything. Not of the man, not of herself.

Yet it lingered there like the warmth of hot tea deep in her belly, making her feel more welcome to be aboard this boat than at any moment until now.

Despite the impossibly convoluted series of circumstances that had her coming back to this boat for a wholly different outfit after two years away, it was a return to exactly the right place at exactly the right time.

Claudia didn't know what to do with that. She'd raised herself with minimal help from her parents and only a little more from their neighbors. It had been up to her alone to consciously form herself into who she wanted to be. She was pretty pleased with the woman she'd built so far.

So what was this instinctual thing that had the Ice Queen kissing a crazy D-boy colonel? One she couldn't even keep out of her head.

His presence seemed to radiate from a quiet center.

Yet as aware as she was of him, he was invisible to so many others. People moved so close that they might have thought him a wall or piece of furniture. Few even greeted him. One actually startled himself when he almost walked into Michael.

~

Michael was always amused at how simple it was to disappear in a room. It wasn't about outer stillness; it was inner stillness. Very few saw past that.

Lieutenant Commander Ramis hadn't even seen him enter the room. Of course with a woman of Claudia's fine looks in front of him, that was little surprise.

Sly was more observant than most.

Claudia turned away from them, but he could still feel her awareness of him. He shifted, fetching a couple cookies from the refreshment table tray for himself and Sly.

Something, something he couldn't see, had caused her to glance back at him as he did so.

She shouldn't be a Night Stalker; she should be a Delta operator, except there weren't any women allowed. Not yet, but the landscape of the military was changing. Even four years ago there hadn't been any female Night Stalkers.

Well, if Captain Claudia Casperson was an example of that change, he was all in favor of it.

In more ways than one, which was a wholly inappropriate thought. But even though he was biting down on a chocolate chip cookie, that wasn't the taste he was remembering.

It was a woman at sunset.

~

Claudia was doing her best to retain names as one person after another arrived. It wasn't like a Marines operation with multiple ground commanders, flight team leaders both jet and helo, and so on. This was definitely a lean-and-mean operation: Night Stalkers, Rangers, Delta, and Navy.

An extremely tall, slender guy strolled in, actually wearing a white cowboy hat tipped back on his head. His easy drawl proved that the hat wasn't just an affectation as he introduced himself.

"Captain Justin Roberts, ma'am. Pilot of the Chinook CH-47 *Calamity Jane* at your service. Nice to have another captain aboard among all this riffraff." He moseyed—a man who actually moseyed—his way over to one of the deep chairs and settled in. In SOAR, a company command didn't necessarily follow rank. Seniority and experience were far more important in a regiment where captains and even majors flew the helicopters.

Of course, a colonel in the field. Maybe Michael was only in planning. No. Last night. Yemen. Leading a four-man fire team himself.

The man was a puzzle.

The last trio to arrive was a very strange set. The man was tall—though shorter than the Texan—and slender, and introduced himself with a very Boston accent, not all that different from Trisha's, as Air Mission Commander Archie Stevenson III. The man Claudia had traded a dozen words with last night before he sent her into Yemen. He moved off to the coffeepot.

If he saw Michael, it was hard to tell. There might have been a brief nod.

The woman he'd entered with just stood there facing Claudia until she rose uneasily to her feet.

"Let me guess," the newcomer addressed Claudia. "This is Trisha's doing."

Claudia knew in that instant who commanded this unit. It was the voice from the DAP Hawk last night. The woman was tall, wore her mahogany hair in a long, flowing wave that framed a stunning face, and had an air of absolute authority.

"Well"—she didn't even wait for Claudia's answer—"when you're conscious tomorrow, you can officially report in. I did send Trisha to guide you in and welcome you aboard ship. She was supposed to lead you to me eventually. I'm Chief Warrant 3 Lola Maloney, by the way." She had a firm handshake.

"Trisha, ah, took me aloft, ma'am."

The woman glared at the gray steel ceiling, clearly counting to ten. Slowly. Possibly twice. "O'Malley..." she ground out between her teeth.

"I had to see." Trisha came over and shoved a cold can of ginger ale into Claudia's hand. "I mean, last night she was good and all, but not like it was a tricky mission or anything. She did great, Lola. Can see something of all those Marine Corps SuperCobra habits, but well integrated. Took to the bird right away, compensated for the stealth characteristics nice and clean. No freeze in a crisis. If it were up to me, I'd sign off on her right now."

Lola glanced down at the pint-sized chief warrant officer.

Unless Claudia was mistaken, Lola's gaze had shifted from anger to interest. So, Trisha might be a certified lunatic, but she was well respected by her commanding officer.

"You, Captain Casperson, are forgiven. We'll talk more after you've slept again. You, O'Malley, just stay out of my face for the rest of the night, please." She didn't speak as if she expected such a request to be obeyed.

She headed off with a nod, leaving the third person who had entered watching Claudia frankly. The girl looked about fifteen, yet she stood with the poise of someone much older. Claudia studied her face. Except for the look in her hazel eyes, the girl was fifteen. But no young girl had ever looked at the world with such old eyes. She was as tall as Trisha but clearly still had some growing to do. Even now, her sleeves were just a little short, unless that was some new style. Her dark, ruffled hair was hanked back in a sloppy ponytail built off a pair of smaller braids that swept back from her temples, revealing her dark skin that matched no one else's in the room.

All of the others were dressed in some variation of combat casual, with only Boyd wearing the Navy tan slacks and shirt open at the throat typical of a boat officer. This girl was dressed in full teen style: black boots, skinny-leg jeans, a red cami under a yellow tank top, and an airy, worn green scarf with dark blue trim draped over her otherwise bare shoulders. She had a smartphone with headphones and an e-reader. She was fully equipped, but for what?

"What are you reading?" Claudia asked to break the stretching silence between them. Other conversations were going on in the room, but they had disappeared into a background buzz that was easy to ignore—except for her awareness that Michael was watching them intently.

Claudia was so tired that it was a relief to focus on only one person at a time.

"*Hunger Games*. A strange title. Hunger is never a game." The teen spoke as if this were a matter of the deepest importance.

"No, it isn't." No one else was paying any attention to the strange conversation. As if casual fifteen-year-olds always appeared on ships in the service. SOAR was definitely far outside the norm. Or perhaps it was just D Company.

The girl continued her inspection of Claudia for a moment longer, then moved over to the end of a couch next to AMC Archie Stevenson, plugged in and, after waving hello to Michael, began reading. She might as well have been in a suburban living room as in an amphibious-assault-ship briefing room. The way the two leaned together, they clearly were close. Yet Claudia felt as if she'd just been subjected to the toughest test of a tough day with the verdict still outstanding.

The AMC must have noticed her confusion. "My daughter, Dilya." There was no sign of the man in the girl. Maybe she favored the mother, about a hundred percent. No explanation of what she was doing here, but no one seemed bothered by her presence.

And Michael was being nice to the kid. He'd actually smiled and waved back. He had an amazing smile, which made her glad that he hadn't tried it on her yet. It had a genuineness that shone right through him.

The final person arrived quietly and slipped into a seat beside Claudia. She required a second look. She had a Mediterranean complexion of dusky olive. Her straight hair, as dark as her eyes, reached to her lower back, accentuating her long frame. Special Operations Forces allowed some leeway in hair style, but Claudia's own hair length, brushing past her shoulders, was the normal limit. This woman really stood out.

The woman offered a nod and a fine-fingered handshake.

"Captain Kara Moretti, SOAR," the Italian beauty offered with a distinct Brooklyn accent that almost provoked a laugh from Claudia. The woman didn't offer any further explanation or any hint that humor would be welcome.

Claudia hadn't heard the name before, and it made the count wrong. She knew exactly how many women were in the regiment.

By the side glances from the others, no one else knew who Captain Moretti was either. Justin, the Texan pilot, didn't bother to glance; he simply stared as if he'd been struck by lightning. Only Michael didn't react. He simply accepted her presence. Chief Warrant Lola Maloney also knew who the woman was.

Well, if Colonel Michael Gibson was attracted to sheer beauty, he would be a goner on this one. It was ridiculous, but Claudia found herself a little irritated that Captain Moretti had some connection to Michael. More than a little irritated, which was beyond ridiculous.

Boyd Ramis rose and everyone settled. "Michael came to me this afternoon with an interesting idea that I'll leave for him to explain. Before he does, I just want to say I think it's a great idea. I rang up Roger at EU NAVFOR, and he said it sounds 'top-notch.' But I'll leave it up to you experts to decide."

Roger at…that would be Dutch Commodore Roger Hamstein, the afloat commander for the entire Operation Atalanta—the operation against Somali piracy that stretched over much of the Indian Ocean. So, the mission hadn't even been explained yet, and now command was expecting it to happen. Michael didn't look pleased, but he managed to hide it from Boyd, if not from her.

Michael rose to speak. "Six months ago we flew Operation Heavy Hand."

It was Claudia's first chance to notice his voice when it was meant for a group and not just for her. It was low and soft. He was the sort of man who never had to shout because when he went really quiet, he scared the crap out of you. But at least at the moment it was a gentle voice, as if he were whispering to a horse. Or maybe a redwood. Everyone went dead silent to listen.

"We took out over sixty pirates including four pirate lords, recovered five ships and forty-seven hostages, and lost only one person." All eyes in the room traveled to Trisha, though most shied away before they got there.

Claudia didn't see any accusation; it was all sympathy. So, no one even questioned if it might be Trisha's fault. Good. It made her think a little better of the woman. "Pulled a Roland" on her—that was one hell of a coping mechanism, reenacting the death of her copilot as a test.

But that also matched the way they were using the mission as a teaching tool at SOAR training. Every step of the operation had been dissected and analyzed: on the classroom board, in three-dimensional simulations, and as specific techniques in the field. They'd spent a full week studying something that had been planned in a day and taken barely ten hours to execute. All but forty-seven minutes of that had been transit time.

To this day, SOAR hadn't been mentioned in any news story relating to the operation. Nor Delta, yet clearly Michael had been a part of it as well.

Michael made a quick assessment of the room. Most of the people here had been involved in that mission. The Texan Chinook pilot and Kara Moretti hadn't been here and clearly didn't know what he was referring to.

Claudia did. He could see her connecting the pieces of her recent training with the people in the room. He actually waited, giving her a moment of silence.

At seven seconds, her attention shot to him, shifted to Billy and Trisha, then back to him. That fast she'd put together exactly who had been deepest in country.

Damn! He really needed a new word for her, but she was impressing the hell out of him in more ways than one.

She made him feel...hopeful. Hopeful of what, he'd analyze later.

He'd thought to keep her in the background for this mission, toward the safer rearguard positions until she had her feet down. He wondered if he'd ever met anyone whose feet were so clearly down solidly.

On the fly, he made a change to the plan's flight assignments. He considered if it might be a personal bias, but he didn't think so.

He forced his attention back to the briefing but felt as if he was presenting to Claudia alone despite his previous conclusion.

Claudia studied the map of the western half of the Indian Ocean that Michael had put up on the projector.

"Al-Shabaab militants have been driven out of Mogadishu. They are still fighting an active war in the south but losing against the new government with the assistance of AMISOM, the African Union Mission to Somalia. The south only holds one ship at present, one that apparently no one is interested in paying a ransom for. They've been using her as a long-range mother ship to deliver pirate teams up to fifteen hundred miles away in the Maldives and—"

"Give me a break, Michael." Trisha, of course. "How are we supposed to find one mother ship in two million square miles of ocean?"

"O'Malley." Lola made it sound like a wounded plea. "Shut up and let the man speak for once."

But Claudia could see there was no real heat behind the request. Even through her exhaustion-hazed view, she could start to see how tight this team was. Trisha might have ticked off her commander, but they'd chosen to sit side by side on one of the couches.

Over the next two hours, Michael laid out his plan. Thirty-eight hostages from four ships were spread across five locations in southern Somalia. Even though the boats were gone—two accidentally sunk, one more lost in a storm, and one recaptured at sea while being used as a mother ship—the hostages were still ashore.

Unlike the northern territories where professional criminals had replaced the original fisherman-pirates attempting to protect their fishing rights, the southern piracy was run by religious jihadists. Al-Shabaab embarrassed most of the Muslim world with its extreme practices. Even Al-Qaeda had parted ways with the group. Kidnapping seven-year-old boys and arming them as shock troops was but one of many travesties.

"Taking back these hostages will be a very different operation from the one we used in the north. I've spent two of the last six months on the ground and—" A gasp rippled around the room.

Michael let it run, waiting for a silence that didn't quickly return. A white guy walking into the wrong side of the widely acknowledged most dangerous area of the most dangerous country on earth. Somalia's white population, especially out in the desert, was near enough to zero to make him completely stand out. He'd have been better off walking through downtown Tehran wearing an American flag on his back.

Yet she could see him doing it, moving so softly that no one noticed him. Though how could you not notice a man who looked that good? There was nothing extraneous about Michael: not motion, not energy, not focus. He was—well she was just tired enough to be totally crass, at least in the privacy her own thoughts—one amazing man-package.

Only three people in the room didn't react. Billy and Trisha's lack of surprise only confirmed her conclusion that the three of them had been at the heart of Operation Heavy Hand.

The third one in the room who didn't react was the teen, Dilya. No longer lost in her book and music world, she was nodding her head as if this information somehow made sense or was at least familiar. She was a sharp one.

"There were five sites in-country," Michael resumed

once the surprise had settled. "Unlike Bill's fine work in Heavy Hand, I was able to only partially foment a consolidation of the hostages so we will have to recover them in three separate strikes. One of the sites is on the coast. We'll be leaving that to Chief Petty Officer Stowell's amphibious craft, supported by Lieutenant Barstowe's Rangers."

The grim look Bill shared with Michael was enough to tell her that even if Bill had taken the lead on Heavy Hand, he and Michael had been in it together—and in it deep.

"There is," Michael continued, "a higher level of prestige among the al-Shabaab factions for those who hold hostages over those who don't, and any attempt to circumvent that posed too high a risk to the hostages themselves. However, a recent takeover of one militia group by another has combined two of those targets, so we only have two in-country. We hope. Our latest intelligence is nearly ten days old."

A glance around the room revealed that no one was balking at the stakes. This is what they did.

"Captain Kara Moretti"—Michael finally acknowledged the quiet Italian-New Yorker seated beside Claudia—"will be flying a MQ-1C Gray Eagle for us. This unmanned aerial vehicle, UAV, has a duration of forty hours, and its camera offers infrared body recognition of individuals from three kilometers up. Her command-and-control gear will be arriving tomorrow."

Claudia knew the Gray Eagle UAV also offered four Hellfire missiles, each capable of taking out your average tank or building. SOAR had added the Gray Eagle team in late 2013 so that they'd no longer have to rely on the Air Force for intelligence operations. The UAVs were now being organically embedded into SOAR operations, though she'd never flown with one before.

That's why Claudia hadn't heard of her; she was an NFO, a non-flying officer. The acronym also stood for "no future occupation." Though the UAVs were finally breaking that. Traditionally, only combat officers advanced to the higher ranks.

They'd need something new to call the drone pilots, who really wanted their craft to be known as remotely piloted aircraft or RPAs. "Fly in a can?" That's what they did. It explained how Kara was able to get away with such amazing hair, which would be too much trouble in a helmet and flight suit. Claudia's was pretty much the manageable limit.

"And if Captain Casperson is cleared for operations"—Michael interrupted her wandering thoughts—"we'll be flying a very nonstandard configuration."

"When are we planning to have an operational 'go'?" There was no way she was going to miss her first real mission. Though last night had been real. She was tired enough that her thoughts were muddling, but if she had to get it all done in a week, she would.

No matter what it took.

"The new moon will give us a fully dark night in forty-eight hours. The op is a tentative 'go' for the day after tomorrow."

If she hadn't already been awake, that certainly would have snapped her to.

Chapter 4

It would take them two days of hustling southward at *Peleliu*'s top speed before they'd be in position just over the horizon from Merca, south of Mogadishu. Claudia spent much of the first day asleep, catching up and getting in sync. Michael had again helped her to find her quarters. She'd been too disoriented when Trisha had come to get her to pay attention to where she'd started.

Through the weaving haze of her exhaustion, she wanted to kiss Michael good night, just to… Well, just to do it.

Instead, she behaved and finally repeated the face plant she'd so been looking forward to, this time between the sheets. Too tired to be more than momentarily grumpy at Michael for not taking advantage of her weakened defenses.

A dozen hours of sleep later, she was mostly awake. It was late afternoon, but as she was finally shifted over to the Night Stalkers clock of fight at night, she opted for breakfast. Claudia had eaten alone with the Navy shift, enjoying the comparative peace of not having to interact with anyone. Lola caught up with her as she delivered her tray to the scrub buckets.

"We're passing abreast of the aircraft carrier *Harry S. Truman* and her attendant group of destroyers and cruisers. Suit up and get aft." Lola was gone before Claudia could do more than nod her understanding.

The carrier group wasn't part of Operation Atalanta, focused instead on the Arabian Peninsula, probably Yemen and the several terrorist-harboring nations in the region. But apparently her proximity to the *Peleliu*'s course wasn't pure chance.

Claudia had dragged on a flight suit and tucked her helmet under her arm before reporting to the *Calamity Jane*, the Chinook parked at the *Peleliu*'s stern. The deck plating had been absorbing heat all afternoon, just dying to find someone to re-radiate it into. Apparently Claudia was the chosen sacrificial victim offered to the blaze. Crossing the hundred yards of steel was a very long trudge.

Justin was just starting the preflight on the monstrous bird and walked her through it. The Chinook was the heavy lifter of SOAR. It was a hundred-foot-long, twin-rotor monster. It could have a Humvee driven right up the rear loading ramp, carry forty troops with full gear, or hoist anything that just happened to be lying about and weighed under fourteen tons.

Once inside she introduced herself to the three crew chiefs: a ramp gunner and the two gunners stationed right behind the pilot and copilot.

"Y'all ready to do a bit o' flying, Captain?" Justin's accent was nearly incomprehensible.

"As soon as your copilot arrives."

"We-ell, we must be ready then." He grinned down at her. Not many people could make her feel short, but he certainly succeeded. He still wore his cowboy hat, which made him even taller.

Claudia spotted Captain Moretti coming up the back ramp into the helicopter, her hair a straight fall that floated along behind her. "Oh, I didn't know you flew a Chinook as well as the UAV."

Kara looked surprised. "I don't."

"Nope, she don't," Justin agreed cheerfully enough. "But y'all will today or my name ain't Winnie the Pooh."

"I thought you were Captain Justin Roberts."

"Dang! You caught me." Then he dropped about half of his accent, which had been getting a little thick. "Well, you're flying copilot today anyway. Lola wants you to fly in different types of birds, and your Chinook hours are way too low."

"As in zero."

"Ouch, Captain. What have you been flying anyway, them there little pea-patch-hoppers?" The accent returned as he waved a disgusted hand out the open ramp at Trisha's helicopter tied down on the deck.

Claudia shared a grin with Kara and then moved up to the left-side copilot's seat to get them moving out of the heat. It was clear that with two pretty women to entertain, Justin would be glad to go on dishing out the charm all afternoon and right into the evening.

Once Justin was in his seat, Kara sat on a small jump seat just aft of their positions.

The Chinook could lift eight Little Birds, even if each had a full load of fuel, munitions, and personnel. But the big helo handled just as delicately. Other than the engine controls and all of the elbow room, the cockpit didn't feel as foreign as Claudia had expected. The strangest thing was the seats, which were like loungers compared to Trisha's. Of course a Little Bird was intended for short-strike missions while the Chinook could stay up for six hours and a thousand miles, even without midair refueling.

With Justin not making it too obvious that he was worrying about his baby, Claudia lifted it into the sky. The way the mass of the bird behaved, it felt as if she were wearing a suit of medieval armor.

The aircraft carrier *Truman* was only a hundred miles and forty minutes away, hardly enough to get a feel for the Chinook. But with a lot of guidance from Justin, Claudia managed a landing without hammering it down onto the deck of the carrier. She'd never landed on one of the big carriers before, and certainly never a bird of this size.

In the Marine Corps she'd flown a lot of their craft, but never the big Sea Stallion. In the Corps you got good in your craft and they kept you there. In the 5D apparently, you'd better be good at everything or they'd get you there fast.

The *Truman* was only two hundred feet longer than the *Peleliu*, but she was twice as wide, had three times the displacement, and could carry five times the number of aircraft. Her air-wing personnel alone outnumbered the maximum staff of the *Peleliu*, and the total ship's personnel was upward of six thousand.

Bumble Bee had a population of nineteen. Sixteen now that Dad was dead, Mom was in Flagstaff, and she herself was mostly gone.

Crews descended on them in well-coordinated mayhem. In minutes, a shipping container had been rolled into the cargo bay, clearly designed to slip in neatly. Six and a half feet tall, seven and a half wide, and twenty feet long.

To Claudia it was just a big steel box. To Kara Moretti, it was clearly her reason for living. She fussed and hovered as the crew chiefs slipped the container aboard, checked the load points, and locked it down.

That was about the time Claudia picked up on where Justin's attention was focused. His attention to her was merely a strategy to spread some of his Texas charm over to the sultry Kara Moretti. He was clearly smitten.

Claudia felt amused rather than offended.

If Kara noticed, she gave no sign.

Next the carrier's cargo and helicopter handlers—dressed in bright green to distinguish them from all of the other crews aboard a carrier in active operations—trundled over a second container of similar size. It was addressed to her.

Befuddled, she had to sign for it before they would hand her the key to the padlock on the door.

"Do I unwrap it now or later?"

Kara and Justin stood to either side of her and inspected the paperwork. "Captain Claudia Jean Casperson. Personal." Other than her duffel bag and pack, all of her life's belongings presently resided in a back bedroom in an empty house at one end of an Arizona ghost town and wouldn't fill three cardboard boxes. She didn't even own a car, so what the hell personal belongings could possibly fill this container?

"Uh"—Kara tipped her head—"I dunno, Claudia. I always open personal stuff in private. You know, in case it's a box of my mom's cookies and I don't want to share." Then she stared up at the container. "Of course, this would hold a hell of a lot of cookies."

Justin tapped the paper in Claudia's hands. "There's the only number that matters. It weighs under a ton, three with the container. I can pick it up easy. Let's keep it in the box and take it home."

So they did, dangling the load on a long line attached to one of the undercarriage lifting hooks as they returned to the *Peleliu*.

"She's brand-new." Trisha patted the nose of the new helicopter they'd found inside the container. A stealth bird, which explained the "personal" label on the box to keep its arrival quiet.

Claudia stood with Trisha and Chief Warrant Lola Maloney as they all inspected the helicopter. She was beautiful. After their return from the carrier, the SOAR mechanics had whisked it out of her hands before she'd had a proper chance to admire it.

Kara Moretti at least had her command-and-control box, nicknamed "the coffin," to set up. They'd used the big elevator to take it down to the hangar deck. Kara and her assistant, Santiago, had spent the night wiring the coffin into the *Peleliu*'s radar and communications systems.

Every time Claudia had gone near her new bird, the service team had shooed her away. But overnight they'd put her helicopter together and now the bird sat on the *Peleliu*'s deck shining in the morning sun. Claudia couldn't stop grinning at it. She'd wanted to fly an AH-6M attack Little Bird and here she was, staring at a stealth one of her own.

"She's yours to name, Claudia," Lola Maloney told her. "Needs to start with an *M,* but otherwise it's up to you."

"Why an *M*?"

"Tradition." Trisha cut off her commanding officer. She made the interruption look like her normal operating procedure, but Claudia would be willing to bet Tricia knew exactly what she was doing—pushing the edge just because it was there. "Henderson and Beale started it with *Viper* and *Vengeance* for their DAP Hawks. We Little Birds went with *M* just to be contrary. *Mad Max* is flown by Max Engel, *Merchant*—as in *Merchant of Death*—is Dennis Hakawa's, and mine is the *May*."

Claudia could feel the trap in Trisha's smile. Yeah, this woman did nothing by accident. She was just waiting for the question of why a hotshot like her would name her bird *May*. So not the *Merry Month of*... Not a compression of *Mockingjay* from the book Dilya was reading. No, it had to be..."*Mayhem*." It fit Trisha perfectly.

The woman in question offered a pout at how fast Claudia solved the riddle.

Little Bird *Michael*. Now there was a good image. Lean and dangerous.

Trisha began making suggestions, "*Maverick* is too clichéd. *Mabel* like the female version of Abel and Cain. Or how about—"

"*Maven*."

"Uh..." Trisha had to stop and think about that one.

Longer than Claudia had taken on *Mayhem*, she was pleased to note.

"Like a wise woman dispensing knowledge in the form of ammunition?"

"Like Catwoman's friend and sidekick from the animated series. I always felt she had a secret identity of her own that she never revealed. The woman had serious moxie."

Trisha's low whistle of appreciation was approval enough. "Now that's seriously obscure. I like it."

Actually, if Trisha had guessed the Catwoman reference, Claudia would have claimed the other. Someone had to keep that woman on her toes. Besides, she had yet to pay Trisha back for scaring the shit out of her on that first flight.

Apparently not trusting anyone, the SOAR mechanics who'd put her bird together in under an hour had taken another six hours before they'd sign off on the airworthiness certification. Dozens of small parts had been replaced as "not up to specification" despite being factory new. There'd also been a complete recalibration of all of the onboard systems including a series of questions for her on preferred sensitivity settings and even a few adjustments based on measurements of her hands as well as hip-to-foot length.

When at last they were satisfied, Claudia took the bird up. This time she sat in the pilot's right-hand seat and Lola Maloney in the left seat. The Little Bird was so small that their inside shoulders constantly bumped until they synchronized their actions a bit. If it was Michael beside her, maybe she'd—get her head examined. She barely knew the man.

Then, as Claudia lifted off the flight deck, she noticed him. Michael leaned against a wall of an upper level of the communications platform superstructure, his arms folded over his chest, clearly watching her aloft once again. Her skin prickled with the attention. Everywhere she'd turned in these first two days she either ran into Michael or someone else would start talking about him.

As far as she could tell, it wasn't a conspiracy to make

her totally insane, because they'd also managed to not exchange a single personal word or even share a meal. They were rushing toward and planning for his mission, which kept him at the center of the storm. Everyone's pulse rate was up and climbing, especially hers. Which was really making her crazy.

No kiss was that good. It had to be an illusion or a devious Delta trick or something.

Fly. Focus on the flight.

The admonishment helped, barely.

In the SuperCobra, the pilot sat behind and above the copilot shooter, both wrapped in as much armor as the bird could carry. In the Little Bird, she was more exposed to the right due to the lack of a door, and the copilot blocked much of her view to the left. In compensation, she had a vastly better forward and down view than in a Snake.

Her new bird also had the new ADAS camera system that projected an all-around view from external cameras onto the inside of her helmet's visor. Whatever direction she turned, she could see as if she were sitting in open space with nothing but a rotor attached. Then merely changing where she focused her eyes allowed her to see the real world beyond her visor when she needed to.

Unlike Trisha, Lola Maloney had a specific set of tasks and check-offs to be accomplished. This gave Claudia an excellent chance to settle into her new helicopter and find out what its limits were. She did wonder which was a better test of skills and decided that if she ever drilled a new pilot, she'd try a bit of both—planned drill mixed with a touch of unholy mayhem.

"Sukhoi Su-30 Flanker on your tail. Bird away!" Lola shouted.

Claudia kicked out flares and chaff, and hauled back on the cyclic, then did a climb-and-flip to point her weapons at the attacker. How had she missed? Nothing there! A Russian fighter capable of cracking Mach 2 was not sneaking up on her tail. Okay, another test, though this one had pumped in a load of adrenaline.

"Why did you climb, pilot?" Chief Maloney sounded ticked.

"Unexpected response, ma'am. They'd expect a dive. And it blocks me from any ground-based surveillance or targeting systems, especially when I cross above my own chaff and flares."

"Why didn't you wait for me to release the countermeasures?"

"Because"—Claudia had been through too many proficiency tests to bristle at the Chief Warrant's tone—"you hadn't already done so, and my ability to outrun a Mach 4.5 R-77 air-to-air missile for more than a second or two is nonexistent."

"Give me a full dive."

Claudia had been thinking a lot about that maneuver Trisha had pulled on her. She crossed the cyclic and rudder control and snap-rolled into an inverted dive, making it a spiral just for good measure. It felt right, just ever so slightly nausea-inducing, which she corrected with pedal trim. She kept the blades at full climb, which, because she was upside down, made their descent very fast.

They fell five thousand feet in far too few seconds, while she kept her eyes on the altimeter and then ran force loading calculations in her head to not overstrain the new rotor blades as she did the rollout. She was five hundred feet up, instead of Trisha's two hundred, but she'd take the extra caution on her first attempt. She did a loop-the-loop, climbing up over the top until the Little Bird lay on its back and all of the controls were functioning backward due to inverted flight.

Allowing for a longer drop, she came out at two hundred and fifty feet above sea level and felt pretty damn pleased with herself.

"Shit!" was Maloney's first comment. "You learned that from Trisha, didn't you? Just what I need, another hot-rodder."

"No, ma'am. Not a hot-rodder. Just trying to be the best."

"If you weren't, you wouldn't be in SOAR. And the Training Battalion wouldn't have specifically recommended you to D company of the 5th Battalion."

That was news to her. She was wondering how she'd made it into the notorious 5D.

"The worst part, Casperson, the part that's really pissing me off—"

Claudia tensed and waited for the verdict. Had she done something wrong? She couldn't think of what.

"I hate having to admit to O'Malley that she was right. You're ready and are hereby cleared for all flight operations."

Claudia added a victory roll on her way back to the ship.

Michael had invited himself into the air plot room aboard the *Peleliu* by hinting to Lieutenant Commander

Ramis that's where the LCDR wanted to go. It was only natural for security to admit the man walking at Boyd's side into the most secure room on the ship. Sometimes stealth was not the required technique when performing an infiltration.

He wanted to see Claudia's flight. He didn't analyze why; he simply knew that he did and followed instinct just as he would on any assignment. Michael had long since learned to trust that little voice of experience.

He then suggested that one of the duty officers might want to use the stealth Little Bird presently aloft as a training exercise for tracking hostile inbounds. That kept three primary radar screens focused on what Claudia was doing up there. For good measure they added a visual follow with an automated tracking telescope. They had a very hard time keeping a lock on the craft because its radar shielding was very good. Even the visual scope was radar steered, so it fared no better than the strictly electronic systems.

Michael suggested the infrared targeting system used on the deck guns. That finally gave them a moderately reliable track of her antics on the gun-sight camera, but she still slipped out of frame at least once a minute because her hot engine exhaust was also shielded and even the infrared lock would be lost.

The blast of flares startled the team and the cloud of chaff punched a hole in the ship's constant scan for incoming raiders. They all began scanning below the chaff for the helicopter's new location. Michael spotted Claudia climbing clear over the top but didn't point her out. She was barely a faint echo on the distant side of the chaff cloud, well hidden even accounting for her stealth gear. If the *Peleliu* had ridden just a few more kilometers to the west, she'd have been invisible behind the spinning bits of foil.

The staff only spotted her as she was rolling off into a dive. A crazy damn dive.

"Get the scope back on her and magnify," the watch officer called out. "C'mon, team. She's dusting you again."

The buzz in the room disappeared when her image came up on the screen, plummeting downward in a spiraling inverted flight. Her rollout and loop finally made the senior flight controller be the first to break the silence. "Damn!"

When she did the snap roll, losing no altitude as she did so, Michael couldn't think of a better description.

He knew how it felt to always strive to be the best.

He also knew how it looked when he saw it because he was always looking for it in himself and others.

"Damn!" indeed.

Claudia could really fly.

Chapter 5

The entire flight of helicopters flew deep into Kenya before doubling back toward the Somali border. The helos settled beside Justin's Chinook helicopter, *Calamity Jane*. The *Jane* had flown in ahead of them and parked deep in the desert to set up a FARP, a forward area refueling-rearming point—a mobile gas station for short-range helicopters like the Little Birds.

Claudia flexed her hands after she shut down the *Maven*.

In moments, a crew swarmed them from the MH-47G Chinook with long fuel hoses that connected back to a massive rubber bladder of fuel in the *Jane*'s cargo bay. The big Black Hawks could refuel from a KC-135 Stratotanker in flight, but the Little Birds couldn't waste their limited weight-carrying ability on a heavy refueling probe. And tonight they needed to start the operation with full tanks. Even freshly fueled, they'd have little left over for unpredicted problems along the way.

Eastern Kenya wasn't Claudia's Arizona desert. It was too flat, white instead of red, the trees were all the wrong shapes. It was terribly disorienting and she didn't even want to step down on it, just in case it wasn't there in some strange way.

The sun was an hour from sunset, two hours until full dark. She should stretch her legs, but her nerves were at full jangle. Normally she flew smooth and clean. After six years with the Marines and two more in SOAR training, flight was her natural state. Being on the ground was what felt disjointed.

"Come with me." Michael had ridden copilot with her for this first leg. He'd been deep in his strong-and-silent routine. She'd been so busy worrying at the details of the mission like a sore tooth that she'd also had nothing to say. It had been a very quiet ride. Trisha and Bill, paired in the other stealth Little Bird, had probably spent the whole flight chatting about, she didn't know, China patterns or frag grenades or something equally prosaic.

Knowing she had to move, she forced herself out of her seat and checked that the ground crew was behaving. After all, this brand-new bird was all hers and she'd spent years working for it. The man and woman of the fuel team wore bright purple vests over their armor, marking them clearly as fuelies, also called grapes because of their vest color.

Even though she hadn't fired a shot, a two-man, red-vested ammunition team inspected her craft carefully. These reds kept trying to relabel themselves as "the Red Hot team" and even though one of them was pretty damn handsome, it didn't stick. The not-quite-so-hot one, but with a better smile, asked her to please double-check that her weapon and the spare ammo pouches along her thighs were fully stocked. He also ensured that the FN-SCAR combat assault rifle strapped across her chest and her Marine Corps M9 in her hip holster were loaded.

Once they finally stopped hovering, Michael came around from the other side of the helicopter. She noticed that they didn't bother to question his readiness. Was it because he was a D-boy and they'd learned not to ask, or was it because she was a woman? Maybe it was just that she was new and they didn't trust her to have a clue out here in the real world. After almost a decade in the service, she was always ready, so they were going to be disappointed on that point.

By the look in Michael's eye, Claudia could see what he was up to. Okay, some things she wasn't ready for. She cut him off.

"Please, no. I can't stand to review the mission one more time. My brain will short-circuit and I'll be useless."

Michael closed his mouth and considered her for a long moment. Then with one of those silent, sideways nods, he turned and led her away from the bustling impromptu airport.

They'd landed in the deep desert, a dozen miles from anywhere except some trackless stretch of the Somali border. Low scrub trees that Claudia didn't recognize were scattered every few hundred meters. Bushes under a meter high might have been related to the creosote ones that dotted the hills of Bumble Bee. Here the sands were very white, rather than the yellow and red of her home hills. And instead of hills, there were just miles of flat land that would be of use to no one except perhaps a really desperate camel.

Michael came to a stop just over the first rise.

Claudia walked up until they were standing side by side looking out at the endless expanse of dusty green brush, white sand, and dusty blue sky. With the helicopters out of sight behind them, and even the fuel pump noises muted by the shallow rise, she felt as if she could suddenly breathe for the first time in ages.

She hadn't missed the feeling when she was in the middle of it all. There'd been no time to just stop in months. The final part of Green Platoon training for SOAR was no easier than the beginning part. Helicopters, tactics, explosives, language, first aid...the trainers had inundated her with information, methodologies, and endless practice during every second they'd had her in their control.

That had been followed by an immediate assignment to Operation Atalanta, travel, the Yemeni terrorist camp, and all of the intensity of mission planning before she even had met most of the flight crews.

Five days ago, she'd been signing out of her billet in Fort Campbell, Kentucky, sweating beneath the moist heat of a May afternoon. Now she was sweating like a dog beneath the setting sun in the arid furnace of the African desert.

Finally, for a brief moment, there was peace in her world. The soft breeze, though not enough to cool her brow, occasionally rustled the dry branches together. Some small animal chirruped in the distance. Far aloft, a scavenger circled, perhaps wondering if the new visitors would have the decency to die here so that it could feed.

"There will be dead enough this night," she told it. Just follow the Night Stalkers. A grim thought for the start of a mission, no matter how true. She just needed to remind herself that some of these hostages had been three and four years in captivity. Someone who would do that to another human being didn't deserve to live.

Most of the hostages belonged to various uninsured ships with owners who had disappeared rather than pay the multimillion-dollar ransoms. For some reason, the

Somali pirates held on, hoping that somehow money would fall out of the skies. Well, tonight something certainly would. The Night Stalkers would be delivering the weight of the American military.

—∞—

"Stop thinking about the mission. Just listen to the desert." Michael kept his voice to a whisper.

Claudia nodded once, then again before appearing to finally relax the tensed-up line of her shoulders.

He waited a while longer.

"I grew up here. Became a woman in the desert."

He had become a man climbing the trees. First the maples and oaks of his backyard, then the towering Douglas firs that often reached a hundred or more feet above the ground and grew around the campus where his parents were professors. The redwoods had been inevitable in his quest to go highest, to be the best. The few who ascended the Titans, as the biggest trees of them all were called, were a small community and not a one of them could outclimb him.

Claudia's experience must be different. It would be—

"My parents weren't real involved. My father had a bad back injury and was on lifetime disability. He was a real bummer." Claudia momentarily remembered how her father's shroud of silence lay over the house like suppressive fire, killing off all expression and action. It wasn't a gentle or benign peace. "The man really should have taken antidepressants or something."

He smiled but did not laugh.

"Yeah, some joke," she acknowledged. "I spent a lot of time on my old horse, Squib. We'd ride up into the hills for hours, sometimes days. Just the two of us alone in the Castle Creek Wilderness or camping at Upper Dead Cow Spring."

Michael had never been to Arizona, but he'd been in several war games in the Nevada desert—he'd even designed a couple of games until the Navy, Army, and Air Force got together and asked the Joint Special Operations Command for a challenge their people had some chance of achieving. The point was to find a way to achieve the impossible, but that day he'd learned that regular forces weren't Delta and needed different standards.

And he'd certainly fought in many other deserts all over the world. This one's smell of mineral, salt, and sand would be wrong to her. She'd have ridden among sweet lupine, astringent juniper, and biting creosote over iron-tinged sands.

"I read a lot," she continued softly. "Anything I could lay my hands on, including local history. It is called Yavapai County for a reason. The Yavapai were a people forced onto reservations with the Apache. I read that there they adopted the Sunrise Dance ceremony. When a woman reaches puberty, there is a four-day ritual of dance and blessings to welcome the girl to womanhood. I liked the sound of that."

Michael's transition to manhood had probably been his first solo Titan ascent. He'd been fourteen, and his parents had become too old and cautious to climb the big trees any more. At three hundred feet above the ground, he'd laughed. He'd also wept there for the last time, with no one there to see what he had achieved.

Solo.

"You were alone."

She nodded, then, after a long time, continued.

"I was thirteen when I spent four days in the desert. Four days and nights I danced and did not sleep. There was no medicine man or godmother, so I made up my own blessings. And I ran."

Claudia pointed east. "They run each morning of the ceremony, so I ran for the child." She turned north. "The girl." She continued around the compass. "The woman, and finally old age. I ran for hours every day. I finally realized that I was running toward something rather than away. That is where I learned that I was the only one responsible for my journey. That is the day I made myself and knew that no matter what team I joined, I did it alone."

Michael had learned the same lesson as a child and then searched until he found it again in the armed forces.

"For the first month of the Delta Selection Process, you have no name among the instructors. You're Green Five, Red Three; it changes every day. There are no team or buddy activities like the other forces. It is completely a solo effort, every brutal inch of it."

"Which you loved."

"Which I loved," he admitted.

Claudia turned to face him. Framed by the sunset light rippling over the Kenyan desert, she was golden.

"I've never told anyone about that. Or about the silence." Her voice was a caress. "I thought only I could hear it, but you can too."

He nodded. He did hear it. Even a single heartbeat before battle. Perhaps especially then he could hear the small moments of silence.

"I've never met anyone like you," she said softly.

Claudia could feel herself going soft in the head for Colonel Michael Gibson. He was like a guy wearing a tool belt taken to the hundredth power.

Michael stood beside her in the Kenyan desert with the gentle evening breeze riffling his hair. He wore Crye Precision MultiCam camouflage beneath his heavy weapons harness. He carried minimal survival gear and maximum ammunition. Silenced rifle, submachine gun, two handguns, a big knife, grenades…

He looked dangerous, like death walking the land.

Yet he was also beautiful in the quiet sunset as they waited for the last of it to give way to the moment when the stars would command the sky.

As a D-boy colonel, he was perhaps the most effective field soldier alive. Those skills didn't show on the surface. There was no hardness of expression to go with his hardness of body. His hands didn't clutch his weapons, nor were his thumbs tucked in with his ammo magazines.

He stood at peace and watched her. Even that watching wasn't some deep assessment. Rather it was as if he simply saw all of her.

There was a question she wanted to ask, but this time she didn't.

It was too big.

Perhaps too dangerous.

She didn't even dare to ask it of herself.

Instead, she simply hooked a finger through the D-ring at the center of his harness and pulled him toward her.

Before their lips touched, she knew this wasn't going to be some little kiss of testing and tasting.

A heat rose up from within her. The heat of the desert. The fire of upcoming battle. The need to prove that she was alive. That however true the image of the Ice Queen might be to the rest of the world, for this man in this moment, she could be far more.

She held on to his harness and drove into the kiss only to feel every bit of the heat returned tenfold. In moments her only ability was to hang on as Michael overwhelmed her senses.

He'd dug one hand into her hair and fisted it there, not as if he was trapping her, but rather as if he was holding on for all he was worth.

The other hand dragged her against him so powerfully that she might have been naked beneath the moonless night. The strength of his arms was beyond imagining.

She groaned and clung and fought to get closer as if she drank of his essence only to have him take it back and return it tenfold.

Claudia wanted to rend and tear. Toss weapons, armor, and battle clothes aside. To lose herself.

There was neither rending nor a sudden step back to break the heat.

One moment they were going at each other like wildcats, then the next like lovers suddenly gone gentle.

A last, painfully soft brush of lips, and they once again faced the desert as it quieted into full darkness, this time over each other's shoulders as they kept the embrace.

His hand now cradled her head, hers held on to his powerful arms rather than his harness.

Out there in the dark somewhere lay a question.

A final brief hug and they let go, turning once more to stand side by side.

The question she didn't dare ask.

She ran her tongue over her swollen lips and relished Michael's taste.

What if you didn't have to do it alone?

Chapter 6

Michael could feel the mission building inside him as he listened to the desert. After all of his years in Delta, it was a familiar pattern, one he knew and welcomed.

Though he'd rarely been kissed breathless the moment before a mission began. Oddly, he felt he was somehow more than he really was due to how she saw him, rather than less. As if he was even more ready for this mission than any prior one.

The first layer of a mission-centric mind-set—the goal and mission that was the purpose—formed during the briefing. It didn't matter if it was training or reality, he treated them exactly the same. If there was a 10k morning run, he gave it the same focus as when they slid into Libya and "helped" the locals track down Muammar Gaddafi. Though, if it hadn't been for the locals, they could have done it a damn sight faster and the man wouldn't have been beaten to death, then shot in the head, no matter how much he deserved it.

The next layer—shutting off the outside world—overlaid that base. All that mattered was the moment and the mission. Nothing outside that focus existed. Not the Presidential orders authorizing the action, now in the past. Not the news networks always looking for a juicy "in" but finding out about fewer than one in a hundred Delta operations.

Next layer included the operational aspects that he no longer needed. The *Peleliu* had no meaning until the end of the operation. Captain Kara Moretti had some relevance still, but he was close to forgetting about her as well. She'd kept the Gray Eagle UAV aloft for most of the last two days, watching their first target deep in the Somali desert. They didn't want to lose track of the group if they decided to move. They hadn't. So, her task and usefulness to this night's mission were almost over. All he needed to know about her right now would be embodied by a clean data feed.

The Gray Eagle was up there now, with a full load of four air-to-surface Hellfire missiles just in case, but they weren't anticipating any need for that capability tonight, so he let it wash out of his mind.

Some days this task of focusing down was easier and some days harder. Today, the next layer of mental preparation was giving him definite problems.

He'd selected Claudia as his pilot because he liked the way she flew, that perfect steadiness and the creativity he'd seen during her flight test.

But Claudia in the desert silence was a revelation. Michael enjoyed women. They were fun, interesting, and often a challenge—all of which he found to be motivators.

Claudia in the desert throwing herself at him had left him spinning, a feeling he definitely didn't have much experience with. He was always three steps ahead of the women he was with, could see their plans long before they even became conscious of them. Every time he thought he had Claudia pegged, she slipped quietly to the side.

She was about much more than flight. In the four days they'd known each other, they had yet to say a single word about piloting or past missions. Yet the few things he had told her, no one else knew.

He knew that she smelled of moonlight and new-grown conifer.

And tasted, dear sweet gods. The way that woman could kiss, with her whole heart and her whole body. He…

Focus.

They returned as full darkness settled on the desert. And he thought of their frantic kiss. Until that moment, Claudia had been remote, fascinating, and so beautiful that his heart beat strangely around her, but remote.

He had dismissed her first night's embrace as an aberration she'd thankfully been too exhausted to recall and he was still too dumb to stop reliving.

But that first kiss on the ship's deck and the discovery of the softness and warmth of her lips had made the woman instantly, intensely real. Flesh and blood. Not a distant object to be admired and appreciated, but a living, breathing woman.

And now, after… If he were to bed this woman, and he couldn't wait to do just that, would he even come out the other side alive?

Claudia wanted to laugh at them. They were both so carefully outwardly sedate and calm. Yet inside she was torn between a desire to grab Michael and try a repeat of their kiss out of sight of their impromptu helibase, and simply ripping his clothes off right here in the middle of everything and not giving a damn who watched.

She wondered if she was really screwing up his mental preparation. Part of her hoped so. To have that kind of power over a man like Colonel Gibson, well, it would certainly be something.

But if it made him even the smallest bit less likely to walk away from this, she was going to kick her own ass but good.

It was comic, their movements in such silent, perfect unison. Climbing into the small helicopter from either side as if choreographed. Seat harnesses clicking loudly at the same moment, both checking their gear.

She should say something, or he should. You didn't just kiss someone like that and then…nothing.

She lifted off with the other helos, climbing as high as they could into the night sky.

Or maybe "nothing" was the only thing to say after a moment like that.

She watched the night sky outside the bird as they climbed near the upper limits for high-and-hot operation of the fully loaded Little Bird. Much higher and they'd burn fuel at a prodigious rate that tonight's operation could ill afford and didn't require.

A glance at the mission clock told her she was out of time for words.

Ten seconds.

Michael released his seat harness and checked his parachute harness.

Five.

He double-checked all of his weapons.

Then he reached out and squeezed her arm briefly before stepping out of the helicopter at fifteen thousand feet.

A moment too late, she knew what she wanted to say.

Michael didn't reject her or laugh at her. He didn't see her as a target or as the Ice Queen. As far as she could tell, he looked at her and saw Claudia Jean Casperson.

Which was a first for her.

"Thank you."

She said it to the dark and hoped that he somehow heard it as he fell through the sky.

~

Michael fell until the wind was a full-throated roar in his ears, then pulled his rip cord. His black, night-flying chute deployed with a sharp *ka-phump* and jerked his body sharply.

It was only then that he realized he never before had done that with a pilot. A shared nod or a tap on arm, and he'd be gone. Instead, through her flight suit, he'd felt the strength of Claudia's forearm as she worked the collective. Been aware of the miniscule flexings of her muscles as she adjusted the controls even in the instant they were in contact. Could feel once more the strength with which she'd grabbed him.

Michael pulled down his night-vision gear and looked about the dark sky. Five others flew their chutes nearby—Bill and four other Deltas. A glance up revealed that the *Maven* was already far above him, lost in the stars except for the slightest trace of her engine's heat signature. His team formed up above him in a stack; he was the flight's primary navigator.

He checked the infrared readout from Moretti's Gray Eagle on the small screen he wore on the inside of his wrist. The objective was ten miles northeast. An easy flight—the oversized parachute providing plenty of lift above the still-hot desert—as they moved in absolute radio silence. Five minutes from the jump point, a half mile from the landing zone, he scanned the horizon with his own night-vision gear instead of the UAV's. Exactly where anticipated, he saw a dozen heat signatures a thousand yards past the preselected landing point.

The team hit in unison, spread at fifty-foot intervals across the desert. Thirty seconds later, they'd packed their chutes, unslung their HK416 rifles, and set out at a dead run. Five minutes in, they slowed, spread out, and began scanning for sentries. Moretti had circled her UAV down from four miles up to just one to improve her sensing accuracy. Her tight focus showed his team of six encircling the camp, with no other sentries out in the bushes.

This al-Shabaab group had become complacent because of their remote location. They'd set up camp under the largest tree in the area and scavenged almost everything around them for firewood. The small nightly plume of smoke was how he'd finally located them in the heart of the desert.

While scouting the cities, he'd overheard a mention of periodic food deliveries to a camp out in this direction. He'd traced the Range Rover driver using the local food market and managed to get the general location from him by buying him liberal amounts of the khat drug that seemed to fuel all of Somalia.

This lone remaining tree offered the jailers a wide range of vision and made escape difficult for the prisoners. During the day it would also be the only shade in the area.

However, at night, it offered Michael's team clear visibility of what was occurring in the camp. The only guard still awake sat by the dwindling fire for warmth, facing the flames so his night vision would be nonexistent. Fifteen bodies slept on the ground, most huddled into themselves against the relative chill of the desert night. All in rags.

Michael waited until he could see the five other Deltas standing around the edge of the clearing. They showed as soft green outlines in the infrared night-vision gear. Even in the NVGs the D-boys were barely visible. Their clothing was heat-reflecting and their faces were only exposed from their goggles to their chin.

He raised his arm and waited. Five arms were raised in answer. Everyone was ready. He swung his arm down and they began walking forward in unison, careful to avoid twig, stone, or shifting sand. The last hundred feet took another three minutes.

By the time the guard noticed them, Michael's men were standing scattered in and among the sleeping bodies and had already picked their targets.

The guard looked up startled when Michael stepped between him and the fire. He reached for his gun.

The soft double-spit of a silenced HK416 dropped him where he sat.

Two seconds later, before the hostages were even awake, the other four guards were dead, each with a double tap to the head and a "sure shot" to the heart.

Ten seconds more to check off the guards and the hostages versus the gathered intelligence.

Bill informed the hostages that this was a rescue by the U.S. Navy. Which was partially correct; after all, the *Peleliu* was a Navy ship. Of course, everyone would automatically assume that meant the SEALs. It seemed only fair to burden their brothers-in-arms with yet more unwanted publicity. Couldn't happen to a nicer bunch of guys.

"Stay together. Stay quiet."

The other four D-boys moved back into the night to watch for stray sentries or unexpected arrivals. It was possible to fool the Gray Eagle's eye—not easy, but possible. Fooling an operator on the ground with the latest NVGs and desert skills was not something your average Somali nomad-turned-jihadist could manage.

A quick scan assured Michael that the area was secure. There was little chance of any radio transmission being monitored from out here, but radio silence was the protocol. The watching helos above would only break silence if they saw the heat signature of another moving body or an unexpected arrival.

He pulled out his infrared beacon, a trio of LEDs snapped onto the top of a nine-volt battery—that also fit his emergency radio—and set it to a three-second flash. Otherwise invisible, it would paint a distinctive signal for the waiting helicopters.

While the helos were flying in, he gathered up the weapons. The sole radio operator was lying beside his gear, which Michael grabbed. If the man had any codes or contact frequencies other than the latest one tuned into the radio, he had taken them to the grave. Michael noted the frequency; they'd monitor it from the helos just in case.

He mounted a camera in the trees with a microphone and satellite antenna. It took him under three minutes to mount, test, and hide it under a cloth that would look like bark except under the closest examination. Chances were low of it being useful, but someone back in ops wanted to test their cool, new eavesdropping system.

They'd tried this surveillance strategy once before in Mogadishu harbor, sending in a team at night to mount cameras in removed sections of wooden pilings that held the docks. A couple hundred thousand dollars of hardware that he'd told them was stupid, but his team had been ordered to install it anyway. Guess what? It had been stupid. The target had to walk in front of the stationary cameras to be seen. By the time the image was received and interpreted, the target was long gone—assuming that a satellite was even in position to pick up the signal before the batteries died. This at least stood a chance because Kara Moretti's Gray Eagle would be listening in for the next two days.

Calamity Jane hammered down out of the sky accompanied by the four Little Birds. Lola Maloney aboard the *Vengeance*, their main Black Hawk gun platform, wasn't needed for this and remained aloft, keeping a watchful eye.

He and Bill hustled the eleven hostages onto the Chinook. They only had to carry two of them—too weak to walk themselves. They were all frightfully thin but appeared healthy, other than a dazed disbelief that their long nightmare was actually ending. SOAR would have a pair of combat search-and-rescue medics aboard to help them. The CSARs could do anything that didn't require a fully equipped operating theater.

The *Vicious*, a transport Black Hawk flown by Chief Warrant Dusty James, arrived and swept the pirates into body bags while his boys cleared the site of weapons and refuse. Hopefully the clean wipe of the site would waste someone's time when they went looking for what had happened to the group and wondering if they'd moved on of their own accord.

They hadn't.

And maybe his little camera rig would snap their photo.

He stowed his chute and reserve in the back of Claudia's helicopter less than twenty-three minutes after he stepped out of it, fifteen thousand feet up and ten miles away.

Eleven hostages recovered, check.

Twenty-seven to go.

The next site would require different tactics.

Chapter 7

Claudia was used to thinking in sorties. When the Marines went in somewhere heavy—where the lines were drawn and the troops engaged—helicopters flew sorties. Load up with ammo, fly in to provide close fire support, cycle back to the airbase or the ship when out of ammo or fuel, then repeat as often as necessary.

SOAR thought in strikes and operations. Need a hostage rescued? A bad guy targeted? Intel gathered? The 160th was your team. She knew her role during the first strike of this operation was to deliver and retrieve, assuming everything went according to plan, which it had.

Now the flying would become more interesting.

"We lost starlight. The storm front is moving in as predicted." Claudia greeted Michael as he climbed aboard. "A night parachute jump, one kilometer sprint, and sanitizing a hostage site; you've had a very busy twenty minutes."

"Had worse." Michael began reloading his weapon as she lifted back into the night. As last aloft, her rotor wash erased any final impression of the Little Bird's skids or the now-rescued hostages. She noticed that Michael didn't need many rounds to reload his rifle. Generally, a great deal of lead flew through a battle scene for each person who was injured or killed. With Delta, two shots equaled a life almost every time.

Claudia had thought she was inured to it, to the price of battle. With Delta it was very up close and personal. That's what they were good at and known for. That would take some getting used to on her part.

"Why?" Michael reseated the full magazine into his rifle.

She tried to unravel what question Michael could possibly be asking. The storm front had been part of Michael's plan, so that wouldn't be it. Guessing was what Michael wanted her to be doing. So…not. It was probably about why she'd kissed him, but if that was it, he was going to have to ask. And maybe that would give her a little more time to decide why she had. No matter how right it felt, it had been stupid in many, many ways—one of which included a potential court martial and the ending of one or both of their careers.

"Use your words, Michael. Ask me the whole question."

He leaned forward to look up at the pitch-black of the moonless and starless night as she turned southeast. This time she remained nap-of-earth—her maximum height fifty feet from the ground to the top of her rotor—and only then to clear a line of trees. Power lines in the deep Somali countryside weren't much of an issue. Mostly she stayed under twenty-five feet, which kept her skids about fifteen off the ground.

Claudia kept a special eye on the *Mayhem* to see what Trisha was doing. She was another five feet lower than Claudia, but they had a thirty-minute flight ahead and there was simply no need to work that hard until they were closer. Flying at that level used up "edge" too quickly. It was why snipers were only allowed to be "on target" for fifteen minutes at a time. After that, their skills decreased if they didn't get a rest break. Of course, Trisha appeared to be nothing but "edge." Maybe she could sustain it forever.

Michael's protracted silence told her exactly what he was asking. It was about the kiss. Well, she certainly wasn't about to volunteer any more there. She should never have done it in the first place, but she'd been overwhelmed by the simple gift of silence he'd given her. It didn't hurt that he had so much integrity that it poured out of his very fingertips. So damn handsome too.

It wasn't an excuse—there was no sufficient cause for her to have crossed that line—but it was hard to regret that kiss. He hadn't pulled back either, not that she'd given him much chance.

The problem was that it was going to go further, much further. That fact was both beyond stupid and contained not the least little bit of regret. She'd start by...

She really had to stop thinking about it. But if it meant nothing, why could she remember every... Crap! She really was a basket case. *Just fly the damn machine, Claudia*.

At ten minutes and thirty miles out, Michael still hadn't asked the rest of his question and the feed from the Gray Eagle went dark. That meant the cloud ceiling was below the pre-agreed limit. Kara would keep the drone in the area, but it probably had done its duty for this operation. The first spattering raindrops struck the windscreen, then increased rapidly as he and Claudia flew toward the target area and deeper into the storm.

The night was so dark that Claudia was relying solely on instruments anyway and didn't need to see.

The display from the ADAS made for a very clear grayscale image of exactly what lay ahead. The cameras mounted outside her craft were offering her an exceptionally detailed real-time image of the terrain around her. Terrain-following radar simply couldn't match this, though she did appreciate its warnings when some obstacle cropped up.

She was on course and on mission plan. One of the skills drilled into her during training was how to hit any target within a thirty-second window, whether it was over the ridge or across the country.

At least she was on profile for her flight. Where she herself was going was anybody's guess. SOAR was supposed to help her life make more sense, not less. That was another reason she'd come over from the Marines. The distractions were supposed to be less in SOAR—her mission here would be to fly, not to follow a hundred Marine Corps rules and procedures. That part was off to a good start.

But after just forty-eight hours in theater, her own life was, for the first time since she'd held her own desert ceremony at thirteen, starting to spin out of her control.

Michael had counted on the rainstorm, now striking the laminate-glass windscreen as loudly as hail. Rainfall was a rare and inconsistent event throughout Somalia. The Mog, with its surrounding area, was the garden spot of the country, receiving almost twenty inches of rain each year—about the same as southern California, only without the major irrigation systems. In Somalia, the rain didn't even come all in one season.

But for tonight, the weather forecasters aboard the *Peleliu* had tracked a decaying cyclone and predicted it would be pushing some rough weather over southern Somalia.

Michael had been squatting in a hut in Buurhakaba last month when rainfall hit. At first, everyone streamed outside to wash themselves in the warm rain and collect water. Once they were clean and the water barrels were filled, they'd retreated inside—every single one. Even the al-Shabaab guards on the hostages he'd located at the outskirts of town.

And this storm was pushing a cold front along in the squall line. It would be sixty degrees, fifteen degrees cooler than the average low of seventy-five, for several hours as the storm passed through. No sane Somali would go out in such weather. He'd probably get frostbitten, or as good as, if he tried. The Somalis' circulation just wasn't up to fending off sixty-degree weather.

That's what he was counting on.

He tried to see ahead. He tried to anticipate each variation of the attack scenario. If the rain hadn't come… but it had, allowing him to shed a whole set of contingencies. He checked the gauge on the dash… Yes, the outside air temperature was also falling as predicted. The rain was heavier than anticipated. He considered flooding problems, visibility, effects of the moisture on firing accuracy.

Michael thought about the woman beside him and how she'd felt in his arms, offering him the best kiss of his life, and also that brief moment when he'd rested his hand on her arm and the powerful connection he'd felt to her.

He'd long since learned to let such thoughts flow over and through him, to acknowledge their existence and move on. Shoving them aside rarely worked; then they simply came back twofold.

Instead, he said thank you for the reminder of his own humanness and moved on.

"Use your words, Michael." As if she were talking to a child. She knew exactly what he was asking and was making it clear he was going to have to work for it if he wanted to taste her stillness again. That was fine with him. One thing he'd learned when he joined The Unit all those years ago was that he knew how to get what he wanted. At the moment, that was two things: a mission and the woman beside him.

He also knew that Claudia would understand that the mission had to come first, which made him appreciate her all the more.

Three minutes and eight miles out, twenty-seven hostages to go, he double-checked his weapon. The weather was bucking the Little Bird. He stuck an elbow out into the wind through the missing door. The rain pounded against his battle gear with the force of a .22 shell—hard enough to knock his elbow back out of the airstream. Even with them moving at more than a hundred and fifty miles per hour, that was a heavy rainfall.

Two minutes out, he checked the other birds. The *May*, with Bill and Trisha aboard, had the point lead by two rotor diameters. Claudia was mirroring her closely, without all of that twitchy magic that was a part of Trisha's flying. A part of him wondered, just intellectual curiosity, if Claudia made love the way she flew, smooth and steady.

To his left were *Merchant* and *Mad Max*. They each toted along two more D-boys in their tiny rear seats. There was no way they could have ridden the outside benches at these speeds in this storm. It would delay their exits from the aircraft for several seconds, but that had been accounted for.

One minute out. Claudia dropped another ten feet of altitude. If someone stood up unexpectedly from the occasional scrub brush, he was likely to get a skid in the head.

The rain continued to pound on the windscreen. Tin roofs—all of the huts in the key section of Buurhakaba had tin roofs. The driving rain would make a thunderous racket on the roofs, one far louder than the landing of the stealth helicopters in their courtyard. If the rain hadn't come, the D-boys would have fast-roped down three blocks away, but it had arrived and arrived hard.

Ten seconds out, the outskirts of town came into view. They flashed over the poorest houses with rough-thatched conical roofs over circular huts of stick and mud. Michael dropped his seat harness, raised his weapon to ready position, and stepped one foot out onto the skid as Claudia slowed. He ignored the bug-like stings of the flight-driven rain.

The conical buildings gave way to rectangular adobe ones with peaked tin roofs. The target square in front of the building that had held the hostages a week before appeared below. Thermal scans had confirmed that the main building still had a much higher than standard occupancy rate—which was saying something in Somalia—based on the heat radiation coming off the tin roof just before dawn this morning.

Claudia backed the helicopter from full flight to a standstill so sharply that he was almost thrown into the forward windscreen, would have been if he hadn't been expecting it.

He used that last gift of forward momentum to hit the ground running.

Claudia slid the cyclic forward and eased up on the collective even as the rear end of her skid brushed the earth. She rolled onto the front tip and climbed aloft again before Michael took three steps away.

Damn the man for not following up on his question. Damn him for having such perfect timing and athletic ability that she simply had to appreciate him anyway.

A big truck had been parked in the middle of the square. It was a large, flatbed cargo truck with wood-slat sides, probably for hauling al-Shabaab's illegal charcoal down to the Kismayu port. A smuggling operation that made a quarter of a billion dollars a year for the extremists, despite UN and Somali governmental sanctions.

One of the D-boys tried to hot-wire the truck, but it apparently wasn't going anywhere. That was going to be a problem.

Trisha was several seconds slower getting off the ground than Claudia had been, which did some nice things for Claudia's ego. Which also meant that she drew first fire. Rounds began pinging off *Maven*'s windscreen.

The projection on the inside of her visor traced the rifle to the third window of the hostage building. Hitting it with a missile would be an unreasonable risk. Then in her night vision she saw the figure jerk backward, then collapse over the windowsill. She'd wager that he had a neat double-shot wound in his head.

Even masked by the rain, the shot had been enough to draw attention. A half-dozen buildings erupted with gunfire, most of it in no particular direction.

She needed permission to target them.

"Count is four low," Michael squawked over the radio.

Crap! That meant that four hostages had been moved. It also meant no firing back at whole-building targets until the other four had been located. Now they had to back off and let the six D-boys do what they did. The streets were only going to heat up.

"Leave northwest route clear," Michael ordered less than thirty seconds later. So, he'd learned something, and learned it fast. She would never ask how.

There were three other entrances to the square.

Claudia double-checked the compass because the four roads entering the courtyard were at odd angles. Then she launched a pair of FFAR Hydra rockets into the southwest intersection and two more to the south. Trisha gave the southeast approach the same treatment. The combined pairs of rockets delivered ten pounds of high explosive. That cut a deep enough crater to stop most vehicles. It also caught surrounding buildings on fire and would slow down anyone else coming in.

"We have thirteen ready for the square." There were supposed to be seventeen, damn these militants. Couldn't they cooperate in their own demise any better than that?

Cataclysm, another big Chinook, was supposed to come in. Justin in the *Calamity Jane* was running the rescuees from the desert site out to the coast. No point in putting them at risk again. But there was no way that the *Cat* would fit with the big truck there.

"Fire in the hole," Claudia called out and watched as the gathered team of Delta and hostages ducked back into a building. No need for him to ask what she was thinking. No need for her to tell him to clear the street and then wait. They were in perfect sync. She didn't need to know it to feel its truth.

"Do it," Michael called.

Didn't have to tell her twice. She hammered a Hellfire antitank missile into the truck, aiming for the driver's cab. The Little Bird twitched as three percent of her weight took off in a rocket-propelled flare. The Hellfire did its best to break the sound barrier before it pummeled into the truck.

A pillar of fire erupted and momentarily blanked Claudia's night vision. The cameras compensated and recovered from the change in ambient light fast enough for her to see the engine block embed in the wall of a building across the square. The rear of the truck had been flattened. The cab was nowhere to be seen, probably just tiny shreds in the bottom of the crater.

There was no secondary explosion of a fuel tank. That's why the D-boy couldn't hot-wire it—no gas.

She spotted a rooftop water tank. Ignoring the rifle fire, most of which was missing her blacked-out bird, she slid sideways across the courtyard to change her angle on the tank. A quick burst with the minigun punched a hole in the side facing the square. A couple thousand gallons of carefully hoarded water splashed into the square and killed off the worst of the flames.

Cataclysm came down fast. Her rotor wash fanned the flames, but there was too little left to matter. She had her rear gangway lowered and aimed toward the doorway where the hostages had taken refuge. The pilot kept her front end flying rather than setting down the front wheels, as there were a crater and some lingering fires where his front end should land. The hostages were aboard in moments and *Cat* clawed back aloft.

The D-boys moved fast out of the northwest corner of the square. That meant that the last four were being held close by, if their information was good. With a lone surviving militant facing a ring of angry Delta Force operators, their information was bound to be as good as it could be.

Claudia punched down a pair of rockets to close the courtyard exit behind them.

A hail of fire from the south side of the square was cut off when Trisha replied with two more rockets right through the front door.

Claudia pulled back up until she was high enough to be invisible in the dark but could shadow the team's movement on the ground.

They fought at a dead run. Despite the suppression on the rifles knocking off most of the visual flash, she could see the small flashes of heat signature with each doubled shot. The two men at the rear ran mostly backward, actively firing as they moved. Even the best of the Marines didn't do that trick. Not if they were hitting their targets.

A pair of technicals figured out how to circle around the destroyed main square. These Toyota pickups each had big machine guns mounted in their beds and a half-dozen other gunman perched along the sides of the truck bed.

"These are mine," Trisha declared in a voice so harsh that it couldn't be just an effect of the encrypted radio. This sounded personal.

Claudia watched as Trisha zoomed straight up over them, flipped the *May*'s tail up, and dove straight down from only a couple hundred feet above. On the descent, she fired a rocket into each and then tore up what remained with her M134 miniguns. She only had a few seconds, which was a couple hundred rounds from each gun. For a solo pilot, it was an incredible maneuver backed up by perfect gunnery.

Claudia added that to her mental list of Trisha-tricks to practice.

The technicals disintegrated as men dove clear, those still capable of doing so. Trisha had already recovered from her radical move and had switched over to clean up on the gun crews who had managed to dive aside.

Claudia turned her attention back to the team. Wherever they were heading, they were sure of themselves. She held back to provide them with air cover but not so close that she'd give away their presence to whoever waited ahead.

Michael could feel Claudia flying over his right shoulder as they approached the building one of the guards had revealed, after the two rounds in the shoulder that made him drop his rifle and his eyes crossed to stare at the barrel pressed against his forehead.

Fifth house on the left. Four women—the other hostages hadn't seen them in a week. He couldn't think about what might have happened to them; he simply needed to get them aloft and out to the carrier. They would be taken care of there.

His job was to get them out.

The gunfire had died behind them and nothing new had opened up before them. Not yet. The driving rain had muffled the battle in the square. The building ahead was a two-story affair, perhaps eight or ten rooms, a mansion by local standards. He wished he could get up on the roof, but he didn't have time. Or did he?

Michael wound his arm over his head in the signal for a crane lift and then pointed back at the intersection they'd just crossed through. He tapped Bill on the shoulder. With hand signs he told Bill to lead the assault into the building in twenty seconds, then turned and sprinted back just as Claudia touched down in a space that couldn't be more than a yard past her rotor tips.

He jumped on the skid and grabbed the door frame for a handhold.

No instruction needed, she moved over the building. He could see her clearly in his night vision, so integrated into her helicopter that he almost couldn't tell where woman ended and mechanical extension of the woman's will began. And Claudia packed a lot of will.

She didn't take him in close, but crossed over the building at seventy feet up. He wanted to arrive as undetected as possible. She had a fast rope on the copilot's side of the bird.

With a jerk, he pulled the rope loose. Twenty meters of forty-millimeter line uncoiled to dangle from where one end attached just above the door frame.

He wrapped his gloved hands around the rope even as it uncoiled. Sliding down, he was standing on the building's roof three seconds later. Claudia kept moving, releasing the rope into the street below as she continued flying along. Anyone inside who'd heard her would think she'd passed them by.

Despite her beautiful exterior and quiet manner, she was deeply battle experienced and thought very fast. He wasn't sure he'd have come up with hitting the water tank to suppress the truck fire even if he'd been in position to see it.

Michael found a trapdoor and dropped through to the second story, doing a land and roll on the floor. The two guards sleeping there never managed to reach their weapons.

He heard gunfire below as he cleared the hall, and then the next room. It was the third room on the right where he found what he'd been hoping wasn't there. It was against al-Shabaab rules and typical pirate practice, but that hadn't stopped these kidnappers. Four narrow beds with straw-tick mattresses, and the four women naked and tied in place.

The one man in the room died with his pants pulled only halfway up his legs. Michael pulled out a knife and slashed all of the women's bonds, keeping a close eye on the door. The battle below gained volume.

How could he move four women?

"This is a U.S. military rescue operation. Can any of you walk?"

"Walk?" one of the women spat out. "Show us where, and we can run."

Two of them had to help a third, but the one who'd spoken almost charged out into the hall ahead of him.

"Upper hall, northeast corner, four in tow," he announced over the radio.

~

"Confirm northeast," Claudia replied.

"Confirm," Michael told her.

In answer, she shot a gaping hole in the second story of the south face of the building.

"*Cat*," she called over the radio. "Tailgate on the south face now. Now. Now." There was no courtyard in the immediate area big enough for the big M-47G to land. There was also still a gun battle on the floor below, not a good place for hostages.

She pulled back out of the way and into the darkness as the Chinook came to hover with her rear ramp against the second-story wall and her rotor swirling mere feet over the roof. The pilot had nailed his position without hesitation, despite sitting sixty feet away in the cockpit with his back turned toward the wall and being wholly dependent on the ramp gunner's directions. Damn, but she loved flying with SOAR.

She and Trisha focused on taking out the shooters who were cropping up to either side.

"Four clear," Michael announced as the Chinook pulled away.

Claudia closed her eyes for a moment in relief. Wait! "Four clear." That meant Michael was still… Damn him!

She could see by the flashes from the ground-floor windows of the building that a full-scale firefight was going on inside the lower story. Of course Michael would go back in to help his team. But how could she help him?

She hovered, safely fifty feet into the dark above the roof, and glared down at it. Any action she took against the building would threaten the D-boy team.

He'd be coming down the stairs behind the Somali pirates. These weren't even pirates; these were professional criminals who had crossed the wrong military force.

All she could do was make sure that no one else joined the fight. So she set herself to a circling fire patrol, using a hail of bullets to warn off any who approached the building. Trisha set up to circle directly opposite her. Between them, they kept the main building isolated despite the rapidly escalating interest and gunfire from the surrounding areas.

The firefight didn't last long. Caught between Bill and the other D-boys' hammer and Michael's knife, it was over…in the longest sixty seconds of Claudia's life.

The full team returned to the roof, and the Black Hawk *Vicious* came down and scooped them all aboard. Then the whole flight, as a group, turned for the coast with her and Trisha flying rearguard.

They'd departed to the east, which would make sense for the closest part of the coast, in case anyone was left alive to report where they were heading. Then they curved around to due south. That should make anyone looking for them search the wrong piece of the sky. Still, they stayed low for the thirty minutes it took to reach their final goal.

Right on cue, as they crossed over Barawe and the coast, Sly Stowell reported the successful recovery of the last ten hostages from the heart of that city. They'd timed it so that if there were problems, the SOAR and Delta contingent would be directly overhead to help.

They weren't needed.

Exactly as he had in the attack six months before, Sly had driven his hundred-ton hovercraft over the beach and right up the main street. He'd knocked a few houses down and crushed any vehicles that were in the way. Ramming straight through the security wall, he drove right into the compound where the hostages had been held.

Dropping the forward ramp, he'd disgorged fifty U.S. Rangers backed up by a pair of armored Humvees each carrying twin M2 .50-caliber machine guns. He also had a pair of ten-foot-long GAU-13 30 mm rotary cannons that he'd "been dying to try out." The Somalis gave him plenty of excuses, but not for long.

The city that had successfully repulsed SEAL Team Six in 2013, when they'd come after these same hostages, gave them up to Operation Sleight of Hand.

Claudia and Trisha, with Lola above them in the DAP Hawk *Vengeance*, flew escort until the massive landing hovercraft was once again skimming over the ocean waves at seventy knots with every person accounted for.

Claudia still had more than twenty minutes of fuel, though very little of her ammunition left by the time they reached the *Peleliu*.

She also carried a whole lot more to think about than when she'd started the night.

Chapter 8

BACK ON THE *PELELIU*, ROCKING ON THE ROUGH SEAS just beyond the tail end of the storm, Chief Warrant Lola Maloney stalked across the wet deck toward Claudia before she even had a chance to shut down her craft.

"Captain Casperson!"

Claudia snapped to attention and barely resisted saluting at her commander's sharp tone. "Ma'am!"

"You're really pissing me off, Casperson."

Claudia let herself relax just a little. Last time Maloney had used that tone, it had turned out to be a compliment. She really hoped that was the case this time as well.

"Do you know what that is?" Lola was pointing back toward the *Vengeance*. She didn't give Claudia time to answer, punching her words at her. "*That* is a Direct Action Penetrator Black Hawk. It is the most lethal helicopter this planet has ever produced. It is presently the one and only stealth model in existence. Now how am I supposed to explain to *my* commander that an entire operation was successfully completed from which I returned with a hundred percent of my ammunition still in my bird. Between you and Trisha, you didn't leave me one lousy, goddamned shot. Would that have killed you?"

"Uh." Was her commander crazy? Or did she just have a really twisted sense of humor? Claudia rolled the dice and decided to bank on the latter. "Apparently, ma'am, yes. It would have killed me to leave a shot for you. I would have been deeply shamed and laughed at throughout not just the 5D, but all of SOAR as well. I'm just happy to have a commander willing to bear that burden of becoming a laughingstock for me, ma'am." She kept her tone serious and remained at attention.

"Shee-it!" Lola drawled out in an expressive sound that could only come from the depths of the Louisiana swamp. The smile that broke out across her features showed that Lola Maloney could also have pursued a career as a highly successful model if she'd so chosen. "Keep that crap up, Casperson, and I just might get to like you. You're supposed to really screw up a couple times so that I can straighten you out."

"What?" Claudia tried to unravel the last part of that but couldn't make sense of it.

Lola leaned back against the nose of the *Maven*, suddenly as at ease as if they'd been sitting in a diner rather than on the deck of a ship of war.

"There's kind of a SOAR tradition in the Black Adders."

"Black Adders?" Claudia relaxed into parade rest. Totally adrift, she didn't feel comfortable mirroring Lola's casual attitude. Claudia's years in the Marines had made parade rest a wholly comfortable position anyway, even for casual conversation.

"A holdover from when Major Mark 'Viper' Henderson formed the 5D. Before my time, but I hear that there was some rather heated debate about what kind of viper he was. We were almost named the Death Adders. Cobras were out for obvious reasons having to do with those piddling little helicopters you used to fly for the jarheads."

Only a woman who flew a DAP Hawk for a living would call the lethal SuperCobras flown by the Marine Corps "piddling."

"I guess 'asp' wasn't considered macho enough because it would connect him to Cleopatra's death and Elizabeth Taylor's breasts. Though you think they'd have chosen the asps for that reason alone. Anyway, they wound up as the Black Adders. My husband actually has a tattoo of a flying snake with Mr. Bean's nose."

Claudia couldn't stop her snort of laughter. She'd been totally addicted to Rowan Atkinson's British comedies including *Black Adder*. It had been her one, unforgivably geeky vice as a kid. The show was also on PBS, one of the only television channels to make it through the hills to Bumble Bee.

"I know. Tim is pitiful, but I love him anyway. And what he can do with an M134 minigun is just poetry. He'd be our best shot if it wasn't for Kee. Back to my point. Something about the Black Adders attracts all of the real misfits. Kee, Connie, Trisha, and myself—all unholy messes. Tradition is, Major Emily Beale always straightened us out. When she retired, I kind of took over the role. If you keep flying clean and true, I'm worried that you won't fit in, and I won't have anything to do at all, especially since you won't let me shoot."

"I'll try to screw up soon. Just for you, ma'am."

"You do that." Lola stood and stretched, highlighting her exceptional figure despite her flight suit. Then she looked Claudia square in the eye. "Great job tonight."

And Claudia felt about ten feet tall and able to leap small buildings with only a little assistance.

Michael felt a little ashamed at how disappointed he felt the instant that it was clear Claudia had set her lunch tray down with the other women of SOAR for the after-mission meal. It was the first meal they hadn't shared in the three days she'd been aboard. Of course the last two days had included nothing but mission planning.

Oh-two-hundred—close enough to call it lunch-time in their flipped-clock world. They weren't even supposed to be starting the mission until now, but the weather's arrival at Buurhakaba had pushed the time-table forward. Now their birds were already put away and everyone was showered and changed.

He shouldn't feel quite so put out. Trisha was married to Bill, yet she too sat with the other women. That left Michael and Bill to eat alone in their corner. There was a scattering of women in the ship's mess, as there always was. Navy ships had been skewing that way a lot longer than other services. Special Operations? Not so much.

But the five women of SOAR were a real standout group. Not a one of them fit the "classic" military mold any more than a Delta operator fit it. They all wore their hair long and loose, except for Claudia's ponytail, and they were all more casual than any of the other women. Captain Moretti's hair down to her waist was the most impressive, but she struck him as exactly the sort of wildcard who would do something like that given the least excuse.

Special Operations Forces, especially the highly

specialized teams like SEALs and Delta, broke the mold partly to blend in while on an undercover mission and partly because they could get away with it. He knew from studies that the ability to thumb their noses at the military establishment was a key element in most Special Operations Forces' psychological profiles.

Some SOAR fliers followed suit to more closely identify with their customers. The men and women of the 5D had taken that opportunity completely to heart.

The fact that every one of them had a minimum eight years in the service and thousands upon thousands of flight hours, in a type of craft where fifteen hundred hours was a common career high-water mark, seemed to shine off them. Special Ops automatically selected for exceptional physical ability and endurance, as well as significantly above-average intelligence. Genetically, this often led to particularly handsome individuals as well. But even with that, these women were incredible.

And each was as distinct as her looks.

Trisha with her nearly ADHD mannerisms that only seemed to quiet around her husband.

Lola Maloney, who was casually everyone's best friend while remaining the unquestioned commander.

Kee Stevenson who, in addition to being a crack shot, was the sharp edge of the knife, softening only around her adoptive daughter, Dilya.

Connie Davis was even more silent than Claudia, but it was a different silence. Even looking at Connie, you could see her watching and processing everything, and storing all of it in her capacious photographic memory for careful consideration.

Even young Dilya was distinct—practically the sixth

woman of SOAR at the rate she was growing up—displaying some of Connie's quiet observation mixed with her adoptive father's playfulness. She didn't radiate teenage angst, but she'd had to grow up young and fast just to survive. Still unformed in many ways, she was becoming an interesting young woman in her own right. It would be fun to see how she grew and changed over the years. He'd probably still be friends with Kee and could see Dilya grow, Michael thought.

Friends.

He didn't think about friends much. He'd separated from his original team in Delta to become a permanent liaison to the 5D after Emily Beale had saved him on a cliff high in the Hindu Kush. He'd made sure she was awarded the Silver Star for that particular maneuver; it was the bravest and hairiest piece of flying he'd seen, ever.

When she and Mark retired from SOAR, he'd thought about leaving the 5D and returning to The Unit. But he'd shared a lot of meals with Kee Smith, right through her finding Dilya and falling in love with Archie Stevenson. Connie's father had saved his life years before at the cost of his own. And though he and Connie spoke little, he felt an obligation to watch over Ron Davis's daughter. Trisha was an ex-lover and a good friend. As good as any he had. Then Bill had come aboard—amazing Delta material with the right training—and married Trisha.

For the first time in his career, he'd made friends outside Delta. Pretty much the first time in his life. Like Dilya, he'd been raised around adults. His parents were professors, and the youngest kids he hung around with, even as a little boy, were college students.

By eighteen, he'd sat in on enough classes that he managed to test out for a college degree, graduating with top scores at nineteen with a degree in military history—a first for the university—built almost wholly of independent study. He'd also done ROTC just to keep himself busy and discovered that he liked the structure and the discipline. But to call any of the college kids friends would be a stretch. He'd been too young and too good. He hadn't been popular, but young Michael Gibson had been too tough for any of them to mess with despite his youth.

He returned his attention to Claudia and tried to analyze his feelings about her. It wasn't a familiar exercise.

Women, in his world, simply "were." If they performed their duties well, gender wasn't an issue for him. If they wanted to share some time together, well, he certainly enjoyed that part of it too, as long as they were outside his command structure. One of the advantages of serving in The Unit was that there were no women in his command structure, none at all.

When the relationships ended after a dinner, a night, or a month, then they were over and it was time to move along.

Claudia wasn't a friend, or didn't feel like one. She'd been here three days, and they barely knew each other. Yet it felt as if they did.

"Kinda smacks you upside the head, doesn't it?"

Michael looked up at Bill, who sat beside him facing the room. "Up" was the operative word. At six-three, Bill was one of the biggest soldiers in The Unit. Hell, at five-ten, Michael was bigger than most operators. The demands of Delta selection and missions trended toward the light and wiry. It had given Michael pause when recruiting Bill from the SEALs, but the man had kept proving himself several times over.

"What smacks you?"

Bill nodded toward the table of SOAR women. "I know the look."

"What look?" Michael didn't have a look...did he?

"The look like someone just smacked you upside the head. I remember the first time I met Trisha. Goddamn little Irish spitfire who insisted on rescuing my sorry Scottish ass no matter how much I complained about it. The moment she pulled off her helmet and I saw she wasn't another air jock, I knew I was gone. The spark way she looked and the way she moved... Well, I was so gone from that moment that I fought against it way past common sense. You've got that look."

Michael studied his lunch, a roast beef sandwich au jus with all the trimmings. It sat there mostly uneaten, accusing him of being deeply distracted. The op had been intense. The hyperawareness necessary to rescue three separate hostage groups, two of them in heavy firefights, should have his body screaming for calories.

He took an experimental bite of his sandwich. He could feel his body absorbing the calories greedily, so the problem lay in his brain. He looked back up as he chewed and noted Claudia watching him.

She didn't shy off, look away, or play coy.

"What about her?" He soft-voiced his question to Bill even though no one else sat at their table. No hard consonants and a higher tone kept his voice from carrying more than a few feet.

"What do you mean?"

"Does she have the look?"

Bill studied her without studying her, a practiced Delta skill. After too long a pause, he huffed out a breath.

"Damned if I can tell, Michael. I didn't know that Trisha could even stand me until we kissed the first time. Surprised the shit out of me."

"Yeah, I know that feeling."

Bill eyed him over the next bite of his burger, but Michael wasn't about to explain.

Claudia felt that it was far too adolescent to simply go and sit with him at his corner table and fawn all over Michael.

Besides, the women had invited her to their table. It was…unusual. In the Marine Corps, women mostly avoided one another to avoid being pigeonholed as a "chick squad." If you said, "Hey," to another woman as you passed her on the running track, half the guys assumed you were lesbian lovers. And those were the nicest versions.

The next nicest phrase for an all-female crew was a "boob-bird." A SuperCobra with two women was "grab a two-pack." A Black Hawk with four women was a "four-bush bird." Then it got raunchy.

For two years at SOAR, there weren't any women in her training section. Some behind her, none with her.

These women of SOAR either didn't care or were so competent that no one dared say any of that to them. These women didn't have that feel, and the looks they were getting weren't about whether or not they were lovers. It felt like a community, like a potluck in Bumble Bee—just gathered together because they wanted to be.

And those around them?

She checked out the room. No one, other than Michael before he left the mess hall, was paying them any particular attention.

"I know, it's strange, isn't it." Kee Stevenson spoke to her over Dilya's head, which was bowed down as she read her book. "I actually cursed out Major Henderson on my first day for trying to put me on some 'goddamn girlie bird.' Then he tricked me into flying with Emily Beale. The bastard. Best thing that ever happened to me."

Claudia had never met the man, but his reputation did not include great tolerance. Yet this little woman had cursed him to his face and survived. That had to be a good story.

"I could get to like this."

Kee nodded an easy acknowledgment, her pitch-black, chin-length hair slicing forward and back as she did so. "Hard flying and hard men. Gotta love it."

Connie leaned forward from across the table. "Are you really going after Michael?" Her voice was soft, and those were the first words Claudia had heard her say. But by pure chance they dropped into a gap in the multiple conversations going around the table. The following silence was resounding, and she was abruptly the center of every woman's attention.

Even Dilya looked up at her.

"No." She wasn't going after anybody. All she'd done was…kiss him. "No," she repeated, but it wasn't carrying quite the confidence she wished to communicate. "What makes you say that?"

Kee rolled her eyes, and Lola offered her a knowing smile.

Connie Davis blinked for a moment, glaring briefly at her friends who were clearly waiting for something. "Okay, I won't make a list. I'll simply note the inordinate amount of time he spent over this meal watching you."

"Your back was to him," Claudia protested. Now Lola was shaking her head: What had Claudia just stepped in?

"Your attention throughout the meal has primarily been focused ten degrees off my left shoulder. Of the men you've met that I'm aware of, only two were seated in that line of sight. As one of them is Lieutenant Bill Bruce, and I know Trisha's propensity for pointing out her recent marriage at every opportunity, I can only assume that you were observing Colonel Gibson, with whom you have flown two operational missions in the last sixty-three hours."

The others were now smirking at her. Not about Michael, but about Connie. She'd been warned that this woman functioned in a different way, and apparently she had just received a lesson in that. Connie clearly observed everything. The others' looks indicated that they too had all learned that particular lesson the hard way.

Except Dilya. Dilya simply inspected Claudia a moment longer, offered a nod to Connie as if agreeing with her conclusion, then returned to her reading.

Was she interested in Michael? Sure. As a friend. Then why had she kissed him? Twice. And why was she looking for an excuse to go way beyond that?

"I didn't think I was going after him," she amended

her earlier response. "Why? Is it a problem? Someone I don't know about?"

All of the women at the table sobered.

"He's a good man." "He's special." "You walk carefully there." The last didn't sound like a warning about him, but rather a warning to her. So, this whole circle of women were suddenly on his side instead of hers.

Her sense of belonging here was a false one. She was still the outsider. Still suspect.

Of course they knew him and didn't know her. But it still didn't seem fair.

"I'm not stupid," she informed them, then rose and took her tray to the cleanup window. She could feel their eyes on her back as she left the room. Not threatening, but suddenly all very interested in her next action.

Chapter 9

Claudia wasn't stupid, and she most certainly wasn't going to get stupid about some guy, no matter how handsome. No matter how her body and mind reacted to his presence.

In a way she'd spent her entire career getting to this place, this ship, this company, and she wasn't about to jeopardize that with some ill-conceived affair with a man who couldn't even complete a question. Not that a single scorching kiss and a bit of wondering lust counted as anything.

Which apparently was the case. For the first three days of her service in the 5D, she'd run into Michael at every turn. Now, as her first days turned into her first week, she'd only seen him at a distance. And not even that very often. Yes, he'd spent three days of that on the carrier, but the *Peleliu* wasn't that big a ship.

He was avoiding her. Fine. It had only been a kiss.

She wished she sounded more convinced inside her own head.

So she did what she came to do—she flew. They kept her scrambling, and she had no complaints. It's what she'd been born to do. She'd gone up with Mr. Johns in his tiny Korean War–vintage Bell 47 'copter when he'd gone looking for stray cattle that had broken out into the vast wilderness west of Bumble Bee.

By the time she was fifteen, he was letting her do

the flying whenever she was with him. Perched side by side on the little bench seat of the tiny helicopter, she had learned to hug the dry arroyos and search the steep hills as if born to it. At seventeen, when Mr. John's leg was broken by a kicking horse, she had started flying solo. At Annapolis she'd taken a flight test as part of initial qualification assessment, and there had never been another question about her being a flier for the Corps.

Now the Marine Corps had led to SOAR. There was nowhere higher to go, not in the U.S. military or anywhere else on the planet. But she was far from bored.

In some ways she'd come full circle. The Little Bird was roughly the same size and weight as the old 47. Faster, far more sophisticated, and incomparably more lethal than the little Angel of Mercy, the Little Bird still felt deeply familiar. Shifting from the SuperCobra to the Little Bird had been like rediscovering who she'd always been.

But there was no resting on any sort of laurels with this group of women. A highly successful mission didn't mean they had the next night off, or the one after that. At times she wondered if the women of SOAR were intentionally trying to keep her too busy to find Michael. Either it was working, or Michael wasn't even interested and she'd imagined the whole thing.

The more she worked with them, the more she came to like them. That was almost as surprising as her overwhelming attraction to Michael. The women of SOAR welcomed her.

On the nights they weren't flying a mission, Trisha would sit her down at a tactical display or take her aloft, and they'd spend hours discussing and testing techniques. Surprisingly, Trisha was as open to learning tactics Claudia had brought over from the SuperCobra as she was intent on imparting knowledge. On the next night's sweep, they'd test new ideas on the Little Birds.

Trisha shifted from being an irritant to a friend on those night flights. However flaky she might seem, there was no questioning her skills or commitment to the craft. Or the very sharp mind behind that big pile of attitude.

They tried talking about their pasts, but they were too different and neither could make sense of the other. This, Claudia discovered, was true of all of the crew.

Trisha was a rich city girl to the core. Even if she didn't "buy into any of it," as she said, it was a natural part of who she was. She hadn't been lying about running with street gangs, but she'd always been able to go home to her comfortable and safe home after doing so.

Lola and Kee both had grown up on the streets of large cities. Their world was just as foreign to Claudia as Trisha's had been.

Connie had grown up in the Army, following her single dad from base to base, assignment to assignment.

Kara was a big-city girl from a large and close Italian family. Even the legendary Emily Beale had been DC born and bred.

Claudia had grown up in the Sonoran Desert and been homeschooled. The nearest elementary school had been a dozen miles one way and the high school twenty-five miles the other. The only child in that entire area, she had been left to teach herself.

Her dad never talked about his government disability. Mom once joked that he'd been a parking-lot attendant who had his back broken by a congressman drunk behind the wheel at a Redskins game. Claudia had never asked if it was true; she didn't want to know. He'd mostly sat at home and didn't do much or speak much.

Her mom hadn't even finished high school and didn't know what to do with her daughter. She worked at Mr. Johns's ranch milking cows, mucking stalls, and riding fence lines and had simply taken Claudia along. Once she'd learned to avoid rattlesnakes and the bull's pen, there were certainly no need for a babysitter in Bumble Bee, Arizona.

So, Claudia had run wild, for she was never happier than when she was in the high desert. She'd have stayed that way, except for Mrs. Kaye. A retired third-grade teacher, she had taken on Claudia's education. Once Mrs. Kaye had tamed Claudia from her near wild-child state, they had explored far past any standard curricula. The teacher was often only a step ahead of the student, and Claudia's education could best be called eclectic.

But flying with Mr. Johns had caught Claudia's passion. Bless those lost cattle. And Mr. Johns, who'd flown the Angels of Mercy and later the Green Hornets in Vietnam, had sponsored her to the state senator and to Annapolis.

And here with SOAR, she flew as she never had before.

The Black Adders had started as a mash-up of assets from three separate companies for a specific set of missions. Over time, they'd grown so effective that they'd been formed into their own company, the Fifth Battalion, D Company. Normally each company flew only one type of bird and then they'd select assets as needed from the whole battalion, or even the whole regiment.

Not the 5D. The Black Hawk and Little Bird mechanics had cross-certified, so there wasn't any duplication of personnel. They were also working on their Chinook certifications. The 5D had been the first and so far the only company to receive stealth upgrade packages for their helicopters.

And now, with the arrival of Captain Kara Moretti, they had their own Gray Eagle UAV. Nothing like a thirty-million-dollar drone to lend a hand in gathering intel. Flying with the 5D was an even more complex task because of it. Pilots and crews had to integrate the UAVs technically as well as tactically. The trick was to turn such a vast quantity of data into digestible quality information, and that was Kara Moretti's genius skill.

All of the birds had been converted to a standardized CAAS cockpit. The common aviation architecture system provided a consistency of controls, but the solid, twin-turbine, four-member-crew Black Hawks were very different creatures from the AH-6M Little Birds. The Chinook was another animal entirely.

Chief Warrant Maloney wanted Claudia cross-trained by yesterday. That meant a lot of left-seat Black Hawk and Chinook missions in her first week aboard the *Peleliu*.

Michael had backed off.

Claudia didn't know whether to be happy or sad about that. But even if he hadn't, she would have had to.

The training was hectic. Two years to mission-qualified left her barely ready for the 5D's own standards. They were stretching her to the limits. When she wasn't flying with Trisha or Lola, Tim Maloney—Lola's husband, a very handsome Latino gunner—or Kee had Claudia out on the deck working on her shooting skills with pistol and rifle. Trisha was also a fierce hand-to-hand combat instructor and the whole crew worked out on that together.

Sometimes Michael would come and watch those sessions. Trisha would tease him, but he never joined in. Which was probably lucky for them. She couldn't imagine wrestling with a D-boy—well, not in that way.

Rather than feeling self-conscious or overexposed in her shorts and T-shirt when he was watching her, Claudia found a deeper focus and was better able to fend off whatever Trisha was throwing her way. The woman was fast, but she didn't think more than a move or two ahead. Several times Claudia was able to set Trisha up for a failure that the petite redhead didn't see coming.

But in the end, Claudia always ended up flat on her back. Trisha was just that good despite her small size.

They also flew ocean sweeps.

The SOAR helos would go aloft, spread out into a long line, and fly four or five hundred miles of coastline each night like a giant garden rake. Claudia sometimes flew copilot in a bigger bird or solo in the *Maven* beside Trisha in the *May*. They always had a few D-boys or Rangers along on one of the birds, but Michael never seemed to end up on hers.

At first they were spooking up pirate boats every night, which sallied forth in hopes of replacing the lost hostages with fresh fodder. They had a cash flow from ransom money that they wanted to maintain.

But after a solid week of the SOAR and Delta team turning back boat after boat relieved of their weapons and their big outboard engines, the life seemed to be knocked out of the pirates.

Somalia was estimated to have fourteen million weapons for its ten million inhabitants, but the supply of fishing boats and men willing to sacrifice themselves on the chance of a successful piracy mission was rapidly dwindling. Especially with so many of the lords having been taken down in the recent attacks.

It was just before sunset while Claudia was on the patrol, solo in the *Maven* this flight, when they stumbled upon the last unaccounted-for pirated vessel of significant size. Despite Trisha's scoffing at that first briefing, they'd actually found her.

The forty-meter-long North Korean fishing boat *Hong 4* had been pirated in 2010. No one had offered to ransom the ship or the crew. The crew had finally been released, but not the ship. The pirates had taken to using it as a mother ship throughout the Indian Ocean, delivering small, agile attack boats deep into international shipping lanes.

The *Hong 4* had eluded EU NAVFOR forces for the last two years. She spent long stretches at anchor off Somali beaches, rusting and looking as if she'd never move again, interrupted by blacked-out late-night departures for deep waters.

SOAR didn't need reasonable cause to take down the ship for two reasons. One, the ship had been reported as pirated, and even though decaying from rust, she was still recognizable. The second reason arrived as Claudia and Trisha overflew the ship side by side in the *Maven* and the *May*.

A rocket-propelled grenade shot up out of the bridge

of the ship through a missing window. It must have filled the bridge with a choking fog of rocket exhaust fumes. The helicopter's warning system gave her sufficient time to pop flares and dive to just above the ocean as soon as she cleared the edge of the *Hong*'s deck. The RPG wasn't heat-seeking. It simply passed through the flares and arced out over the ocean, creating a small geyser where it impacted the waves. The experience still rattled her nerves, RPGs having taken down more helicopters in war than any other weapon.

"Rolling in, four o'clock," Trisha called.

Claudia recovered from her surprise and banked for the ship's stern to be well clear and set up her own defense from that position.

Trisha didn't even bother being subtle about it. She fired a pair of rockets into the control bridge where the RPG had come from. At the direct hit, the bridge's roof and windows exploded outward. Moments later, columns of flame shot skyward.

Claudia kept a sharp eye on the deck. Sure enough, someone came up from below swinging an RPG to try to target Trisha's Little Bird. Sitting directly off the stern, Claudia unleashed a burst from her minigun to cut him and two other pirates down.

The fire that Trisha had started torched the bridge, but it didn't spread downward. Several pirates dashed out of the lower levels, headed for their small motorboats, but Claudia tore up the boats where they hung in the davits, cutting off any escape.

By this time, almost twenty men had gathered on the deck, many of them still armed. With a twist applied by using her rudder pedals, Claudia unleashed a long burst from her minigun that swept over the deck mere feet above the men's heads.

They began casting their weapons overboard, as if they could then pose as innocent fishermen. Another burst, and they simply dropped the weapons to the deck and clustered together by one of the cargo hatches.

With no one at the controls, without even any controls remaining, for that matter, the ship continued to steam ahead. She and Trisha set up a circling pattern, jinking high and low in case there was still someone aboard crazy enough to try to target them.

A call to the *Peleliu* had a strike team en route in minutes.

She held her breath as Michael, Bill, and the other D-boys fast-roped down to the deck from the Black Hawk *Vicious* and took control just as full dark descended. Apparently, no more Somalis had death wishes and Delta soon had the vessel cleared. Sly arrived in his LCAC with a load of Rangers. They boarded, took the Somalis into custody, doused the fire, and turned the ship once they had control of the engine room.

Just seeing Michael in action did things to Claudia that she couldn't ignore. She had never been one to continue playing games or lying to herself, once she became aware that she had been. She wasn't stupid and she did want Michael, no matter what she'd told the women of SOAR.

And somehow she knew Michael well enough to know that he was avoiding her for her own sake. In that twisted, overly logical soldier brain of his, he'd assessed that she was too busy to be distracted by…

Well, she'd had enough of that.

Thoughts of him had grown to be a constant companion at her side. As if he sat in her two-seat helicopter even when she flew solo. Rather than scattering her attention, thoughts of him steadied her, making her feel sharper and more complete.

She and Trisha flew their Little Birds back toward the *Peleliu* before they ran out of fuel. But as she pulled away from the *Hong 4*, she flew backward for the first few hundred yards before turning the helo. It wasn't to keep her guns aimed at the ship, which was completely under control. She reversed out because she so enjoyed watching Michael prowl the deck.

She'd been waiting for him to come to her, but it wasn't going to work that way. Not with Michael—she understood that now. It wasn't how he'd think. He'd think that it was the woman's choice to come to him or not.

The guy was just too damn decent.

Or too damned smart.

He'd now waited long enough that she no longer had any choice in the matter. She felt lassoed. But she didn't feel any desire to fight the rope.

~

Michael sat, not eating yet another meal, and considered the many things he had learned about Captain Casperson over the last week. Not one of them had made her the least bit less attractive. It was like the woman had been assigned to him as a mission to unravel. She not only occupied too many of his waking thoughts, but she'd started to occupy his sleeping ones as well.

He could attribute his initial reaction to her

physicality. Blond hair that floated behind her like a banner. Blue eyes that never let him look away because they drilled past all of his guards. A shape that, well, that he simply couldn't wait to get his hands on.

She worked out constantly enough to be a Delta operator. If he went for a run, she'd be there circling the hangar deck, as light-footed as any soldier he'd ever seen. He couldn't hit the aircraft-spares cargo space that had been turned into a weight room without finding her on the bench moving an impressive amount of weight up and down.

And there was no way in hell he was going to trust himself on a wrestling mat with a woman sporting such perfect curves. At least not with an audience. Even thinking of her was causing body reactions stronger than the ones he felt anywhere outside a bedroom or an actual mission. She looked like both a model soldier and a soldier model.

Damn. He wanted her so badly. He'd never wanted anyone or anything as much, other than his desire to always be the best. And now that he'd assessed her as being the very best, it only added to his desire to have her.

She kept infiltrating his thoughts. Another portion of her insidious and, he was sure, unconscious methodology to achieve that was how the woman flew. Claudia Casperson was such a joy to watch in the air.

Michael had been leaning out the cargo bay door of the Black Hawk as they flew up to take control of the *Hong 4*. For the first time all week, he was actually glad that he wasn't flying with Claudia, simply so that he had this chance to see her in action.

She had set up a slewing, jinky pattern around the *Hong* that made her almost impossible to target, but kept her guns oriented at the ship. Trisha was doing something similar, but not with the same panache—a panache that would make for a very uncomfortable ride.

It took him a moment to understand what she was doing. She was treating the waves themselves as if they were trees to be hopped over in a nap-of-earth flight that followed their asymmetric curves, except she was doing it while flying sideways with all of her weapons pointed inward.

The woman was absolute magic aloft.

And then there was the way she went quiet. Not quiet and closed like the shy Connie Davis. Nor quiet and thoughtful like Bill. Instead she simply became peaceful.

He was going to be in serious trouble the next time they were alone together. And he knew he couldn't wait much longer. If she didn't decide to find him soon, he'd have to break his own rules about good manners and go find her.

She'd been in the mess hall after he returned from the *Hong*. A Danish destroyer had come alongside to take the ship in tow. They were talking about pumping out what little fuel oil remained and scuttling the ship. She was in terrible shape and no one, least of all the Korean owners, wanted her back.

Seeking patience, Michael left the mess hall before Claudia was done eating and went to sit at one of his favorite spots aboard the *Peleliu*. He'd found "the beach" during his first explorations of the eight-hundred-foot-long, nineteen-deck-high amphibious assault ship.

It lay deep in the heart of the ship, right at sea level.

Sly Stowell's landing craft lived inside the well deck of the ship, a cavernous space open to the sea and awash in a few scant feet of water. Landing craft were driven up to the steel ramp—the beach—for storage in the garages above. Also parked there were the Humvees, tanks, and other vehicles that Sly transported ashore. Without the Marines aboard, most of the hardware had been offloaded and the area was quite isolated.

When not in use, the steel ramp made for a quiet, sloping, sand-less beach deep in the heart of the ship. Dead astern, the massive rear gate was raised only a few feet, exposing the dark night sea but not allowing any following waves to sweep the well deck. Behind him, soft red work lights, the better to maintain night vision, offered the only light, filling the space with shadows and rumors.

He barely heard the approaching footsteps. The pattern wasn't right for someone being stealthy; they were just light-footed. His pulse rose along with his ridiculous hopes. This ship was big enough to carry twenty-five hundred personnel, even if it carried well under five hundred at the moment. The chances of Claudia being that special one of five hundred coming here…

The steps halted at the top of the ramp for a moment, then came down from behind him. It was her—he'd recognize that rhythm anywhere. He could easily imagine the soft sway of her hips and the swish of her ponytail as Claudia came down the ramp, but he resisted the urge to turn and watch.

"Michael." Her voice hadn't a tone of surprise or greeting, just an acceptance that of course he was here, of all places.

The timing wasn't right for her to have hunted him from the mess hall to here. This was simply a place she too had found and liked. She settled on the hard steel about a foot to his side. Despite the smell of sea salt and ship's steel, her fragrance stood out, offering the same freshness of life she'd brought to the Somali desert.

They sat some time in silence in the cavernous space, listening to the soft slap of the foot of water in the well deck slopping against the walls. Beyond the partially raised stern hatch, the phosphorescent wake rolled off into the night.

"Why." He didn't make it a question this time. "All week I've been trying to puzzle out why you kissed me. I'm not complaining. I'm simply trying to understand."

"Do you need a why?"

He was used to missions where he didn't know why. The orders simply said, "Go there, do that, and come back alive *after* you've accomplished the mission." And he did. As a colonel, he didn't often receive orders without a why anymore, but they still happened on occasion.

He wasn't used to a woman without a why. The why usually had to do with sex and not much else. Even with—

No, he was done with comparing Claudia to anyone else, because it simply didn't work. She was in a whole different class from any woman he'd ever met—a class he certainly wasn't any part of. She was the sophisticate. He knew nothing about her past beyond the desert. She was obviously well educated by a very good school, maybe even West Point, and well read. He was a kid from the Oregon woods who'd graduated from college without attending much of it and had been fighting his way upward ever since. She had more poise and built-in class than any woman he'd ever sat beside.

"You make me feel…scruffy."

Her quick laugh mirrored his own feelings of surprise.

"I meant—"

"No," she cut him off. "Don't try to explain. It's too perfect. The most skilled field soldier on the planet, totally flummoxed by a kiss. Picturing you as a scruffy puppy dog is simply too perfect. I once knew a Yorkshire terrier named Bailey. Maybe I'll just call you Bailey from now on."

He smiled in response. He was half tempted to dance around her and bark just to hear that laugh again. It lit up her face like…an emergency flare? Damn, but he was crappy at metaphors. And she was the first woman who ever made him wish he knew how to use them, because normal words just didn't describe how he felt around her.

"You are about the least scruffy person on the planet, Michael. You're like this shining beacon of what a man should be. It's no big surprise that every man on the entire ship looks up to you and doesn't dare speak to you."

"Say what?" That made no sense at all.

"See, that's part of it. You don't even see it in yourself. You certainly don't brag about it. You already *are* what every soldier wants to be. That's why most of them don't speak to you. It's not because you're such a reticent bastard, though that's a part of it. It's that they're too in awe. Now you know why I find it so delightful that I flummoxed you with a kiss."

"It was a hell of a kiss. And I'm not totally flummoxed.

I'm just..." He trailed off, trying to think of just what he was. She was eyeing him with a slight twist of her head that really showed off the shape of her neck. He wanted to run his fingers along it just to see how it felt. To see if she shivered when he did so.

"Okay," he finally had to admit. "That does describe the feeling pretty well."

He turned to watch the waves continue to roll past the stern of the *Peleliu* as she made her way lazily eastward in a broad circling pattern of holding station in the area. The quarter moon was setting directly astern, filling the well deck with the last of its cool light. Since last week's mission...or had it been two weeks? Anyway, since then, the ship had continued on a leisurely patrol, letting the helicopters and drone do most of the flying.

The ship's silence extended until it lay upon them as if they were alone in all the ocean. The thrum of the ship's engines, now running at little more than an idle, was a barely defined bass note that only served to emphasize their remoteness.

Claudia brushed her fingers ever so lightly along his arm.

When he turned to look at her, she leaned forward and kissed him. It was no testing brush of warmth on the ship's deck. It was no blaze of heat that launched a mission.

Instead it was a soft opening, a bloom of warmth and heat and flavor like the finest dish ever served. It built slowly, like a timer fuse, but struck with the heat of a flash-bang distracter charge that echoed down through his bloodstream. He'd have winced at the lousy comparisons if one hundred percent of his attention wasn't busy being consumed. Just as his body had earlier craved calories, now his nervous system craved more of Claudia Casperson.

He did brush his hand down that exquisite neck, but she wasn't the only one who shivered. In that timeless passage, though they touched only at lips and fingertips, he felt transformed—as if he really could do anything. As if he just might be as she saw him.

He'd never in his life felt as powerful as he did kissing Claudia Jean Casperson.

She rested a hand on his chest. Not pushing him away, rather anchoring him in place.

When at last they broke apart—though she didn't remove her hand, for which he was grateful—and he could again think, he whispered to her softly.

"Okay, 'flummoxed' doesn't begin to cover that."

"No," she agreed easily. "But 'lovely' covers it very nicely."

No one had ever described something he'd done as "lovely." He liked the way that made him sound. He was a man capable of making a woman feel lovely. It sounded like a truly amazing achievement when spoken in such a soft, husky whisper, as if she were short of breath from a training run.

More important, he was capable of making this particular woman feel lovely, which counted for much, much more. She had a way with words that he lacked. She didn't use them as barrage weapons—that was Trisha's game—but rather as highlights. Her words were targeted strikes that went straight to the point. And she did feel absolutely lovely.

"Ah-hem." Someone cleared their throat from the head of the ramp.

Michael twisted around to see one of the female petty officers watching them curiously. He hadn't even heard her approach, despite her booted feet. And he'd just been kissing an officer of inferior rank, granted in a different regiment of the Army, but still, it was completely out of line. At least Claudia wasn't an enlisted, but it was still a punishable offense.

"Excuse me, sirs, but we have a craft inbound."

They both scrambled to the head of the ramp and joined the petty officer. As if by some mutual agreement, they didn't make a hasty exit like blushing teenagers. He felt giddy enough to be one, but that didn't mean he had to show it.

The petty officer moved to the ramp controls, lowering the rear gate of the well deck until it dipped into the waves, making a "wet beach" at the ship's stern two hundred feet away.

A small black dot appeared in the low moonlight still skimming across the sea. In moments, the black dot became defined by red, green, and white running lights. It skidded strangely across the waves as if sliding.

"The LCAC," Claudia said before he could. She must have felt his next question. "I served almost a full tour aboard the *Peleliu* when I was still in the Corps. Rode Petty Officer Stowell's landing craft air cushion several times."

She'd been a Marine. That meant Annapolis rather than West Point. He hadn't known that, but he should have—could feel it in her manners and stance. Not gung-ho Marine, but a confidence that was still unmistakable.

In so many of the Tier 2 outfits—the Marine Corps, Green Berets, and Rangers—that confidence shifted over into cocky.

Not in Claudia.

In her it had moved over to powerful. She was perhaps the most powerful woman he'd ever met, maybe even more so than Major Emily Beale, which was a comparison well worth making.

The name "Claudia" didn't quite fit her. At least not in his head, where he had to admit she was becoming immovably stuck. Trisha's "CC" was even worse. "Casperson" didn't do it for him. She wasn't the sort of woman who invited a nickname.

Neither had he. He'd always been Michael. To his parents. To the older kids in school. To his teammates. As a result, nicknames always felt a little phony to him.

Billy, Archie, Trisha…even Kee was a nickname. He'd once overheard Kee whispering to Dilya and learned both of their full names that were never spoken to anyone else. It had the feeling of a deep and significant exchange, and he'd been careful to not appear privy to it. Maybe nicknames did serve a purpose at times, but this one felt off.

The magnificent woman standing beside him deserved more than a nickname. But you didn't want to dress it up either. "CC" was too little but "Claudia Jean" was too much and yet only half enough.

"Claudia." Simple and completely her. He liked that.

"Yes?"

"Claudia Jean Casperson."

She didn't respond this time.

"Your name fits you, either way. Simplicity in one,

completeness in the other. I like the way it feels like you when I say either one."

The small black dot had resolved itself into a speeding hovercraft as it approached the ship's lights. The well deck acted like a giant audio collecting horn, gathering every sound that occurred directly behind the ship. It filled the space with the roar of the heavy turbines and big fans of the LCAC even as it slowed for its final approach.

"It sounds wonderful." Her voice gauged perfectly to be just barely louder than the ambient noise.

"What are you doing to me, Claudia Jean Casperson?" He'd never had a woman so occupy his thoughts. Not even when they were lying with him and he was—

Ordering his brain to shut up didn't help much.

"Hopefully, I'm confusing you as much as you're confusing me. I came here to fly. Not to—"

At least she had the decency to not finish that alliterative sentence. Besides, he'd bet that he couldn't just have sex with Claudia. He suspected that even now, it would have meaning.

Who was he kidding? If? Yeah, right. The thing he wanted most in the world right now was to take Claudia into his arms and see just what they could discover about each other. To sate both of them until they were too exhausted to even breathe.

That was about the stupidest and, he sighed to himself, truest statement on the planet.

~

Claudia was glad for the distraction of the incoming hovercraft. It gave her a moment to attempt to get some control over her runaway heart rate. She had just flashed on the image of making love with Michael. Not that she hadn't thought about it. But now, with the dark, forest taste of him on her tongue and the feel of his heart pounding beneath her palm under that splendid muscled chest—now it was much more real.

Making love to Colonel Michael Gibson was no longer a pleasant daydream to pass the time between duties. It had become a need that coursed through her body, making it difficult not to grab him right now—and to hell with the petty officer.

The big hovercraft blotted out the stern entryway. The *Peleliu* was the only ship of the Tarawa class modified to fit the monstrous craft.

They pulled on the hearing muffs that the petty officer offered. The LCAC's turbines were still at high roar to keep the hundred-ton craft floating on its cushion of air. It nudged its way in, like a warhorse threading through the back alley of a medieval village.

The LCAC sidled up to the dry metal beach at their feet and shut down her engines. From cry to roar to whine and finally silence. With a great gasp and sigh, the forward air bag deflated, then the front of the hovercraft opened and lowered its own ramp down onto the sloping ramp of the *Peleliu* beach.

She and Michael moved to the side as the Rangers came off the craft. Once the Rangers were clear, Sly Stowell came up with the other four men of his crew.

He saluted the duty officer as she raised the well-deck rear door to block out the sea, then he came over to greet them. He was almost as big as Bill, towering over both of them.

"Hey, Sly," Claudia greeted him. "Where are your pirates?"

"Didn't need 'em," he rumbled in his deep voice, "so we chucked 'em overboard."

Michael's face showed absolute shock until Sly burst out laughing.

"Damn, Michael, you are such a perfect straight man." He slapped Michael on the arm in a jovial way. "The Danes took 'em. Shipping them to the Hague for trial as pirates on the high seas. Just a bunch of scared kids really. The main honcho was in the bridge when Claudia took it out."

"Actually, that was Trisha."

"Either way, it was still a good piece of work taking down the *Hong*. She's been making all sorts of trouble as far out as the Maldives." Then Sly sobered for a moment and looked right at her.

"Michael may be the perfect straight man, but he's also the best man I know, Claudia. No matter what he says otherwise."

She opened her mouth to protest against any impropriety, but he cut her off.

"Even if you weren't standing there holding hands, it would still be just as obvious." Then he was gone.

They turned to look at each other carefully and then looked down in unison. It had felt so natural, she hadn't even noticed it. He squeezed her fingers briefly and let go.

She knew that Sly was immensely respected aboard ship. He was gregarious but never one to give compliments lightly. He was one of the old Navy dogs, and his approval carried weight with everyone right up to

Lieutenant Commander Boyd Ramis. Sly was a sea dog who hadn't gone to seed but had rather become a core of the crew, so deeply embedded that he was a part of the *Peleliu* herself.

Claudia looked right and left. Service crews were descending to refuel and rearm the LCAC.

The best man Sly knew. Well, she was ready to find out a whole lot more about that man.

"I need to get you somewhere, Michael. Somewhere alone that we won't be disturbed."

He waited to see if she had more to say, but she didn't. She had lots of need but no words.

Michael nodded once and turned to lead the way.

Thank God.

A man of action.

Chapter 10

"Do you have a problem with heights?"

Claudia looked at Michael like he was nuts, but he wasn't joking. "I fly helicopters for a living. I'm Airborne jump-qualified."

"That doesn't mean—"

"I don't have a problem with heights. What does that have to do with…?"

Michael tipped his head back and looked aloft.

Claudia had understood when they'd passed by his quarters and he'd ducked in for a moment. Decent of him to deal with protection without making any issue of it or assuming the woman would deal with it. But when he'd led her onto the flight deck of the *Peleliu*, she'd been less sure.

The deck was quiet, with no flight operations in these last few hours of darkness, but there would still be officers in navigation, communications, and the two antiaircraft control towers perched high in the *Peleliu*'s superstructure. Besides, even if no one was watching, there wasn't enough room in her helicopter to try making love, no matter how flexible they were. A sports car had more generous spaces.

But Michael wasn't looking at any helicopter, nor anywhere in the communications or control platforms that were the first two stories of the superstructure towering above the ship's deck. He was looking up into the starry night's darkness, high aloft at…

"You're joking."

He returned his attention to her and brushed his fingertips down from her ear, along her neck and then the line of her collarbone. Exactly as that brush had done the first time, it sent a pulse of energy surging through her so strongly that she couldn't speak.

She looked aloft once more and had to admit it was something no man had ever asked before. Actually, not many had dared even make a lewd suggestion to the Ice Queen. It was one of the main reasons she'd promoted the moniker after she was tagged with it the first time; it kept the usual, expected approaches cordoned off.

Well, Michael was never what she expected. He acted as if the Ice Queen didn't even exist.

He led her to the ocean side of the six-story superstructure, and they climbed the stairs past the first two levels. The gentle sway of the ship on the now-quiet sea could be felt here, but she'd spent too many years aboard ships to be bothered by such mild seas. She'd never climbed the ladder to the upper levels, but she knew the way.

Michael didn't stop at the roof of the navigation bridge or the searchlight platform as she'd expected. She'd been unsure of those because of the possible arrival of personnel.

No. He continued right up to the top of the uptake enclosure. The uptake engine stacks and the thin radio main mast were the only things that continued above the small space. The enclosure itself was a maintenance platform that offered a narrow walkway and a handrail around the ship's towering exhaust stacks. On the forward side of the stacks, only the forward radar platform was higher. To the rear of the ship, the space opened up to an area about five feet square. Astern—the view was magnificent, and very private.

She and Michael leaned on the handrail together as she drank in the view. All ship's lights were below them. The moon had set, and only the stars and the two masthead blinkers were higher than their present aerie. The height and isolation were so liberating. They made her want to shout out, "I'm an eagle!" But she didn't.

"We're fifty feet above the flight deck and a hundred and twenty above the water. That's why I asked about heights. Some people can't take the swaying motion even though they—"

She turned into his arms and kissed him to shut him up. The simple kiss grew and expanded to a level she'd never before experienced. Kissing Michael was better than sex with most men. It kept building. Okay, kissing Michael was better than sex with any man. And he hadn't even moved his hands from stroking her back yet. He just held her as if she were somehow precious and important.

When she couldn't take it anymore, she shifted to lay her cheek against his. She liked that they were nearly the same height so that she could whisper into his ear, "It's magnificent, Michael."

"It's not the redwoods, but I like it."

"Then you'll have to show me the trees someday."

His cloak of stillness, as she'd come to think of it, settled over him. He simply stopped moving, stopped vibrating the air with his energy. It almost felt as if he were going invisible in her arms. She pulled back, not out of his arms in case he could somehow dematerialize, but far enough that she could have seen his face if there had been more than the pale starlight.

"I'm sorry," she apologized. "That was too forward of me. This whole thing is too forward. I just got caught up in the moment and how good you feel and smell, and now I'm babbling which I never do except to myself and—"

"I'd love to show them to you." His voice stopped her run-on panic that had built out of nowhere.

"And you show them to..." She had to ask.

"No one."

Her breath caught in her chest, trapped there trying to choke her. She wasn't ready for this. She wasn't prepared for this to mean something. Yet Michael had obviously just opened the vault closest to his heart.

And he'd opened it for her.

They were already way past this not meaning anything. Had been since—

"I'm thinking too much, Michael. Make me stop."

"Is that an order, ma'am?" She could hear the soft laugh that lurked so enticingly in his voice but had yet to escape.

"I think it is more me begging you."

"I thought that was my role. You know, as the scruffy dog named Bailey."

"Oh God. I'll never live that one down, will I?"

In answer he kissed her again and her mind shut off as her body roared to life. His hands, those rough, callus-worn hands, brushed her skin so gently that she would beg for more if she could speak. She wanted so much. Wanted to, even if just for this one moment, shed the Ice Queen and lose herself.

Michael made that easy. He turned her until she lay back against the warm steel of the uptake stack and all she could see were the stars. She braced her feet wide and let the swaying of the ship take her.

He took full advantage of his position, slowly discovering her reactions to him, which rose from deep inside with an intensity that would have alarmed and surprised her in any more normal setting. But here, so high in the night sky, they weren't their own mundane selves. They were somehow more. Somehow other.

Here she could let herself go. It wasn't something she had much experience with. Even on the rare occasions when the Ice Queen took a lover, she kept a piece of herself closed off, tucked away.

Here, standing so close to the sky, that seemed unimportant, perhaps even impossible.

Dragging off his T-shirt, she discovered that his chest was everything she'd thought it would be since she'd first glimpsed it from the helicopter. As she ran her hands over him, she discovered both the strength and the weaknesses. For though he was magnificently muscled, he also wore several battle scars. The round scars of bullet holes, the long thin slices left by the surgeon's knife, and the inexplicable feeling of safety those gave her. If this man could survive so much, maybe he could somehow protect her as well.

She wasn't sure what she needed protection from, but it didn't change the feeling. Not as he unclothed her with those strong-gentle hands. Not as she lay back naked against the warm steel and reveled in the depth of his investigation of her.

When she could stand it no longer, couldn't tolerate

the separateness another moment, Michael somehow knew. At that perfect moment, he sheathed himself and she welcomed him in. Her own soft groan against the base of his neck was the first sound she'd made.

Claudia's moan of passion echoed deep inside Michael's own chest. His traitorous body had known, had waited his whole life for this ecstatic moment of coupling. Their bodies fit together in perfect alignment like a new barrel on his HK rifle, a combination that could never be broken asunder. One hand cradled and supported her as she wrapped her legs about his hips; the other he kept buried in hair even softer than he'd imagined.

Her body thrummed and pulsed against his. Her hands, those hands that had traced over, found, and accepted each of his many injuries and scars, were now buried in his hair. Women were repulsed by his scars or wanted to know the story behind each one or… Claudia was the first who had simply accepted them as part of him.

Her mouth delivered each fresh moan into his core where their lips shared their emotions.

He was fooling himself. He had to be. Somehow. No woman felt this good. No one had ever responded to him this way.

And he had never responded this way to any woman.

Continuing to stroke deep into her, he found places that he had never felt before. The sensations ripped at him like a storm when you're high in a tree—part of you praying you'll survive and part of you flying high on the unbelievable experience.

Claudia's unquestioning welcome and trust were something he'd rarely experienced outside an action team. And even then he'd never told about the redwoods. That past he'd always kept as a closed door to protect something so precious. And Claudia Jean Casperson had walked through it as if the lock wasn't there and shown her glorious light upon him like sunbeams striking through the thick canopy to illuminate the world.

She rose for him, climbing a long peak that left her only able to clutch him and shudder as it roared through her.

He'd always liked to think that he was a good lover. Women seemed to enjoy his attentions.

Claudia's reactions made him feel masterful. Buried deep inside her, he could feel every pulse that echoed the length of her magnificent form, shaking her to the core.

She crested, bloomed, exploded.

And didn't stop.

She wrapped her legs more tightly about him to draw him even deeper within her. No one had ever opened to him so selflessly, so completely.

It wasn't ownership. It wasn't possession. It was a welcome like coming home, though not to any place he'd ever dreamed of.

Then he took her up again. Drove himself as he never had before to a place he'd never been. Her second flashover took them together until the only thing he could do was hold on to her or he'd be lost himself. She was his safety line, the only thing guiding him back from where he'd just been.

How long he held her there, buried deep within her… how long she simply clung to him seemed to last forever.

And he was the happiest he had ever been.

They clambered down before first light, before the Milky Way had begun to fade from the night sky. When they reached the main flight deck, Claudia had to sit. There wasn't a chance her knees were solid enough for something as mundane as walking. Not after flying so high among the stars that now swept horizon to horizon.

At the handrail, she slipped her legs through the lowest opening to dangle them over the water still many stories below. Michael could probably recite the feet and inches from memory. She leaned on the safety lines of the handrail and watched the sky as it shifted from star-spangled black to the deepest blue.

Michael settled beside her. They hadn't spoken a word. Not the first time, not the second, nor the third. She would be sore, they both would, but she'd never had such an experience—never mind three of them.

"You are a magnificent lover." Even as a whisper, she felt she was shouting loudly enough for the whole world to hear.

As voluble as ever, Michael simply brushed a hand down her back along her spine, a simple gesture that left her breathless and told her she'd been answered in kind. There had been no questioning his response to her; she'd woken something in him that was deep and feral. Where their first lovemaking had been exploratory, the second had been almost savage with its shared need, and the third so gentle she'd almost wept with the sheer joy of it. And he hadn't spoken a single word since her fingers had first brushed over his chest, and his over hers.

She'd struck a speechless man speechless. She smiled at her own joke.

"What?" he asked just to prove her wrong.

"For a man who uses so few words, you are one of the most expressive individuals I've ever known."

"For a—"

"Careful there." She could feel him about to dig himself a hole. She should have just let him. It would've been fun watching him try to climb out of it.

He harrumphed, then continued anyway. "For a woman I've known barely a week, you are mesmerizing."

Next time she'd keep her mouth shut and just let him speak. The horizon shifted to pale blue, then pink as the arch of the sky shifted from black to blue. The last stars winked out only moments before the sun crested the horizon.

After checking that the coast was clear and no orderly or petty officer had snuck up on them, she leaned over enough to kiss him on the cheek.

"Thank you for sharing the sky with me."

Michael looked back at Claudia as the rising sun changed her hair from blond to gold. He'd been trying to make sense of her and was even more adrift than when he'd been merely confused by her.

She had driven him to a place he'd never thought to approach, hadn't known it even existed. He had never let himself go and simply taken a woman. She'd enticed and teased him with her body and her hands and her throaty moans until he had lost all control and simply taken.

She'd fallen back upon their piled clothes, and he'd gone at her with his mouth, his hands, and after suckling her breasts like a man dying of thirst led to an endless fountain, he'd driven her down into the deck until he'd exploded inside her. She'd dug strong fingers into hard shoulder muscles and clamped her mouth on his as she came again and again until he could taste the changes in her with each release.

And rather than pushing him away, she'd stroked and held him for a long time. He might have slept except for the wonder of discovering her face, the way her eyelids fluttered closed when he kissed them, the way the tip of her nose was ever so slightly squared off.

Though he was long past recovery, she had coaxed him to give more. With a laugh and a languid stroke of her hand, she had finally made his need for her desperate, and he was never desperate. She'd risen and stood magnificent in the night. Then she'd turned away from him, clothed only in starlight, to place both hands on the safety rail and stare out over the phosphorescent green track that the ship awoke in the ocean.

When he had done no more than trace a single finger down her back, she had shivered despite the warm night. When he reached around to cup her, she'd moaned like a lost soul. And when he'd been able to stand it no longer and, grabbing her hips, drove into her, she'd laughed. Actually laughed with joy that spread over him as well when he'd thrust forward with his need for her and she in turn had strained back against him.

The frantic part of their need was gone, momentarily sated for now by the way he'd attacked her and been attacked in return.

Now, with a gentleness as deep as the night and as perfect as the slow-waving trees, they rode one more time aloft.

He could never get enough of her—not the heat that poured off her body, not the way she pressed her breasts into his hands when he reached for them, not the way her joy of life washed away any dark memories.

Delta were "other." They didn't belong in the military any more than they belonged anywhere else in the world. They were cut off from every chain of command below the Chief of Staff and the President himself. They wore no uniforms except when they wore their combat gear. They told no civilians that they existed.

Yet Claudia gave him a sense of belonging and welcome that he didn't know how to understand. All he could do was accept or reject, and there was nothing in him that wanted to reject any gift this precious woman gave him.

She provided a core of safety that no Special Ops soldier ever dared feel—the moment you felt safe was the instant that someone got past your guard. That described Claudia well enough.

Nothing in his training, nothing in his life had prepared him for the woman he had held this night or who now sat beside him at the ship's rail, lit like a goddess by the sunrise.

After he had so lost himself in her, he had been uncertain about touching her. He'd gone too far, done too much. After they'd dressed but before they'd descended, they had stood a breath apart for a long time just watching the ocean pass in silence.

Afraid she would be repulsed by the animal he had become in his desperation for her, he had waited. Afraid he would be lost after this and never find a way to return, he had left it for her to choose the next step.

As if they really were in perfect alignment, she'd brushed her hand over his and guided him back into her arms. She'd simply held him, her head on his shoulder, her nose nestled against the base of his neck. They let the soothing sway of the ship...of the rolling waves... lull them with its rhythm until the slightest fading of the stars warned him that this moment was ending.

Even now, seated beside her, not touching, he wanted nothing more than to cradle her close and tell her how perfect she was.

Was this wanting what his parents felt? Was this why they always looked at him sadly when he came home for leave, alone? They thought he didn't notice because they always welcomed him with open arms despite his choice to serve, which they truly didn't understand. But he could detect it in their odd silences and shifting looks when they stood arm-in-arm, as they so often did, and thought he wasn't watching.

What would they think of Claudia Jean Casperson when they met her? For they would meet her, that much he knew.

He turned to survey the woman sitting beside him and tried to see her with another's eyes. But it didn't work. He'd learned too much, knew her too well. Every shape defined by muscle and training. She was an athlete in a way that so few pilots, male or female, ever were.

And her physical power was a perfect reflection of the woman within.

She humbled him.

Her vision was so clear and pure that he actually did feel scruffy around her. He knew he had her up on a pedestal, but he couldn't seem to do anything about it. If she had one flaw, it was that he couldn't get enough of her.

"Next time. In the trees."

She nodded without turning from the shining ocean.

Whatever she was seeing out there, he hoped that it included him.

Chapter 11

Over the next two weeks, the patrols dredged up nothing but two unarmed and underpowered skiffs that were turned back easily.

Michael kept thinking that he and Claudia really needed to talk about what was happening between them, but every time they entered each other's presence, his world went so quiet that he couldn't imagine breaking the silence. They didn't go aloft again, but it was a rare day they didn't find some time to spend in each other's arms, even if it was just to lie there and marvel that the feelings weren't wearing thin with time.

They ran 10k every morning and at least 5k more every evening on the hangar deck. Sometimes he ran with Bill, and Claudia ran with Trisha. By unspoken mutual consent, he and Bill would hang back to simply admire the women who shared their beds—both Trisha's full-on charge-ahead run and Claudia's easy lope. Free weights at midnight if they were back from patrol.

At times they just read together, for Claudia was always reading. They'd meet on deck in the warm night air or in the ship's library or even in the echoing quiet of the mess hall between meals. She was reading some book about child warriors battling for food. "Dilya assigned it to me," was her explanation. When she asked, he showed her his weapon's manual.

"You're reading about the PSG1 sniper rifle for recreation? Don't you already know that thing cold?"

"I was considering some recommendations to include in the next upgrade."

"You're trying to figure out how to improve on a ten-thousand-dollar sniper rifle, one of the best in the world?"

And he would tell her about the floating barrel interlock, and she would listen to how he thought he could get another ten percent decrease in the minute of arc variation on successive shots. He had never so enjoyed explaining his ideas.

They were having a quiet dinner together, as quiet as such meals ever were when Trisha was at the table, when Michael heard the sound of the ship change. Trisha kept right on with a story about a midshipman who'd accidentally walked in on her shower and how the poor boy would never recover, but Claudia and Bill both noted the change. Dilya, over at the other table, did as well, slipping off her headphones and looking about for the cause. Then the Navy people.

The engines, which had done little more than idle since the ship's run down the Somali coast, awoke with a slow climb to a deep throb. The ship heeled into a turn. Not a hard emergency turn, but enough of a one to make the ice tea in his glass appear tipped.

The ship's comm squawked for "All Hands" attention. Everyone went silent, except Trisha who they had to shush because her story remained unfinished.

"This is Lieutenant Commander Boyd Ramis. We have been asked to move the *Peleliu* for a possible new mission. That is all of the information I am free to disclose at this time, except to say that we have been released from Operation Atalanta. I'm sure you'll all miss the Somali coast."

He paused for the small laugh but didn't overextend it. He had good timing.

"We are presently headed for the Suez Canal and will receive further instructions at that time. All key mission personnel, please report to my office in fifteen minutes. I have been authorized to pass on one other message from both USAFRICOM and EU NAVFOR, 'Job well done, *Peleliu.*' Keep it up, team. You done good. That last is from me. Ramis out." Nice touch.

Michael glanced across the tables at Chief Warrant Lola Maloney and Air Mission Commander Stevenson. They exchanged glances and then turned to him. Okay, this was news to everyone. He took a large bite of his crispy fried chicken, sipped some ice tea to soften it further, and rose from his unfinished meal. The others were doing the same.

Ramis had the decency not to look surprised when Michael and the SOAR pilots all arrived at his office in under five minutes. As soon as they were settled, Ramis offered an easy shrug.

"I actually know little more than I've already told the chaps. We're in transit to the Med, then holding stations. We'll pick up resupply from the Sixth Fleet. Where we go after that? My guess is as good as anybody else's."

A couple of the others began asking questions, but Michael simply waited. Claudia did as well. It was obvious that Ramis had another tidbit up his sleeve but wanted to have it coaxed out of him.

"Well," he admitted at length with an easy smile, "I do

know that while we're departing Africa Command, we aren't being attached to either EUCOM or CENTCOM for the Middle East. That positively reeks of special assignment." Clearly he was very pleased by the idea that he and his ship had earned it. "Beyond that, your guess is really as good as mine."

Again with the useless speculation. Again Michael waited. Again Boyd enjoyed himself immensely. He did like his bits of control.

"I am going to have to ask you all to fold up your birds. We want them stowed out of sight on the hangar deck when we transit the Canal five days from now. Then…"

This time no one interrupted.

"I told them that you folks had been too long on station. While we hardworking Navy folk are in transit"—he offered one of his beneficent smiles—"you and your flight teams have leave. You have two hours to clear my decks before a Navy Super Stallion helicopter from Camp Lemonnier shows up to haul you out of here. Once they return to Djibouti airfield, you'll transit across to the civilian side of the airport and can catch a flight anywhere you please from there. Seven days. Sorry, a couple of those will be in transit. Best I could do." As if he'd personally arranged it.

They had been six straight months on this assignment, which only spoke to the horrendous operational tempo that the 5D drew. By all prior standards they ought to be back to Fort Campbell for three months of training or testing new equipment. Perhaps a war game or two to keep their edges sharp. Instead they had a week and then would be back in theater.

A week…

Michael popped his head up and turned to face Claudia.

"You don't have to ask." She spoke in just the sort of normal voice that no one in the suddenly chattering room would notice. "The answer is yes, if you want me to."

He pictured Claudia Jean Casperson standing in the silence of the redwood forest. He pictured making love to her there. He nodded infinitesimally to not draw attention. That was insufficient, so he spoke in an equally nonintrusive voice.

"That was a really big yes."

The rest of the Delta team and SOAR personnel had remained in the mess hall awaiting instructions. The rest of the Navy and Rangers had finished their meals and wandered off to other duties.

At AMC Stevenson's announcement of leave, the waiting SOAR team surged to their feet and practically stampeded to fetch their gear. Way too long in the field, but they'd driven most of the final nails into the Somali piracy coffin that EU NAVFOR had been patiently building these last several years. A week wasn't much, but it sounded like a gift from on high at the moment.

By the time Michael returned to the flight deck to assist, Claudia and Trisha already had their birds' rotors folded back and stowed in line with the tail boom. He helped them clip the wheel trolleys to the center of the skids. The ship's loadmasters came to fetch the Little Birds and wheeled them side by side onto one of the elevators that lowered them to the hangar deck below.

There they'd be hidden from any prying eyes. SOAR was very protective of her stealth helicopters.

In quick order, the DAP and the other birds were also clear of the deck. Even the big Chinook went below, its three big rotor blades at either end folded over the central body until it looked like nothing so much as a kid in bad need of a haircut.

Michael packed a duffel and returned to the deck at the same moment Claudia did. They dropped their bags and sat on them, both well used to the military's hurry-up-and-wait mentality.

He enjoyed listening to the others. Tim and Lola were off to Oklahoma as guests of Big John and Connie. Bill was working on Trisha to go stay with her parents, and she was working on him to spend some time in Budapest because neither of them had ever been there. Michael would lay money on Bill losing that bet. Dusty James was headed to Fort Campbell where his wife was finishing Green Platoon to become a SOAR crew chief. Kee and Archie were already talking about taking Dilya to go sailing with his dad, Archibald the Second.

Dilya wandered over and dropped into the low crouch that she favored, feet flat on the deck, elbows resting on her knees. Michael had seen her sit that way for hours at a time. It was a useful skill, but his own knees didn't appreciate it after the first ten minutes or so. Dilya had been born to it.

"Do you like sailing?" Claudia had clearly picked up the same bits of conversation he had. But she'd thought to turn it into polite conversation. He always marveled at how people thought to do that.

Dilya nodded. "Sailing's fun. My first sailing trip I

think is the first time my parents slept together." She didn't even break stride, but just continued as if such an observation was perfectly normal. "I like the beach better. I know it's little-kid stuff, but I still like making sand castles."

"There's an option for you, Colonel." Claudia had a tease in her voice. "You could show me how to build castles in the sand."

He wondered if she was joking, which she must have read on his features, for she explained without prompting.

"Only time I've really spent on a coast was at Annapolis. Midshipmen were not encouraged to spend time building sand castles at the beach."

"I'll take you."

Dilya was watching him. With a sudden nod of satisfaction, she stood. "Remember, do it soon. You never know when the phone will ring." And she was gone.

"What the hell?"

Claudia was watching the teen's back. "I don't know, Colonel. Sounds like the kid knows what she's talking about."

The massive Marine Corps CH-53 Super Stallion hammered down like thunder out of a blue sky. The *Peleliu* was still driving north across the Arabian Sea, a long way from making the westerly turn at the Horn of Africa.

Claudia knew the helicopter well, even if she'd never flown it. The Super Stallion, the largest bird in U.S. inventory, and the MV-22 Osprey tiltrotor were the main tools of Marine Corps transport.

It took her a moment to identify what was wrong with it. A bird she knew so well, it looked… It was the wrong color. Marine gray rather than SOAR pitch-black. It had the pilot's names painted in large black letters below their windows. The aircraft number and the word "Marines" stretched down the side in yard-tall letters. The SOAR helicopters were unembellished black to be anonymous and blend into the night sky. It felt so old school to purposely fly in the daylight.

That realization was as much a marker of the changes she'd undergone since joining SOAR as any she'd experienced. With its rotors thudding heavily, the past landed in front of her and lowered its rear ramp. The present was safely stored out of sight in the hangar deck below, and the future—

Michael stood and gathered up his duffel to board the aircraft. Unsure of her footing, Claudia stood and picked up her own bag to follow him.

Several of the team went all gooey in the head when they clambered up the rear loading ramp. The Super Stallion was a monster with an eighty-foot-diameter, seven-bladed rotor, but it could only out-lift a Chinook by a ton or so. Still, Dennis Hakawa and Justin Roberts were clearly two of the goners, and they hustled up to stand close behind the pilots and talk shop. Claudia noticed that Kara Moretti also joined in, despite not being a helo pilot. Perhaps Justin's attentions had begun to interest her. Kee and Tim, predictably, started chatting up the ramp gunner.

Everyone else just took one of the seats that lined either side of the cargo bay, which was about the same size as the Chinook despite the buzz it was creating. A few managed to bypass the "Ooo shiny" aspect of the unfamiliar craft and continue the conversation about their plans for leave.

Claudia hadn't really thought through where Michael was taking her. Other than Miramar and Pendleton, she'd never been to California. Her former Marines unit was based in North Carolina, though she'd spent most of her career "feet wet" on some carrier or other.

The redwoods themselves sounded a little mythical to her. The tallest trees in the world, they grew only in one tiny strip of the coastland of Oregon and northern California. That was a world as foreign to her as, well, more foreign than Somalia or Indonesia or Argentina—all of which she'd flown.

Michael also was a strange and foreign land. She danced so carefully around the edge of relationships that she'd had relatively few since high school. The party girls dazzled; the confident ones mystified; even the quiet ones like Connie charmed. Clearly she'd charmed her husband—Big John, at least twice her size. He was absolutely gobsmacked by the widely acknowledged best helicopter mechanic in the 5D, meaning she might well be the best in all of SOAR, or even in the world.

Claudia had never charmed or dazzled or mystified anyone. She'd learned how to repulse the unwanted with freezer burn and remain focused on her career. It had lapsed over into her leaves as well. Her desire to go hang out in a bar near her mom's place in Flagstaff was below zero, and she certainly wasn't going to risk her position by fraternizing within the Corps.

"Claudia. You need a nice boy. I'll introduce you next time you're in Flagstaff." Every leave it was the same. And all it did was guarantee that Claudia's visits were unannounced and brief to leave her mom too little time to strategize any serious matchmaking.

At least her mom didn't harass Claudia about serving in the military as so many of the other women soldiers reported about their families. She just griped about Claudia not having a man, as if that were the key to life. On leave, Claudia would tolerate it as long as she could—she knew it was just because Mom loved her—then she'd go stay in the old house out in Bumble Bee. Squib was long gone, but Mr. Johns still let her borrow a cheerful mare named Penelope and ride the hills until she found the silence she so missed.

So what was she doing following a Delta Colonel into the California redwoods? What in the hell was she doing allowing a superior officer into her bed? Even if they were in different regiments, they were both still Special Operations Forces, though she had no idea how Delta actually attached to the military command structure. Were they technically a different branch of the service? Most rumors said they reported directly to the Joint Chiefs of Staff, circumventing both Fort Bragg command and even Joint Special Operations Command. It wasn't the sort of question one asked; inquiries about Delta were strongly discouraged, even when you were sleeping with one. Especially if.

As they flew, she and Dilya began comparing ideas on the various tactics of the contestants in *The Hunger Games*.

"I like the bow and arrow." Dilya popped up to her feet and made as if she were about to launch an arrow out one of the helicopter's square windows.

Claudia corrected the girl's stance and arm position. She'd hunted rabbit and deer with a bow in the Sonoran hills west of Bumble Bee. She could see Dilya memorizing the corrections and integrating them into her muscle feel very quickly.

Because Annapolis didn't have an archery team, Claudia had started one on her own. The dozen interested midshipmen never went on to compete against other schools, but they'd become quite proficient. She found a former Olympic medalist in town who came out to coach them on occasion.

Despite being self-taught, she somehow had the best technique; it had simply felt right. The team had consistently turned to her for instruction, and she'd had to break it down so that it was teachable. Her Academy instructors knew nothing of archery but soon promoted her into the advanced leadership courses.

By now, with Dilya, it was automatic: straighten and lock the forward elbow with the arm straight in line with both shoulder blades, turn the wrist out slightly to create straight-line pressure to hold the bow, raise the drawing hand to her chin with the elbow horizontally in line with the arrow's flight.

The girl held the position, turning only her head to look at Claudia. Claudia pushed a finger against Dilya's chin until she was back in line.

"Your vision and your chin should be in alignment with the target. Chin stays up, but not so raised that it feels as if you're pointing it at the target. Try for level with the ground."

Dilya tested the angles, wiggling her joints up and down until she settled into roughly the right position, as close as she was likely to get without really holding a bow.

"Where's your weight?" Claudia nudged Dilya's shoulder, and she almost fell over backward. "You want it the same on both feet, so it feels as if you're planted solidly. Then lean forward so you're one-third on your heels, two-thirds on the balls of your feet and the toes. Your stability is in your heels, but your balance lives in your forefoot."

Dilya found her stance and held it easily through several small air pockets that shifted the helicopter about. A good sense of balance, and with the wiry strength Claudia had felt in Dilya's thin arms, she'd make a good archer.

Dilya moved to the center of the cargo bay and waited for the next air pocket to try out her balance.

They'd gathered a small audience without Claudia noticing. Michael watched her intently; he always appeared to be studying her. And Kee watched Claudia's actions with her daughter very closely. The woman didn't smile much at anyone other than her husband and child, but her sharp nod of acknowledgment was filled with appreciation.

Claudia returned Kee's nod with a bit of surprise. In the Corps, she'd always thought about her every action—how she fit in and how she could avoid attracting the wrong sort of attention. There was also a constant awareness of the operational pecking order. Who flew more sorties and in what situations was a constant, unspoken point system of prestige.

This was perhaps the first time she'd thought about that in the weeks since joining the *Peleliu*. And what struck her was that for perhaps the first time in her life, there was only one criterion for approval: competence.

Though the 5D only had five women in the air—Kara Moretti stayed on the deck and watched the flight of her Gray Eagle through a console—the number was more than enough to offset gender bias. Anyone stupid enough to try harassing a female Night Stalker would probably end up living out his days at a VA hospital because of all the little pieces he'd be broken into by both the men and women.

And it wasn't personality; five more diverse military fliers would be difficult to find. Having proven herself in the Somalia operation, Claudia felt welcome among them. There was still discomfort and a bit of unease, but a cohesive team wasn't formed, not even among all Night Stalkers, in only a few weeks.

She glanced over at Michael, who was looking a little lost without his weapons about him. Her relationship with Michael was well known to all. How did that affect her acceptance? Tuned as he always was to her, he brushed his fingers along her arm without turning from his discussion with Bill about the viability of his PSG1 upgrade concepts.

The reactions among the group were interesting. The women who saw it weren't watching him; they were watching her. Again their instant defense of Michael came to mind, as if he was the one who needed protection. It was *her* heart that was exposed for everyone to see. And she definitely wasn't comfortable with that exposure or what it said about how she was feeling herself.

Yet another thing to think about among the trees.

Chapter 12

MICHAEL'S PARENTS HAD BEEN UP IN SEATTLE WHEN Michael and Claudia arrived at their home in Corvallis, Oregon. They'd offered to cut short their guest lectures at the University of Washington, but Michael didn't let them. Instead he'd loaded an old Toyota pickup with enough food to feed an entire action team and enough gear to cripple them, and driven Claudia across the border into northern California.

"Seattle to Corvallis is over six hours," he explained. "They're in their seventies now—I was a late child—so it's a long trip for them, especially with Dad's bum hip. They usually stop overnight in Portland just to break up the time on the road. We'll climb first, meet up with them later. Maybe we'll all go out to the coast and build some sand castles together. Doubt if they've done that in years." It was perhaps the longest speech he'd ever made in her presence. He was positively giddy about returning to the trees.

Now they stood beneath the trees and his use of the word "climb" suddenly came home to roost. They stood at the edge of Jedediah Smith Redwoods State Park and looked up at the trees. Except these weren't trees; these were towers of crenulated red bark tall enough to be called skyscrapers. She simply couldn't take it all in at once.

They stood in a clearing of sun-dappled ferns that

grew as high as her shoulders. With no warning, dozens, perhaps hundreds of tree trunks burst from the earth in a disarray of columns that would have humbled the Greeks with their majesty. Branches and greenery were so far above as to be unimaginable; ten or twenty stories of trunk soared upward.

"Climb?" To her the trees were overwhelming. Far more foreign than she'd ever have guessed. There was more wood in one of these trees than in an entire Sonoran ridgeline. There was more life in this forest than… It was oppressive and squeezed in on her, crowding her aside with its vibrancy. There was no exposed rock here to make her feel anchored to the earth. Any soil was lost beneath layers of pine needle, twig, moss, and who knew what all these plants were.

The air itself was wrong, thick with moisture and moss, redolent with the smell of decaying organic matter. Yet, as she breathed deeply, there was a richness to it as well, every lungful so packed with oxygen that it was like a drug.

A small flock of giant black birds flew by. Ravens. At least they were familiar from her desert, though she'd never seen enough of them at once to be called a flock.

"Yes." Michael had said he lived in the redwoods. Despite his question about heights aboard the *Peleliu*, she hadn't thought he meant that he lived *up* in the redwoods.

"Like you live in a tree house up there?" Jedediah was the first big redwood park south of the Oregon-California border. A tree house was a dizzying prospect—simply looking up at these trees gave her a touch of vertigo. The biggest tree near Bumble Bee, Arizona, stood perhaps twenty feet high and a foot or two thick. These trees were ten and twenty feet in diameter, and their rough, red-brown bark soared a long way aloft before the first branch even bothered to put in an appearance. The tangle of limbs went much higher. You certainly weren't going to climb this with a big loop of rope around the tree and spiked shoes.

"No. You'll see what I mean when we get there."

"These aren't them?"

"Nope." Michael was practically bouncing with energy. They stood just a few dozen feet from the parking lot. He patted the closest tree in a friendly fashion.

As if he couldn't help himself, he jammed his hand deep into a crenellation in the bark that must be close to a foot deep, formed it into a fist, and began walking up the tree. Then he hand-jammed his other fist and in moments was a dozen feet in the air.

Claudia looked up at the vast trunk. There was no way she was hand-jamming her way up a tree. The bark looked as if it was ready to break off in big chunks at the least provocation. Nor was she going to watch Michael do it. One false move and there'd be nothing but a little pile of dead Delta-boy. He'd never struck her as reckless.

He kept talking as he began circling the tree, hand-over-hand, still several yards up in the air. "These are just babies, can't be more than five hundred years old. Their granddaddies are three or four times older."

"Just babies." Someone must have beamed her to an alien planet. Joshua trees in the Sonoran Desert lived hundreds, maybe a thousand years, but they rarely stood higher than Michael presently clambered about.

This was way more foreign than she'd ever have guessed. It wasn't foreign; it was alien!

Michael let go and did a tuck-and-roll down the sloping trunk to land easily beside her. His landing made no noise on the soft duff of needles that surrounded the tree. He was actually grinning.

Claudia kept her mouth shut for the half-hour drive down to Del Norte Coast Redwoods State Park.

Michael chatted away, introducing trees they passed with easy waves to the right and left. "The Monarch stands up a little valley about two miles that way, not that you'd know it. Eärendil and Elwing are about a mile over there, but you could be lost for a week trying to find the right spot."

She kept her mouth firmly shut. Normally she enjoyed listening to him talk—he had one of those voices that was an invitation to daydream, soft and deep as if he'd be the one to sing bass despite his lean frame. She'd never met a tree that had a name, and now Michael was introducing them as if they were personal friends who came over to dinner each weekend.

Claudia had been a bit nervous about meeting his parents, but apparently meeting his trees was the bigger deal.

Without preamble, Michael slowed, finally turning off to park his parents' old Toyota in the tangle of vine maple and sword ferns off the road.

"It'll be fine here. The park rangers will recognize Mom and Pop's truck and leave it alone. The tree hounds, the ones who don't understand how to be careful about climbing the biggest trees, might recognize the truck and try to follow us. Better if we can hide it so that they don't find it in the first place." He began gathering up loose brush, and the truck disappeared rapidly beneath its shield.

"Tree hounds? You hide trees?"

"Sure." He began organizing their gear into two large packs. "The real monster redwoods aren't conveniently in the public parks next to the highway where people can visit them. There are a few big ones along the roads all down the coast, but the true monsters, we call them 'Titans,' are known to very few individuals. The knowledge is handed from one tree climber to the next in order to protect them."

The amount of rope he tied to the outside of the packs was...well, ridiculous. Unless you thought about the height of these trees.

"How is it possible to hide a three-hundred-and-fifty-foot tree, Michael? That can't be right."

"You'll see."

Michael had practically talked her ear off for the five hours from his parents' to the state park. At least for him.

Claudia's brain felt plugged up with the amount of information he dispensed so efficiently. And still she knew nothing at all about what lay ahead of them. She considered going on a sit-down strike. The last time she'd slept had been somewhere over the North Pole on an airliner from Rome to Seattle.

"I want to sleep among the trees," Michael answered Claudia's question of whether or not they could get some sleep first as he finished loading the packs. "We've still got about three hours until sunset. We'll hike in now and then we can climb at first light tomorrow."

Michael tested the fit of her pack. He'd loaded it as lightly as he could, but it still weighed about fifty pounds. It was a fairly typical weight for a training march, though he still felt bad about how heavy it was.

"It's going to be a slog," he warned her, wondering if he could move any more of her gear into his own pack.

"Worse than Green Platoon?"

That stopped him. Claudia had such a way of putting things in perspective. He was used to the climbers who made only a few ascents in a year. For them, their first adventure into the big trees was a physical shock leaving them sore and blistered for weeks, often with pulled muscles and bad sprains. The monsters of the forest, the tallest trees on the planet, were reluctant, shy souls at best. They hid deep in the fog-laced canyons of the Pacific Coast.

Claudia was at a level of fitness few soldiers achieved. Even thinking about that rekindled his desire for this woman. Her body was specifically designed to drive some ancient Italian marble artist into madness as he attempted to carve it into stone. Michael needed to ask her for the name of one of those Greek goddesses. He knew there was one for beauty or strength or something. Venus was just beauty, and Claudia embodied so much more than that. Adonis…or was that one of the male gods? Magnificent, that was her. If he ever found another tree worthy of bearing a name, he'd name it Magnificent in her honor.

"Okay, Magnificent. Then let's do it."

"Magnificent?"

Had he really said that out loud? Crap!

"Well, you are." He turned for the trees before her mere presence confused him further. Claudia Jean Casperson in the redwoods was an adventure into the amazing that he'd never imagined. She shouldered her pack and settled it properly without any corrections of course.

The hip belt only emphasized the trimness of her waist and the chest strap the splendid form of her breasts beneath her T-shirt. The strength that always so impressed him combined with her wood-nymph agility to make her blend into the forest as if she'd always been there. She'd tied a folded-over, forest-green kerchief on her forehead to keep sweat and her hair out of her eyes. The green emphasized her bright hair until she glowed fairy bright when a stray sunbeam found her. She was the most beautiful woman he had ever seen.

Forcing himself to turn from the spectacle that was Claudia, he led her along the road a few hundred yards to the north until it crossed a small creek. Looking both ways to make sure no cars were in sight, he clambered down into the creek bed and turned upstream, skirting along the edge of a rocky pool. Based on the water flow, there hadn't been much rain in the last few weeks, and now in mid-May, the snowmelt was tapering off.

He kept checking on her, but she moved over the moss-slick boulders with easy care. In most places they could straddle this little creek, and most of it was shallow enough to not risk wet feet in their boots.

"Low bridge," he called out and ducked low under a fallen trunk that spanned the stream. The trunk was only a yard thick here, but the ferns sprouting atop it and the moss dangling below would hide their departure in the first few steps.

After that, no sound penetrated from the outside world. Birdcall, the skitter of a hunting squirrel, and the clacking of branches in the gentle winds were the only sounds aside from their own breathing and footsteps. Michael could feel the world dropping away from him. And as it did, he appreciated all the more the one precious piece of it that hiked in with him. It felt right that she was here.

An hour in, they'd only twice had to lie on their bellies in tree mulch and drag the packs along behind them to clear the blackberry bushes. As they moved farther and farther from the road, the forest grew thicker, though Claudia's hair still seemed to catch the light even when he thought there was none.

Then the forest brightened ahead, indicating a larger opening in the canopy. They came upon a fallen redwood tree that crossed their path. This hadn't been here before. It was a big one, though not one of the Titans of the forest.

"By the scars of the detonation zone, it's been down only a year or two." Michael hadn't visited this particular grove in a while.

"Detonation zone?" Claudia was weary, he could see, but hadn't offered a single word of complaint or shown any sign of slowing. What word was better than "magnificent"?

"See?" He swung his arm in a vertical arc to imitate the line of the fall. Perhaps two hundred and fifty feet long and twenty feet in diameter, the redwood had ripped a slice out of the forest canopy where the sun now shone through. "It dragged about a dozen trees down with it. Stripped the branches off those there and there, and probably buried another dozen or so trees beneath when it finally crashed in. Look at the ground to either side of the trunk."

The trees all around lay on the ground pointing outward, as if blown over by a bomb.

"Ground shock. First, the sound wave would hit, probably audible a mile or more away. Then the earth would buck and ripple just like an earthquake. She's probably a quarter million board feet."

"Board feet?"

"Imagine a board one inch thick, a foot wide, and fifty miles long, but it all landed right here. All three thousand tons of it, thankfully not in a single-point three-kiloton explosion, which would be a quarter of the Hiroshima bomb, but still bad enough."

"Okay." Claudia sounded a little breathless. "I'll buy the 'detonation zone' phrase and just be glad I wasn't here."

"It probably happened two years ago, based on the growth of the ferns and berries along the trunk. See the big sheets of bark starting to fall off and compost? That's about right on the time. The trunk itself will be here for decades."

Rather than circling around it through the debris field, Michael led her up and onto the trunk along a shattered branch a couple yards across. They stopped for dinner on top of the fallen giant. The trunk was so big around that the surface was practically flat here.

The silence slowly built around them. No longer disturbed by their tramping through the woods, the forest returned to life. A couple of birds flitted into a Douglas fir that had stood on the edge of the detonation zone. The side exposed to the sun sported a vast array of bright green branch tips brilliant with new growth. After a while, a doe and fawn picked their way into view, nibbling delicately, wholly unaware of the two humans watching them from on high. A raven arrived on the branch of a maple sapling that bobbed and wove under the unexpected weight. The majestic bird inspected them at length over one side, then the other of its long beak before departing.

Claudia didn't make a sound as she moved to straddle Michael where he sat. Her hair a halo in the shining sun, she leaned down to kiss him. Ever so gently, she tipped him over backward until he lay on the sun-baked bark. They'd both shed their jackets when the sun had found them, and now she removed his shirt.

She did not trace his chest with her hands, nor tease him with her kisses. Instead, she pulled her hair from its ponytail and let it fall about her face and onto his skin. Softer than a kiss, she brushed it over him until he ached for her.

When he reached, she pushed his hands aside. Pinned them to either side of his head with her fingers interlaced with his. Not releasing him, she continued her journey over him. She moved over him, at times languid and enticing, at times sensuous and erotic.

She moved to offer him her breast and hissed when he took its tip between his teeth. Only her T-shirt separated them as he nuzzled and teased her.

Michael would have spoken, if he'd been able to

think of anything to say. Instead, he did something he'd never done before—he let go, allowing himself to exist only to follow where Claudia led.

When they each shed their clothes, it was her doing, not his. Here, in the wilderness, the soft breezes of the woodland floor brushed over him as lightly as her hair. They cooled him where her kisses had left moisture and heated him where he and Claudia touched.

He lay and watched the forest, a thousand trunks rocketing skyward. Watched the slice of blue sky that revealed a window into a world beyond. And drank in the woman who knelt over him. Claudia was truly the finest sight he'd ever seen in his life.

She knelt over him and commanded a loving experience that was not about man and woman but rather about Michael and Claudia. She sent him flying, and he let her.

When they were done, when they had taken their fill of each other, she descended upon him with a sigh rather than a crash.

She lay down upon him, and they remained there together until there were only trees, sunlight, a glorious woman, and the man who loved her.

Michael had been strangely silent after they'd woken to the cooling evening. Even by Michael standards, his reticence was notable.

Claudia tried not to feel put out by it, but it was difficult. The best sex of her life, the first time she'd ever made love out of doors—because the masthead of the *Peleliu* didn't really count for that—and she felt a need to talk about it. To somehow validate that it was real.

Michael had woken her with a gentle though brief kiss. Without a word he had dug into their packs and set up a small stove to make them a soup of freeze-dried stew with a chocolate bar for dessert.

The silence had continued to echo as full dark set in and he led her along the length of the horizontal trunk toward the branches of the fallen tree. After a little exploration by flashlight, he found whatever he was looking for. In minutes he had a large hammock hung just a few feet over the trunk, tied off to branches now sticking up into the air rather than outward. The hammock included a layer of insulation below, and he tossed in a pair of sleeping bags.

She was no longer sure she wanted to share a hammock with him.

"Michael."

He continued his preparations as if he hadn't heard her.

"Michael!" Her sharp tone elicited a surprised retort from an owl perched somewhere nearby.

He stopped and turned to face her, but it was dark and she couldn't see his face to read his expression.

"Speak, damn you!" She could see his shrug and almost lit into him. No! She'd asked for this. She'd chosen as her lover a man who barely spoke—and certainly not about his feelings.

Claudia wanted to storm away, go back to the truck and drive far away. Back to the desert she understood. But it was dark night in the middle of an uncomfortable wilderness that smelled of green growing things and the rotting damp of wood and moss. Even if it were full light, she wasn't sure she could find her way. They'd left the stream long before reaching this tree, following some signs only Michael could read.

"What do you want me to say?"

"Goddamn it, Michael!" She'd known he was like this, so why was it suddenly pissing her off? Turning, she stalked off along the trunk until she lost any assistance from the flashlight Michael had propped in the bark in order to hang the hammock. For fear of making a misstep and falling two stories to the ground, she stopped and sat.

Claudia didn't know how long she remained there before Michael came up behind her; long enough to get cold without her jacket. His tread so soft that she didn't feel him walking along the trunk until he was almost upon her. She hunched her shoulders more, as if that would fend him off. Possessed of some superior form of night vision, he circled around her to sit in the darkness facing her. At least she assumed the vague silhouette in the night was turned toward her rather than away.

Too bad he didn't walk off the side of the trunk. She'd enjoy hearing him thud down into the moss and ferns.

"I don't know what to say or why you're upset. I know that you are, and I'm sorry for causing that because I can only assume it was my doing."

"And how did you reach that conclusion, Colonel?" She never spoke like that. She wasn't one of those bitchy women who spoke in vitriolic tones.

"Well, there are only the two of us here. And I can only guess that you aren't mad at yourself."

Oh, but she was. Mad at herself for… That stopped her. She was angry, horribly. Was it for the lovemaking they'd done? No. Michael had done an exceptional job of ruining her for any other man on the planet. His body fit hers like it had been custom made to her exact specifications and his thoughtfulness was, well, outside her experience.

She was mad at herself because…

Still the answer eluded her. She hugged her legs more tightly against her and tucked her hands between her knees, trying to warm them.

Michael waited her out, which didn't help in the least. If she could see him…but not even the starlight reached this far through the rent in the forest canopy. And the moon wouldn't be up for hours, and who knew when it would find the break in the trees. Why did the woods have to be so dense and dark?

"I'm angry"—she started in hopes that would help her find the rest of her sentence—"because…I have no idea what you're feeling." She also had no idea what she was feeling, which wasn't helping matters in the slightest.

Michael offered a low chuckle. "Well, that makes two of us."

"It…what?"

He must have reached out because she felt a hand brush down her jeans from knee to mid-calf before withdrawing. Now that she had some guess as to her distance from a likely target, she had to resist the urge to kick it.

"Captain Claudia Jean Casperson, you are a jumble in my brain. You are making me feel things I don't understand and don't know how to interpret."

"Is that why you aren't speaking to me?"

His silence was eloquent.

"I'm not wearing any goddamn night-vision gear, Colonel. I can't see shit! Was that a negligent shrug?"

Again that soft, warm laugh that fought back against her shivers. "I'd say perplexed rather than negligent, but yes."

"Care to try explaining that one to me? Simple words. Any words. I just don't know what to do with your bloody silence." She was shivering pretty continuously now. January and February in Fort Rucker, Alabama, where she finished her SOAR training, had been warmer than this. The Horn of Africa was about a thousand degrees warmer than this damp forest in the middle of the night. Who knew any part of California was this cold in early May?

Michael took his time. Just as she was about to lambast him one last time, he started to speak.

"I've never met anyone like you. Frankly, I never thought I would. I enjoy women. I appreciate them when they choose to spend time with me. But you are the only woman who ever made me wonder if perhaps I've been missing something."

Claudia held her breath so that she didn't risk interrupting him.

"You are a lover like none ever born or imagined."

If he was about to go on and call what was going on between them "sex," then she was going to push him off this damn log and find her own way home.

"You make me think about more than this week or this month."

His silence stretched so long that she had to breathe.

"Or this year..." His voice was a whisper of surprise at his own statement.

He was right. That's what was wrong with her. She'd occasionally wondered if she'd find someone after she retired from the service. But he made her want to be with him for a lot more than that.

"That's why you went silent on me?"

"I guess. I suppose I was on a mission of trying to understand what I was feeling. It's good, I know that much. But you are confusing as hell, Claudia."

She tried chafing her arms to no avail. Blowing on her cupped fingers just made them damp and cold. Then the damp made them even colder.

"Well, next time you set off on an internal mission like that, know that going silent doesn't work. There are two of us in...whatever this relationship is. Now and again I need to hear from you, just like you probably need to hear from me. Are we clear, soldier?"

"Yes, ma'am!"

She could imagine his salute with that smile that always warmed her insides. But it wasn't enough. Not tonight.

"Your next order, soldier..."

"Yes, ma'am?"

"Get me into a damned sleeping bag before I die of hypothermia."

He cursed as he scrambled to his feet.

Chapter 13

THEY'D WOKEN WITH THE BIRDS AT DAWN. THEY WERE wrapped together, naked together in two sleeping bags zipped together. Claudia didn't remember falling asleep. The last thing she could sort out of her sleepy mind was Michael stripping them both naked before climbing into the hammock. She had burrowed against his warmth and let the shivers take her until she slept.

Aboard ship, they'd always returned to their own berths. She'd never woken in his arms, not after a night together. Definitely not to the sounds of birdsong.

Well, there was a potential advantage to their current state of undress. She kissed him awake, enjoying his rapid shift from sleep through surprise and into full participation. They didn't need any words afterward to agree that it was a glorious way to wake up.

Their clothes, strewn about beneath the hammock, were damp with dew. Resigned, she shrugged into them and did her best to warm up with a cup of instant coffee while Michael packed the Treeboat.

"Treeboat?"

"The best hammocks made, designed specifically for tree climbers. Four-point harness made of four-thousand-pound test nylon webbing with..." And he was off on one of his geek rants. Damn, but the man knew how to charm her even if he didn't know he knew.

It took two more hours of march and scrabble as

tough as any route ever set by the most hard-assed drill sergeant before they reached where Michael was headed. At the bottom of a notch canyon—a stream trickled by not a dozen feet from her toes, hidden behind a wall of sword ferns and lesser trees—stood a monster.

"I found and measured this tree when I was fourteen. She ranks as *the* true Titan, the tallest tree ever measured. I haven't even told the other climbers how to find her. By chance she was also the first tree I ever pioneered in a solo climb."

Claudia gazed upward. "You climbed that at fourteen?" She couldn't even imagine climbing the tree now.

"I named her Nell."

She looked back down at Michael. "And who the hell is Nell that she gets such a huge tree named after her?"

"Uh, Nell Fenwick."

"And who was she?" She could feel herself steaming up again. What was wrong with her emotions that they'd gone all chaotic on her?

"The true love of Dudley Do-Right."

She opened her mouth but, not knowing what to say with it, closed it again.

"Mom and Pop are huge fans of *The Rocky and Bullwinkle Show*. They had all five seasons on VHS way back when, then got the DVDs when the old tapes wore out. I kind of grew up with them."

More like he grew up to *be* him. Michael was everything Dudley had aspired to be: handsome, trustworthy, and ever victorious.

"Guess I fell a little in love with Nell Fenwick myself. Me and Horse."

Claudia bit the inside of her cheek. Laughing in the

man's face probably wasn't the best of choices, but it was hard to resist.

"You look a bit like her actually. Taller and more beautiful, but you do."

"You're comparing your 'magnificent' lover to a cartoon character or a tree?"

"The cartoon character." Michael looked at her seriously, turned back to inspect his precious tree, then back at her. "Is that a bad thing?"

She lost it. There was no chance of keeping it inside. The laughter cut her down at the knees as she struggled for breath. She finally had to lie down and curled up beneath a sword fern that towered and nodded above her in agreement.

It was several minutes before she could stop gasping for air enough to massage her sides and whimper out, "Oh my."

"You"—she managed around a fresh wince of pain in her side—"are a ceaseless wonder, Mr. Colonel Gibson."

He sat patiently on his pack that he'd dropped near her.

"Okay. Perhaps I should have said that differently."

She leaned her head back against Nell's heavy bark and closed her eyes as her breathing slowed.

"Wait." She opened one eye and looked at him. "I thought Nell Fenwick had red hair."

"She's a blond in the comic books, which my parents had collected as kids and hung on to. I read those first, so I always think of her as being blond. More yellow than yours, but still blond."

"Not red like Trisha O'Malley?"

His eyes slid aside and she jerked upright.

"You and—" She couldn't even say it. But she didn't need to. He wasn't a stupid man and knew he had to explain quickly.

"Before she met Bill. It only lasted a couple nights. It was fun, but she—" Then he actually flapped his hands in confusion. A gesture she'd never seen before from Michael and would wager that she'd never get to see again. Well, if ever a mismatch was made on earth, it would be the fiery redhead and the quiet colonel.

Oh God. She could feel the giggles trying to reemerge and did her best to fight them back.

"What?"

"The image." She took a careful breath. "The two of you." She swallowed hard and steeled her stomach. "Bet you..." It didn't help, so she finished on a single gasp of breath, "Made-each-other-totally-nuts."

At his reluctant nod, she lost it again.

Michael had expected Claudia to be offended, but not to laugh in his face. He liked Trisha O'Malley and respected her as well. Though Claudia was right—he'd certainly never understood her. Half of what she expended energy on struck him as totally senseless, but it seemed to work for her and for Bill. He'd married her after all.

"Does Bill know about the two of you?"

Michael shrugged uncertainly.

"Don't you dare tell him. Ever. For any reason."

He glanced over, but she looked abruptly dead serious. Okay, at least he wouldn't have to worry about that decision any longer. He trusted Claudia's judgment far more than his own when it came to personalities. She'd proven time and again that she was far more observant on that point than he was.

Digging through the gear, he found his collapsible recurve bow. He folded the arms into place, locked them down, and strung it. Clipping the fishing reel on the lower part of the bow, he tied the free end onto a blunt-tipped arrow. He studied the tree. Nell was not kind about accepting his arrows, but he didn't want to look sloppy in front of Claudia.

Then he had an evil idea. He considered for a moment. Thinking such thoughts wasn't typical for him, but as he and Claudia had already acknowledged, nothing between them was typical.

"You're the archer. You want to make the first attempt?" He wouldn't tell her it often took him five to ten shots to loft the arrow over the lowest branch—and that was on a good day. Nell's trunk ran up true and clean to a hundred and sixty-seven feet. "You have to get it over that big limb there on the left."

Claudia took the bow and plucked the string a few times. "Never shot a folding bow before."

"Excuses, excuses," he teased. That too was new. Claudia didn't appear to notice, so he let it go by.

First, she jerked out a length of fishing line, wound it back onto the spool, and jerked it again. He knew from experience that the monofilament offered little resistance to the arrow's flight. Then she pulled the first full draw, testing the bow's flex, and he appreciated anew the way her muscles flowed and aligned on her frame.

It was as she moved about the forest floor to find the best angle that she revealed a new Claudia.

He had analyzed and could catalog each of her mannerisms: the smooth pilot, the silent observer in groups, the uninhibited lover. Last night he'd added the infuriated woman and this morning the most unexpected, the spontaneity of her humor and the accompanying complete loss of composure.

This one was different.

She was steadier, but it wasn't just the steadiness of the pilot. A flicker of morning sunlight reached down through the trees and cloaked her in glory as she nocked an arrow and drew the bow in earnest. Every muscle shifted into the alignment she'd shown Dilya on the Chinook. But it wasn't the alignment of practice; instead it was the way the best D-boys ran and fired their rifles, as if it was instilled in Claudia's very soul.

Every muscle was defined through her thin T-shirt. No bra strap broke the smooth lines. She was so skilled that he could watch the balance and her aim shift, could even see her pulse beat in the tiniest shifts of the bow. Then, on an exhaled breath, she loosed the bolt skyward.

The arrow roared aloft with a sharp whistle he'd never achieved and the high whine of the fishing line spooling so fast. He didn't have to look up to know that it had flown true over the branch. There was no discouraging *plonk* as the arrow bounced off branch or bark. The fishing line continued to hiss out as the arrow fell toward the underbrush on the far side of the tree. He didn't turn from the magnificent woman to see where it fell.

No, that simply wasn't enough.

He was going to have to find a new word to describe her.

~

Claudia enjoyed watching Michael flail about in the huckleberry underbrush to retrieve the arrow. Once he'd scrabbled around and dragged it back to the tree base, he tied on the thin line of accessory cord. Next, as Claudia wound the line back into the spool, he used the fishing monofilament to drag the light pulling line over the branch and back down to them. Then he lashed on a hank of nine-millimeter black tactical rope used throughout Special Ops and dragged that up and over with the pulling line.

He lashed one end to a stout tree nearby, only a half-dozen feet through, rather than the thirty-foot-diameter monster they were about to ascend. The knot looked good to her. To the other end, he attached their packs and then began fishing through them.

"Have you ever worn a harness?" He held up a knot of buckles and straps.

"I've put one on a horse and I've worn a parachute—Airborne qualified to be in SOAR, remember?" She enjoyed sassing him. "Neither tells me what to do with that thing you're waving at me."

With a flick of his wrist as he came over to her, it untangled and fell into place.

"Oh, that looks comfortable." But when he held it out, she braced herself on his shoulder and stepped through the double loops—first one leg, then the other. They slid up, one to mid-thigh and the upper one to just below her crotch. Then he raised the wide belt past her hips and fastened it around her waist. He made a series of adjustments, then clipped a large carabineer ring to the front and gave it a sharp tug.

"Once you leave the ground, this ring is always attached to a line that is attached to the tree. Always!" He tugged it again for emphasis, forcing her to stagger forward as he practically lifted her clear off the ground. The man's unconscious strength felt as if it tugged at something far deeper and far more carnal. She let her momentum take the extra step and moved into his arms.

When she finally let him move back a half step, he drew in a deep breath. "You keep doing that and we'll never get up this tree."

"That's okay. Nell's a sweet girl; she can take care of herself."

He hauled her back against him using the harness ring as leverage. By the time he stopped, her lips were sore and her head was spinning. He climbed into his own harness before she recovered.

"Cheater!"

He grinned at her and kept pulling out gear.

"These are called Jumars." He handed two to her. It was a metal loop about twice the size of her hand. The outer part had clearly been shaped to grab on to. The other side was a confusing cluster of gaps and adjusters. Below them dangled a strap that ended in a loop about a foot across.

He snapped them onto the main rope—that's what the gaps and adjusters were for—and showed her that while they wouldn't pull down, they could slip up the rope easily.

"See, you hold on and push them up the rope. Then you can't slide back down," he explained as he put keeper rings through holes. He then hung with both hands on one of the Jumars to prove his point.

She could feel that foreign world descending over her once again. She knew how to parachute down, but now she was being asked to climb up a rope. It was the size of her pinkie and hung a good three feet away from Nell's trunk. When she tried to follow the rope upward with her eyes, all it did was make her head spin.

"Step into the lower loops. Hands on the handles. This is a little old school, but it's the way my parents and I climbed when I was a kid. That was back before someone thought up boot cleats and all that."

Greek. Greek. Greek. Why did he think he was speaking any form of a language that she understood? Though the analogy failed as she understood Greek, or as much as she'd been able to pick up during a two-month training exercise with their navy.

Urdu. Urdu. Urdu.

When she stepped into the loops lying on the ground, he tied two short lines to the harness ring at her waist and tied the other ends to the two Jumars, obviously safety lines.

He slapped a hard-shell helmet on her head and fastened it under her chin. That was actually the first comforting element of the whole episode so far; it reminded her of her pilot's helmet. That took away a tiny bit of the mass of foreign newness that surrounded everything about Michael and this whole experience.

He'd become a different man in the woods. He still moved with that easy, sliding pace that all the D-boys had, even Billy the ex-SEAL. But he was somehow lighter here, younger—as if he'd never gone to war and seen what he must have seen and done. Perhaps here he could just be himself instead of "Colonel Gibson, the country's most skilled soldier."

He clipped a long line to the back of her harness. It looked complexly tied and included several more safety rings.

"Just ignore this. It's called a split-tail lanyard, and you won't need it until we're up there. Now, raise your right foot as if you're climbing a ladder."

She did so. "I feel stupid standing here on one foot like some seagull."

"Think heron or flamingo. You're beautiful." He kissed her briefly and she took absolute advantage of her raised foot by wrapping it around his waist, as much as the harness allowed.

She really was losing it about this man. How many more times could she throw herself at him? Not that he appeared to be complaining.

Maybe she too was different in the woods.

"Now slide your right-hand Jumar up about a foot."

As she did so, the right-hand foot loop was now tight against her boot.

"Good. Stand in the loop."

Pushing down with her right leg, as if she were climbing stairs, her left foot came off the ground and she began to swing and spin. Michael's hands on her waist stabilized the disconcerting motion. It felt nothing at all like dangling from a parachute or sliding down a fast rope.

"Now the same on the left."

She raised her left foot and slid the left Jumar up against the bottom of the right one. It also raised the left loop so that she was once again standing on two feet—in two straps just over a foot above the ground.

"Again, try to do them in unison. Right hand and right foot together."

Right and right. Left and left. Now she was two feet in the air.

"Now let go of the Jumars with both hands."

"What? Are you nuts? I don't—"

"Do it!"

At the sharp command her instincts from years of drill instructors cut in and she did. She fell about a foot, her harness jerked tight around her hips and thighs. Her feet, still in the Jumar loops kicked out sideways. Now she dangled from the safety lines on her belt, most of the way to upside down.

"That's called a bat hang. You're not a bat, so get yourself back into position."

It took her a bit to figure out how to do it, but with a knee bend and a pull on the safety line at her waist, she was once again standing upright with her hands on the Jumars.

"I shouldn't say this, but you're good at this."

"Gee, thanks, Michael."

"Do it again."

"Yes, sir." She let go.

As she fell back, he gave her a sharp push. It flipped her once more into a bat hang, but also knocked her feet out of the Jumar straps, and set her to both swinging and spinning.

"Recover!" he commanded as she cursed at him.

Her shoulder swung hard enough against the tree to hurt. On the next swing, she managed to plant her feet against the tree, but she did it so stiff-leggedly that she bounced back off. It took her a lesser bang on the other shoulder to recover, but by the time she was back in the right position, she felt fairly secure on the rope despite its tiny size.

"Good. Do another jug up."

"Jug?" She slid up the Jumars until her feet were even with his chest.

"That's what you're doing, jugging up a line. Now go. When you get to the top, sit on the branch. Do not detach from the line until I get there. Repeat that."

She repeated the whole speech verbatim out of spite and jugged up once more—right, left.

Then he turned away to see to his own harness.

As silently as she could, she tipped herself over into a bat hang, until her face was even with the back of his head, except that she was upside down. She tapped him on the shoulder.

When he turned in surprise, she wrapped her arms around his neck and gave him a serious upside-down kiss.

He started to reach for her, but she flipped back upright and did a quick couple of jugs up.

"Gotta be faster than that if you're gonna catch me, soldier boy."

His laugh as she headed aloft was one of pure joy.

Michael watched Claudia jug upward. He tried to ignore the spectacular view the harness provided of her exceptional ass. And then he figured that as her lover, he had a right to admire such a fine display.

For most beginners, he'd apply tension to the bottom of the climbing line to steady it. She was moving well without it, even though this was clearly her first rope ascent. She really would make an exceptional Delta recruit.

So, with nothing to do but wait until she reached the high branch, he lay back on a bed of ferns and watched the show.

About halfway up, she stopped and looked down.

"Holy shit!"

"What did I tell you about not looking down?" Michael shouted up to her.

"Not a thing!"

"Well, don't look down."

"Thanks so much for the great advice, soldier boy." And then she continued aloft.

When she reached the branch, he didn't volunteer any information, but waited for her to puzzle it out. It didn't take her long before she disappeared up and onto the top of the branch. Easily six feet across, it stuck sideways out of the tree a good ten or fifteen feet, then turned upward and shot into the green canopy. All by itself it would make a plenty impressive tree, except that this one was rooted a hundred and sixty feet up into the side of Nell.

He was about to shout up additional instructions when he saw the lanyard he'd clipped to the back of her harness disappear as well. It took her a few tries, but she was soon lashed to the tree rather than the ascent rope.

Maybe it was time Delta reconsidered its no-women policy. If there were more women out there like Claudia... Well, no, there weren't. But ones with her skills. He'd have to pass on the suggestion to The Unit's commander about it next time they met.

"I'm clear." Her voice drifted down to him across some impossible distance.

By the time he reached her, she was eating an energy bar and admiring the little orchid that grew in the cleft where the branch left Nell's main trunk.

With another bow shot, she managed to catch a branch another hundred feet up and probably only two feet across. It took her only two tries.

"I'm not used to shooting from a sitting position fifty yards up a tree. I'm sure you, Mr. Perfect Soldier, can do it first time every time."

He decided it would be best to make no comment. He always went for the far closer branch behind them, and even that one occasionally eluded him for a time.

"Okay, Mr. Smarty Pants. What are you going to do about that?" She pointed to where the arrow dangled at the end of the fishing line. After passing over the branch above them, it had descended to dangle opposite their position, but almost twenty feet away.

"Easy."

"You're not going to do some crazy hand-jam thing in the bark to try and get over there, are you?"

Trying to keep a straight face, Michael pulled out a tiny, folding grappling hook, attached it to another bit of line, and managed to snag the arrow on his first try.

"Show-off," she muttered. "I get to try the next one."

He did flash her a grin at that. "But it's my grapple."

Claudia slid a hand up his neck and pulled him in. The kiss built and progressed until she'd guided him down to nuzzle her breasts through the thin T-shirt she wore.

It wasn't until they had again climbed and were

recovering the next arrow shot that he noticed she was the one who now had the grapple attached to her gear.

Michael's parents had taught him proper climbing and safety techniques when he was a kid. They themselves had begun recreational tree-climbing in college. Their masters' work was based on research done in the forest canopy. Mom was a botanist and Pop an arboreal biologist.

Michael couldn't remember not climbing trees. Not like every other little kid—clambering aloft and scaring their parents to death—rather with ropes, helmets, and safety lines ascending the sixty-foot madrone tree that lived in their backyard.

Through high school and college he'd made his spending money teaching students how to climb the big Doug firs on the OSU campus. Oregon State hadn't appreciated it for insurance reasons, so he'd found a couple of giants in the Coast Range and held his classes there.

In the years since, he'd trained dozens and dozens of Delta operators safe rope techniques. Though tree climbing wasn't typically involved, he was definitely the Delta rope guy. But no one had ever taken to it the way Claudia had.

They'd lunched on a wide branch after the second jug up. She sat at ease with her feet dangling twenty-five stories above the ground. Definitely no problem with heights, but he'd keep an eye out. He'd seen acrophobia strike at the oddest of moments. And if the fear of heights slapped you even once high in the branches, it was unlikely you'd ever climb over ten feet again. She was such a wonder to watch, so at ease aloft, that he didn't want to ever lose that.

They spent the afternoon exploring the forest at the top of Nell. It was a maze of buttresses, suckers that had turned into their own trees, and the detours required by broken debris barely clinging to the structure. It really was another forest in the air, with hundreds of trunks, deadwood, and snags. And because they could traverse it vertically for a hundred feet up as well as horizontally, it wasn't all that hard to become lost.

Nell's crown was an active, messy, biological world that had nothing to do with weapons and ships and crazy pirates. He could feel all of that leaking out of him, tumbling thirty stories to splash onto the forest floor and seep into the earth, to never be seen again as long as he remained aloft.

He showed Claudia the double-ended split-tail lanyard that confused every beginner. He should have taught her on the ground, but he'd been too eager to get aloft. In under an hour, she was skywalking through the canopy, using the lanyard to move herself through space between major trunks in three dimensions.

After that, it had become a game of tag. He'd lose her in the branches, only to have her surprise him around the next vertical trunk. One time she did a long, controlled descent past him, tantalizingly a mere foot or two out of reach. Tantalizing because she had pulled off her T-shirt and tucked it into her belt. She made a gesture like a fainting damsel in distress as she passed him, then disappeared from view.

And, damn it, he couldn't do a thing about it because she still had his grapple.

By the time he was properly tied to chase her, she was gone off in some other direction.

He took her to "the Garden." At three hundred feet, Nell's "leader"—that fastest growing point of the tree—had broken off the main trunk. It was typical that the sixty-foot top broke away after the first eight hundred to thousand years of growth. After that, the main tree trunk became thicker but no taller. Instead, it sent side branches aloft forming the forest of the canopy. Losing the leader also created damage in the top center of the main trunk. Rain collected there and rotted the wood. Fungi and mosses arrived, soil started to form, and the process kept going.

"Nell's Garden," he told the woman hanging close enough now that he could brush her skin and watch her body react, "is growing on about three feet of what is called canopy soil. It's regular composted material that has turned to dirt three hundred feet in the air. Pop's best estimate is that a couple thousand liters of water are trapped here as well. We're too early for huckleberries—that's those little bushes over there—but look, the early rhododendrons are blooming."

"Can we walk there?"

"Not really. Don't want to kill anything. Who knows how many hundred years it took to get up here and grow from some bird who dropped a seed or a bit of wind-borne pollen."

"It's like a miniature forest grove. Look, it even has little evergreen bonsais. Let's just sit and watch it."

And they did. Each dangling in their own vee of lashed-off ropes, using their safety harness as a hanging chair, they sat in silence.

"It's different than the desert. The smells are so different. In the desert, the breeze is just as clean, but it's achingly dry and carries only hints of what it has passed over, not this hard slap of smells. Here it's so lush and alive." Her voice was a caress as soft as that breeze. They swayed slowly back and forth. Occasionally bumping their knees together. "Not many birds."

Even as she said it, a raven landed to inspect them curiously. The birds didn't come near most climbers; Michael rarely saw them except when he was alone. This one didn't seem to mind Claudia in the least.

"Redwood is poisonous to insects," he explained. "There's not much food here for them in a redwood. Every now and then you'll find a raven like that bold chap."

"Is he the same as last night?"

"Could be. He's big, maybe he's king of the forest."

"You gonna take him on, Mr. Delta Colonel? Mano-a-Corvus?"

"Nah." He winked at her. "Wouldn't want to risk having my butt whipped in front of my girl."

Her sparkling laugh spooked off the raven, and then she pulled Michael to her as they hung there in space. This time there was no shirt barring his way to her glorious shapes, nothing but the feel of her, the taste of her. Not a thing impeded his study of every nuance of womanly curves.

Her breathing was ragged as he suckled her, and she locked both arms behind his head to hold him there. He drove her upward with hand and mouth, with whisper and need.

There was never a purer moment in his life than

Claudia Jean Casperson's shattering cry as an orgasm ripped through her while they hung over the garden in the sky.

Claudia clung to him a long time, holding his ear to her chest. If she let go, their two harnesses would have them dangling apart and she couldn't bear that much separation from Michael.

He in turn clung to her, those ever-so-powerful, ever-so-gentle arms wrapped about her waist. He too had shed his shirt in the warm sunlight reaching into the treetops.

But the light was fading now. The soft sound of breakers on the Pacific Ocean was a constant murmur in the background. Michael had said they were just three miles away, though they couldn't see the ocean from here.

She brushed a hand over his face and released him slowly. "I hate to leave, but the sun is setting and it's a long way down."

"So?" He smiled at her.

"So, when the sun sets, it gets dark. I'm not climbing down in the dark."

"Me neither."

Since when had Michael discovered how to tease her? She could see him doing it, but couldn't see why this time. Claudia would have to play straight girl until she figured out what he was up to.

"So, we need to go down."

With a little kick, he managed to swing forward just enough to grab the loop on the front of her safety harness once more. He pulled her in and kissed her. He took his time about it. It was another of those things that he did exceptionally well.

"I will never tire of doing that," he whispered when at length he'd shifted back just a little and rested his forehead against hers.

"I promise I'll never tire of you doing that." Then she looked over his shoulder. "But the sun has moved a lot closer to the horizon. We really need to go."

"Why would you want to leave this?"

"I don't want to!" Her voice was practically a whine, but she couldn't help it. "It's so lovely up here that I could stay forever."

He looked surprised, no, shocked. He opened his mouth two or three times before he finally spoke.

"Then don't leave. I brought up the hammock and sleeping bags as well." The teasing was gone.

She'd pay a pretty penny to know what he'd been on the verge of saying before changing his mind.

"Sleep up here?" Now it was her turn to pretend she was shocked.

"Do you want to?" He missed the tease.

This time she was the one who pulled him in. "That's a big yes."

"How do we do this?" Claudia lay curled against Michael's chest in the Treeboat hammock after they'd watched the first planets come out. Jupiter and Venus were now both well above the horizon to the west. The first stars would be following shortly.

"Do what?" She heard his voice as much through his chest as through her ears.

"Make love at three hundred and fifty feet without dying in the process."

"We're only around three thirty."

She rolled her head enough to plant a kiss in the center of his chest. "Then how do we make love at three hundred and thirty feet without dying in the process, Mr. Smarty Pants?"

"Well, I, uh…"

She propped herself up enough to look at him in the last of the day's fading light. "You're kidding me, right? Don't tell me you've never thought about how to make love up here."

He shook his head.

"But—"

"I never thought I'd ever bring a woman here. I never thought I'd find one who wanted to be here."

"Well, I'm here, so you better start thinking. Because we sure can't do anything like this." She reached down into the sleeping bag and shook the front of his safety harness suggestively. Like hers, it was wrapped over his pants, encasing his pelvic region in thick nylon straps, and had a rope that led out of the sleeping bag, off the edge of the Treeboat hammock, and was tied off to a nearby trunk.

She didn't have to wait long. It was as if she could watch his mind work. He was so forthright and straight ahead that he really was the perfect straight man.

But once a problem was laid out before him, he was definitely the best man for the job, no matter what it was.

In the dark, he sat up from the sleeping bag and reached for the small rucksack of supplies they'd left dangling from the edge of the hammock. This time when he let the forest air into the sleeping bag, it didn't feel cold. Instead it teased an enticing caress across her unclothed torso. There was no space in the Treeboat to not feel every motion her companion made, and she enjoyed the sensations.

He leaned forward and started doing something down by her feet. He worked his way up the hammock, the slick sounds of rope sliding back and forth as he did whatever he was doing to guarantee their safety.

She didn't even try to follow his motions; she merely enjoyed them. Then she took advantage of them.

Perhaps not the wisest thing, trying to distract a man tying them in, but she had fun. She slid a hand up his leg when he went to brace it against her for balance. When he bent over again, she ran her tongue over his nipple and ticked her fingernails along his pants zipper. When he mostly lay beside her, working on the ropes at the head of the hammock, she nibbled her way over his chest until he had to brush her aside in order to focus.

She didn't stay brushed aside longer than it took her to regain her balance.

He growled, a rumbling sound that echoed from deep in his chest.

She worked harder to distract him.

He worked faster to finish his task.

She bit him through his jeans, and he groaned at his frustration.

It was perhaps the strangest foreplay she'd ever experienced, being tied into a hammock a hundred meters into the sky, but it was certainly affecting her as much as it was him. By the time he finished and lay once again beside her, she was ready to tear off his clothes.

"We're ready. Just no violent maneuvers."

"No promises. What did you do?" She reached up and felt a latticework of the smooth tactical rope mere inches above them. It not only crossed side to side every foot, but there were also lines running head to toe with funny twists at all of the junctions.

"I made a running barrel hitch up the length of the Treeboat. Theoretically, we could flip over and be safe, though I'd rather not try that. Don't try to sit up. We can't."

She wouldn't know a running barrel hitch from a Blake's hitch, though he'd demonstrated and explained the latter at length. And right now, she didn't care. She reached to undress him.

"No," was all Michael said. No steel of command entered his voice, but in his deep voice the mandate was just as solid and unquestionable. Claudia didn't even think to ask why not.

Then he put his hands on her and she forgot how to speak. How they undressed in the small space, she could never quite remember. Every time she thought about it later, all she could recall what this man could do with his hands and his lips.

He didn't make love to her; he worshipped her beneath the sky. Except they weren't beneath the sky, they were in it. They were as alone as two people could be and still be on the earth. In a desert or out at sea, someone could walk in on you or sail up to you. Above them now were only the distant lights of the occasional high-flying jetliner and the bright glitter of a satellite.

It was Claudia Jean Casperson, Michael Gibson, and the stars.

She let go and lay back and let him have his way with her.

When he brushed her legs apart, she opened for him.

When he drove her upward with the ministrations of his hand, she arched against his fingers with desperate need and dragged his mouth to her breast.

When he kissed her so lightly at the base of her throat that she could barely feel it, she groaned like a woman whose heart had been too long cast in stone. Or ice. And when at long last he entered her, her cry lit the night sky until she outshone the stars and the rising moon.

She never cried out during sex, but then this was so much more than that.

The two of them had climbed atop the world together, driving each other upward. Only Michael could have led her here; Claudia tried not to be too smug about her ability to follow.

When turnabout was fair play and she had scooted down enough to pin him between her breasts, she knew that she controlled both the warrior and the man. Not with his body, though she did that as well. It was his perfect openness to her that echoed in the darkness. And she knew that it was a mountain no one before her had ever conquered.

Michael made her feel special without making her feel less.

She tasted him, ever so lightly, and he growled out his need.

He made her feel more than she ever had before. Men didn't do that; they thought about themselves and it was up to the woman alone to not feel less.

But Michael was different. He made her feel worthy

of being with him, of being that incredibly exceptional. Well, she would do her best to return the favor.

This time she took him long, slow, and deep. Took him until his body shuddered. Until his infinite control shattered and what few words he normally had were lost to him. Until his breath ran rough and, when at long last she allowed it, his release hammered at her as his body writhed.

She held him a long time, leaving him there with a kiss.

When he finally came back to himself, he pulled her back up into his arms before collapsing into a well-deserved slumber.

Claudia discovered herself to be wide-awake, paralyzed by the wonders her body had just experienced, both the taking and the giving. She held Michael as he slept, listened to the silence of the trees, and let the gentle motion of the tree lull her blood until it no longer pounded through her veins.

Then she felt it, that perfect rhythm of the tree, easing ever so slowly back and forth in the still night air: tap, pause, tap, pause. The most natural motion of them all. The one Michael had done after the battle in Yemen, the one she had felt as she stood in the Somali desert.

She let the feeling wash through her as she watched the constellation of Orion the hunter set, soon followed by his faithful dog Canis Major. She watched Leo the mighty lion fly high above them with Virgo chasing close behind, the symbol for fertility of both land and woman.

The sky she knew so well kept her company as she held the sleeping warrior and attempted to unravel her own feelings about him.

Michael was such a gift to her and such a constant surprise. He gave her his passion, and he shared himself so openly. Not with words—that would never be one of his skills—but with his heart. He had taken her into the sky, the one place he went to be alone, and shared it with her.

Thinking over last night, just last night?—when she had raged at him in the forest below—perhaps she could now understand some of what she was feeling for the man who sighed in his sleep and nestled more comfortably upon her breast.

Her father's mute sullenness and her mother's resulting silence had given their child no idea of what to do with the emotions now swirling and fluttering about her and seeking somewhere to roost. The heart of the Ice Queen was a deeply protected and chilly bastion—armed and safe against all mortals, including against the one named Claudia Jean Casperson.

Yet one superhuman had found a passage to that deep core and revealed not just warmth, but passion.

Who knew.

It was not a part of her that she knew anything about. Turbine hot, it burned from within until she wondered that it didn't consume them both with its fire, even Nell the tree.

Instead, she lay quietly beneath the spring sky, holding the man she loved. It was a new word for her, one never applied by either parent or by herself. And certainly not by the ever-so-expressive wordless man wrapped around her.

Claudia tested it. Despite the newness and the unfamiliarity, she knew it to be true. On her first day with the

5D, in her first hour, hadn't she pitied Trisha for falling in love with a D-boy operator? What kind of fool did that make her? She'd fallen in love with the best one of them all.

She combed her fingers through Michael's hair, relishing the nearness, the familiarity, the joy that such a simple action evoked.

Yes, Claudia Jean Casperson loved.

She wanted to wake Michael and tell him. Instead she slipped into a peaceful slumber before the constellation of Corvus the Raven had fully flown his nightly adventure across the southern sky.

Chapter 14

THE SHARP BLEAT OF A RINGING CELL PHONE WOKE HER up. Claudia grabbed for her hip, but instead found her arm pinned down and nerveless, burdened by the man who had slept on it all night.

Michael opened his eyes at the second ring and tried to sit up. He was stopped by the black tactical rope woven over their sky-high cocoon and collapsed back onto her, placing an elbow in her overfull kidney.

After a bit more scrabbling around, she managed to get her arm free and began rubbing it back to life. He reached out through the rope lacing and found the tied-off rucksack to extract the cruelly ringing phone.

Michael mumbled something about cell reception before he answered.

"Michael Gibson?"

Claudia could hear the woman's voice easily since they were still crammed together in the sleeping bag and trapped by the rope lines.

While he mumbled an affirmative, she started wondering how many women had his private number. She didn't. She knew that much.

"Glad we found you." The woman sounded very pleased with herself.

"How did you find me? There are no cell towers around Nell."

"I was told you were with a Captain Claudia Casperson.

Who's Nell? There's a cell repeater in the craft circling above your location."

Claudia would have been getting pissed if not for the total perplexity on Michael's face. Watching him try to figure out how to explain that Nell was an entirely different species was actually pretty funny.

"Emily?" Michael's face showed a dawning comprehension.

The only Emily that Claudia knew of was Emily Beale, who had retired from SOAR over a year ago. The chances that it was her were negli—

A small, black UAV slashed by so close overhead that Claudia flinched. The drone was painted with a garish set of red and orange flames.

"Oh, there you are. Very cozy. Why are you tied in?" Despite the departing buzz of the small drone's engine, Claudia could hear the woman's amusement. "Wait. Never mind. Sometimes I'm a little slow."

Emily clearly had a bird's-eye view of their little aerial love nest. So much for feeling safely separate from the rest of the world. Any burgeoning sense of amusement at the situation had just been bludgeoned out of Claudia.

Michael glared up at the now-circling drone as the woman continued speaking.

"We'll be at your location in twenty minutes."

"I'm on vacation," he practically snarled. He even had the decency to mouth a "sorry" to her.

That's when Claudia realized that his irritation was at least partly on her behalf. Yes, he disliked the intrusion of the outside world, but it was the interruption of their own personal idyll that was making him so unusually irritable. His voice had gone low and dangerous. Michael was not a man she'd ever want to make angry at her, but it was pretty flattering to watch him be angry on her behalf.

"Sorry, I know. Peter's calling."

Whatever that meant to Michael, it washed any doubt from his face.

"We'll drive out and—"

"We'll be there in twenty minutes," Emily cut him off. It didn't make any sense, but it had to be Emily Beale.

"I have a truck—"

"Your parents have already provided the spare keys to someone or other, and they're headed down to fetch it. They say they know where it would be parked."

Claudia watched Michael's face as he made some quick calculations.

"Better make it thirty minutes." Then he hung up the phone and looked down at her from inches away. "We have to go."

"Why?" She wanted to explore Nell some more, as well as this man who impossibly owned her heart.

"Peter."

"And I care about that because?"

"Because"—Michael offered her a brief smile and brushed his fingertips down the curve of her neck—"he's our Commander-in-Chief."

President Peter Matthews.

"Peter?"

"It's a safe way to refer to the President when we're on unencrypted comms. Emily Beale is one of his best friends. I think they grew up next door to each other."

"Oh," was all she managed, and she began squirming

around in the sleeping bag to find what had happened to her clothes.

Michael's estimated thirty minutes took closer to forty. Getting dressed with Claudia Jean Casperson in a Treeboat was too much fun, and she hadn't complained when he'd interrupted her attempts to unsnarl her clothes from his in the tiny space. He just hoped the drone had indeed departed the area at the end of the call.

He helped her pack their aerial camp, then left her securely anchored to a stout limb before he abseiled all of the way down to the forest floor. There is no way he was leaving any indication on the ground that Nell was a Titan worthy of note. Unlashing the ground end from the anchor tree, he did a double-rope ascent, clearing each successive line upward behind him as he went. He had never departed upward out of a tree before.

Emily had to circle her garishly painted Firehawk for several minutes. The Firehawk was a Black Hawk rigged for dumping water or retardant on forest fires in thousand-gallon loads. A garishly bright Mount Hood Aviation flaming logo was splashed down the glossy black helicopter's length, a stark contrast to the unmarked, matte black birds Emily had flown for SOAR.

Once Michael returned to the branch beside Claudia, Emily began lowering several very long lines out of the Firehawk's cargo bay doors. She'd tried to come in low, but Michael had waved her back aloft to protect Nell from the downdraft of the helicopter's rotor. While Emily repositioned well above them, he took Claudia's hand and looked at her. Really looked at her.

"You belong here in so many ways."

Her laugh charmed him as it always did. "Yep! Feel just like I'm sitting on the bench waiting for the Amtrak Southwest Chief out of Phoenix." She looked down at her feet and wiggled them around as if they were on a floor and not three hundred and fifty feet above ground.

"There's a storm coming." He pointed west over the Pacific. "A big one by the looks of those clouds. We'd have had to descend this morning anyway. I've ridden one out in a tree. It's not something I'd ever do on purpose."

"So, let's hitch a ride outta here." She looked upward and stuck out a thumb as if hitchhiking.

Then she slowly turned to him and her face went serious.

"Kiss me, Michael. Before she hauls us away from Nell. Really kiss me."

As lines hissed down from the sky to slap against them, as the downdraft whipped near storm-level winds into the tree and their branch weaved and bobbed in the induced wind, Michael found a sense of peace and belonging in how Claudia clung to him, gave herself to him, and how he gave himself right back to her.

They sent the packs up first.

Then, once the lines were back down and attached to their climbing harnesses, they carefully unlashed their safety lines. It was the first time he'd ever been at the top of a tree and not firmly tied to it. Even the lifting line from the helicopter didn't offset the strangeness of the sensation.

There had been a world to discover here, but he and Claudia had been snatched back to reality. He hoped it wasn't forever lost, whatever they had begun to explore here among the treetops.

As Emily began to winch them aboard, he felt the initial tug on his harness. With a well-placed departing push-off, he was able to swing over and brush his fingers along the very highest and thinnest spire of Nell. It was the newest bright-green spring growth, soft conifer against his palm.

He'd finally, after all these years of trying, reached the very pinnacle of a tree. Three hundred and eighty-two feet, Nell was the unreported holder of the title of tallest living thing. The most glorious being on the planet.

Save one.

Chapter 15

THEIR ARRIVAL IN THE HELICOPTER WAS A HARSH SURprise. Claudia winced when she first touched the metal outer hull, and after climbing inside, settling on the lifeless steel decking was a body shock. In a single moment she'd gone from a world where the loudest thing was a breeze or Michael's call from fifty feet away, checking in on her through heavy branches, to thudding helicopters, headsets, and three-meter monkey-lines to secure their climbing harnesses to the inside frame of the bird.

The transition was too fast, and now this was the world that felt foreign. Who had she turned into over these last forty-eight hours?

For the first time ever, she'd gone more than a day without once thinking about her career and her position. And now she was screwing a Delta Force colonel at every chance? In the tops of trees? Where was the Captain Casperson she'd built so carefully?

She considered checking her pockets but didn't, just in case she couldn't find herself when she went looking.

"My crew chief today is Steve Mercer." Emily's voice was smooth over the intercom. "He's my drone pilot. Steve, these folks are both third contract. Not a word goes out about this."

"Roger, boss." A guy with dark hair and an easy smile shook their hands as he helped them get squared away. He carefully didn't ask their names.

"Why you, Emily?" was Michael's greeting. Claudia really needed to talk to him about some basic manners.

"I guess Peter is into something nasty. He wasn't explaining, but I'm guessing that he's trying to keep the circle of knowledge really small. I'm delivering you to a tiny airport up on the coast where a Gulfstream will be waiting for you. Now that I'm on the outside, that's all I know." After glancing back to make sure everyone was secure and the lines were all in, she slammed the cyclic forward and left, and wrenched up on the collective. The Firehawk responded with a throaty burst of power that jerked them aloft.

Apparently Emily cared as little about manners as Michael did. She was also clearly frustrated at not being on the inside of whatever was happening. Claudia wondered if she herself would be sorry to *be* on the inside by the time this was over, assuming she was. She decided to just keep her mouth shut.

"Our gear—" Michael started.

"Your parents will have to ship you anything at the house or in that truck. I can drop your climbing packs at Corvallis airport for your parents to fetch."

Michael dropped the headset and waved Claudia to the back of the helicopter's cargo bay. He pulled an empty Mount Hood Aviation gear bag with a flaming logo from a hook. Together, she and Michael began sorting through the packs, pulling out their little bits of personal gear and stuffing them into the sack. Neither of their duffels sitting in the truck had carried much more than an extra change of clothes.

Claudia tried not to read any significance into her and Michael's clothes now being combined in a single bag.

She was still breathless from the transition and couldn't seem to get her head working again. Not until her fingers closed around a pair of two-foot-long nylon cases.

The folding bow and the blunt arrows. She held them and tried to remember the woman who just yesterday morning had fired them into the redwood. She hadn't been so focused on the shot that she'd missed the look on Michael's face. No one had ever, not in her whole life, looked on her with awe before. Lust, anger, totally despising her trespass in this man's army, sure. But not awe. She'd felt like Diana, the Roman goddess of the hunt.

Twenty-four hours later she was a woman who had climbed to the top of a redwood and fallen in love with the best man she'd ever met. Whatever Michael was doing to her, it was thorough. She'd had lovers, but definitely never one she loved. Well, she wasn't actually willing to declare it, but a part of her acknowledged that it was true nonetheless.

She held the two slim cases out to Michael and mouthed Dilya's name.

He didn't hesitate or even bother to nod in acknowledgment. He simply took them from her hand and slipped them into the gear bag.

Military service was such that she didn't know if she'd ever see the girl again, but Claudia's guess was that the 5D was too good a team to break up from one assignment to the next. It wouldn't be all that long before she and Dilya ran into each other again.

Once she and Michael were packed, they moved back to the front of the cargo bay and pulled the headsets back on.

"One other thing, Emily," Michael continued as if they hadn't just been off the intercom for five minutes.

Claudia wondered how to introduce herself to the retired major and thank her for trailblazing the way into SOAR. And do it without sounding like a total fan girl.

Then Michael got that implacable tone in his voice. "You and Steve will erase any and all GPS and flight-path information to do with the location of that tree."

"Michael, why does it—"

"And you'll do it now!" No drill sergeant had ever mustered such a tone of absolute authority.

Claudia watched between the seats as Emily Beale, without further comment, began punching buttons on her console. Steve Mercer did the same to his drone guidance console. Nobody messed with Colonel Michael Gibson, not when he was in that mode.

Maybe she'd just keep her mouth shut.

She didn't get a chance to talk with Emily Beale until they landed at a tiny airstrip just outside a coastal Oregon town.

"Wow!" Emily sounded impressed. "They sent the 650 for you. They want you two in Washington fast. You're in for a very cozy ride."

Claudia peered out the cargo bay door at the sleek Gulfstream jet. The G650 was the fastest small passenger jet built, soaring through the sky at just under Mach 1. It looked as if it was at full-tilt boogie just sitting there.

Emily left the Firehawk's rotor ticking over on fast idle and climbed down. She snapped a sharp salute to Michael. Claudia noted that the one he returned was equally sharp. Then she hugged him. By his delayed response it was easy to read his surprise. So, Major Emily Beale (retired) unwound for very few people, but Michael was one of them.

He moved over to the Gulfstream parked on the age-cracked tarmac of the taxiway. At a small hand signal from Emily, Claudia waited. The immaculate blond with steel blue eyes suddenly turned her full attention on Claudia. In that instant, Claudia saw the truth of every story Lola and the others had told about their former commander. Emily was tall, slender, stunning, and in such absolute command of everyone around her that it was hard to believe she wasn't still in the Army.

Beale was studying her just as closely, which didn't bother Claudia in the least. She didn't know Emily Beale from Adam. Except she did. The woman had been the most respected helicopter pilot on the planet, for those who knew of her existence. That set Claudia back on her heels a bit, though she did her best not to show it. Beale had not only the respect of her colleagues but, more tellingly, of Colonel Michael Gibson as well.

"So you're the one, Captain Casperson."

Claudia was getting tired of people assuming something that she was barely beginning to figure out for herself.

"Claudia. And that means what to you?"

Emily smiled to herself before answering. The smile looked a little sad. "It means that I wish I was still in the service so that I could get to know you, for you must be someone very special, Claudia. I think that Mark and I are the only other people who know about Michael's trees. He's never invited us there."

Claudia tried not to feel foolish for her initial acerbic manner.

"He's…" She didn't have the words to describe him to herself, so how could she to this woman she didn't know? "Amazing."

Emily turned and they both looked over to where Michael was waiting patiently by the lowered steps of the sleek jet.

"Also remember, Captain," Beale said without turning, "that he is a man. Just as unsure of himself as any other when it comes to women. The good ones know how to be a soldier, but they have only the slightest notion of what to do with the woman they love."

"He…" Claudia attempted to protest, but couldn't. She had only just figured out that she loved him. She'd thought that was a nice addition to a relationship that would be best kept to herself. But the concept that Michael might love her back struck her with a quick succession of emotions as rapid as gunfire on full auto: absurd but not, possible, possibly encouraging, even desired…

She settled on "totally unnerved" and would leave it at that.

"Of course, I doubt if he realizes it yet." Emily was clearly not aware of the madness that had just been unleashed inside Claudia's brain. Abruptly Claudia no more wanted to climb aboard a jet with Michael for several hours than she wanted to fly with a caged tiger.

She'd been overdosing on Michael and that, she was beginning to understand, was a dangerous drug.

That would explain it.

The Yemeni exfiltration; planning, then executing the

mission in Somalia; making love at every chance… She could recall his smell of darkness and safety better than she remembered the smell of gunpowder or Jet A fuel.

Claudia needed to detox.

To get away from him for even a little while to find out what she was really feeling.

"Did they, uh, call us both back to DC?"

Emily looked at her with as absolute an understanding as if Claudia had spoken all of her thoughts aloud. "Both of you."

Well, so much for that escape.

Emily took her by the shoulders and looked her in the eye for a long moment before nodding to herself.

Then, much to Claudia's surprise, the woman hugged her and whispered in her ear. "I suspect that Michael has indeed chosen well. Tell him to call us next time you're both on leave. We'll all go fishing together."

"But I don't fish…" Claudia pulled back, unable to make sense of what Emily was talking about or the sudden kindness she offered.

The jet's engines grumbled and then whined to life, starting low but climbing the scale rapidly in a long glissando.

"Neither do I, but he and Mark love to fish together. If you stay with him, you'll discover what it means to lie along a stream for a long, lazy afternoon. Day after day." Her wry smile indicated the woman's humor behind the observation.

"They'll fish and we'll become friends, Claudia. Now go." With no further acknowledgment, not a handshake or even a look, Emily climbed back aboard her helicopter. Mere seconds later, the rotor's downwash was driving Claudia toward the waiting jet and the waiting man.

By the time she reached the jet, Emily was aloft. A waggle of rotor blades and she was gone over the trees.

Michael let Claudia head first up the stairs.

Chapter 16

A HUGE MAN IN A BLACK SUIT WITH THE TRADEMARK coil of wire to his ear greeted Claudia as she stepped into the Gulfstream jet's cabin.

United States Secret Service. Had to be.

"Captain Casperson. Colonel Gibson. Welcome aboard. You may leave your bag with me."

There was no question of not obeying. Michael handed over the bag.

"Are either of you armed?"

Michael bent down to untie the hunting knife from around his calf and dropped it into the bag. Then he added a folding knife and a Colt Defender 9 mm that she somehow hadn't noticed.

She didn't even have a Swiss Army knife with her.

"The rest is in the gear bag."

The rest? A romantic idyll in the tops of the redwoods and Michael came loaded to personally fend off the Taliban. Always ready for anything. A good lesson that she'd have to remember. Always be ready for anything.

How was it that Michael just kept getting better?

"Thank you, sir. You may both take a seat."

He closed the door behind them and then retreated forward as the engines began to wind up in earnest.

The cabin was beautiful. It was the same size as a Chinook's, six-and-a-half feet high and over eight wide. It looked even longer than the helicopter's thirty-foot bay…and that's where any similarity stopped. Instead of the utilitarian dark gray that could seat fifty troops on hard fold-down seats or carry a Humvee strapped to load points along the steel cargo-bay floor, there were a dozen seats of plush white leather sitting on white, deep-pile carpet.

There was also a forward group of four seats, two to either side, with highly polished fold-out tables of dark burl wood. Then six more grouped around a large table. Beyond that were couches long enough to stretch out and sleep on. That sounded pretty good at the moment.

There were two other passengers, seated with their backs to her approach, three if you counted the baby she could see over of the man's shoulder, asleep in his lap.

In profile, as she came down the aisle and passed alongside the seated couple, she could see that they were elegantly dressed. She wanted to brush at her jeans and T-shirt but was afraid of shedding dirt or stray bits of Nell onto the white carpet. She'd had a bra somewhere in her pack but hadn't thought to put it on. It was probably even now being inspected for hidden weapons by the Secret Service agent.

She moved past the seated couple so that she and Michael could both greet them and then turned.

Ready for anything?

Claudia was absolutely not ready for this.

"Good morning, Mr. President, ma'am." Michael saluted President Peter Matthews and First Lady Genevieve Matthews.

Unexpected, but not a total surprise when Frank

Adams, the head of the President's personal protection detail, had greeted them at the door. Besides, all of Delta's training was about adapting quickly to changing situations.

The President saluted from his seat. "Pardon me for not getting up, Michael." He waved at the First Daughter asleep in his lap.

"No problem, sir."

The President indicated for them to sit across the table.

Michael moved to do so and found Claudia blocking his way. She'd dropped her salute but remained immobile in the aisle.

"I'm sorry I missed Emily," the President continued, "but my detail wants to keep this excursion as low profile as possible."

Michael nudged Claudia with his hip, and she as much collapsed as sat in the chair across from the President. Michael sat across from the First Lady and clipped Claudia's seat belt and then his own as the plane began taxiing for takeoff.

"I'm assuming this isn't a social call." The First Family traveling at large without Air Force One and the normal phalanx of four to five hundred agents probably meant this was about to become the worst kind of operation there was.

"Afraid not, Michael," the President acknowledged. "This one is strictly black-in-black."

"Black-in-black." Claudia was recovering from her initial shock very quickly. He knew Delta operators who didn't recover this quickly. Yet more to admire about her.

"Is that what you call a black op in SOAR?"

Oh no.

Michael reached out to squeeze her hand for a moment in comfort. The poor woman had no idea what was about to happen to them.

"What am I missing, sir?" She shook off Michael's hand, even if she appreciated it, and it was out of sight below the table that separated them from the First Family. The President appeared to have missed it, but his wife most certainly hadn't.

President Peter Matthews was the youngest President in history, elected shortly after his thirty-fifth birthday. Tall, handsome, and photogenic. He wore his dark hair past his ears and was immensely popular despite having already served a full term. He was considered a shoo-in for the fall.

His wife was a French beauty from Vietnam who had shocked the world two years ago when the President married her. She was also a senior director at UNESCO and a major player at the World Heritage Centre.

"Captain Casperson"—the President offered her one of his million-watt television smiles—"a pleasure to meet you at last." It was far more potent in person than on any screen; in person you could feel that the smile was completely genuine to the core.

"At last, sir?" How on earth had she gone in under an hour from being a simple SOAR pilot sleeping three hundred and thirty feet aloft in a redwood with the world's number one soldier in her arms to sitting across from her Commander-in-Chief? No escape—the plane roared down the runway and rotated aloft even as the President answered.

"I have very good reports on you. I try to keep an eye on Emily's old unit."

"Emily?" Wow! She was so out of her depth here. She really needed something to hold on to. Anything. Like her original question.

"Black-in-black, sir?"

Michael sighed.

The President looked chagrined. "I take it you've never flown one."

"Black ops, a couple. Most that fall to the Marine Corps are dealt with by MARSOC, but I flew a few."

White ops were secret during planning but typically went public afterward. Grenada, Panama, the taking of bin Laden, and even their recent Somalia strike—though that was wholly attributed to the U.S. Rangers and "other Special Operations Forces assets," with unconfirmed rumors of SEAL Team Six's involvement, when it made international headlines.

Black ops never went public intentionally. Delta's crossing into the Iraqi desert a week ahead of Desert Storm to find and kill dozens of Scud missile installations long before the invasion ever happened. Those attacks and false radar reports Delta had generated in Western Iraq before the start of the invasion had made Hussein think the allied forces were coming from the west rather than the south. It kept him from escaping into Syria.

"Black-in-black is different." Michael again reached for her but apparently thought better of it when she scowled at him. "They're very restricted and very tough."

"What are the differences?"

"Have you ever lied to a commander?"

"Not about anything important." That won her a quick smile from everyone at the table. She glanced at the President and wished that she'd simply said, "No, sir." He was her commander, the in-chief one.

"If your commander is not inside a black-in-black operation, you can't speak to them about it—ever. Not during an interview, not when drunk together, not when under oath during your court martial. No one outside the team. Ever. No black-in-black has ever been leaked."

"Oh." Claudia wanted to be back in Nell so badly she could taste it. "Okay."

So *not* okay, but the look on her Commander-in-Chief's face said that she didn't have a lot of choice in the matter.

"I'll bet the 5D gets most of them."

The awkward silence around the table told her that was a bet she'd win.

"This will be your operation, Michael."

Michael nodded and kept his own counsel, knowing the President would have his presentation of the facts neatly planned out.

"We think that this mission will be handled most appropriately by Little Bird assets rather than heavier helicopters, but that will be up to you. Based on that assumption, we are making Captain Casperson your SOAR liaison. We feel this is a safe choice based on her initial successes with SOAR, the reports of her Marine commanders, and the fact that she achieved the highest training scores in SOAR history. With—"

"Wait, I did what?" Claudia jerked upright in her chair, at least as far as her seat belt allowed.

Michael hadn't known that about her, but he wasn't surprised.

The President's smile was radiant. "Yes. You even beat out Em's old records; bet that would tick her off no end if she were still cleared to know. I just might have to tell her anyway."

"Wouldn't Chief Warrant Maloney be better qualified?"

"You and Michael may choose to add assets to your team that you deem necessary. But I'm guessing this mission will be less a matter of force and more one of finesse."

She looked at Michael.

He could see it in her eyes. Yes, their Commander-in-Chief was guessing.

She blew out a breath and scrubbed at her face before running her fingers back through her hair.

Neither of them needing to speak, he nodded to answer her unspoken question: *Yes, all black-in-black feels this way*.

"And then it gets worse," she said aloud.

"And then it gets worse," he agreed.

Claudia needed a minute to gather her thoughts, but that clearly wasn't going to happen.

The President nodded to his wife, who began.

"I was visiting in Tehran for a checkup on the Golestan Palace, which was recently added to the UNESCO World Heritage List."

The First Lady, who was also a UNESCO senior director, had traveled to Iran. Claudia wondered what the Secret Service detail on that one had been like.

"It is such a beautiful interconnected series of palaces. We only managed to place it on the list in 2013. I was very glad to finally see it for myself. I met there the President of Iran, Javad Madani, a very pleasant and forward-thinking man, and he asked for our discreet help."

Claudia considered the geography of that. Iran reached from the Caspian Sea down to the Persian Gulf and Arabian Sea. The *Peleliu* had been less than a thousand miles from southern Iran before she'd started her race north to transit the Suez for a "possible" operation.

"The *Peleliu*," she whispered it to Michael and saw his eyes widen briefly, then his confirming nod.

What was unique about the *Peleliu* that set it apart from other warships in the Mediterranean? There had to be some reason she was involved. Oh, the shadow assets of the 5D and Delta.

"So, you need us in the Caspian Sea as a favor to Iran." Claudia hadn't meant it to be a flat statement, but it fit the facts. "Not just SOAR, but Michael's abilities as well. What's the target?"

"How did you do that?" The President leaned forward, which woke his daughter. The First Lady extracted the girl from his lap. She didn't want to settle, so the First Lady began walking up and down the aisle with her, but staying close enough to hear over the well-muted engine noise of the racing jet.

"It"—Claudia clamped down on her tongue—"it just seemed obvious, sir."

Michael and the President exchanged a look. Michael's nod confirmed something in guy speak. Normally she could follow guy speak—six years in the Marines did that to a girl—but not this time.

The President cleared his throat and continued, "Azerbaijan is an extremely gas- and oil-rich nation. They have numerous pipelines that run through Georgia, Armenia, and Turkey, providing access to the West. Turkmenistan wants to develop a pipeline under the Caspian Sea to facilitate exports of its own massive reserves along a similar route."

Claudia closed her eyes for a moment to picture the Caspian Sea. Azerbaijan to the west and Turkmenistan to the east. Iran to the south. To the north, Kazakhstan and Russia. With Russia controlling the only waterway, a northern route would mean a difficult passage through the thirteen locks of the Volga-Don Canal system.

"But why would Iran be upset by—" And then she saw it.

Even Michael didn't follow her this time. Oddly, that made sense. He might be the most flexible soldier on the planet, but the man didn't have a devious bone in his body. Of course what did that say about her?

"Russia." She made it a flat statement.

"Russia," the President confirmed. "Iran would prefer to have the pipeline loop south of the Caspian, but even more than that..." He left it dangling as a test.

But Claudia didn't find it to be a trick question.

"Even more than wanting it themselves," she answered, "they don't want Russia having control. Which we would agree with."

The President sighed. "As odd as it may sound, we

are almost on better terms with Iran than Russia at this time."

"So who is stopping the Trans-Caspian Gas Pipeline?"

"The Russian Navy, specifically the Caspian flotilla. My Chief of Staff and his wife, she's a CIA analyst, will have details for you when you arrive in Washington, DC. You'll be dropping us off in Colorado Springs where we are supposedly in high-level meetings prior to a speech at the Air Force Academy."

Michael was nodding as if it all somehow made sense.

Claudia was still missing a dozen pieces. She waited until the First Lady was once again walking past their seats and raised a hand to stop her. Mrs. Matthews arched one elegant eyebrow.

"Based on some past association, you, Mr. President, are inclined to believe the message President Madani sent to you through the First Lady."

He nodded.

She waited, but that was all either of them offered.

Michael was also very quiet. In one of those states that was unnaturally quiet rather than his usual silent self.

"Therefore, your trust of President Madani of Iran is based on prior experience that all three of you are aware of but not discussing—meaning it is from a prior black-in-black operation."

No one corrected her assumption.

The President nodded as if such convoluted processes were the norm. Maybe they were in his world. Not in hers.

"And so you, Mr. President, involved Dr. Darlington who called in his wife, a CIA analyst, to perform background and authentication research. You also are shifting the USS *Peleliu* 'just in case' by sending her on a high-speed run through the busiest seas on the planet."

Again the pleasant nod from the President.

"And this is a well-contained, black-in-black operation by what definition?"

That sobered the expressions around the table.

Perhaps sarcasm hadn't been the right approach. She tried again.

"I know I'm the new person here, but how much farther has this proliferated? How reliable are the Iranian security teams that might have overheard President Madani and the First Lady speaking? Has it spread through to CIA's assistant researchers? Who in the 5D is cleared for this level of operation if we need an asset? Can we recruit Lieutenant Bill Bruce if we need another Delta asset? How big do these operations get, and how in the world do you keep them secret?"

She bit down on her tongue to stop herself. Here she was, questioning the integrity of the country's leader, but she had to know.

"Crap!" President Matthews dropped back in his chair and his wife settled beside him cradling the once-again sleeping girl. "I wish Emily was here. She ran four of these things, and she knew how to make them work. When I assigned them to her, they never failed."

Claudia smiled, feeling oddly relaxed for the first time since boarding. "Don't you love it when there's no pressure?"

That won her a look of chagrin from the President.

"She was an amazing strategist." Michael's tone held nothing but respect.

"And you and Mark were her tactical geniuses."

Michael nodded his agreement to her assessment.

The President looked back and forth between them, then he shifted. That was the only way Claudia could think to describe it.

Up until this moment, he'd been casual and easygoing. So much at ease that Claudia found it difficult to believe that he was the President of the United States, Commander-in-Chief of the planet's best military force.

No longer.

Now he looked at her with deeply assessing dark eyes, studying her in the same way he probably studied his adversaries across the table at a G8 summit meeting. For a full minute, the silence stretched and it was hard to meet his frank scrutiny. When he finally turned aside to look at Michael, the pressure on her didn't ease.

Again that silent question she couldn't read, not even after she saw Michael's confirming nod in her peripheral vision. Then the Commander-in-Chief was facing her once more.

"You don't know me or my people, Captain Casperson, but I do know them. We also know you very well, far better than we did forty-eight hours ago. I'm about to do something that you're really going to hate."

"Oh great!" She couldn't stop it. It just came out. It earned her a smile that did nothing to soften the cabin's unexpected pressure-cooker atmosphere.

"I can guarantee you that the inner circle of this operation is presently the four people around this table plus two in Washington. The head of my wife's personal protection detail is the woman who originally recruited the man who has headed my detail since before my nomination. If my wife wanted a private moment with President

Madani, then I can promise you that it would have been truly private; she's very good at what she does."

Claudia was used to the high stakes of military actions. But now she'd crossed into something "other." She was now inside the Bubble, as the President's tight area of personal security was known. She'd wandered in unaware. But if there were truly only the six of them...

"Oh shit!" she said aloud and no one even blinked. She now understood the question that the President had just asked Michael, but could see no way to avoid the answer.

"Here's the part you're going to hate, Captain."

She knew it!

Claudia tried to hold her breath, only to discover she already was. She had to blow it out and gasp back in to keep from passing out.

"From this moment forward"—the President tapped the table between them for emphasis—"no one will be authorized to expand the scope of this operation without your express permission. Not me, not Michael. I'm going to trust my instincts and pull this from Michael's tactical hands and put it in your strategic ones. You are under no obligation to report who your team members are to any other person, not to the other members, not even myself. It will be up to you how you compartmentalize that information, both up- and down-channel. Are we clear?"

At first all she managed was a nod. Then, digging deep, she sat up as straight as the seat and the table allowed and offered him her best salute. He returned it as smartly.

Then he shifted back to being the man she'd first

been introduced to. He did it so effortlessly that he left her stumbling along behind. "So, Claudia, where were you when I blew apart your and Michael's vacation? Emily wouldn't say over the radio when I had our pilot ask, something about erasing it from her memory."

Chapter 17

THEY DROPPED THE FIRST FAMILY AT THE U.S. AIR Force Academy, unloading their passengers in the shadowed corner of a heavily guarded hangar.

They hadn't returned to discussing the mission for the remaining two hours of the flight.

When the First Lady discovered that they hadn't had breakfast, she'd gone to the galley herself to serve them: toaster waffles with blueberry syrup and steaming mugs of coffee. That was just fine with Claudia.

"When does the public get to see your daughter?" She'd hit the perfect note. It was straight from the Lieutenant Commander Boyd Ramis playbook of how to deal with impossibly awkward moments. She'd have to remember to thank him. No, because she'd then have to explain how she'd met the President, and Boyd was on the wrong side of a black-in-black operation. She'd get the hang of this eventually. Claudia just hoped it wouldn't be too late by the time she did so.

"Not just yet," Genevieve Matthews replied in her softly French-accented voice. "We are perhaps too much enjoying keeping her to ourselves. But you are right. She is the first Presidential birth in the White House since 1893. It must be soon."

"She is such a beautiful little girl."

"That is her name." The First Lady cooed at her daughter as she slept. "Adele for my mother just as I am named for my grandmother, Gloria for Peter's mother, Sebiya Matthews. Sebiya means 'little sister.' A young friend of ours said she once had a cat named that. She looked both so sad and yet pleased when she told us about it that we gave our own girl that as a second middle name. It sounds so beautiful. And I think Dilya was really touched."

"Dilya." Claudia was clearly going nuts. "Adopted daughter of..."

"Kee and Archie," the President acknowledged when she couldn't finish the sentence. "Little scamp was here with her father and grandmother right after the birth. You know her?"

Clearly not! "A little bit." She wouldn't mention that the Secret Service was presently storing a folding bow and some arrows that were to be a gift to Dilya.

"Great kid." The Commander-in-Chief was smiling—no, grinning—at even the mention of her.

"That girl," Claudia felt compelled to remark, "was never a kid. And growing up on a Navy assault ship, she isn't getting any younger." Then she heard her own tone. "Not being critical. Just an observation."

"I understand what you are saying." The First Lady shook her head. "I keep telling Archibald that it is not so good a way to raise his child. He is here in Washington so much, he should bring Dilya here full time. Perhaps you"—she addressed her husband—"can convince Kee she should work here as well. I think that just perhaps our protection details have need of another sniper on one of those teams of theirs."

"Maybe." The President clearly liked the idea.

After some thought, the First Lady startled and took her husband's hand.

"Oh, Peter, this we must do. Little Addie doesn't need a nurse much longer, but she needs a babysitter, an au pair." She clapped her hands together. "It will be *parfait*! Dilya will go to local school and meet others her age, and she can help me. Then, when her parents must travel, she can stay with us."

By the time they landed at Colorado Springs, Claudia decided that in addition to respecting her Commander-in-Chief, she also rather liked Peter Matthews and his wife.

Minutes later they were aloft and bound for DC.

Her brain was crammed with ideas and questions. The exhaustion of missing so much of last night's sleep was the last thing that mattered. She had an upcoming meeting with the CIA and the White House Chief of Staff.

How in the world was she supposed to command an operation half a world away when she had no idea of what the assets were or the people involved?

When the jet's landing gear squealed on the runway at Andrews Air Force Base, she jerked upright and checked her watch.

Impossibly, she'd just had three solid hours of sleep.

It still didn't make her feel one bit better.

Chapter 18

AFTER THE LENGTHY MEETING WITH THE CHIEF OF Staff and his wife aboard the echoingly empty backup of Air Force One in the hangar at Andrews, Claudia's need to get away had hit its limit.

Michael drove her along the Potomac to the Marines' HMX-1—the group who flew the Marine One helicopters for the President—where she "commandeered" a utility helicopter from General Arnson by using the simple technique of begging. After serving three tours as a Marine flier, she'd gotten to know the commander enough to borrow an old Black Hawk they used as a trainer. She needed to go somewhere private, and she needed to straighten some things out in her head.

Michael sat silently in the copilot's seat while she flew and the insane jangles of the last twelve hours slowly drained out of her.

"Just twelve hours?"

She could see Michael nod in her peripheral vision. "I'm sorry." His voice was a soft caress over the intercom and the beating of the rotor blades.

"For what?" She flew south down the Chesapeake Bay, enjoying the setting sun and the dark blues and soft grays it brought out in the water.

"For how our trip ended. Dilya will be upset that I didn't get you to a beach for sand castling. Kid was right. You never know when the phone will ring."

"You like her too?" Dilya was more adult than many of the soldiers she'd served with.

"Yes." Michael's voice was sad. "Even that first day when Kee brought her in half starved to death, that girl was clearly smarter than most of us. But you're right, that girl was never a child."

"What about you, Michael?" She took a vector off the Langley and Norfolk TACANs just for practice. She managed to verify her location within two hundred feet of where her GPS reported her. "Do you want children?" Where in the hell had that question come from? She knew she was just avoiding the larger issues at hand, but now that she'd asked, she found that she did want to know.

His silence stretched a long time. It was actually comforting in its familiarity. Far too many words had been thrown at her in the last few hours.

"I never expected to live long enough to have them." Again, that odd sense of wonder in his tone as he discovered something new about himself. "But…I think… that I do. Especially—"

"What?"

This silence was different. This was his stron silent-guy silence, and she wasn't having anything do with that.

"What?" She pushed him again.

"Especially since I've met someone I'd like them with."

Okay, that she hadn't been ready for. She c asking "Who?" just to tease him. But Micha a straight man that he'd probably answer, ar really wasn't ready for that.

They continued south in silence past the Virginia border and over the Outer Banks islands of North Carolina. If she could fly forever and not run out of fuel, she'd be tempted, but regrettably running away had never been her style.

Finally, about an hour south of DC, she brought the helo down out of the sky and settled it in the dunes twenty miles north of where the Wright brothers had first flown in the Kill Devil Hills.

Michael had watched the last of the sunset bleed from the sky while they flew. Acknowledging that he wanted children had opened some hole in him. For twenty years he had thrown himself at every dangerous situation as if it were a game. Roll the dice, dive in, and prove that he could walk out the other side when not another soul could.

He'd hunted terrorists from Baghdad to Tokyo. Had walked the streets of Somalia and crawled through the opium fields of Myanmar's Golden Triangle. He was the man to get it done.

At ten, he could scale anything. At fourteen, he had discovered and measured the tallest redwood Titan there was, and told no one but his parents. They, in turn, had hecked the height with a trusted friend to verify it was ie tallest without revealing Nell's location. The day 'd signed up for the U.S. military, his parents had de Nell their last climb to honor his find. They were heir mid-fifties by then, and the big trees were get- beyond them. He hadn't been back to the top of Nell he took Claudia.

But now she'd made him think about children, a possibility he'd never considered before. With Claudia such things seemed possible, even desirable. He was still younger than his parents had been when they'd had him.

Did that mean he'd retire from the service like Emily and Mark? That was wholly unimaginable. But he was certainly at the very senior end of being a field operative. SOAR pilots often flew right through their forties and fifties, but Delta was a younger man's game. He didn't want to leave the field, perhaps no more than Emily and Mark had wanted to.

Maybe he could make the same shift that Archie Stevenson had made. After his injury, he'd shifted to an Air Mission Commander role, even though his wife had remained in forward operations. If the President did pull him back to the White House as a full-time advisor, would Michael be willing to step into a similar role for the 5D? Could he, as Archie often did, design a mission that would send the woman he loved into harm's way?

Perhaps that was too high a price.

But to have children by Claudia? It was an opportunity that he'd definitely have to think about at some length.

She settled them in the dunes above a moonlit beach that stretched wide and empty in both directions. He followed when she climbed out of the helicopter and strolled down the beach and toward the ocean. She began shedding her clothes, first shoes, then socks, so that she walked barefoot on the shining white sand. Her T-shirt, pants, and underwear soon followed, scattered as if they were bread crumbs for him to follow. How could he not?

The woman's bare skin and light hair glowed beneath

the quarter moon rising out of the Atlantic until she might well have been a goddess of old brought to life before him. He had never seen such beauty as Claudia strolling forward into the waves. And that she shared that beauty so freely with him humbled him.

Yet one more feeling that was new to him.

He was the best tree climber, the best ROTC student, had consistently been promoted at each rank on the first day he was eligible. Had managed to unravel the Delta training until he was always the maximum performer, the heart of each team he served with, and now their most senior officer ever to serve in the field.

But Claudia humbled him.

She outflew Emily Beale. She thought as quickly as any Delta operator in a crisis situation, a skill she'd proven several times in Somalia. And she'd taken to skywalking as if born to it.

Of course the President had seen that in her, giving her command of the present operation. He had been on the verge of making precisely that recommendation. He knew his own strengths—flexibility and reaction. He was only beginning to know hers—clear-sightedness and always thinking. Everything he did by instinct, she did by being smarter than everyone around her.

Only when the first wave broke warm over his shoes and soaked his pants up to the knees did he realize that he was following her mindlessly. He trotted back up the beach above the waves' reach and shed his own clothes. Then he followed her into the waves glittering in the moonlight.

They floated and swam in the warm Gulf Stream waters of North Carolina. He cataloged the time by the movement of the stars and moon across the sky because he couldn't help himself. He wanted to hold and cherish each precious hour he spent with her, even if it was only to swim in companionable silence.

Emerging from the water, she was lit as if by a thousand sparkles of light, each water droplet catching the moon and accenting a curve, a moment of motion. Unable to resist, he reached out and touched her incredible skin for the first time since he'd touched her hand on the Gulfstream. He had to prove to himself that she was real. He could feel her, but he still wasn't quite sure about the reality part. He'd had as many fantasies as the next man, but none matched Claudia in the flesh.

In answer to his touch, she turned and flowed into his arms. She lay her head on his shoulder and simply stopped there as if they were caught mid-moment in an infinite slow dance. The warm spring evening felt chilly on his drying skin, but neither of them moved to dry themselves off or get dressed. She simply leaned into him.

When his body's inevitable reaction to her occurred, she still didn't move from his arms. He'd never been so unself-conscious around a woman.

"I need you to be strong for me, Michael. I don't know how to do this." Her voice was weary and soft as moonlight.

That she would ask such a thing of him made him feel stronger than perhaps he ever had before. He scooped her up in his arms and carried her back to where their clothes lay scattered. He set her on the pile of clothes and fetched the light jacket he'd been wearing to drape over her shoulders. Then he sat beside her and simply held her with no idea of what to do next.

"You are the most capable person I've ever met, Claudia. And that's saying something as I've known and flown with some exceptional people. You are the best of them."

She patted his chest, keeping her head on his shoulder, her damp hair against his cheek. "That's sweet of you to say, my lover."

He was going to protest that it was the truth, but her last words tied his chest up in knots. He had made love to many women, or at least had had highly consensual and enjoyable sex. A few had even called him their lover. But never before had it meant so much. He wanted to explain, to insist, to spill forth words until he was wrung dry, but he couldn't think of where or how to begin. So he kept it simple.

"You are the very best…my lover." And merely saying the words aloud anchored the feeling like a grapple even deeper within him.

Again she patted his chest.

Well, what she needed most right now wasn't his adoration, but his strength. That's what she'd said, and he knew her well enough to believe her. For that, he damned well did know where to begin.

"Okay." He kissed her atop her salt-damp hair to gather his own strength and stave off something of his body's need for hers. "Let's start with the beginning. First, what assets do we know, positively, that we need?"

Claudia's tight embrace, as close as she'd ever held him even during sex, told him that he'd done something right.

"We know we need Trisha and Bill." Her voice sounded a little more like the confident woman he knew so well.

It was the most surreal mission planning session he'd ever held—in this case, literally. He'd done them in The Unit's headquarters just a couple hundred miles inland from here at Fort Bragg. He'd met teams in bombed-out Belgrade, in a cardboard hut in a Shanghai ghetto, and an upscale Brazilian condo. He had never before planned one while sitting mostly naked with a beautiful woman filling his arms on a moonlit beach.

Claudia eventually stood and pulled on her jeans. He did his best not to be disappointed, though she continued to wear his jacket unzipped, offering him the occasional heart-stopping glimpse of skin-colored moon shadow. He shrugged into his pants and T-shirt.

She began drawing in the sand. "This is the Caspian Sea, two hundred miles long and seven hundred north to south. Azerbaijan is in the west, sitting on top of one of the largest oil and gas reserves on the planet and friendly to the United States; Iran south, Turkmenistan to the east. Up north, Kazakhstan and then Russia completing the circle back to Azerbaijan." A third of the way up from the bottom, she slashed a sideways line across the narrowest part of the sea.

"The Trans-Caspian Gas Pipeline," Michael acknowledged.

"Proposed," she amended.

"Proposed. And deeply opposed by both Iran and Russia on a supposedly environmental basis. Iran actually wants the pipeline to run overland through their country for the taxes, and Russia wants ships to pay large tariffs to use the thirteen locks of the Volga-Don Canal system."

He knew he was simply repeating their briefing, but that was how the process worked: reinforce the familiar, then build on that to create the next layer of the known.

They never did build a sand castle, but about the time that dawn graced the deep Atlantic, he did help her remove his jacket.

They made slow, gentle love as if they weren't surrounded by a dozen drawings of an impossibly dangerous mission plan against a friendly foreign power. A mission that if it went wrong was going to kill them and start a war, a big one. A mission plan that would soon be erased by the incoming tide.

Chapter 19

UNABLE TO SETTLE THE ARGUMENT OF WHERE TO GO, Bill and Trisha were in neither Budapest nor Boston. Fort Campbell exchange tracked them down in Scotland, and Claudia and Michael flew in on a commercial airliner to meet up with them.

Claudia set the meeting in a warm Edinburgh pub, because May sure wasn't as warm here as on the North Carolina beaches. The problem was the bottle-to-throttle rule. In civil aviation, there was a required minimum of eight hours from your last drink to wheels up. In SOAR, it was twenty-four. And since SOAR pilots were technically on call twenty-four by three-sixty-five, that didn't leave a lot of chances for a drink.

She finally decided that if she was in charge of this mission, she'd make sure they didn't fly within the next day, because she definitely needed a beer.

They met at a pub just off Grassmarket Square below the castle. It was an old place built of heavy, dark wood beams and worn flooring. The sign over the door said "Here William and Robert shared a pint." She thought it would tacky to ask whether they meant William Wallace and Robert the Bruce seven hundred years before or the current owners' dads.

Several regulars sat at the long bar. But unlike in an American bar, there was no morose feeling as if that's where the patrons moldered over the years. These folks were all cheerfully debating a soccer game on the television. "Football on the telly," she corrected herself.

"I'm sooo glad you called." Trisha dropped down in the tall-backed booth isolated in a dim corner. She landed across from Michael and leaned over the table to punch his shoulder in greeting. "Not only has this bloody Scotsman that I married"—she hooked a thumb at Bill—"never been to his homeland, but he knows almost nothing about it. That means I've had to play tour guide in his bloody country."

Claudia tried to read more into Trisha's greeting of Michael, but it didn't work. Trisha clearly liked Michael a great deal, but she loved her husband, even if he was the subject of her welcoming diatribe.

Bill nodded a greeting as he sat beside his wife. "It's been, uh, an education." He easily blocked Trisha's elbow shot to the ribs.

Claudia had actually missed them. Not that she wasn't instantly wishing she were back in the trees or lying happily in Michael's arms listening to the shorebirds come awake in the Outer Banks sand dunes, but she did miss them.

"So, what brings you two to Scotland? Where did you two go anyway?"

"Michael took me somewhere lovely." She smiled at him as she thought about Nell.

"Oh God, she's going all gooey on us." Trisha finally leaned back and slowed down. "You two really are a good fit. How the hell did that happen, Michael?"

"Don't know, but I'm not complaining."

"No. No, you aren't." Trisha gave him a warm smile. "I'm glad."

It was one of the first times Claudia had heard warmth in the woman's voice, yet another unexpectedly likable characteristic.

"You were on the ground under four days," Bill observed. Claudia kept forgetting how much he was like Michael. They were so different in size—Bill half a foot taller and his shoulders at least that much wider—that it was easy to forget they were both top Special Operations Forces soldiers with very similar training. Of course Bill would reconstruct the travel times that had led them to California and back to Scotland.

"Two days, then we visited Peter." Never saying "the President" in public helped make the ongoing mission discussions she'd had with Michael sound casual to any passing stranger. After meeting the President, she didn't feel that awkward about referring to the Commander-in-Chief by his first name—at least not out of his presence.

At their blank expressions, Claudia glanced over at Michael. His brow knit in concentration lines for a moment and then cleared.

"Oh, it must be their first time." He was kind enough to avoid mentioning that it was also Claudia's first time as he described the meaning of a black-in-black operation to them.

As expected, Bill looked appropriately grim, and Trisha looked as gung-ho and excited as always. So much so that Claudia wondered if they could involve Bill without Trisha. It didn't seem likely, and the sand-drawn plans washed away by the Atlantic's waves did require both of them.

When the barmaid came over, Claudia ordered

bangers with mashies and a pint of stout. Trisha tried to disgrace them by ordering an Irish stew, but the barmaid was cheerfully pleasant about being disdainful.

"She's had me trying everything," Bill whispered confidentially. "Boiled mutton, neeps and tatties, elver cakes—which are made out of baby eels, by the way, though she didn't tell me until after." His shudder explained why he'd ordered a burger and chips with his lager. Michael simply nodded toward Claudia and held up two fingers.

"So, Michael, what's the gig?" Trisha barely waited until the waitress was out of earshot.

He repeated his nod to Claudia, which caused Trisha's expression to blank for a moment, and then, instead of looking surprised or defensive, she became much quieter. Okay, Claudia felt a bit better about including the woman.

"Damn," Trisha whispered half to herself. "This just got a whole lot more serious if they put you in charge. Who are *they* anyway? Wait." She narrowed her eyes and then they popped wide.

"Peter? As in—"

"Yes," Claudia cut her off.

"Damn girl." Trisha whistled at her. "You *are* hot shit."

Claudia laughed. "More like in it over my head."

"Yeah, I can buy into that. But still hot shit. So, is he really as handsome as on television?"

"Yes," she answered before she could stop herself. She could feel Michael's smile without turning to see it. "But his wife makes you wonder why any men even look at us."

"Too perfect," Michael commented dryly. "We like our women to be real."

"Like real flawed?" Trisha teased him.

Michael opened his mouth, but Claudia stopped him with a light touch on his arm and a gentle shake of her head. "Don't even go there. No way to win that one."

Trisha offered Claudia a pout for ruining her fun.

~

Claudia laid out where her thinking had gone so far, drawing pictures with her fingertip through a little salt she'd scattered on the scarred tabletop. Their conversation was easily masked by the increasing evening crowd and the growing tension of the televised match. Apparently not important enough to pack the bar, but exciting enough that no one was paying any attention to the four tourists at a back table.

Bill's plate was sparkling clean by the time he pushed it toward the center of the table. "Now that's what I call good Scottish food."

"I'll order you a Scotch egg next time. You'll like that." Trisha spoke absently as she returned to studying the latest sketch of Baku port in Azerbaijan. Actually no more than a vee that pointed east and a dot near the wide end along the lower arm. The capital city sat on a stubby peninsula that reached a couple dozen miles out into the Caspian Sea.

"I was in Baku back in 2004 when I was just a baby SEAL," Bill continued, as if this weren't a complete revelation that made him the only one of their tiny team who'd ever been there. "My squad was sent over on a training mission with their navy. When the Soviet Union collapsed, Russia grabbed most of the Caspian flotilla. They've since geared up and are definitely the powerhouse fleet on the Caspian. Azerbaijan is number two, and they say number two tries harder."

Apparently Trisha had actually learned something about silence, or at least giving her husband room to speak his thoughts. Though he was about a dozen times more voluble than Michael, Claudia suspected that the degree of restraint still must challenge Trisha to the core. Bill sipped his beer and stared at the wall over Claudia's head for at least a minute.

"You were looking to bring in the Chinooks and a SEAL submersible. That would be a Havas boat, by the way. Very serviceable little craft."

"But?" Claudia prompted him.

"But, that expands the operational crew by a dozen people or more."

"A dozen?"

"Five crew on the Chinook. The delivery and maintenance team on the sub itself. They're going to want to provide the pilot, even with me there. So, we're looking at two subs to do this as they're only two-person boats."

Claudia wanted to put her head down on the table and scream. She wanted to go fly against forest fires and make Emily come back and do this. She wanted...

"So back to that training mission in Baku. Russia didn't get the whole of the Caspian flotilla. Azerbaijan was able to grab and hold on to many vehicles that the Soviet Union had based at Baku, but that were manned by Azeri. That includes four miniature submarines, both Triton class. Two were dash-one, which is a two-man craft good for six knots at five hours."

"We'll probably need something with a bigger range than that."

"The other two," Bill continued as if she hadn't spoken, "are dash-2Ms. Six-man wet sub. It can go twice the distance. Pressure-balanced, which means you can take it deep without having to decompress on the way back up. Has onboard air. I could check through channels, but I'd wager they're still sitting at the naval base outside Baku. Their navy is still too small to afford throwing anything away. And if one went quietly missing, maybe they wouldn't notice for a while."

"That's good, Bill." Michael nodded to him. "That puts us back to a four-person team."

"Yeah," Trisha remarked dryly and waved for another round of beer. "Four people and a kajillion-year-old miniature submarine against the Russian Navy on behalf of Iran. No worries."

Chapter 20

MICHAEL AND CLAUDIA SPENT MOST OF THE NIGHT SITting up in the small room they'd rented at a local B and B. Thankfully they'd had to walk a couple of kilometers to get there, which cleared their heads as well as worked off the heavy meal.

The B and B was a three-story stone house dating back centuries. Purple lupines lined the neatly kept garden. It even had a little garden gate to admit them. The proprietor was right out of a brochure: pleasantly round, very cheerful, matronly gray, and offering a traditional breakfast with or without haggis. "Mostly just for the tourists, dearie. We don't eat it ourselves."

Michael could tell that the room was exactly Claudia's kind of luxury. Rich quilts on the dark-framed beds. Comfortable wingback chairs and a pretty little gas fireplace. She fit here as if it had been designed with her in mind.

Michael could feel the beer, the meal, and even the accommodations slowing him down, but he often felt slow around Claudia. Actually, that wasn't right. Claudia made him feel as if he was going exactly the right speed. Trisha's mercurial shifts of thought left him exhausted. Someday he'd have to ask Bill why it worked for him, just out of curiosity. Trisha's approach was to throw down a thousand ideas and see if any of them survived even cursory inspection.

Claudia, thankfully, had an approach similar to his own for tackling these sorts of problems. Find exactly what was needed, and only then start looking outside the box to solve that. He also liked her low-tech approach. Always make do with the simplest item you could to solve the issue at hand. Bill's suggestion of simply stealing an Azerbaijani naval asset had been exactly that. When it still didn't have sufficient range, Trisha had started talking about ways to recharge the batteries in the middle of the sea at night.

"When we're done with it," Claudia had answered, "we'll steal a fishing boat to finish the trip out of sight. Or we'll hijack a boat early on to tow it the first leg of the journey."

Low-tech—he liked it. But there were still too many pieces of the plan that weren't there and the clock was running.

Once they were in the room, Claudia dropped down into one of the chairs without even turning on a light, like a puppet with all of its strings suddenly cut. He'd been on the verge of trying to puzzle out what came next, but she looked so tired where a shaft of moonlight found her that he suddenly felt very protective. Exhaustion wracked her face, making her even paler than her fair skin usually was. The solid woman who was winning his heart was almost ethereal in the moonlight.

For a half second she didn't even look alive, and that scared the shit out of him. Then she moved and the fear slipped away almost unnoticed, but it left behind a very uncomfortable itch.

When was the last time they'd slept? He traced back. He'd slept on the transatlantic flight, but he was guessing she hadn't. Thinking back, the last place she'd slept, other than a couple hours from Denver to DC, was a third of a world away at the top of Nell.

Well, the strongest woman he'd ever met had asked him to be strong for her. Right now, she was past functioning and it was up to him. She barely protested as he lifted her up and placed her on the bed. She struggled a little as he unclothed her, but stopped after he tucked her in. He nudged her onto her belly and began digging at the knots in her shoulders.

"Ow! Hey! Ow!" She half rose. With a halfhearted glare, she flopped back down on the pillow.

Right. This wasn't some brute strong soldier fighting a cramp and needing the muscle seizure broken up in order to continue the march. No matter her strength, she was still a woman with a woman's frame and musculature.

He started much more gently. She released a soft sigh. Then a small hum of pleasure. By the time he shifted from her neck to her shoulders, the sound had changed to a soft snore. After a brief debate, he continued, knowing her muscles would loosen even if she wasn't awake to be part of it. Deep sleep is what she needed.

What she *needed*. He would think about that in a bit, but for the moment, he kept going.

Working all the way down the glutes and calves, even working the muscles in the arch of her foot and between her toes. It felt as if she were turning to liquid behind him, each muscle and joint loosening. When he reached the end, he slid the covers back over her.

With the lights off, the moon shone cold through the window, casting her face in chill relief. So deeply asleep that she appeared lifeless. Not able to stand the image, he finally placed his hand just in front of her mouth. He had to wait several heart-stopping seconds before a faint warm brush of air across his fingertips proved that she still lived.

Again the image.

He pulled over a chair to look at her, to watch her sleep beneath a handmade quilt in a bed that probably dated back as far as the house; it was old with ornate woodwork. He leaned back in the brocaded wing-back armchair and felt the lacework doilies over the chair arms.

He would watch over his lover.

His lover.

No. That was no longer sufficient. The passing thought in the trees had turned real, concrete until it was a solid thing inside him…lover.

He was watching the woman he loved.

As he watched her sleep, he tried to picture a future… and couldn't. He'd always known he was going to die out here. If not this mission, then the next. He was a man who was born to die in the saddle, not in some VA home. He wasn't going to live beholden to any man.

That was one of his favorite parts of The Unit. They were self-selected for being independent thinkers who were willing to walk into the darkness. "Alone and unafraid" was one of their unofficial mottoes. One they trained hard to prepare for.

She was one of his team, and his duty was to stand watch, to protect her as she requested. Well, first he would make sure that she survived this mission.

And after that? What would be best for her after that?

What would happen to her if—no, *when*—he died in action? She had a kind and generous heart. He could see that in how seamlessly she'd slipped into everyone's life. The women of SOAR, Dilya, Emily, the First Family: each had welcomed her in with little question.

No one invaded his life. No one. Not even his parents. Bill and Trisha were the closest friends he had, kept at a specific distance—this close and no closer.

Claudia Jean Casperson did not stay where he placed her. She'd slipped in close under his guard when he wasn't watching, past every roadblock. She had left no markers that he could use to retrace her route and brush out the footprints as if it had never happened. She was a part of how he breathed. Her scent of spring and the moonlight that even now had found another way to brush its light upon her sleeping form.

Michael knew what was best for her.

He would protect her as no other before. For Claudia Jean Casperson, he would do anything and bear the pain gladly.

Not at the cost of his life, rather at the cost of his heart.

Claudia woke in the lap of luxury—a deep bed and heavy quilts. She felt better than she had in days. Out the window, sunlight was just slipping into the sky and casting its light on Arthur's Seat, the high, green hill where the king was rumored to have sat ever so long ago.

And she woke to the sight of Michael asleep in the chair facing her. His feet were propped on the foot of the bed and his head tipped over against the side of the wingback. She considered dragging him down into the covers, but she'd had an idea in the night. With a time difference of eight hours, she had to place the call soon.

She slipped out of bed, dressed, and left the room to stroll the streets of Edinburgh while she placed her call. Breakfast wouldn't be for an hour anyway. She found a turn that opened into Holyrood Park, which was deserted at this hour except for a few people who had caught the morning jogging disease from America.

The cell number she was calling rang a number of times before a sleepy voice mumbled, "What?"

"Emily. I'm sorry. It's only about 2100 your time. I didn't think that would be too late to call."

"I'm visiting my parents in DC. It's past midnight. Who the hell is this?" Then she heard Emily telling someone in the background to go back to sleep and the motions of her probably leaving the room, all of which made Claudia feel even worse.

Emily's voice echoed, from hard bathroom walls by the sound of it, when she continued. "Uh, I think my brain is starting to wake up. Captain Casperson?"

"Yes. Sorry. I can call back in the morning..." But that would be six or seven hours from now, and the thought of waiting that long made her head hurt.

"No. Go ahead. What can I do for you?" Emily's voice was slowly growing clearer.

"I, uh..." Claudia wasn't sure what it was safe to say over the phone. "I wanted to talk to you about that fishing trip you mentioned. And I'd like to talk about it real soon. I could use some advice." That should cover it if Emily was as sharp as her reputation.

"The fishing trip?" Emily sounded perplexed.

"Your friend Peter—"

"Oh no! That bastard!"

Claudia flinched as Emily cursed the President. Yep, Emily was that sharp.

"He gave you one, didn't he? I knew it. I should have lied and told him I thought you were a total screwup when I met you. I'm so sorry."

Claudia appreciated the sympathy. "I was hoping we could talk."

"Not over the phone." Emily sounded wide-awake and absolutely sure of herself.

"I know that. I was thinking I could catch a flight and—"

"Where are you?"

Claudia looked around, suddenly feeling as if she'd been beamed to a foreign land. She'd come to a stop among the park's trees and could see the towering stone height of Edinburgh Castle beyond them.

"I'm lost in the woods." She blinked and focused on being rational. "Scotland, Edinburgh."

"I'll come to you. How's your timeline?" Emily was all business from her parents' bathroom.

"Getting tight. I'm thinking I have three or at most four days before we need to, ah, go fishing."

"Which probably means two. Okay. Mark can take Tessa for the day. I'll be there in a couple hours. I'll need to find a Hornet F."

Claudia pulled the phone from her ear and stared at it. Then she put it back to her ear. "A Hornet?"

"An F/A-18F—" Emily began explaining.

"I know what one is." It was a supersonic fighter jet that could make the Atlantic crossing in two hours, but it would need a midair refuel over the Azores. The "F" was a two-seater version. "How would you—"

Emily laughed at her. "You don't get it yet. Did he give you a letter?"

"Yeah. He said it was a toned-down version of an 'Emily letter,' whatever that means."

"After I hang up, read it again and think about it. I'll be there by lunch. Do you need Mark as well?"

"Uh, I don't know. I have Michael and—"

"Don't tell me!" Emily cut her off again. "If you have Michael, you're covered. See you soon."

And the woman was gone. Again Claudia pulled away her phone to look at it, but all it said was "Call Ended" and then it turned back to showing the time before the screen blanked.

A Super Hornet F/A-18F? She stuffed the phone into a back pocket and blew on her fingertips to warm them because the sun still hadn't reached over the high peak of Arthur's Seat and down into the park where she stood. Then she pulled the crumpled letter out of her other pocket and read it again, even though she knew all of the words on the paper.

Please afford any and all assistance requested by Captain Claudia Casperson.

President Peter Matthews

Below it was White House Chief of Staff Daniel Darlington's name and direct phone number. She hadn't quite appreciated what that meant until Emily said she'd requisition a ride in a fifty-million-dollar fighter jet on no notice and arrange for a refueling tanker to meet her halfway across the Atlantic.

At full speed, she'd be here well before lunch, which meant Claudia had some real hustling to do. She headed back to the B and B. Michael was out of time for his beauty rest. And she wouldn't even have time to wake him with a proper tumble beneath the covers.

Chapter 21

Based on his rapid responses the last two times they'd woken up together, Claudia knew that by the time Michael's feet hit the floor, he'd be awake enough to take in instructions.

"Good morning. By end of today we're going to need to find out exactly where the Triton-2M submarines are moored and if they still work. Can you do that?"

Michael rubbed a hand along his jaw as if testing his beard and eyed her warily.

"I should be able to. I have some buddies in the 22 SAS Regiment. We do exchange training with the British often enough that they'll help me."

"They can't know why you're asking. Then while they're chasing that, I want to be headed for the *Peleliu* by dinner." She wasn't quite sure why she felt such an urgent need to hurry up all of a sudden, but she wasn't going to ignore the instinct.

"Have Bill and Trisha arrange us the fastest possible route. Commandeer a jet if you have to." He didn't even blink at that, as if of course that's what you'd do in a black-in-black operation. Well, she knew that now.

"Also make sure the *Peleliu* isn't stuck behind traffic in the Suez or something stupid. If Ramis is anywhere near close enough, have him drive hard for the far east end of the Black Sea. I want to be there by sunset tomorrow. Got it all?"

He looked at her strangely, as if it hurt him to look at her. "Got it." His answer was clear and sharp.

She'd apologize later for being so abrupt. But she now understood what was expected and felt as if she'd been lazy and gotten nothing done these last thirty-six hours. She had also figured out that the only way to keep this whole thing black-in-black was to have the mission completed before the rest of the crews were back from leave. That meant she had barely five days to defeat the Russian Navy and make it look like it wasn't anyone's fault.

Claudia took the rental car and drove across the Forth Bridge to pick up the M90 north to RAF Station Leuchars an hour away. Renting a helicopter would draw unwanted attention. Besides, she needed time to think.

However, she spent the first half of the trip thinking about how many wrong turns you could make in a country where they drove on the left side of the road. Once she was on the highway, she had to concentrate on moving left for the slow lane rather than right. Thank God the car was an automatic or she'd have been totally screwed up.

Around the middle of the trip, she got the hang of it. It was like flying a helicopter. A helicopter pilot usually flew from the right-hand seat so that she could take the less-critical left hand off the collective to reach any control panel settings and still keep her hand firmly on the cyclic. By the time she was passing Kirkcaldy, she considered the chances for success in asking President Matthews to change the laws about which side of the road Americans drove on. This made far more sense.

The last part of the trip was spent continuing the recalibration of her thinking. For two days she'd been locked into old thinking. Plan this, figure this out, find the right asset, get it in place. Then rehearse the whole thing until you had it right. She'd flown hundreds of missions of exactly that type in Iraq and Afghanistan. Clear objectives, clear targets, team fully briefed and engaged.

She'd only started adapting to Special Operations Forces thinking, despite two years of training. In the training environment, you know your mission. Tougher than anything a Marine flew, but still it was known and carefully planned.

SOF missions weren't necessarily more dangerous, but they were flown much farther from help or backup. One of her SOAR "training" missions had included assisting in the planning and flying copilot for the takedown of four Colombian turboprops on four successive nights. They'd flown four different routes, but each plane was confirmed to be packed solid with drugs. None of the Colombian planes made it more than a mile into international waters before they went down forever, radios jammed so that their dispatchers never knew what happened.

Black-in-black was another layer again, but she still couldn't get a handle on it. She knew it was different, but she didn't quite know how to think about it.

After another series of wrong turns—maybe she'd stick with left-hand drive for cars—she reached the gate to the RAF Leuchars. She hadn't thought this through. First, the guard didn't look friendly at all. Second, Michael probably could have fixed this, but she'd decided to keep Emily in her own compartmented cell for some reason. President Matthews had said it was up to her how she chose to allocate her team, and some instinct had said to keep this part of it private. Third, the guard still didn't look very friendly.

"I need to see your company commander. I'm meeting an inbound flight." When planning wasn't in place, go for bravado.

"This isn't Gatwick, missy. Now turn around your little rental and move your civilian backside out of my sight." On him, the Scottish burr that she usually enjoyed simply sounded nasty.

Claudia looked down at herself. SOAR didn't wear uniforms much. She wasn't even sure if Michael owned a uniform; Delta blended into civilian scenarios rather than parading into military ones. She wore tight jeans, a blue silk blouse—a gift from the First Lady to replace her lone T-shirt—and bright red sneakers—a gift from Alice the CIA analyst. A windbreaker that she'd picked up at a shop in Edinburgh lay across the passenger seat.

She dug out her wallet and handed her U.S. military ID to the guard, hoping that it worked somehow.

The guard read it carefully, then disappeared inside his hut for a moment and placed a call. He hung up quickly and hustled back to the car, returning her ID smartly, then offering her one of those palm-out British salutes.

"You're cleared directly to the field, ma'am. That's your flight on short-final now. They'll be deplaning at Hanger 14 on the left there, ma'am."

She returned the salute and drove slowly down the access road wondering what had just happened.

Emily Beale is what had happened.

Claudia had so damn much to learn.

She pulled up beside Hanger 14, which was completely empty. Maybe they were having her on. A glance out the window proved otherwise. An F/A-18F Super Hornet hammered down right on the numbers painted at the end of the runway. With a roar of thrust reversers that echoed across the field, it slowed abruptly. So abruptly that it was able to turn at the first taxiway and pull straight into the hangar.

When Emily Beale climbed down from the rear cockpit, Claudia couldn't think of anyone that she'd ever been happier to see. Emily's strong handshake made her think that maybe, just maybe, this was all possible.

"God, thank you so much for coming."

They settled in a back corner of the hangar. Just the two of them, a large mission-briefing table, and a pad of paper. Claudia had also brought the file that Daniel had given her aboard the backup Air Force One, but she left that in her case beside her chair. The pilot was hanging out at the front of the hangar with his airplane, waiting for a fuel truck. As good security as they needed.

"Your first one, Claudia?" Emily didn't have to say that she was talking about a black-in-black mission.

All Claudia could do was nod.

"Michael's in charge? Where is he?"

"He was going to be in charge, with me as the SOAR liaison. Then something changed the President's mind and he assigned it to me."

"What changed his mind?" Emily poured them both

coffee and took an oatmeal scone off the plate someone had provided.

"Something about my record, field recommendations, that I outflew you on the SOAR training tests..." Claudia didn't have a good enough feel for this woman yet and dropped that tidbit to test her reaction.

She hadn't expected a laugh in response.

"So that's what Peter was hinting around about. We're having dinner tonight, and he's bound to unload it then. You beat my test scores? Well done, you. Doesn't actually prepare you for squat compared to the real thing, does it?"

Claudia shook her head. "Better than the Marines, but no, not even close."

"I had the same thoughts coming in from the Screaming Eagles. Well, we'll have to figure out a way to totally turn this one back on Peter. He loves it when he thinks he can trip me up."

"Does he ever succeed?"

Emily smiled. "Not very often."

"I'm sorry to make you miss dinner, and sorry I woke you."

Emily glanced at her watch. "It's only about five a.m. East Coast time. I should be back in plenty of time. Now, how much can you tell me and why am I here?"

The fuel truck rumbled up outside the hangar and began running grounding lines and hoses.

"Uh, I'm not sure how much I can say. I've already learned more about what I'm doing from your thirty-second phone call than I did in the two days of work prior." Claudia rubbed her eyes, wishing she hadn't had the second beer last night. SOAR had turned her into a total lightweight. In the Marines, when you were on leave, you were actually on leave, and a beer or two with dinner was pretty standard. Some of the guys really loaded up. A lot of them actually.

Emily waited for Claudia to organize her questions.

"Okay, let's start with the process. I get that black-in-black is different. I just don't quite understand how it's supposed to feel."

Emily's smile was empathetic. "If it feels like you're in hell, you're on the right track."

"Check on that one."

"Black-in-black can't be controlled. Don't think it will go as planned—it won't. Don't think you can anticipate how it will turn out—you can't. So don't overplan. Instead prepare to be very flexible."

"Like Delta."

"Yes. I learned a lot about that just by working with Michael. Use that."

"Okay, next question. How did you successfully run four of them?"

"Eight. But four were for a prior administration and Peter doesn't know about them." Emily sighed. "Nine if you count this one, but I don't since there is no way I can fly with you, much as I'd enjoy it."

"Enjoy it?" Claudia practically shouted it out. If this was Emily's idea of fun…

"I miss the edge. I have a good job flying against wildfires, a great husband, and I know that I'll most likely be alive to watch my daughter grow up. But I do miss the edge. The other reason I couldn't fly with you, you already know. That edge takes constant practice. I fly a lot of hours, but they aren't SOAR hours.

Especially a mission like one of these." Emily looked around the empty hangar as if looking for some way to explain.

Claudia waited.

"These are a whole different animal from normal operations. The real key to making a black-in-black work is pigheaded stubbornness. You simply decide that you and your team are going to survive no matter what. Then you do whatever it takes. That's the only way to do it."

Claudia sat with that for a moment. She was good at stubborn. And flexibility might not be her primary trait, but it certainly was at the core of each of her teammates. Even Trisha exuded that ability.

"How big is your team?" Emily was toying with her scone but hadn't eaten any of it yet.

"Uh, four in DC and four in the field, so far. Michael, Tr—"

"No. I don't want to know." Emily stared up at the steel trusses holding up the roof. "I once did an op with two inside and two outside. I should have added a third, but he was both inside and outside, and I didn't understand how to use him. I've apologized a dozen times since, and I still don't think Frank has forgiven me."

Emily was watching Claudia for a reaction on that. So, she must be referring to Frank Adams, the head of the presidential protection detail. Unsure what Emily was expecting, Claudia kept her conclusions and her reaction to herself.

"Good." Emily surprised her. "That thing you just did is very good. Keep your own counsel. Listen to others, but do your own math. That's another key element to surviving these things. But don't shut out help. If my second outside person had been anyone less skilled than Mark, I'd be dead. Four is good—fire-team size. Don't ever go over a squad of eight. You need to be able to hold every string yourself and make changes on the fly. What can you tell me about the mission?"

"We need to defeat the Russian Navy."

Emily looked at her askance to see if she was joking. She only wished she was.

"Uh." Emily blinked. "Maybe you'll need more than four."

"I only have to defeat the Caspian Sea flotilla. So what do you think? Five should be able to do that, right?"

Emily looked at her wide-eyed and then burst out with a laugh that rang off the hangar's metal walls and had the pilot glancing their direction from the front of the hanger where he was overseeing the refueling of his craft.

"Damn, Claudia. I can't wait to go on that fishing trip for real. We'll have a great time."

They did settle on five. It took them two hours to hash it out. There were only two interruptions. One when Claudia called the White House Chief of Staff to get Kara Moretti, the UAV pilot, back to the *Peleliu* by tomorrow. Her copilot had stayed aboard to oversee the moving of the Gray Eagle from Somali airspace to Turkey.

The other interruption was the pilot bringing over a couple of "packed" lunches: sausage and onion sandwiches, a bag of crisps, and a small sealed container of cubed pineapple. The Coke was what finally cleared

Claudia's head. The sandwich she found a little strange, and the crisps turned out to be just potato chips by another name.

Emily hadn't eaten breakfast and only picked at her lunch, complaining of a queasy stomach from the flight.

"Either that or you're about to have another kid," Claudia teased her.

Emily looked down at her perfectly flat stomach and then began swearing. "I'm going to kill Mark. I'm just going to kill him."

"You don't want another kid?" Claudia didn't know whether to laugh or be shocked.

"The man is so insatiable, not that I'm complaining. We ran out of protection and figured one time without wasn't going to…" She sighed and then rubbed her belly gently. "It'll be alright," she told her midriff. "You just won't have a father."

The goofy smile that bloomed on the woman's face did something to Claudia.

Michael had said that he could imagine having children with her. Well, for the first time in her life, she could certainly see having children—as long as they were Michael's. Actually, now that she thought about it, she couldn't imagine not having his children. Her father had been a silent and closed-off man, but she knew that while Michael would never be chatty, his heart would be wide open to his offspring.

"Now you're looking like I'm feeling, Claudia," Emily kidded her.

Maybe she was. And maybe it was okay.

By fourteen hundred hours Greenwich Mean Time, Emily was aloft and headed back to DC in time for dinner. She'd left behind a warm hug and the feeling that they really would be friends.

She'd also identified a key fact that said they didn't have five to six days. They needed to be in place on the Caspian Sea in under forty-eight hours. Emily had been right about that even before she knew the mission.

By fifteen thirty, Claudia had made only half as many wrong turns as the trip out and arrived back in Edinburgh. They were waiting for her in the room and had even packed her few items. Most of her belongings were supposedly still following from behind, left in a truck in the woods. Probably end up as lost luggage somewhere. The First Lady's Secret Service agent had given her a small knapsack, so she had her change of clothes, toothbrush, and the bow and arrows stowed in her own bag.

By four o'clock they were aboard a small Cessna charter jet, without cabin attendant. This morning it would have seemed like an unconscionable luxury. Since Emily had helped her fully grasp the scope of what they would have to do, this seemed the least of issues. The six saved hours were well worth the expense, as well as the freedom to continue their planning conference. Actually, those six hours were now crucial to their plans.

As soon as they were aloft from Edinburgh and the Firth of Forth was pointing their way over the English Channel, they grouped around the small table between the facing leather seats.

"A helo will meet us at Istanbul to take us out to the ship," Bill reported. "Ramis made good time and was waiting halfway between Athens and Istanbul. I've directed him into the Black Sea. He wanted official orders."

"I told him to goose it through the Bosporus and send me a bill." Trisha knocked back her Coke like it was a shot of whiskey. Red can, caffeinated and with real sugar, Claudia noticed. Trisha was gonna be a wonder to deal with in about twenty minutes—though maybe you couldn't tell the difference between a hyped-up Trisha and a normal one. "He should actually be through the straits and into the Black Sea before we arrive for our 'training exercise.'"

Claudia sent a message to Daniel at the White House to get the orders sent out so that Boyd was covered.

"The subs are still there." Michael gave the good news. "My man is pretty sure they're operational." He was a hundred percent focused. Hadn't even greeted her with a soft look, just a sharp nod. Well, Bill and Trisha had been there and they were both in full-on mission mode, which was fine with her.

Mostly.

Michael's blank expression, per typical, didn't reveal his thoughts. Not per typical, she couldn't read was going on behind that expression.

She tried not to picture how Michael's face would look if she had the news that Emily would be telling her husband in a few hours. It caused a lack of focus that she definitely didn't have the time or privacy to deal with. So, she shunted aside any private thoughts until after the operation was complete.

"We have a fifth team member running about ten hours behind us. Let me show you what I've come up with." Claudia began laying out the details. It was still based on what she and Michael had drawn on the sandy beach of North Carolina the night before last. With a couple of exceptional variations that she and Emily had worked out.

"We need to blame this on somebody, and I think the safest people to blame are the Russians themselves. Here's how I think we can do this."

Once through the plan, and after a few more refinements were suggested, the excitement rose in the plane. Led by Trisha, even Bill and Michael were soon cautiously optimistic.

Without specific details of how she'd come by them, Emily had showed Claudia the bullet wound in her arm, mentioned another in her butt, and told of a third black-in-black after which both Dusty James and Archie Stevenson had spent three months in the hospital, and another when her copilot had been shot and killed.

Claudia had done everything she could to prepare, but she couldn't help watching the sky through the small window of the jet. The sun was setting beyond the layer of clouds below them that hid most of Central Europe. By this time tomorrow, they'd be committed and the only way out, for any of the team that survived, would be through.

Chapter 22

DANIEL DARLINGTON HAD FOUND ANOTHER F/A-18 TO launch Kara Moretti from New York. She arrived in Istanbul an hour ahead of them, and then they all bundled aboard a Eurocopter AS532 Cougar of the Turkish Air Force.

"Exercise," Claudia had said, cutting off the others' eagerness to explain the situation to Kara. "Sorry to pull you just for this, but you know Army thinking." Even though there was no way they'd be overheard, she wasn't going to risk it.

"It's all good." Kara pronounced it "gud" in her soft Brooklyn-Italian accent. "Carlo, he gets these ideas. This gave me an excuse, you know, to be nice about the fact that none of his ideas were ever gonna happen. Just because he's now this hotshot opera singer, he thinks I'm gonna fall for the same lines that didn't work on me in high school. But he's a friend, so I wanted to let him down nice."

Claudia could appreciate that some man would keep trying year after year. Kara had inherited whatever Italian genes made her long, dark, and slender. She was a knockout who had clearly just KO'd an opera singer.

Kara also showed, with the simplest of glances, that she wasn't buying for a second that a Navy Hornet had flown her straight through from New York with two midair refuels just to deliver her to an exercise.

Trisha was chatting up the pilots the moment they were aloft. SOAR had at least one helicopter of almost every type, either at Fort Campbell or down at Mother Rucker, as Fort Rucker Army Aviation Center for Excellence was known. The instructors there definitely lived up to their brutal reputation. This let Army fliers, especially SOAR, constantly test the capabilities of any heli-aviation opponents they were likely to meet. And every pilot made sure to get type-certified in anything they were likely to need to "borrow" in an emergency.

But the occasional training flight didn't equal continuous experience in type, so Trisha charmed the pilots with her usual cheerful manners and a bit of flirting and was soon getting the down-and-dirty on the Cougar's strengths and shortcomings from men who flew her for a living.

Claudia spent the thirty-minute flight to the north of the Bosporus doing her job: worrying.

They were aboard the *Peleliu* by midnight. She set Trisha to unpacking and checking their helicopters. Bill and Michael went off to prepare their assault packages. Meanwhile, she and Kara took over a corner of the empty mess hall and began working through the details.

The Gray Eagle UAV could be aloft for forty hours without refuel, thirty-six hours of it on station from the U.S. airbase at Incirlik in southern Turkey. It took some fussing to decide which packages to place aboard. A pair of Hellfires—in case a heavy hit was needed—were an obvious choice, but most of the UAV's mission would be intelligence and tracking, so they went with only two of the four possible missiles to instead load up heavier sensing gear.

With Kara's advice, Claudia selected a day-and-night video package as well as high-resolution, static image capture. Rather than trust the sporadic coverage of low-orbit satellites, they loaded a communications-relay package that could feed directly from the helicopters to Kara even on-site.

Claudia considered an ASW—antisubmarine warfare—set of sensors, but as she hoped to have the only submarine operating in the area, they left that off to save weight. In addition to a signals intelligence package to intercept any radio communication, they also selected a broadband ELINT—ELectronic INTelligence—package just in case other coded communication was occurring. A small radio-jamming set would back up the one Trisha was installing on the *May*.

The last piece was a second drone, a small ScanEagle with only one package, a communications relay. The Gray Eagle could operate either line-of-sight or through a satellite. To keep their signal isolated and wholly in their control, they needed the second bird aloft because the Gray Eagle would be flying both beyond the Caucasus Mountains and the curvature of the Earth. Kara would loft the ScanEagle UAV to circle high above the *Peleliu* as a relay.

For foreign communications, if there had to be any, they were well set. Michael and Claudia both spoke Russian, though his was far better. Trisha had Persian, which would cover most of the Iranian communications, and had been learning Azerbaijani. It was a rare Special Operations operative who didn't have a minimum of two or three languages under their belt—at least well enough to monitor communications…and always enough to curse fluently.

But Trisha seemed to inhale languages for sport, like Archie Stevenson. Southwest Asia was a massive hodgepodge of languages, and Trisha seemed determined to grind her way through them all, forcing Bill to learn some of each as she went through them. They'd considered bringing aboard a specific translator, but Trisha had insisted she was up to the task as long as they weren't doing any peace negotiations.

"No, not peaceful ones," Claudia had assured her.

By sunrise, Claudia had Kara squared away. She found Trisha at the Little Birds and clearly fussing enough for both of them, which was a bit of a relief. Claudia had too much worrying of her own to do and was glad to leave this part of it to Trisha.

"One can is full." Trisha thumped on the ammunition can for the port-side minigun. "I pulled out the can for the other gun when I dropped off the other mini so there's enough space for the amount of gear Billy said they'd need. So, on both your and my helicopter's four hard points I've got: a seven-rocket Hydra launcher, a minigun, an extended-range fuel tank, and a pair of Hellfires. I think that's the best rig for this trip. I double-checked the math, and no matter how we cut it, we need the extra fuel tank. But I was thinking, if we planned on refueling on the way out as well, I really think that we don't need two of them."

Claudia inspected the setup and liked it. Several times they'd discussed which weapons to sacrifice in order to mount the second external tank. Not knowing much of the scenario they were entering, they hadn't found a happy choice. Trisha had found a way for them to keep some of each type of weapon.

"Well done, Trisha. Really well done."

They'd high-fived in the morning light, Trisha's face aglow with excitement. No matter what Claudia had initially thought, she now understood she had a true friend there. All she had to do was survive this mission and she might actually start feeling as if she belonged in the 5D. She headed off to find Michael and Bill.

They were in the Delta equipment locker, a small but impressively stocked ten-by-ten-foot space way at the stern of the ship. It was filled with everything from crowbars to sniper rifles—just the sort of room any growing boy dreamed about when he was playing superhero. Radios, hand-launchable drones, several sizes and styles of parachutes, and breathing gear for underwater as well as for high-altitude parachute jumps... It was a dizzying array of cool toys.

From it, Michael and Bill had assembled assault packages that would bury a normal human. Closed-loop scuba gear so they wouldn't leave a trail of bubbles, an array of explosives from lead-sheath door-breaching charges to blocks of C4 for punching large holes through thick steel, and even items that Claudia didn't recognize but was too tired to ask about. Each D-boy also had two handguns, a combat rifle, and a sniper rifle with large stocks of ammunition.

"Uh, food and water, guys?"

Bill smiled up at her and dangled something the size of a small fanny pack: room for two water bottles and a handful of energy bars. She supposed that he was right.

If it went well, they'd be in and out between tonight sunset and sunrise thirty-six hours later. If it didn't go well, there'd be little time to eat.

Michael knew what he had to do, but he couldn't stop watching Claudia. He so enjoyed observing the way she moved, the way she thought. As she tried to solve the puzzle of this mission, her tenacity and clear vision had shown through in the way she thought calmly, step by step, without being boxed in by the protocols of her Marine Corps past. He wanted to tell her how proud he was of her…if he could think of how to do it without sounding stupid.

By the time they finished a full-gear review, she was clearly weaving on her feet again from lack of sleep. He appreciated her as a leader though, in the way she'd retained focus and was willing to go through the process with them.

She was the one who came up with the idea of phase packages. What if, she'd asked, he and Bill rearranged the gear so that they'd use one package to liberate the submarine and then drop any of that particular package they didn't use by the wayside? Then the next package for the fishing boat attack and so on.

It was a different arrangement than he would normally use, arranging the gear by category. But this mission was going to be a long haul. They'd be exhausted by the end of it, assuming they were still alive, and with this arrangement their load would lighten with each successive step of the operation. It was innovative and he should have thought of it himself.

"You need to get some sleep." They were the first words he'd been able to speak directly to her since her arrival, since the Edinburgh pub really. And they sounded lame and pointless even to his own ears.

She'd slid down to sit with her back against the one open bit of wall in the Deltas' equipment locker. In most situations, the Delta team would return to Fort Bragg between missions to reevaluate, restock, and move on to the next assignment.

With the 5D, one mission led to the next. So they had supplied themselves with an arsenal. Lieutenant Commander Ramis would have a stroke if he realized how much weapons-grade material was sitting so close to his hull. It was all safely inert except if there was a direct hit from a big shell. But if someone wanted to sink the *Peleliu* from the inside, they could do so from right here.

"I'm fine," Claudia mumbled from where she was curling up against a case containing one of the PSG1 sniper rifles.

Michael exchanged a look with Bill that informed him this was Michael's duty. Of course it was. He pulled the last strap on his reloaded field pack and tipped it against the doorjamb.

"I'll be back for this in a minute."

"Take your time, Michael." Bill's easy grin didn't sit well with him, but he turned to deal with Claudia. Easier to think of her that way.

He coaxed her to her feet and managed to get her aimed the right way down the corridor. She made it about ten feet to the first junction and then looked around, dazedly seeking a clue as to where she was. Not many came all of the way aft to the pyrotechnic stowage at the very stern of second deck. It was as far from everything critical as possible just in case there was an accident. At this rate she was going to walk into the machinery pit for the aircraft elevator and never be seen again.

Moving to her, he placed a hand on her elbow and gently guided Claudia toward her quarters in the bow. It was a long eight-hundred-foot trek. The warmth of her skin tingled along his fingers, reminding him of that first walk when he'd led her to her cabin after Yemen.

She also evoked warm beaches and tall trees. Her scent of moonlight and mystery—so unexpected in a woman so fair—told more of the story: the archer beneath the trees; the woman with eyes closed and standing in the desert with her arms rising unconsciously as if she could fly; her hair now fluttering behind her, brushing his face as it caught even the slightest breeze.

He tried to close himself to it all, but he couldn't. So instead, he opened himself to it all the way. He drank her in as he guided her forward. Stored her away in his own deepest lockers where the memories would lie safe.

At her door, he stopped and let her continue to the bed. Unlike last night, which was almost two days ago now, he did not undress her and tuck her in.

Claudia stopped, half a step from collapsing onto the bed, and turned to look at him. The question was clear in her eyes. No need for an invitation, rather surprise that he wasn't simply joining her.

"You need to sleep."

This time, he didn't even wait for her to collapse onto her bunk. He merely closed the door quietly and began the long trek back.

Chapter 23

Claudia woke quietly but the peace didn't last long. She was on top of her sheets, wearing the clothes she'd put on forever ago…aboard the Gulfstream maybe? She'd also woken alone with little memory of how she'd arrived, but she was in her quarters aboard the *Peleliu*. By her watch it was one hour to sunset and mission launch. She grabbed a shower and pulled on her flight suit.

One thing was clear as she tightened the covers of the bed she'd never climbed into—she'd slept alone. How had that happened? She hadn't slept alone in weeks. It felt so right to sleep with Michael that it seemed to her they always slept together. Missing him was jarring.

Deal with it, Claudia. And she would. That's what life with Michael would be like. One or the other of them would disappear on a mission for a week or a month with no notice and no ability to communicate once on the mission. It's just how it would be. But it would be worth it.

Well, this was one of those times when she needed to focus.

Fifty minutes to launch. Her first stop was the weather office up on the communications platform at the base of the main structure. The aerological officer assured her of several days of "spring typical" weather for her "exercise"—a high overcast with a low chance of rain. About perfect. Moonrise, if it was visible, would be a crescent around oh-three-hundred hours. Next stop was to see Lieutenant Commander Ramis who was at his desk in the flight-deck-level office where that first briefing on Somalia had occurred forever and a month ago.

"Good evening, Captain Casperson." He offered her the coffee that her body was craving and waved her to a seat. She grabbed a handy blueberry muffin as well. "We have reached the eastern end of the Black Sea. New territory for me, I can assure you. Always a pleasure to see some new terrain. Nice set of mountains there in the distance, I must say. Too bad we can't go climb them. The Sochi Winter Olympics of 2014 were held just over the horizon to the northwest. Would have enjoyed seeing that. Are you a fan of figure skating, Captain?"

"I'm more of a Summer Olympics person, sir."

"Right. You grew up in the desert. Used to ride if I recall."

"Still do on occasion."

"Good, good. Well, I can see that you're setting up something." He nodded toward the flight deck where Trisha's and her helicopters were tied down. "So, what's the plan?"

"Please don't take this wrong, sir. But the plan on your end is very simple. We will be departing"—she checked her watch—"in thirty-four minutes. If all goes well, we will be returning before dawn on the following night."

He waited for her to continue.

When she didn't, Claudia could see the frustration building up in him.

"Excuse me. You're implying that I drove my ship and crew over four thousand miles to just sit here?"

"I'm afraid so, sir." Before he could complain further, she added, "Should you need to contact me, I anticipate being available through Captain Kara Moretti. You'll find her in the coffin, the Gray Eagle's command-and-control container, stored at the aft end of the hangar deck. I'm sorry, sir. I have to go now. I appreciate the coffee."

He looked at her balefully for several seconds as she stood, then laughed for a moment.

"Well, if that doesn't put me in my place for sticking my nose where it doesn't belong." He rose and held out his hand to shake hers. "I wish you the very best of luck, Captain. If you should need anything of me, simply have Captain Moretti ask." His handshake was firm and sincere.

In that moment she knew. She finally understood why Boyd Ramis would always be a second-rate commander. Taking that last bit of responsibility for the lives of your team wholly on your shoulders was a weight he couldn't bear, so he spread it around, laying what he could on the shoulders of those around him.

Well, she didn't have a choice. Tonight, she and three team members would live or die based on a plan she had developed and taken full ownership of. She could at least absolve the LCDR of this mission if it went wrong.

She returned the handshake. "If I have need of you, Commander Ramis, I fear I will be beyond helping."

"Nonetheless, the offer stands." And in one of those things Boyd Ramis somehow did so well and that won him the support of those he could depend upon, he made it sound as if it was for her alone that he'd do this.

Dropping down several stories to the hangar deck, she knocked on the coffin and smiled up at the tiny security camera perched over the door. Kara let her in and started briefing her the moment the seal was set.

"I've been aloft for three hours as we planned. I'm presently on station at thirty thousand feet. Let me show you." Kara led her over to the command-and-control station.

The coffin was the size of a short shipping container. The racks at the front could contain a disassembled Gray Eagle and its parts kit. Those had been left at Incirlik with the small launch team who didn't need to know anything about the mission. At the far end of the console were a pair of chairs, each of which looked like a cross between a Barcalounger and the captain's chair on the starship *Enterprise*. The chairs were on pivots in front of side-by-side curved consoles that made a Black Hawk look seriously under-equipped.

Santiago, Kara's copilot, a rather intense and silent young sergeant, sat in one chair. Kara leaned on the back of the other.

Large screens across the top gave several views as seen by the Gray Eagle. Below that were readouts from the nonvisual gear: radio frequency intercepts, quiescent screens that could fill in moments with Hellfire targeting data, and several that Claudia didn't recognize at all. Below that was a full set of flight instruments giving the status of the bird and then a joystick control with just as many shortcut buttons as she had on the head of her helicopter's cyclic. They even had mixture and throttle controls just like any plane would. In the narrow space between the two consoles was a whole rack of radios.

"We found your subs." She pointed at the top right screen. Exactly as reported, two long, thin shapes sat low in the water alongside a pier in the south bay at Bibi-Heybat. "I've already given confirmation to Colonel Gibson. *Tosca* done good."

"Good. Who's *Tosca*?"

"Opera heroine. Not the smartest of ladies, but when the bad guy betrays her trust and kills her lover, she executes the villain herself."

"You sure you're over this singer Carlo?" It didn't sound much like it to Claudia if Kara was naming her equipment after operatic heroines.

"Oh sure, totally done with him. But he does sing beautifully."

She gave a small sigh that totally confused Claudia. She'd have bet it was a sad sigh. So she dropped the subject.

"Santiago, bring up the view of Karachala." Kara moved to lean against the back of her assistant's chair; the casual lean clearly one of Kara Moretti's natural states that made her look even more elegant. On Trisha it would rapidly decay into a sloppy slouch. On Claudia such a move would look clumsy, one of the reasons she'd trained herself to sit and stand straight and tall.

In moments, a view of dusty Karachala airport at Salyan, Azerbaijan, showed up on one of the main screens. Santiago did something and a red circle showed up at the northwest corner of the runway. "There's your first target."

Claudia felt the relief coursing through her. Their first two steps were in place. They were two of the only three fixed assets in the whole mission. Everything else they'd have to make up as they went. After Claudia offered a final thanks, Kara let her out of the coffin and resealed it with a sharp clack of locks.

Claudia breezed through the chow line. Most of the SOAR fliers were still on leave, so no one was around to ask questions there. The Rangers who'd stayed aboard for the transit showed a halfhearted interest in her being suited up for flight.

"Training flight. We're just warming up for some training work with the Turks next week." A set of exercises that the White House Chief of Staff was rapidly arranging at this very moment as a cover.

Groans greeted her explanation. These guys were used to action, and after the high-mission tempo of Somali, steaming for a week was making them kind of cranky.

A handful of energy bars, a few bottles of water, and a sausage-and-egg English muffin sandwich, which she began eating as she walked, were all in keeping with her cover story.

On deck with ten minutes to go until flight, Trisha and the boys were already prepped.

"Hi. Did you get some of that sleep you needed?" Michael's smile was soft and protective.

Right, now she recalled him guiding her to bed last night. She must have really been out of it. Had she even hugged him this time? Not that she recalled. She could only smile and nod; her voice somehow eluded her.

Michael always looked good to her. But now he

looked really amazing—her own personal guardian angel. One who looked like no other. Nighttime desert camo, pouches bulging with ammunition. His chest expanded by the swim gear and bulletproof vest under the shirt. No bulky survival vest like Trisha's and her SARVSO survival gear with pockets filled with food, compass, maps, med-kit, and a dozen other essentials if they were to crash.

A D-boy stayed lean and mean. Michael's vest had five pockets across the front, each stuffed with four rifle magazines. His handgun wasn't at his hip, rather it too was across his front below the magazine pockets. Michael had claimed that it typically saved a half second or more on the draw. He had a silenced HK416 machine gun draped across his chest and a silenced PSG1 sniper rifle hanging over his shoulder. His MICH Kevlar helmet had a set of four-tube panoramic night-vision goggles, the same that were worn by the team that took down bin Laden's compound.

He appeared impossibly strong and powerful, exactly how she'd want her guardian angel to look. It made her feel suddenly shy before him, not one of her natural states. She turned away to inspect her own gear.

"I already preflighted your bird," Trisha commented with a smile.

"Don't take this wrong, but—even though I now know who the hell you are, Chief Warrant—I don't fly a bird I didn't preflight."

"Be my guest." Trisha completed the ritual.

How far they'd come since that first flight. Claudia knew now that she could trust Trisha in any situation, no matter how ugly. And while she might fly like a maniac, she flew like an immensely skilled one. It took Claudia only minutes to check out her *Maven*. She really was clean. She patted the Little Bird's nose and asked the wise women to lead them all home safe and sound and Catwoman's sidekick to boot some butt.

Five minutes later, exactly at sunset, they were ready to head out: Bill with Trisha and Michael beside Claudia. Kara and Santiago in the coffin. That was her action team. She wondered if it was good luck or bad that the mission didn't have a name. Maybe all black-in-black operations remained nameless as a part of being invisible. Or maybe they all happened so fast that no one had time to think of one—she certainly hadn't.

Ramis had apparently gone up to primary fly control because his voice answered when she radioed PriFly for departure clearance.

"Roger. Cleared for exercise, Omega Four. Good hunting, Captain."

As with any clearance for flight, the proper response was simply to take off and depart from the ship's flight pattern. So Claudia did just that, pulling up the collective and nosing the cyclic forward. Trisha came off the deck the same instant she did.

"Omega Four?" Michael asked over the intercom. Bulked up with all his gear, he barely fit beside her. His pack was crammed in beside the big ammo cans that filled the helicopter's backseat.

"Got me. Something Ramis cooked up. Omega is 'the ending' and there are four of us. At least that's all I can think of. I didn't brief him on the mission other than to say we'd be gone for a few days, but he's not stupid. He knows that we're why he moved his ship."

As she slid down to wave height and set course for an uninhabited strip of the Georgia coast, Claudia decided that wasn't a bad name for this flight. She just hoped it was a lucky one.

"Let's hope it is not the ending of us." Michael echoed her own silent thought as he so often did.

A glance over at him in the last of the light didn't reveal whether or not he was joking. She didn't think he told jokes, or if he did, they were too subtle for her to notice.

They were compatible in that way too. Trisha always had something to say and some tone to say it in: wry, amused, teasing, flirty… All that did was make Claudia tired. She'd take Michael's forthrightness any day.

"How did Bill and Trisha meet?"

"She rescued him from a Somali pirate attack, and he wasn't very happy about it."

He must have noticed the sideways turn of her head despite the darkening cabin.

"Honestly. He was undercover on Somali soil as a mercenary to track the hostages. She refused to leave without him. Turned out that without question, she saved his life."

"So, then smack, it was happy ever after?"

"Took them a bit to get over being angry at each other. Then no one ever thought Trisha would settle down, her probably least of all. It took a bit, but yeah, it was pretty fast."

"Like us. We're happening so fast that you're still making my head spin, Colonel Gibson."

They crossed over the beach. They were now unwelcome and illegal invaders of the country of Georgia.

If they were caught, an international incident was the least of what would happen and "we were just passing through" wouldn't be an acceptable excuse, not without special permission and not in heavily armed helicopters packed with exotic gear.

"Feet dry."

Michael was glad that the cabin was dark enough that she couldn't see him flinch. He literally was in the dark. His PNVGs were turned off to conserve their batteries, and he wore the wrong type of helmet to plug into the Little Bird's ADAS camera gear. All he could see were the faint lights of the console, tuned to work with her night-vision gear, not his unenhanced eyes.

Claudia was racing them along a bare ten feet over the Georgian soil. In moments they were flying the ridges and valleys of the mountains that lined the Black Sea. Helicopters would be rare at night here, but not impossible. The Georgian Air Force owned approximately a hundred helicopters, though none would sound like a stealth-silenced Little Bird. Thankfully, the average person on the ground wouldn't know that their unique sound signature indicated a foreign power aloft. This first leg of the mission was considered low risk.

With no visual reference points, Michael had to clench his jaw against the nausea. Claudia was jerking and twisting the craft to retain her flying altitude.

Cut the bullshit, Gibson. It wasn't the flight that was making him feel sick to the pit of his stomach.

It was Claudia, and there was no point fooling himself. She really thought they had a future. And why wouldn't she? He hadn't said anything to disabuse her of the notion. They'd even talked about children, for crying out loud!

She nosed over a ridge and plunged down the far side, leaving his stomach still gaining altitude somewhere behind him.

He had to face it. He didn't dare let her get any closer, because he knew he was losing his survival edge, slowing down. Someday soon, maybe tonight, at some critical instant, he'd no longer be the fastest one. A kid with a tenth his experience but possessed of a nervous system wired up on speed-texting and full-immersion video games would be that hundredth of a second faster, and it would all be over for him.

There was no way that he could do that to Claudia. And yet she deserved to be told. Soon. He knew enough about soldiers to know that now was even a worse time to come clean than while she'd been planning the mission. She needed to be out on the edge if they were going to succeed.

Unlike Trisha who thought "edge" was a place you were supposed to live every minute of your day, even unlike a D-boy who hunted for "edge" as surely as he hunted the Taliban, Claudia used "edge" as a tool. Like a knife sharpened and honed, she had built up layers of skills and planning until she was so ready that "edge" would emerge at the moment it was needed.

If he told her they were over, he'd blunt that edge past recovery, at least for this mission, hopefully not for longer. If they were going to survive this, it wasn't because of his and Bill's skills any more than it would be Trisha or Claudia's flying. If they survived, it would be the perfect wielding of Claudia's intense mental edge.

"How fast we moved makes my head spin too," he told her. The bitterness of the half-truth was very hard to swallow.

~

Claudia focused on the flying. Her helicopter's systems included a highly accurate terrain map of the entire region that was synchronized and superimposed with what she was seeing. The stored map showed as a line-figure glimmer behind the night-vision infrared reality. There were problems with it though. Unlike Pakistan, Afghanistan, and Iraq, the map had holes. There were gaps where no analyst had reviewed and resolved conflicting readings. It was also several years since the file had been updated for Georgia and Azerbaijan as they were "friendly" nations. New buildings, bridges, power lines, and the like weren't necessarily on the map.

So, she flew more by instinct, following the terrain she could see rather than anticipating her route from a map she didn't dare trust.

It was a good analogy. She and Michael had moved into a new phase of their relationship. He'd begun as a lover but had shifted over to the role of protector as if they were a committed couple. It had occurred so smoothly and seamlessly that she hadn't even noticed the transition point.

She'd always been her own protector, and to have someone else in that role was surprising. It would take some thinking about. She'd been a loner for thirty years, the only child of a pretty checked-out family, her safety and her education mostly in her own hands. Fitting in had been just another skill, one learned at Annapolis that had transferred to the Marine Corps as easily as to SOAR.

Yes, she wanted to be with Michael so badly her body ached with it even now. But they needed to work out a few things, just so that she was clear about them.

Now was not the time. Too much of her concentration was needed to avoid flying them into the side of a barn, but after the mission maybe they could finish their interrupted leave. Then they would have a talk. And if it came out the way she expected—the way she hoped—it was going to move them to a whole new level.

She threaded through the dense population centers around Tbilisi without having to cross into Armenian airspace, then began descending into the flatter, more arid lands of Western Azerbaijan. At least Georgia was behind them. Azerbaijan was U.S. friendly and could probably be talked out of executing the task force if they came down on Azeri soil.

The main risk now was oil-well derricks. They grew thicker here than the desert grass. There were more than two thousand working wells within the Baku greater metropolitan area alone, and that wasn't counting the offshore rigs.

She couldn't climb. Anything over fifty feet and her detection avoidance system would start stuttering with intermittent traffic radar warnings. Near Baku, between the international airport and the military bases, she'd have to stay under twenty feet.

But the oil derricks were everywhere. She'd never seen anything like it.

She felt like she was flying a slalom course worthy of the Sochi Olympics after all.

Chapter 24

Michael noted that they weren't quite on fumes, but Claudia was well into the extended-range gas tank by the time they slid into Karachala Airport fifty miles southwest of Baku. Kara Moretti confirmed no flights inbound or outbound from the small airstrip. It had no commercial flights at all, and only a few private craft were parked there. The airport was a Soviet holdover used by few and nearly forgotten.

But not totally, which Michael had been counting on since his buddy at the SAS had happened to mention it as a quiet, out-of-the-way spot he knew if someone—oh, he had no idea who—might just want to land a plane there.

Kara circled her Gray Eagle *Tosca* from six miles high down to three—low enough to confirm no human-sized heat signatures at the airport, though she did spot a small family of deer. As long as Claudia's team kept it quiet, no one should even know they were there. They could just steal some fuel and go. At least things were starting out well.

Claudia and Trisha slid the Little Birds into the airport from the north at barely five feet above the ground and then settled to either side of a fuel tanker truck that was parked beside the field. Kara was the one who'd spotted the truck parked close beside the hangar when they were reviewing the initial satellite images. *Tosca*'s overflight had confirmed that the truck was parked in a different position than in the first reference photo. That meant it was still operational.

Michael flicked on his night vision and hit the ground running the instant the skids touched. He rapped his knuckles up the side of the large tank on the back of the truck as he trotted down the length of it. Over a quarter full. He tried not to think of how old this particular load of fuel might be.

While he hot-wired the tank truck, Bill climbed on top and began a survey of the surrounding neighborhood through his rifle's night scope. At ten at night, the closest light was a half mile distant. The air was still and the temperature was about seventy-five. They'd have accurate shooting to at least a half mile even without the sniper rifles.

By the time the truck was running, Trisha had spooled out the grounding safety line to make sure there were no sparks and Claudia followed close behind with the nozzle.

At her signal Michael hit the pump switch. It caused the fuel truck's engine to falter, then groan with a deeper note as it began pumping fuel from the tank into the *Maven*.

He climbed up onto the tank to help Bill keep watch. Ten minutes to max out the fuel in each bird. Twenty minutes on full alert. The pump was so damn slow—each wheeze and gasp of the old engine worried him—but they got a full load of fuel onboard both Little Birds with no sign of anyone being the wiser. Maybe they could use this stop on the way out as well. It was certainly one of the contingency plans that they'd discussed.

They'd also discussed ditching the helicopters off

the Iranian coast, stealing a truck, and trying to drive out across the desert. A hundred scenarios had been reviewed and the best had been chosen. None had been wholly rejected. Flying back through Karachala was one of the better options, but driving across the Iranian desert was far from the worst. Far.

Once the fuel was loaded, Michael made sure to wind the hose and wire back so that they would look unused. He considered breaking the pump's readout for number of gallons in case anyone tracked it, but he saw that it was already broken. He pulled off his hot-wire tools. The engine idled to a stop, then released a backfire as loud as a mortar barrage. He locked the door and bolted for the helicopter.

A single glance back as they pulled aloft and scooted off to the north showed several houselights flicking on in the distance. Maybe coming back this way wasn't the best option. Either way, they had their fuel and had made it through the first leg of their inbound journey.

Claudia hated this next part, but it was the best idea they'd come up with. It was time for the boys to go swimming and steal a submarine.

The port at Baku's south bay was a naval military base. And as paranoid as the Azeri were about possible attacks, it would be well guarded. Maybe not to U.S. standards, but certainly better watched than the airfield at Karachala they'd just raided.

Now she felt as if she was letting Michael go on without her. Three miles off Baku harbor, she and Trisha settled down to the wave tops. With no heavy weather anywhere on the Caspian Sea, the waves were barely a foot high.

They'd considered skid floats for the helicopters to perform this part of the operation. It would have allowed her and Trisha to wait right where they were. It would also have allowed them to land safely on the Caspian in an emergency. But they simply couldn't justify losing the extra hundred and thirty pounds of ammunition to rig the inflatable pontoons. That would have emptied the seven-rocket launcher. They'd already sacrificed one of those to the extended-range fuel tank. At least that choice of the hundreds she'd made had been an easy one.

She hovered inches off the water while Michael climbed out onto the skid and retrieved his pack from behind his seat. He pulled out goggles and snorkel, and slid out a small rebreather tank.

Then he pulled out something she hadn't seen last night that he'd stowed behind his seat. It was a cylinder about as long as his arm and big around as his leg—a bulbous housing, two handles at the sides, and a caged propeller. It was a DPV, diver propulsion vehicle. Its little electric motor could tow them quietly to their goal faster than they could swim. They also wouldn't be tired out when they arrived at the sub.

He noted her attention in the light of the tiny red flashlight he'd clamped to his swim goggles. "Under four hundred dollars; I bought them online. They have the range we need for this mission."

Claudia had been really worried about the plan of dropping them so far from shore. Michael had kept insisting it was no problem without explaining why. Because he had planned from the beginning to use a

DPV and simply not thought to tell her. And Emily said she'd managed teams up to eight people? Twice this many variables and four times the amount of communication required. The woman was amazing.

Claudia stuck her tongue out at him for not telling her.

He winked and then fell over backward into the water. The last she saw of him was two-raised arms making a circle around his head in a "diver okay" signal before he disappeared under the water.

It was a good moment. Claudia refused to think that it had at least been a good *last* moment. They'd get through this. They had to—there was too much waiting for them on the other side.

She lifted the *Maven* to five feet over the waves and Trisha did the same, which meant Bill must have gotten off as well. It was a short flight to Vulf Island, where they landed on the deserted strip of mud well off Baku harbor. The far end of the island had a small radar installation and a couple of the inevitable oil derricks. But the radar was watching outward for others attacking Baku, not someone parking a bird on the Baku side.

They landed and prepared to do the thing she hated even more than worrying. It was time to sit and wait.

Trisha shuffled her way across the sixty feet of oil-blackened fine sand beach separating their helicopters and slouched down into the copilot's seat, dragging on the headset Michael had been wearing moments before.

"This had better work, Casperson. I'm gonna be really ticked if Billy comes home dead."

"Me too," was all Claudia could think to say in response. She understood Trisha's humor, but it was unnerving. The image of her life if Michael suddenly wasn't in it was one she didn't like.

"Well, if anyone can live through this, it will be those two assholes. Can you imagine how insufferable their egos are going to become if this whole thing succeeds?"

"As big as ours?" Claudia offered.

Trisha laughed. She had the greatest laugh, and it was easy to join in.

They sat in silence and watched the distant lights of Baku. It was barely 2200, and they'd have hours of darkness yet to decide if they had to spend the fuel to retreat back into the desert and hide out through the daylight hours. The earliest they were likely to see the boys was around 2:00 a.m.

"This sure is something," Trisha remarked softly.

It sure was.

Chapter 25

Michael and Bill drove their DPVs elbow to elbow. With no running lights, it was the only way to be sure they didn't lose track of each other. They'd also tied ten meters of line between them, but hadn't needed it yet.

They were three meters underwater, approaching the south port. They couldn't see crap, and Michael's head hurt from the cold. The water was temperate, actually unseasonably warm for May, but still cold. He and Bill both wore thin-skin neoprene suits under their clothes, but he hadn't pulled on his hood. There'd been one in the Phase I package in his pack, but he'd been distracted by looking at Claudia. Dangerous mistake, but too late to rectify.

The DPVs tugged them along relentlessly. They were deep enough that they'd pass below any late-night fishing boats. Only big ships would draw deeper, and they'd hear those easily over the DPV's slight propeller noise.

He checked the GPS readout on his wrist and adjusted a few degrees to the north. The water clarity was only fair. While it was good enough to read the GPS, they'd have to surface for the final stage.

The DPV was attached by a short leash to a D-ring on his harness down at his waist; that did all of the towing. All he had to do was hold on to the handles to steer it. Still, his arms were starting to burn with the effort.

At least, in exchange for the thermal lashing his head

was taking, he had an amazing picture of her in his head. Full gear, in clear command of the mission, hovering as stable as a rock just inches over foreign waters and sticking her tongue out at him. God he loved that woman so much.

The thought chilled him more than the water rushing by. Maybe Bill had some suggestion on how to handle this.

No. Why would he? He was happily married, and if there was one thing the happily married wanted, it was for everyone around them to be in the same state. But that wasn't an option.

So he kept his head down and the motor switch on high rev as they were pulled into Bibi-Heybat harbor.

"I've never seen Michael so happy. Is he good to you?"

Claudia had no experience with woman-talk. The closest she'd ever come was Emily's discovery that she was having a second child. Yet here they sat side by side in a parked helicopter on the oily shore of a country that their team was robbing right at this moment. And the question had been asked.

She considered how to approach Trisha's opener, then decided that what the hell, she'd try honesty.

"He's amazing to me."

"Yeah, he's really good. I mean a good guy. I didn't mean—"

Claudia considered letting Trisha dangle for a while but she sounded so distressed as she dug her hole deeper and deeper that Claudia decided to throw her a rescue line.

"I already know about the two of you."

That didn't slow Trisha down for a second; all it did was change her course. "You do? He told you? Why that low-life slime. Aren't a woman's secrets sacred anymore? Next time I see him, I'll—"

"Say absolutely nothing. He didn't tell me. But there are times that despite being Mr. God of Special Operations Forces, he's actually fairly easy to read."

"Did he, uh… Never mind." Trisha's voice went soft.

"All you need to do is look at how he treats you to know how he feels about you. Maybe it's more like a protective brother now, but he'd defend you right to the grave." Claudia felt a chill at her own words.

"I don't know, Claudia. If he'd do that for me, I can't imagine what he'd do for you."

"Well, whatever it is, I hope he has no intention of dying any time soon."

Their conversation drifted from the men they were awaiting to the mission's plan and alternates, and then on to other missions they'd each flown. The time passed far more easily than Claudia had expected.

Michael and Bill shut down their DPVs before they rounded into the mouth of the south bay. There was a thin sheen of oil on the surface, not enough to coat you, but enough to smell. That's when he realized that he'd been smelling it since they'd approached Baku. His SAS pal had warned him, but he'd thought it was hyperbole.

"The whole place reeks of oil, pal. The air, the water—the banks reek of oil money—but all the rest just smells like oil," the SAS operative had said. And he'd been right. It was thick on the air. The oil was so shallow in places that it had been harvested for millennia using hand-dug wells. And it also was so deep in places that the first offshore undersea oil rig in history had been an Azeri rig in the Caspian Sea, long before the Texans even thought about tapping into the Gulf of Mexico.

They kick-swam into the harbor and surveyed their options. Third pier up on the left would be the Triton subs. They were close when Bill stopped Michael with a hand on his arm.

Michael stopped to tread water and turned in the direction that Bill was staring.

"Now isn't that a pretty sight?"

Michael had to agree. It really was.

Chapter 26

"Hi."

Claudia yelped—she couldn't help herself—and then grabbed for her gun.

Michael had simply appeared right by her shoulder. Even Trisha squealed in surprise. They'd been keeping watch. She had intentionally landed the helicopter facing down the beach. Between the two of them, they'd been watching the whole strip.

He continued to grin at her like an idiot. She checked her watch to see it wasn't even half past eleven.

"What are you doing here?"

"Aren't you glad to see me?" He was teasing her and enjoying himself entirely too much.

Well, two could play at that game. She grabbed the front of his vest by the D-ring mounted there and hauled him in. He tasted and smelled like the rest of Baku, but she was so glad to see him that she really didn't care. The heat flashed through her and she could feel it overcome him as well. Gods but she wanted to just tumble right down onto the beach with him, oil sheen or not.

Trisha whined, "Hey, where's *my* D-boy?"

Michael eased back abruptly, clearly recalling he was on a mission, not a fling. He pointed over his shoulder.

Beyond the point of land that made the west end of the beach, eighty feet of U.S. Coast Guard ship came into view.

"I thought there weren't any U.S. assets in the Caspian. Those bastards lied to us."

"No." Michael was back to looking very pleased with himself. "We sold this one to the Azeri Navy about a decade back. You can't tell at night, but she's dark gray now rather than bright white. So, we thought we'd take the old *Point Brower* for a ride."

"You idiot!" Claudia jabbed her fingers into his collarbone just above his vest and armor. He didn't even flinch. "The whole idea was to remain low profile! That ship is—"

"Going to be invisible because they expect her." His voice was absolutely calm, as if they were having a quiet conversation in a forest canopy. "She's known in these waters. And we have an Azeri officer on board who is only too glad to aid a pair of well-armed caviar smugglers in exchange for his life and a thousand manat, about eight hundred U.S. dollars. Even he doesn't know that he has a Triton-2M submarine in tow. We have it trimmed at about five meters depth."

"Caviar smugglers?" And she'd thought that just his body made her head spin.

"Sure. Big business on the Caspian. The Azeris set very tight catch limits on fishermen to sustain the fish stock. But the smuggling market for Caspian Sea caviar is so lucrative that their mafia can pay the necessary bribes and still turn a nice profit."

"Eight hundred dollars isn't much of a bribe."

"It's okay. He isn't much of an officer. Only one aboard, fast asleep and drunk out of his gourd on vodka. We also may have led him to believe this was just a test run and much more would follow if tonight went well."

Michael was so pleased with himself that he was being positively outgoing.

Claudia remembered Emily's instructions to be flexible and tried to reset her thinking. She checked her watch again. The original plan had them at this point by 0200 if they were lucky, and in position to hunker down for the day by 0400. There just wasn't enough time between 2:00 a.m. and sunrise to execute the plan safely and get out of the area. But they'd gained two and a half hours. If they moved fast...

She grabbed the D-ring on the front of Michael's vest and dragged him back in for a quick-smacking kiss.

"Okay, you done good. Can anyone think why we shouldn't go directly to Phase IV rather than wait out the day?" She gave Michael and Trisha a few moments to catch up with her. When they did, all she got was a "Hunh!" of surprise.

That was the answer she needed. She'd left two of the encrypted radios powered up—one on the team frequency and one that connected to the Gray Eagle circling somewhere above them.

Despite the encryption, she wasn't going to do it in clear speech.

"Hey, Brooklyn," Claudia called. "Talk to me."

Kara caught on to the schedule change faster than Michael or Trisha had, even though she hadn't been expecting that request until tomorrow.

Claudia powered up the display of the Gray Eagle's data that Kara was feeding back to her.

"Patrol on schedule." A flashing red highlight appeared on her display. All two hundred feet of a Russian Buyan-M class warship was right where it needed to be, if this were tomorrow night. The recent powerful addition to the Russians' Caspian Sea flotilla had been cruising the Azerbaijani coast as if the Russians owned it, harassing pipeline construction vessels, violating territorial waters, and generally being a royal pain in the ass. They were making it clear that no one was going to build a pipeline as long as Russia ruled these waters, even if by legal treaty it actually didn't.

With the vessel in place now, Claudia and her team should grab the opportunity in case tomorrow's schedule changed for some reason.

That was the key fact Emily had uncovered that had sent them hustling into Azerbaijan. An apparently unrelated bit of intel on the Russian patrol schedule had said that after tomorrow night, the Russians were going to up the ante by shifting over to day patrols, possibly kidnapping working crews or at least scaring them off.

That change would have made their present plan impossible; they needed the darkness.

Yet another reason to go for it right now.

Claudia smiled to herself. If this worked, the Russians' schedule was going to change a day ahead of schedule—and by a great deal.

"Sting 'em, Bumblebee," came over the radio.

"Will do, Brooklyn."

The Bumblebee nickname took her back to the desert for a moment, her beloved Arizona desert. She'd show it to Michael someday soon. Show him the most magnificent sunsets on the planet and sunrise vistas that made you feel so alive it was hard to hold them in your memory.

"Let's do it."

~

Michael swam back out to the boat, old *Point Brower*. Now it was going to get interesting.

So many times, Delta rehearsed, analyzed, and rehearsed again for a target only to be called off at the last moment. It was always energizing when they received the actual "go" on a mission. It didn't matter if the planning had spanned hours, days, or months; when it all came together, the feeling of satisfaction that all the preparation was actually going to be used was the same.

The old cutter floated off small Vulf Island—where the helicopters were still parked—about five miles to sea from Baku. Except for the distant city lights, the cloudless night was pitch-dark. The wave chop was low enough that he made good time back to the boat, which was little more than an outline against the stars.

On the afterdeck of the *Point Brower*, the Azeri officer greeted him with a hug as if they were long-lost brothers and a sloppy kiss on the cheek, and waved a fresh bottle of Xan Premium vodka, which he immediately forced into Michael's hands.

Michael sucked in a mouthful of vodka and then blew it back into the bottle so that it looked as if he'd taken a huge swallow. The guy was way past minding a little alcohol-sterilized backwash. He didn't have to pretend to gasp afterward; this stuff was high-test. He handed the bottle back and slapped the guy on the back hard enough to send him staggering into the rubber service boat sitting in its cradle on the ship's stern.

He found Bill at the helm.

"You had to give him another bottle? Wasn't he drunk enough yet?"

"No. He was starting to sober up, and we can't let him figure us out. Also, I heard the 'go' message from Claudia, and I had an idea on how to spice it up. We're actually going to use this guy"—he patted the helm of the cutter—"for something more than towing a submarine out to sea."

When Bill told him his plan, Michael didn't even bother to say he approved. It was a great addition.

Then Bill started reciting a message in Azeri for Michael to memorize. Once Bill told him what it meant, Michael gladly began repeating it back phonetically until he had it right.

Bill fed power to the *Brower*'s big engines, accelerating slowly enough to not strain the towline still attached to the submerged submarine. They headed northeast to the far point of the Absheron Peninsula and out toward the deeper parts of the Caspian.

"You'll want to broadcast that phrase starting the moment Phase IV is completed. Remember to sound very charged up."

"Thanks. Real helpful." Michael mumbled the phrase to himself several more times to anchor it in his mind. Bill went back to nursing along the boat that really should have a crew of eight to run her properly.

Michael went to check over his Phase IV kit once more. The only kit below that included an E and E bag. He sincerely hoped they wouldn't be trying to do an escape-and-evade across four hundred miles of hostile countryside. Especially not with the state of alert everything would be in if this worked.

It took most of an hour to steam around to the northern tip of Pirallahi Island at the very easternmost tip of the Absheron Peninsula. They were now at the very limit of where Azerbaijan's land reached out into the Caspian Sea.

On Pirallahi, a couple of smaller pipelines, each a half-dozen feet across, rose out of the ocean and came on land over the northern beaches. The island itself was quite populated, but the northern tip was industrial. The existing pipes led out to the offshore drilling rigs, pumping the oil and gas directly ashore.

There were also some new concrete foundations for unbuilt pipelines that showed up on satellite imaging but weren't in the news yet, which suited the D-boys' needs perfectly. Whether or not the new foundations were for the proposed Trans-Caspian line didn't particularly matter in the overall scheme.

They beached happily snoozing Auxiliary Officer Zadeh in the *Point Brower*'s rubber utility boat—without oars or gas for the engine. They found him a muddy island just a short swim from land and slipped another two thousand manat into his pocket. It should be enough to buy his silence, if he remembered anything at all.

They also left him with a radio—with dead batteries—set to the emergency radio frequency he had provided while still sober enough to do so.

"Part one of my ace in the hole," Bill had practically crowed after Michael had swum back from beaching the Azeri officer.

"Now, for part two." Bill drove the *Point Brower* so close ashore that he was making Michael nervous.

"You do recall that we're towing a submarine."

"Fear not, my friend. Water and I get along just fine." Bill anchored her close ashore.

Right. Never try to tell a SEAL anything about boats, because they already knew it. So, he'd keep his mouth shut. Besides, he had plenty to worry about.

Michael's job waited for him after Bill delivered him by submarine to his point of attack. What happened to the boat they'd used to drag the sub into position wasn't his concern. He trusted Bill to get it right because that's what you did with your team. Bill had proved his worth long before Claudia Jean Casperson came on the scene.

And he'd trust her with his life. Already was. And his heart too, which had become a problem.

He and Bill both pulled on their scuba gear again and slipped over the side to dive down to the sub.

Chapter 27

Claudia and Trisha had debated Bill's final cryptic message as they continued to sit on the beach of Vulf Island awaiting the start of Phase IV.

Bill had said, "Shoot the *Brower* from over the 21631. You'll know when. Into water. Four."

They'd agreed to send no messages in the clear despite the encrypted radio. It was overkill, but that was the right mental image for this whole mission. But there was "not in the clear" and there was cryptic.

The 21631 was the model number of the Russian's Buyan-M missile corvette—two hundred feet of a brand-new and very nasty breed of fighting ship. This one was presently cruising along the Azeri shore. They didn't know which specific ship he was—the Russians always called their ships by the male pronoun—and Claudia didn't care. All that mattered for their purposes was that it was the newer missile model and not the older 21630 gunship.

"Is your husband always so clear about what he wants?" Claudia kicked one of the pedals of her still parked and silent helicopter.

"Into water. Four. At least that part is easy." Trisha slouched lower, which was a hard thing to do in the tight Little Bird seats. "At least we know they're now off the cutter and boarding the sub."

"Phase IV has now begun," Claudia agreed.

"Past the point of no return." Trisha made her voice spooky, which Claudia really didn't need.

Their next signal should come from Moretti. Sure enough, the screen that was set to the Gray Eagle's data feed showed the small submarine moving away from the anchored *Point Brower* Coast Guard boat.

"As to the rest of his message..." Trisha waggled her hand back and forth. "Billy seems to think that we can somehow communicate without actually speaking. Usually he's right, but I think he sees it as a kind of game."

"I don't have time for games." Claudia knew she was snarling at the wrong half of this couple, but couldn't help it. Her attitude didn't appear to faze Trisha in the slightest.

"Oh, I don't know, Captain. That was a pretty damned hot kiss I just saw. Better than he ever gave—Shit! Sorry, Claudia. Didn't mean to say that. Just being envious because Bill wasn't here to give me one just like it."

Claudia left Trisha to squirm, not that she did it for more than a few seconds before continuing.

"Anyway. His message is that when they shoot the primary target, we should be hovering over the missile boat and fire at the poor old *Brower*. I'm guessing he wants to make it look like a two-shot attack by the bad guys."

Claudia considered it. "So...he figures the Russians will be too busy trying to figure out what's going on. They won't spot our stealth bird in the confusion, and we can make it look like a double-shot attack, making it even clearer that they are the guilty party."

"Uh-huh." But Trisha didn't sound any more certain than Claudia felt.

It seemed like a lot of trouble and risk for not much gain. Not Bill or Michael's style. Well, even if she didn't quite know why, she at least knew what to do.

They watched as the submarine disappeared into the depths and out of the *Tosca*'s sensor range. Now she wished she had ordered the ASW package for the Gray Eagle just so they could track the sub, but she couldn't think of what she'd have sacrificed from the payload they'd loaded aboard. No point in second-guessing herself now.

If the Russian ship stayed on track, it would pass five kilometers off the point of the Azeri peninsula. That was what had so upset the Iranians originally.

There were constant disagreements among the five nations bordering the Caspian. They hotly debated the borders for surface rights such as fishing versus subbenthic rights for minerals such as oil and gas. The collapse of the Soviet Union had turned the discussions into a real nightmare because now there were five countries where there had only been two. Proposals had been made and goodwill squandered with almost nothing solved.

The proposed Trans-Caspian pipeline would bypass Iran and Russia, at either end of the Caspian, and cut both countries off from the lucrative transport share. The only thing the two countries wanted more than having the resources routed through their own country was not having the other country receive a hundred percent of the traffic.

Russia had recently become very aggressive in its unwillingness to allow a pipeline to run through Iran or across the Caspian, although neither route encroached on their own resources or territory. The nightly circling patrol by their newest missile warships—deep in territorial waters, down the Azeri coast and back up the Turkmen coast where the other end of the line would begin—was an obvious threat that had worried Iran no end.

No one had been willing to risk confronting the Russians. Finally, Iranian President Madani had asked the U.S. President's wife for help in stopping Russia, even if the price was Iran losing the passage of the pipeline through their own territory.

Claudia would very much like to know someday what was on the other end of that equation. With this mission, the United States was doing a huge favor for the new Iranian president. Maybe that was payoff enough, strengthening the position of a friendly politician. Or maybe it was that all of that gas would be piped directly to U.S.-friendly Azerbaijan.

Looking at the drone image of the old *Point Brower* anchored offshore from Pirallahi still had Claudia perplexed. She wished she knew what her team had been thinking, but that was her answer right there. Her team. These were the best handpicked people she could find. Her job was to stop worrying and make sure the shot happened.

"I'll take the shot," she told Trisha. "You be ready to meet them at the RV." The prearranged rendezvous was a simple set of GPS coordinates another five miles out into the Caspian Sea.

"You get all the fun jobs." Trisha punched her arm. Then she sobered up. "I'm just glad it's not me running this show. I would have long since cracked."

Claudia didn't feel shaky. What she felt was terror, but showing that wasn't going to help anybody, least of all her.

The next step that was most dangerous, and her lover was going to be out there alone when he did it without even Bill to help him.

Chapter 28

MICHAEL DOUBLE-CHECKED AS BILL TOOK A FINAL SET of readings and then bottomed the submarine. They now lay a hundred feet down and five miles off the Azeri coast. The dim instrument lights on the small panel were the only things to look at while they waited.

The Triton-2M could carry up to six divers. It was a wet sub, but it allowed for pressure retention. So, inside the sub, Michael and Bill were only exposed to shallow water pressure and could rise without having to stop for decompression.

At a hundred feet down, they were too deep to receive any signals from the surface. The reason they were here was that they would look like nothing more than a rock on the bottom of the sea to the Buyan missile corvette as it passed overhead. The Russians were unlikely to also be watching astern, since the brand-new missile boat had no fear of attack in these waters. That was why the sub was the perfect solution. Even a small rubber Zodiac would stand a much higher risk of being detected in such a close approach.

For forty-five minutes, they sat on the bottom and waited. The timing was critical. The Buyan was moving at a leisurely pace since its whole purpose here was intimidation. But a missile corvette's leisurely pace was only a little slower than the submarine's top speed. They had to come up close enough behind to catch the Russian warship.

It was 1:00 a.m. when Michael heard the first sound of propellers turning at low speed. Bill floated in the seat beside him in the two-man cockpit of the sub, both of them using breathers hooked into the sub's air system. The air tasted of old fish and crude oil no matter how many times they spit out the mouthpieces and rinsed them in the salt water. A soft red light emanated from the simple instruments of the sub's control panel. Heading, speed, depth, and battery condition: the three-decade-old sub was not a complex craft.

The propeller and motor noise from the Buyan missile corvette up on the surface was growing louder, transmitted through water, the sub's hull, and the water filling the compartment.

He looked at Bill, but the man remained with his hands quietly in his lap. He'd been a SEAL for seven years before Michael had recruited him, so he'd know far more about the sound of a ship's passing than Michael.

So he waited.

Just a moment before Michael couldn't stand it any longer, Bill reached out to take the controls. Battery connected. Motors started at low rpms. Compressed air released into ballast tanks changing their buoyancy, and they began driving up and forward.

Michael released his seat belt and checked his gear for the third time. For Phase IV, he would be traveling very fast and light.

Fifty feet up, fifty to go. It felt like he was climbing a tree with a trunk that would never end. He wished he knew what to say to Claudia. Wished he'd said it. Instead he'd kissed her and simply let the fire that she was ignite inside him until it burned away all his words.

Well, need wasn't enough. Not if he wanted to keep her safe.

Fifteen feet. He shifted until he was crouched on the seat and his hands were on the release wheel for the overhead diver's hatch. The sound of the Buyan's screws was louder. Loud enough that Michael wondered if they were going to rise right into them, damaging both the sub and the ship and aborting their mission and perhaps their lives.

Ten feet.

Rising.

Five.

Rising.

The four hand-wide round portholes that surrounded the cockpit broke free of the water. Bill leveled the sub so that it didn't fully surface but remained high enough to enable them to see ahead. And, exactly per plan, they were looking at the broad, flat stern of the Russian ship *Grad Sviyazhsk* less than a hundred feet ahead.

Michael shot the wheel on the hatch and climbed up into the air. He left behind his face mask and breather. Bill brought the sub up another foot and drove it ahead at full speed.

Michael stripped open a waterproof bag and pulled on the dark-blue work shirt of a Russian navy machinist. He'd worn synthetic poly-blend pants that would still be wet but wouldn't obviously look so without close inspection. He pulled his bandolier of tools on to hold the shirt in place and felt naked without more weapons. He had an old AK-47 dangling over his shoulder and an outdated Marakov PM pistol, both filled with handloads that he'd done himself. Both weapons shot perfectly even after immersion in salt water, and both were silenced.

Bill was winning the race. The moment before he would have nudged the *Grad Sviyazhsk*, Michael ran the three steps to the raised vertical bow fin of the sub, placed his foot on the top, and leaped for the rail. He hung there from the stern rail of the Russian warship until Bill had safely slipped back beneath the waves behind him.

Claudia had seen the small sub surface once more on the Gray Eagle's screen. It was so close behind the Russian ship that it looked like they were the same boat.

Kara zoomed the Gray Eagle's display in for a close-up just in time for Michael to make his jump.

Claudia choked. She slapped her hands over her mouth to stop any sound, but then couldn't remove them.

Trisha placed a comforting hand on her shoulder as they watched the submarine disappear astern and a figure climb up and over the stern rail. Trisha shook her slightly as Michael began creeping along the afterdeck and climbed up between the two turreted 30 mm cannons.

Then she jerked Claudia's hands down and kissed her on the tip of the nose. The surprise was enough to jerk Claudia back to reality.

"What the hell, Trisha?" She pushed the woman away and rubbed the arm of her flight suit over her nose.

"Figured it was better than slapping you. Michael's the very best there is. We gotta go. You up for this?"

Claudia stared down at the digital feed showing the

green outline of a figure moving easily toward the missile launching tubes as if he belonged there. A crew of only thirty men to hide among. Well, he didn't have to hide for long.

"Okay." She nodded to herself. "Okay. I've got this." She grabbed Trisha by taking a handful of her flight suit's sleeve.

"Thanks, Trisha. Now get out of here." And she shoved the woman out of her helicopter so that she tumbled onto the sand.

Trisha hit with a roll and ran for her own bird. Less than a minute later, they were both aloft. The final moves were coming and they had to be in position.

Chapter 29

Michael knelt in the deepest shadow beside a starboard-aimed missile launcher on the *Grad Sviyazhsk* missile corvette. The four angled launch tubes rose out of the deck like a growing thing.

He rolled out his Phase IV kit on the deck. With an electric screwdriver, he had the outer service plate off it in a minute flat. The missile's plate was less forgiving; the missiles weren't designed to be serviced in the tube. He had just pulled the inner cover plate free when a deep voice called down to him in Russian.

"What are you working on, Yuri?"

Michael didn't look up but kept his attention focused ahead of him. In Russian he replied, "There is a warning light that we have a bad seal here. The captain said for me to fix right now. So I'm fixing it."

"You're not Yuri. Step into the light."

Michael sighed. He really hadn't expected the ruse to work.

He stepped forward, and even as the look of surprise crossed the man's face, Michael had his hand over the man's mouth. With a sharp twist, he broke the man's neck. Using the momentum of the man's collapse, Michael dumped him overboard. If the body was found, it would look more like an accident than if he'd put two bullets in the man's forehead.

Michael went back to his task.

Claudia almost caught one of the helicopter's skids in the waves when she saw the body fall over the side of the ship and quickly disappear astern. Catching a skid in the water would be fatal for the *Maven* and possibly for her as well. She had to be more careful. Michael was just coming out of his shell, and it would be cruel if she were to die and leave him only to crawl back into it.

When the figure returned to the missile tube, she calmed down and focused on her flying. Five more minutes and she'd be hovering less than thirty seconds behind the missile boat.

Michael slipped out his Phase IV hot-wire kit. It was much more sophisticated than the wire stripper and clips that he'd used on the fuel truck at Karachala. He jumpered into the programming lead without interrupting it. He didn't want any warning lights going off on the boat's bridge.

It took almost five minutes to program the missile correctly. One of the targeting options was a GPS system. The only problem was that the missile used the Russians' own GLONASS system rather than the American one his controller was set for. He had studied the Russian interface enough to know it well, but it took three full minutes to be sure he had the settings correct.

He set the timer and began closing up the access panels.

Claudia remained in position. Three feet off the wave tops and idling forward at the same leisurely four knots as the Russian ship. The waiting was killing her. The worst was she didn't know exactly what her next task was.

Bill's message had said she'd know when to fire, but that she was to do it from over the missile ship. That way any observers would think her own Hellfire missile had also come from the Russians.

He really could have been a little clearer.

Then she understood.

Bill's message did make perfect sense.

She heard Michael click his microphone key twice, announcing he was ready.

She swung hard to port, out over the Caspian, and then circled around to fly directly at the side of the ship. This time she did let the skids get wet as they cut through the wave tops.

Michael moved to the rail of the Russian ship and counted in his head. He double-clicked his microphone when there were fifteen seconds left on the countdown for the missile launch he'd just hot-wired.

At five seconds, he flipped his radio to the Azeri emergency frequency that Bill had given him.

At one second, he covered his face and eyes to protect his night vision and shifted behind a gun mount to protect himself from any backsplash from the rocket motor's exhaust.

The 3M-54 "Sizzler" lit off with a roar, and he could hear it depart in a big hurry. By the time he looked, it was far to starboard and headed for the land. Thirty feet of rocket was about to make a hell of a bang.

With the missile traveling at just under the speed of sound, he had to wait twenty-nine seconds for it to cross the five miles of ocean and find its target. All hell was already breaking loose on the Russian ship. Everyone was shouting for information that no one had.

The scale of the explosion when it struck the Azeri shore was incredible. Even in Delta, they didn't get to test such large-scale munitions. The tower of fire bloomed upward. The wooden forms-work for the foundation of where the new pipeline would emerge from the depths onto the land would be utterly destroyed.

He keyed his radio and began screaming his memorized message in Azeri.

The sharp sizzle of a Hellfire missile, a sound he knew well, snapped to life mere feet over his head.

He ducked, then looked up and back just in time to see one of the stealth Little Birds briefly lit in the backflash of the rocket motor. They'd fired so low that the Hellfire actually passed below the muzzles of the ship's turreted machine guns as it rushed toward shore.

There was more panicked shouting coming from fore and aft of the Russian ship. That was his cue. He started to repeat his message, then cut it off in mid-word. He pulled on a black mask, crossed his arms over his chest, and let himself fall backward over the rail.

He splashed into the Caspian and did his best to pretend he was an invisible piece of driftwood.

Searchlights and wild gunfire sprouted from the ship even as its big engines roared to life and the propellers dug in. But none of it came near him. As far as he could tell, they were simply firing in all directions in panic, a swath of 30 mm shells cast forth upon the deep.

Then he saw it. The Russians would probably never know they'd made a hit as they roared off into the night, because it wouldn't show on their radar.

By the light of the *Point Brower* patrol boat exploding into flames five miles away, he watched the shadow of a Little Bird helicopter tumble out of the sky.

By the time Michael swam the hundred yards separating them, the Little Bird had already sunk out of sight. He reached the middle of the flotsam and dove. He had to clear his ears twice before he was deep enough to reach the bird. With open sides, the cockpit had trapped no air to keep it afloat and the helo sank quickly.

In the darkness he found an opening and grabbed on. Copilot's side. No one there. He groped across the cockpit as the helicopter jarred hard and slammed into him. They hadn't had time to sink a hundred feet yet.

He ignored everything else and fought his way through the swirling wreckage over to the pilot.

His fingers found a limp figure in the darkness. He slapped the seat harness release and tried to shove the person out the pilot's side door.

Trisha or Claudia. Which would be worse?

Don't think, Gibson!

Something was blocking the pilot's opening. He reached out and felt steel.

If he could see, his vision would be tunneling from lack of oxygen. Years of training were all that kept him from the fatal mistake of gasping for air that every instinct in his body was screaming for.

Locking a fist through the pilot's harness, he dragged the pilot out the copilot's side of the craft. And launched them both into the air.

He gasped in a wracking breath that scraped across his lungs. He kept the pilot afloat, face up. No response. He couldn't tell if she was dead or alive. Or which of the women it was through all the gear.

Which would be worse? Telling Bill or accepting his own loss?

Stop it!

His head cleared from the anoxia.

How had he surfaced so quickly?

The mangled helicopter floated just a few feet away.

But something was different. It didn't float. It lay crumpled across the bow of a small submarine. Bill had dived under it and caught it across his bow.

Michael swam over, dragging the pilot with him.

"Who? Is she alive?" He heard the desperation in Bill's voice as he stuck his head out of the hatch.

"Don't know… Got to—" Breathe.

He handed the pilot to Bill without stopping to look and climbed back into the helicopter. He found the timer on the self-destruct charges, set it for ten minutes, and pulled the pin. He gave the Little Bird a kick, and it slid off the submarine and began its final plunge into the depths.

Bill was looking at him when he turned. "It's Claudia. She's breathing, I think. Hard to tell."

"Give me a harness. We'll run on the surface."

In moments they were rigged and heading east at five

knots. He sat with his back against the rear of the sub's little conning tower. His feet dragged in the water to either side.

And Claudia lay in his arms.

Chapter 30

Michael was thankful that the exfiltration was uneventful, but that was the only good thing.

Trisha waited on the abandoned oil derrick that they'd identified as a rendezvous point. They hadn't dared risk radio traffic. By now, every frequency was being monitored. Azeri patrol boats were circling the wreckage near shore and hunting for any watercraft.

To lighten the load of the *May*, they stripped the ammunition cans out of the backseat and the weapons off the external mounts. They loaded it all into the submarine.

Bill pointed the sub northeast and set it for a slow descent. He rode it down for the first minute to make sure it was on track before surfacing and swimming back to the derrick.

In two hours, ten miles away and five hundred feet down, a demolition charge would destroy the craft along with its load of U.S. military hardware. From that depth, nothing but a few air bubbles would reach the surface.

Michael climbed into the Little Bird's tiny rear seat and cradled Claudia against him. The engine spun up, not fast enough. She took off, not soon enough. Medical help was several hours too far away.

They'd determined that Claudia was breathing and had no external signs of injury. It was all they could do.

It would be four long hours back to the *Peleliu* before they could learn more unless she woke on her own.

She didn't.

Chapter 31

Claudia woke slowly. Sounds, smells, soft voices impinged. Clean sheets. Echoes that told her she was aboard a ship. She opened her eyes to dim lights and Trisha slouched in a nearby chair.

"Hey there."

Trisha jolted upright. "You're awake?"

"No. I'm speaking to you from beyond the grave."

"Uh, okay." Then Trisha offered one of her electric smiles. "As long as you're speaking, I'm cool with it. What's it like over there?"

She inspected the room again. The *Peleliu*'s infirmary. "Safe."

"Safe is good."

Then it crashed back in. She tried to sit up and her head nearly exploded. She collapsed back onto the pillow.

"Yep!" Trisha was back to her merry elfin self. "You should have stayed beyond the pale. On this side of it, you have a really impressive concussion. Doc's been hovering for three days. I should go get her."

"No, wait." Claudia grabbed Trisha's arm to keep her in place, wincing against the wave of nausea even that motion set up. "If you do, they'll want to talk about all that medical crap. What happened?"

"What's the last thing you remember?"

"Falling out of the sky after they shot half a dozen shells into my turbine by pure blind luck."

"Right." Trisha settled back in her chair and propped her feet up on the bed. "I heard that was pretty spectacular. There was at least one shell that didn't hit your turbine. It dug a major groove in your helmet, probably what concussed you. The boys said something about rescuing you with the submarine, but I never did get the whole picture."

"They're okay? And you?"

"We're all fine. They're around somewhere. You were the only one hurt."

"They dragged your sorry behind out to the rendezvous point and we flew back, even hit Karachala airport again to fuel up on the way home. They had to waste the *Maven*, the sub, and every bit of my beautiful arsenal."

"Bill me." Claudia lay back and could feel the sleepies coming over her again.

"The mission was a hundred percent."

Claudia fought back to full consciousness and opened her eyes to show she was listening.

"That radio message that Michael transmitted about the Russian attack was done in the name of that drunken officer they'd bribed, then safely marooned. He has very humbly and quietly accepted commendation as a hero of the Azeri people for crying out his warning, even if the warning came too late." Trisha grinned wickedly. "Apparently he slept right through the whole thing."

"But no one questions a hero."

"But no one questions a hero," Trisha agreed. "Bill and Michael did some quick communicating with the White House. A story was leaked about how the officer had suspected the Russians of preparing an attack on the future Azeri pipeline. His ship's radio broken, he set out solo to defend his home soil but was too late and had his ship shot out from under him. Only the emergency radio in the rubber utility dinghy allowed him to cry his warning."

Exactly what Claudia had figured out as she set up her final attack run. A hero and the loss of his ship gave a focus for the news and the people of Azerbaijan. United for the moment by something deeper than oil. They'd found pride in one of their citizens, a man apparently savvy enough to know when to keep his mouth shut.

"The Russians tried denying it. Right up until a European mapping satellite just, ahem, happened to be making a pass and testing new video technology for the first time. Kara captured crystal-clear images of the two shots and released them directly to a news service from a British lab that no one has ever heard of or will again. Kara says you did great, by the way. She didn't even have to edit the footage to make it look as if both shots came from the Russians."

"So glad I could help." She could feel her voice slurring. She fought against the sleep; she wanted the whole story. "Give me the end."

Trisha leaned forward and took her hand, which helped Claudia focus her attention.

"Russians are backpedaling as fast as they can. The whole crew on that patrol boat are probably going to the gulag or something. The blame went right up the ladder—to levels we'll probably never hear about—laying blame right and left on whoever ordered the aggressive patrols in the first place. Iranian President Javad

Madani has stepped into the breach with a Caspian Sea cooperation accord or some such thing. He's the hero of the hour."

Claudia nodded, letting her eyes drift closed. It had worked. A crazy, impossible gamble that only ten people would ever know about—from Emily Beale to the President to her action team—but it had worked. And they'd made it back.

"Where's Michael?"

If she managed to speak her question aloud, she didn't stay awake for the answer.

For three days Michael, who had never doubted his actions, had come to doubt his sanity. Each hour he sat with Claudia, worrying over her unconscious state, had been torture. Each hour away from her had been worse.

Michael had finally descended into the unused bowels of the ship to get away from everyone. People who'd never spoken to him before were suddenly asking if he was okay, if there was anything they could do for him. He must really look like shit.

Of course, he hadn't slept since that chair in the Scottish B and B.

Until now.

He'd been deep in the back corner of one of the empty barracks spaces usually packed with Marines. He'd sat because his legs were actually shaking with the exhaustion of his pacing.

Michael didn't remember lying down on the bare mattress or the slam of exhaustion that knocked him out.

But he remembered the nightmares.

He never had nightmares.

Claudia falling from the sky, except this time the shell had been through her heart, not her helmet.

Nell breaking a branch beneath Claudia's feet for sheer spite, sending her plummeting to the forest floor.

Worse, watching her face twist in agony as he was the one who fell, Claudia's face staying in perfect focus even as he tumbled away from her to his death.

He woke as he slammed into the Somali desert from fifteen thousand feet, fighting a parachute the whole way, only to remember moments before he hit that he'd forgotten to pack it before he jumped.

It was wrong.

It was so wrong.

There was only one answer for either of them.

He hated it.

But that made it no less true.

The next time Claudia woke, she was surrounded.

Her infirmary room was crowded with the women of SOAR. They were all here, even Dilya. The doctor had to practically fight her way through.

Claudia's head hurt less and she was hungry. A bowl of soup arrived along with an admonishment not to try standing up yet, but she was able to sit up as the others crowded around her, perching on her bed and the empty ones to either side.

"So, you survived one," Lola Maloney said once the doctor was gone.

"I don't know what you're talking about." But then

she studied their faces and could see it. Lola, Connie, Kee—they'd all survived a black-in-black. Of course they had, they'd flown with Emily Beale, the master pilot of the 5D. These were the women who'd flown with her.

Even… "You too?"

Dilya grimaced. "Sort of by accident. I was just trying not to lose my new mom."

Kee wrapped her arm around Dilya's shoulders and softened as she did every time they were together. They were of a similar height, but that was the only thing they had in common. Kee was a curvaceous Eurasian sharpshooter from the streets of LA with narrow dark eyes and severely black straight hair. Dilya was a dark-skinned Uzbekistani war orphan with round eyes of piercing green and had a slenderness that spoke of still having a ways to grow. Yet arm in arm as they presently sat, they were no less family.

Trisha leaned in to whisper with one of her winks and saucy grins. Everyone else leaned in to listen.

"She didn't just survive it. She led it."

"Whoa!" was the universal reaction around the room.

"Only Emily ever led any of ours," Connie observed. The others all looked at Claudia in surprise but, she noted, none of them was asking how Connie knew that. Connie simply knew things and that was enough.

"So, Captain Casperson…" Lola looked down at her as she finished her soup and set it aside. "You led one and brought your team out alive with no one knowing what you did."

Claudia nodded carefully.

"You know how I hate it when Trisha is right, but

I'm thinking that maybe you really are goddamn good enough to belong with the women of SOAR."

~

Michael stood outside the door to the infirmary and listened.

Captain Claudia Jean Casperson really was that good. Her laugh that spilled forth moments later pulled at him. It wasn't the hysterical loss of composure at the base of Nell. Or sheer delight at something new. It was a sound of welcome.

It was not a welcome he could accept, no matter how it drew him. He was Delta. He was "other." He'd been too long in the field and now understood that. There was no path back from so far afield to what was happening in that room.

They were bonding. Stories of Emily, of themselves, of their husbands. They were community.

He was not. He had a team; he had missions. He couldn't afford community. And he wouldn't risk exposing Claudia to that. She deserved better.

She deserved not to wake up at night and wonder if her lover, if her husband, if Colonel Michael Gibson lay dead, bleeding out in some godforsaken hellhole.

Claudia Jean Casperson deserved better than him.

Chapter 32

MICHAEL SAT AT THE TOP OF NELL. THE WARM SUMMER breeze had been replaced by one of the chill fogs on which the redwoods thrived. Yet he stayed. When darkness fell he didn't even bother rigging a Treeboat, merely zipped his jacket up tight to his chin, tucked it down into his safety harness, and dug his fists deep into the pockets.

The storm that had been sweeping in from the Pacific as they left Nell aboard Emily's helicopter had been short but brutally sharp. Several Titans had fallen. Two near Arcata, one up in Jedediah, and another here in Del Norte. It was a devastating loss, four of fewer than fifty.

Nell had survived, but not unscathed. One of her major tops—though not the highest—had broken and crashed down, only to snag in the lower branches. Some of the wreckage had broken through to make a wide debris field around the base. Some of it still hung here, leaving the upper canopy clogged with hangers and widowmakers. He should never have climbed her.

Years ago, a friend had closed the entire Atlas Grove to climbing—including a half-dozen Titans grouped together—because of this exact situation. His friend had waited for years before the branches had finally released their shattered pieces, many two feet across and dozens of yards long, to crash down into a debris ring around the tree's base before he dared climb there again.

Nell was unclimbable now. Michael had never once in his life pointlessly risked his life, not until he'd made this climb. He'd taken a thirty-foot whipper when a branch he'd been anchored on had let go. Only the fact that he'd crossed over to the other side of a main branch before he fell, and that he'd been fast enough with a knife to cut himself free before the broken limb had dragged him down, had saved his life.

So, he sat for the last time atop this tree even though he knew he'd never again find peace here. It would never be the same.

He didn't begrudge Claudia Jean Casperson that loss. Every branch here was filled with the memory of her laughter, of the gifts she'd given him.

His resolve had been softening throughout the mission; he'd been wondering if he was right in his plan to push her aside for her own good. But then he'd seen her fall from the sky. He'd cradled her lifeless form for hours and waited until he knew she'd be okay. He knew the pain of fearing connection to another human being and the loss that could cause.

Michael would never do that to her.

He'd left the infirmary doorway without entering. Packed his gear and arranged transport off the *Peleliu*. One the flight deck, he'd taken Bill aside and told him he was now the lead Delta liaison position with SOAR's 5D.

Bill hadn't understood.

Michael should have expected that. What he hadn't expected was the massive fist that had crashed into his jaw moments later.

He refused to rub it though it still ached. Michael

had put in for some of the massive amounts of leave he'd only rarely taken and come back to the redwoods. To Nell. His parents' kind questions about the woman he'd taken aloft just the week before stung. He'd been unable to answer. He'd simply taken the truck keys, turned around, and walked back out the door.

They even still had her duffel. They'd been unable to reach him to ask where to send it because he'd been in communication lockdown for the mission. It rested on the passenger seat of the truck parked in the brush down by Highway 101.

He sat through a second sunrise and sunset. He should eat. Drink water. Climb into a sleeping bag.

Instead he watched the stars poking in and out of the fog.

Half of what he did was practice for missions; the other half of the time was spent planning for success and analyzing failures. So, perhaps it was time to analyze why he and Claudia Jean Casperson had failed.

Michael climbed down from the tree, stripping the climbing gear behind him as he went and testing each branch thoroughly to make sure he'd reach the ground alive.

He crawled out through the thick brush and dew-wet ferns to the truck. He backed it out of its hiding place and began driving. It wasn't until past Arcata that he realized he was headed south rather than north toward his parents' home.

Somewhere past San Francisco he became aware of where he was going. He wouldn't think about why or what to expect there. He simply drove and waited for enough of the road to pass beneath his wheels for him to arrive.

Bumble Bee was a small town in the desert, but not dusty like Somalia or Azerbaijan. The air had a crisp clarity, dry and clear. To Michael it felt as if he could see forever.

The blue sky above the redwood trees was almost always soft with moisture, sometimes as clouds, sometimes simply as a softening of the blue. In the Arizona desert the blue was a slap in the face. It was as if you'd never seen the true color blue before and now you'd been given a new sense just for that sole purpose.

A bright yellow sign, almost the only color not found in nature here, informed him there were seventeen people, forty-five horses, and a hundred and sixty-one cattle in Bumble Bee. Also that the town had been here since the Civil War a century and a half earlier. Some of the buildings had fallen, some looked as if they would fall the next time an overly stout squirrel ran by. A few were solid though—some of stone, some adobe. Just a scattering of human signs amid the vastness of the arroyo-and-ridge chaparral.

Michael found her home just before sunset. The old wooden house had a tar-shingle roof and "Casperson" carved into a wooden post by the road. It wasn't her home, but it was her house. Like him, she didn't live here; she only came to life out in the desert.

No lights. No car, though the tire tracks in the short driveway were recent, not more than a few days old. It was a small one-story house that might have once been blue. He shaded the window against the bright sunlight and inspected the dim interior. While the outside of the glass was coated with a thin film of dust, the interior looked neat enough.

His knock went unanswered. When he knelt to pick the lock, it looked frozen with age and disuse. He turned the knob and the door swung quietly inward. No need to lock your door in a town of nineteen people. No intruders would come calling.

He looked down at the narrow threshold and hesitated. It should be sacrosanct. None would cross this strip of wood uninvited. No one except a colonel in the U.S. military hoping to find some answers.

There were few answers in the small house.

It was a two-up, two-back arrangement. Enter into the living room, kitchen left. Two bedrooms to the back down a narrow hallway of beige paint, rear exit straight ahead letting in a thin light through the dirty panes of the back door.

The interior was clean, dusty but far from abandoned. A well-worn couch and two equally weary chairs. Claudia's appeared to be the right-hand chair because it had a stack of books, a close reading light, and a small table that would hold a teacup and a small plate of food. The other chair and the sofa hadn't been used in a long time.

In the kitchen he found no food other than some canned goods. The floor creaked down the hallway. Even stepping only on the nailed rafter lines, it still squeaked at his every step. No silent entry here.

The larger bedroom was stripped bare, while the smaller one had a single bed, chair, and dresser. Neat as a pin. No, neat as a soldier's bedroom. There were no certificates, no knickknacks, yet the room was far from barren. The walls had been covered with photographs of the desert: unbelievable sunsets, a racing rabbit with hind legs blurred in movement, a towering saguaro cactus with bold, white blooms on the tip of each arm. An old horse looking at the photographer. Her desert brought to life inside.

In the corner stood a beautiful wooden recurve bow and a worn leather quiver of arrows. The goddess hunter. He could feel her nearby, as if she was watching over him.

Michael returned to the living room from studying the images as the last of the daylight failed. He lay down on the braided rag rug that covered the old wooden floor and settled in to wait for first light.

The heavy tread on the front stoop had Michael rolling to his feet. He had no sidearm, was even disoriented for a moment until he recalled where he was. Claudia's living room.

An old man, once a large one, stood at the front door blocking the late-morning light. Michael didn't recall sleeping. Here in Claudia's house, his sleep had been long and dreamless. Restful. So different from the tortured catnaps that had barely sustained him since leaving the Black Sea.

"You can't be squatting here, son. This house belongs to someone." The big man's voice rasped with age but you could still hear its firm core. A shotgun dangled in the crook of the man's arm; no real threat, as Michael could disarm him long before he could get it raised and his finger to the trigger.

"I'm looking for…a friend."

"What makes you think your friend is here?"

Michael liked that the man was careful enough not to reveal the resident was female.

"I served"—he winced at the past tense, but pushed through—"with Captain Casperson."

The man didn't ease his stance and neither did Michael.

"And would she be pleased to see you asleep on her floor like you owned it?"

Michael had to consider that for a moment. Then he knew the answer to the first of the many questions he had. "I have to say, sir, I rather expect she would not."

The old man harrumphed but still made no move to raise the weapon. "When was the last time you ate, son?"

"Been a while, sir."

"It's coming up lunchtime. You come on over, and we'll see about fixing at least that part of it. Be sure to close the door behind you."

Michael made a guess about who this might be. "Would that be to keep your wandering cows out of her kitchen, sir?"

Mr. Johns nodded as he moved off the stoop and waited for Michael with only the slightest hint of a smile. "That. And she has a habit of shooting vermin with that bow and arrow of hers."

Michael closed the door softly and followed the old man down the road.

They sat out on his back porch talking well into the afternoon. The dry hills rolled out into the distance, with scrub tree, reddish sand, and jutting bare rock defining the steep hills above dry arroyos. The stark, dark green and long stretches of exposed earth were such a sharp contrast to the thickness of a redwood forest that Michael felt as if he were floating just a little above the world and looking down on it.

Long after the tuna fish sandwiches were gone, Mr. Johns admitted that he "might have seen Claudia pass through a few days ago."

"You were the one who taught her to fly?"

"She tell you that?" The man nursed a smoking pipe, Michael a lemonade.

"I can see the old Bell 47 up behind your barn there. She flies like she had an exceptional teacher early on." The front bubble of the helicopter was barely visible from where they sat, but it was enough. It was also enough to see that no rotor blades were still attached to the old craft.

"I taught her how to fly, but the way that girl flies, she found all of that herself."

"Best I've ever seen."

Michael liked the old man. His silences were a comfortable pace for him, no matter how badly he wanted to find Claudia. He was enjoying this time, but he was starting to feel itchy.

"You've seen a lot fly?"

"Yes, sir. The very best. I've seen them not come home too."

Again the heavy nod. Clearly the man had served, but if he didn't want to talk about it, Michael wasn't going to ask.

"She's never had a man come after her before."

Michael pondered that a bit. "Still not sure how she'll take it that I have."

"There's the rub, Colonel." For he'd insisted on calling Michael by his rank once he'd revealed it. "I'm not a big fan of sending extra burdens her way."

"Neither am I. But I have…things I've done that don't feel right. I'm not used to that. Claudia, she has such clear vision. I'm hoping she can see the sense of it."

"And I'm betting that she's at the center of the sense of it."

"She is, sir."

Mr. Johns inspected him a while longer. Then, with his pipe stem, Mr. Johns pointed up into the hills.

"She left two days before you came in. Might be at the Castle Creek Wilderness up that way. I can lend you a horse just as I lent her one. Only seems fair."

"Never learned to ride, sir. Don't really have time now." He rose to his feet.

"You're just going to walk into the desert, young man?"

"Yes, sir."

"That isn't some playground out there."

"I've walked through much worse."

He returned to his truck and assembled a small pack with water, food, and a few other supplies. As he crossed by the back porch on his way toward the hills, the old man stopped him and inspected him closely.

"Are you the one that did it to her?"

There was no need to ask what had been done to her. He still had the lingering ache of Bill's powerful blow if he needed a reminder. He let his silence be his answer.

"Expect you don't want my opinion much, but it

looks like you done the same to yourself, young man. Walk soft. She's the best woman I ever met besides my wife."

Michael nodded and turned for the hills.

Claudia was the best woman he'd ever met too. That was the problem.

Michael started in the general direction that the old cattleman had indicated. Over the rise, he found a worn trail. The thorny brush was dense, unbroken along the sides of the trail, no hoof marks in the dirt. No one had passed this way in a long time.

He backtracked and found two other likely trails. Pulling a shirt out of his pack, he tied it around his head and let it fall over his shoulders to keep the sun off. He ranged a hundred yards up each trail. On the northern track he found a single preserved hoofprint in the soft sand. It had a horseshoe.

Even at a trot it took him until sunset until he knew she must be close. Less erosion of the prints. False leads along a streambed had cost him more than an hour. Guessing that the stream was the last water he was likely to see for a while, he drank his bottles dry, refilled them, and dropped in a couple of purification tablets.

She'd crossed over two ridgelines on her way and skirted the edge of a steep canyon. If the Sonoran Desert was this hot in May, it must be brutal in summer. The shirt he'd been using as a headband was white with salt that he'd sweated out during the long afternoon and evening of tracking. He popped a couple of salt pills.

Michael scanned the three possible trails and two

ridgelines that lay ahead of him in the last of the light but could discern no clues. If she had a fire, she knew how to control the smoke.

He'd lose the trace in the night, so he was forced to stop. He tried a flashlight, but it was insufficient to see trail signs.

He hunkered down to wait.

A whole night…

He wasn't willing to wait another whole night.

In the failing light, he noted and memorized the various marker shapes of the landscape: two ridges lined up due east and a single high hill at three hundred degrees to the northwest by the compass, with a lonely lightning-struck tree clearly marking its crown.

Now he knew he could return to this point in the morning if he had to and start over. He waited until the stars came out so that he could remain sure of his orientation. Thankfully, the desert sunset was as fast as it was dramatic. The evening sky shimmered in oranges, golds, and reds that had come out of the same vivid paint box as the afternoon sky's blue.

Once the show had ended and the few lingering high clouds were too small to obscure the sky, the stars shown like needle pricks in the jet-black night. A crescent moon after a new moon remained aloft, enough for him to see a boulder before he walked into it, but not much more. He'd lose even that bit of light by midnight, so he'd best hurry.

He set off in sweeping arcs that expanded along the most likely lines. Three hours later, the faint scent of fresh horse dung led him to a narrow track cutting up along the side of a steep slope. A quick inspection with his flashlight indicated broken branches to either side, just the kind a rider's boots and stirrups might make. He followed that until again the landscape opened before him.

The moon was setting, so he watched the direction of the stars as he once more began tracing sweeping arcs across the landscape.

It was still an hour to daybreak when he scented the char of a wood fire, though he could spot no light. The breeze was so light and variable that he followed the elusive trace down into steep rocky clefts and into tree tangles. He almost stepped on a family of sleeping deer but was able to back away before they took to their feet and gave away his position.

He was finally close to the campsite when a voice spoke from the darkness. "I hear you out there, Michael. Go the hell away."

She didn't sound angry; she sounded weary. As if she was sick of it all.

Claudia didn't have the energy to look up as Michael stepped from the trees.

"How?"

Of course he'd want to know how his field craft had failed.

"There's a night cricket about a hundred feet over that way that stopped singing twenty minutes ago. You were about fifty feet to my other side when you knocked loose some dirt. Sounded like a deer, but it didn't recur. So it was you. My horse smelled you before either of those, but all she does is let out a huff when she smells something unexpected, so you wouldn't have heard her. But I did. Now go away."

She knew he wouldn't, so she wasn't sure why she even bothered saying it.

They'd given her two weeks' medical leave once she'd stopped falling asleep without intending to. Then Trisha and Bill had come to her together and told her that Michael was gone. She had waited until they left the room in the infirmary to cry herself dry. Now she was an empty husk, hollowed out by the events of the last weeks. She knew where he'd gone, of course—up his goddamn tree. Well, she'd rot in hell before she chased him there.

She'd come to Upper Dead Cow Spring to find the silence once more. It was here that she'd run her way from girl to woman. But how little she'd known then of the heart and the pain of a woman. Now Claudia needed the silence so that she could once more be strong enough to stand the noise of the world again. She wasn't there yet.

Hell! She wasn't even close.

Michael still stood at the edge of the clearing, the only evidence that he stood there was his silhouette against the stars. She'd been watching the remaining coals of her tiny fire, a remote observer to the slow death of its glowing heart.

If she asked him to go away a third time, would he? Claudia considered the question. Based on his stillness alone, he would. The man was so stupid that he would actually listen to her if she told him to go. If she were Trisha, she would call his bluff. If she were Emily, she go up and add her own fist to any damage Bill had already done—Trisha had told her that one when Bill wasn't around to be embarrassed.

But she wasn't either of those women. She was Captain Claudia Jean Casperson. A woman who loved a man who'd walked away without saying good-bye or trying to explain.

Yet still she loved him. That was her weakness. Her failure.

"Why are you here?"

He moved to the fire, squatted on the far side of the glowing embers. He reached out to place a dried branch from her pile onto the glowing coals, to nurse it back to life.

"Don't. Just leave the fire alone and answer the question."

"I'm..." He trailed off for several minutes. "I'm not sure."

"That's not very complimentary, Michael." She'd thought to be sarcastic, but Michael never understood sarcasm.

"It's the truth. I just knew I had to come."

She rubbed her forehead. That was one thing about Michael; he always spoke truth. He'd never said he loved her. He'd barely been willing to acknowledge the word "lover."

"Can you tell me why you left?"

"To protect you." He didn't even hesitate.

"From what?"

"From my death."

For the first time she wished she could see more of him than the soft fire glow that barely reached the toes of his boots.

"Are you dying anytime soon?"

"Not planning to, but it's possible."

"And that's why you left?"

"Yes. Watching you fall from the sky, I knew how I would feel if you died. I don't ever want you to have to feel that."

She'd had many strange conversations in her life, but this was one was definitely the oddest.

"Yet you've come back, but you don't know why."

"Yes."

"Why?"

"Asking me why I don't know why is like asking… why isn't fruit purple?"

"Grapes."

"Oh, right."

Claudia poked at the fire and the embers crumbled. If she didn't feed it soon, it wouldn't make it through to breakfast.

"How did you get here?"

"Well, I was up in Nell thinking about you."

"I liked her." *I wanted to visit her again someday.* Her heart ached with the thought. She couldn't bring herself to say it aloud. It hurt too much even thinking it; the memories of things that were so good but weren't to be.

"I'm glad. I shouldn't have climbed. That storm we saw coming in. She was damaged. Unsafe. I knew before I went up. But I went." His English was becoming stutters of images. "I fell. It's the closest I've ever come to dying in or out of Delta, doing that climb. No one would have known."

I would have. But again there were words she now couldn't say. She added a small stick to the fire. Its bark flared briefly, revealing his shadowed face.

"I knew I'd done the right thing, leaving you so that you wouldn't feel the pain if I died on a mission. But it doesn't feel right. I don't understand why. The more I thought about it, the less sense I was making to myself." He shifted in place as he hunted for words.

She left him the silence to find them and added another small stick. This one didn't flare, but it did start to burn with a sharp resin smell.

"I only knew of one person who would understand, who would see and could explain it to me. That's when I knew I had to find you."

"The most words you've ever spoken to me, and you're telling me that you had to find me so that I could explain why you broke up with me. Without a word."

"Uh…" He toyed with his bootlaces.

She still couldn't see his face and added a bigger branch this time. It would take it a few minutes to catch.

"Sounds pretty lousy when you put it that way…but it's pretty much right."

Claudia looked up at the sky, wishing there was some guidance there. The stars were supposed to lead the way, not confuse the path.

"You're so much better at that sort of thing than I am," he continued in the dark. "You understand how people work. I don't know how you do what you do, but in less than a week you built a team, pulled off a miracle, and got us out alive. I was best man at Bill and Trisha's wedding, and he flattened me on your behalf. I never even had a chance to block it. How?"

"That's not your question. Retain your focus." Because she desperately needed him to answer his prior question.

"Right. Good advice. So, uh, previous question was that I don't understand how something I know to be right could feel so wrong."

"You're still convinced that it was the right thing to walk away from me?" Claudia considered kicking the fire at him: ashes, embers, and all.

"Maybe not the way I did it. I can see that now." This time his silence was that of a man lost and she let him explore it. "It may have been the one…cowardly act of my life. I'm sorry."

"Is that supposed to make it all better?"

"No. But I am."

She was sorry too. And the apology helped. Even more important, how much had it taken out of a man like Michael to admit he'd been cowardly?

"We do dangerous work, Michael."

"I know tha—"

"Shut up. I'm speaking now."

She could just see him nod his head. A glance up showed that the sky was lightening toward dawn.

"We've both chosen that path. I fell in love with you—"

He grunted as if she'd just struck him.

"—knowing that about you. You think I don't understand how close we came to dying on that mission? You think my heart didn't stop when that body fell overboard off the Russian ship? Well, it did. But it went on beating. You know what hurt, Michael? It wasn't watching you risk your life. I was doing the same thing. It wasn't even waking up alone and you weren't there, though that was pain enough."

He shifted, almost reached out to her, but didn't.

It was good that he didn't as she would have laid her own blow atop Bill's. She couldn't quite make out his expression yet in the faint predawn light.

"What hurt was thinking that you could cut yourself off from the joy we shared. It was imagining that wonderful heart of yours closing back in on itself. I think together we offered each other a first glimpse of light." Claudia liked how that sounded.

"I've spent three days sitting here, right here. Going no farther than to find firewood. And I have decided something. I suffer from the same fault as you. I wrapped my heart in ice as much as you hid yours behind danger." She could feel the weight sliding off her shoulders, the armored carapace of the Ice Queen finally melting in the fire's light.

"I'm choosing to embrace that joy. I am a better person for loving you, whether or not you love me back. I know that now, and I'm going to embrace that. I couldn't have survived that mission without you, and I'm not just talking about you dragging me out of the helicopter."

A mountain pygmy owl passing overhead hooted a final call of the night as it sought its nest. The thin trail of smoke spiraled upward against the pinking sky. They sat in silence, the last of the stars fading away.

It was almost dawn before he spoke, though he didn't look up from the low, steady flames. His voice was different. More assured, like the man she'd first met, but also clearer somehow than he'd ever been before.

"I love you, Claudia Jean Casperson. From the first moment I saw you flying us off that beach in Yemen, I loved you. You are magic in the air and in my arms. I don't know how to live without you, but the thing I fear the most is hurting you. Which I've done while trying to protect you from just that. It makes no sense."

"Hurting each other happens, Michael. Between two people, it happens. But it is easier to find the way through it together."

He nodded and looked up at her finally. There was just enough light to see the softness of his dark eyes.

"I get that now. I have only ever been myself, truly myself, in two places: sitting aloft in Nell and being with you."

"I wish we could climb her again." Claudia wished it with all her heart.

"Maybe someday. Another storm a year from now, or maybe a decade, will blow down the broken sections, and we could climb her again. Oh"—he patted his breast pocket—"I brought you a present from Nell. After I survived my fall, I found this." He pulled out a long, black feather and twisted it slowly in his fingers.

It appeared to glisten, though the sun had yet to break the horizon.

"It's a raven feather. You find them on the ground, but it's the first I ever found among the branches. Very powerful magic. The Yurok and Tolowa peoples of the redwoods believe that the raven is one of the few powers who can travel to the land of the deceased and bring back the soul of someone who has died. It made me think of you, reborn after I thought you'd died."

And he didn't see that he too had been reborn from his own passage through the trees. He had come back to her wiser, even more thoughtful.

She loved him without question.

Her problem had been whether or not she could

forgive him. Inside she knew the answer. With his rebirth, there was nothing to forgive. He'd almost sacrificed his own heart to spare hers, but it didn't work that way. That too he now understood.

When he held the feather out to her, she didn't take it. Instead, she moved around the fire and knelt before him. She wrapped her hands over his to keep him from withdrawing so that they held the feather together.

"To the Yavapai and others of Arizona," she told him, "raven is the bird of creation. Raven who flew out of the dark womb of the cosmos and brought the light of the sun. Brought understanding."

Then she looked up into his eyes and saw herself there. Her better self, the one she'd forgotten in the misery of his departure.

"I love you, Michael. There's been no other. I can't imagine one. Whether we have a day or a hundred years, I want to spend those with you."

They leaned together until their foreheads touched. They stayed there in silence as the sun rose and lit the feather they both still held.

"Now might be a good time to use your words, Michael." Claudia could feel her smile growing for she knew what was coming next.

"Uh, what should I say?"

"You could try proposing to me."

"I thought I just did."

"In that case, the answer is yes."

"Good."

She waited. "You can kiss the bride now, Michael."

"Oh, right."

And he did.

Read on for a sneak peek from *Hot Point*, the next book in M.L. Buchman's scorching-hot Firehawks series

The sharp warning buzz of a Critical System's failure crackled through Vern Taylor's headset.

A momentary panic hit him as palpably as the time Mickey Hamilton had gotten drunk and decided that plowing a fist into Vern's chin made some kind of sense.

Vern had just flown his helicopter down into the critical "death zone." Helicopters that broke between fifty and four hundred feet above the ground were in a really bad place—too high to safely crash and too low to stabilize and autorotate in.

A glance out the window didn't improve the news. The Mount Hood Aviation firefighters' airfield was still two miles ahead. Below him was nothing but a sea of hundred-foot fir trees covering rugged thousand-foot ridges.

So screwed!

Meanwhile, the more rational part of his brain—that the U.S. Coast Guard had spent six years investing so heavily in training and that four more years of flying to fire had honed—was occupied with checking his main screen on the helicopter's console.

He located the flashing, bright red warning. Hydraulic failure in the primary circuit.

He smelled no burning rubber or hot metal.

Several things happened simultaneously.

The first thing was being seriously ticked off that the helicopter was trying to kill him.

Vern had been type-certified in the massive, ten-thousand-pound firefighting helicopter for precisely thirty-two hours and—a glance at the console clock—seventeen minutes. It simply wasn't fair to be killed on his second day flying this sweet machine.

The second thing that happened was he actually read the flashing message: *#2 PRI SERVO PRESS*. The backup hydraulic pressure warning system wasn't reporting any problems which meant it was still running to cover the failure of the pump's pressure.

Vern double-checked.

No secondary alarm.

He wiggled the cyclic joystick control with his right hand, which altered the pitch of the blades to control his direction of flight.

His chopper wiggled exactly as it should. The back pressure of the controls against his dry palm felt normal.

He tried restarting his breathing. That worked as well.

Then—with the practice of a hundred drills that had felt like a thousand under MHA chief pilot Emily Beale's watchful eye—his left hand came off the collective control alongside his seat long enough to grab the correct circuit breaker among the eighty other breakers, switches, and controls that made up the overhead console attached to the chopper's ceiling.

He pulled on the breaker which shut down the number two Primary Servo pump.

The alarm went silent and the blinking red warning on the screen shifted to a steady red glow. Then his hand returned to the collective, completing everything that really needed doing.

The third thing that happened—all in the same moment as far as he could ever recall—was the thought that Denise Conroy, Mount Hood Aviation's chief mechanic, was going to kill him even if the helicopter had decided not to. Breaking one of Denise's birds on your second day flying it solo and expecting to survive unscathed was downright foolhardy.

Among the pilots it was generally agreed that upsetting the head of MHA's helicopter maintenance team was not to be considered a life-prolonging experience.

Nor was disappointing Emily Beale, who had only certified him in the Firehawk yesterday morning. The four years he'd been flying the little MD500 for MHA wouldn't count for squat if he dinged up their newest twenty-million dollar bird.

He followed the other two Firehawks back into camp. They were the massive Type I juggernauts of the helitack firefighting world able to deliver a thousand gallons of water and foam or retardant to a wildfire. There were only a few helicopters that could carry more, and those were all far less agile machines. This chopper ruled the wildfire helitack sweet spot.

The Mount Hood Aviation Firehawks were painted gloss black with the red-and-orange racing flames of the MHA logo running from the nose and down the sides, they looked as cool and powerful as they really were.

The Firehawks were built from Sikorsky Black Hawk helicopters. Each one was an eight-foot-high, ten-foot-wide, and forty-foot-long nasty-looking machine. Black Hawks, no matter how prettily painted, always appeared to be looking for a fight. They were the tough boys on the block, even if the two in front of him were flown by women: Emily, ex-military and kind of terrifying truth be told, and Jeannie, one of the most competent and pretty fliers he'd ever met.

How in the hell had some photographer guy snapped her up? Jeannie was awesome. Not that they'd ever done more than fly together—it wasn't like that between them—but seeing her look so damn happy had really emphasized how totally lame his own relationships had been.

Closing his eyes for a moment, he braced himself. Stepping on the rudder pedal, he twisted the tail of the five-ton helicraft to the side. He shifted the cyclic joystick in his right hand to compensate. Again, it felt completely normal, proving that indeed the backup hydraulic system was operational even if his breathing still sounded harsh over the headset and microphone system he wore. Now he flew mostly sideways but remained in formation with the other choppers in order to look behind him.

He opened one eye. A cloud of black smoke was streaming from his chopper. No sign of a fire warning on the instrument panel, so it was just burning off some hydraulic fluid that had spilled before the pressure loss was detected and he'd shut down the pump. They were under two minutes from Mount Hood Aviation's Hoodie One Base Camp.

Not enough time to burn everything off. Thankfully none of the fumes—nasty, astringent stuff—had leaked into the cabin. Vern realigned the controls to once again face forward and retain his position in the flight. He managed to also convince his breathing that he was back in control.

The MHA airfield and base camp lay less than a mile ahead now. It was perched low on the northern side of the towering mass of Mount Hood—eleven thousand feet of dormant, mostly, ice-capped volcano. It was easy to miss the airfield in among the towering fir trees and the vibrant yellows and reds of September aspens and maples.

It was the end of day, the mountain's shadow already lay long across the camp, and the grass airstrip was not empty like he'd hoped. The four smaller choppers of MHA's seven-bird fleet had already returned, parked along the north side of the strip up close to the towering Douglas fir trees that defined that side of the base. Pilots and ground crew were milling around them.

Along the other side of the field were the low buildings of the long-since defunct kid's summer camp that had been taken over by MHA. Though much of the structures' dark wood was covered with green moss, like so much else in the Pacific Northwest, they were dry and warm inside.

But were the other pilots, ground crew, and smokejumpers tucked away safe and warm?

No such luck.

They seemed to think that just because it was a beautiful late September afternoon everyone should be out at the cluster of picnic tables that served as the camp's main hangout. As he neared, he could see the dots of their bright faces turning like damned daisies following the sun—all tracking the path of his smoking flight.

And sure enough, the nightmare awaited.

There at the end of the row of four already parked choppers and the two smokejumper delivery planes was the maintenance truck. In front of the truck, stood five feet and four inches of livid woman with dark blond hair down her back—her feet planted as if part of the mountain's basalt shield. Though not close enough to see, he knew she'd be standing with her arms crossed over one of the nicest chests he'd ever seen.

He could feel the burn of her glare at a thousand yards out.

Vern followed the other two Firehawks in for a landing, Denise coming into focus as he approached. Jeans, T-shirt, and a canvas vest that had once been beige before it spent years being worn around broken helicopters. She wore a tool belt like an Old West gunslinger. Damn, she was gorgeous and cute at the same time. And about the most unapproachable woman he'd ever met.

A single drop of salty sweat dripped into his eye and stung. He sniffed the air again, no smell of fire other than the bit of wood char that you always picked up flying over a wildland fire.

A glance back as he hovered, spun into place, and set his bird down on the markers. Yep, still smoking black.

Denise was going to do more than kill him; that would be too kind.

She was going to outright annihilate him.

He hoped that she at least waited until after he was done landing before she did so.

"What did you do to my poor bird?" Denise Conroy heaved open the cargo bay door and spoke to Vern

Taylor's back in the pilot seat. She reached up and pulled down on the gust lock in the middle of the rear cabin's ceiling. It would keep the rotor blades from turning unexpectedly once she climbed atop the helicopter to check the engine.

"Broke it," was his sassy reply.

"I guessed that much. Confirm ignition key in the off position," she called out even though she could see forward between the seats to the center console that it already was. Outside the front windscreen she could see Mickey and Bruce pressing their faces up against the windscreen and making funny faces at Vern, blowing out their cheeks like puffer fish or three-year-olds.

"Confirm off and out." Vern pulled the key free and dropped it on the center console of radios that ran between the pilot and copilot's seats. Then he gave the finger to his juvenile buddies who laughed and moved on. She made a mental note to wash the outside of the pilot's side windscreen—while wearing gloves.

She stepped back outside, slid the big door shut with perhaps a bit more force than she should have, and climbed on top of the Firehawk helicopter using the notches built into the section of the helicopter's hull that had been covered by the door. Denise began peeling off the cowling of the number two turbine engine, being careful of the still blazing-hot exhaust; she could feel the radiant heat on her cheeks as soon as the sheet metal was shifted aside.

The stink of scorched, hi-temp phosphate hydraulic fluid made her glad for the slight breeze that was wafting it away. She pulled on goggles and neoprene gloves so that the acidic fluid wouldn't splash in her eyes or sting her hands.

The failure was instantly apparent from the spray pattern. The side of a hose had split and shot out a broad fan of pressurized fluid. Some of it puddled, some of it had struck the engine and been vaporized.

Vern finished filling out his log as if everything was absolutely normal before climbing down from his seat.

"You do know, Vern, busting a bird when you've had it less than two days really puts you on my bad list?" Denise jerked out a wrench to loosen the blown hose, but scattered several other tools as she did so in her nervousness. How had she even spoken that way to a pilot?

Vern didn't sound the least put out by her tone. "The few, the proud, the helitack firefighter pilots of MHA. We're all in the crapper with you, Wrench. How are we supposed to fly to fire without actually using your helicopters? That's the puzzle, isn't it?"

She shifted her scowl from the engine and aimed it down at him.

Vern leaned with his back against the pilot's door of the helicopter, staring off into the distance as if completely unconcerned about the midair breakdown and oblivious to her conflicted emotions.

It was her fault that the pilot had been placed in danger.

And Vern was teasing her about it. He was tall enough that the top of his head was almost close enough for her to swing down and rap it sharply with the wrench in her hand, which might cheer her up a bit. But he wasn't the problem, so she rammed the wrench back into her tool belt and knocked a few other tools loose that she had to retrieve from the helicopter's innards.

She really shouldn't be aiming her anger at him; it

was herself she was furious with. She'd sent a bird aloft that had broken in the sky. That was wholly unforgivable. Her pilots counted on her to provide safe, airworthy equipment and she'd failed them.

Firehawk Oh-Three had been in the Mount Hood Aviation inventory for less than a month and now it had blown a hydraulic line. Thankfully, Vern hadn't been in any danger from the failure—the backup system had taken the load. But she'd thought it was clean when she'd signed off the airworthiness certificate; something she'd done every day for a month.

It definitely wasn't clean at the moment. In addition to the blown hose itself, hydraulic leaks were messy and took time to clean up. Furthermore, the fluid that sprayed into the engine had caused the trail of acrid black smoke that had scared the daylights out of her. She'd had to wrap her arms around herself to hold herself together until Vern set the bird safely on the ground. The burn-off of fluid also added to the mess with sticky exhaust particulate sheathing the rear half of the pretty black-and-flame paint job.

"I can feel you aiming nasty thoughts down at me." Vern rubbed a hand on the top of his head as if it was getting hot. Then he turned to look up at her. His lean face was rich with a summer's tan. His mirrored shades hid the dark eyes that matched his hair she'd occasionally fantasized toying with in her more psychotic moments. "Anything I can do to help?"

"Not unless you're planning to break something else on my helicopter, Slick. Go away. You're distracting me." And he was. Denise had some principles and those included not getting sucked in by the charm of a handsome flyboy. The last time she had let that happen was…a long time ago, and it wouldn't be happening now.

"Yes, ma'am, Wrench, sir." Then he saluted, hitting his forehead hard enough to pretend knocking himself silly.

No matter *how* handsome and charming, she would *not* be tempted.

She raised the exact implement that had earned most mechanics the Wrench nickname, and he stumbled back, raising his hands in mock terror.

He pulled a black Mount Hood Aviation billed hat out of his back pocket and tugged it on before shooting her one of his cockeyed grins. The blazing red-and-orange MHA logo offered her a tempting target. Maybe if she had a tennis ball handy, she'd bean him one.

"Make me proud, Wrench."

"Fall down a gopher hole, Slick." Again? Had she really sassed a pilot? That wasn't anything the Denise she knew would ever do.

He tipped his hat and headed across the narrow grass airstrip of the Hoodie base camp. On his third step he stumbled badly, pretending to fall into a gopher hole.

Denise laughed. Of the many jokers among the crews, Vern was the only one who consistently made her want to laugh. Though not usually out loud.

She watched him walk off. Had she just been flirting with him? She'd never been any good at it, so she couldn't be sure. He didn't fly a Huey UH-1 "Slick" helicopter, but she liked how the nickname fit him. Nicknames were another thing she rarely used correctly. Yet another reason not to become involved with flyboys who seemed to live by them. For example, Mickey was usually…she couldn't even remember. Hopeless. Absolutely hopeless.

Pilots also had these unspoken rules and codes that the women they picked up in the bars seemed to already know. It was as if every one of them had gone to the same training course, but no one had told her she needed to enroll to understand men.

Denise understood none of them.

Once he was gone, she could relax a little. She sat back on her heels atop the helicopter. It was one of her favorite times of day and she took a moment to enjoy it.

Malcolm shot her a wave when he noticed her watching. He'd finished servicing one of the Twin Hueys and was moving to the other one. Brenna, her other assistant, was deep in an MD500 and didn't look up. No need to worry though. Brenna could handle almost anything on the smaller birds; she was good.

The sun was setting into the Oregon wilderness over the massive shoulder of the glacier-capped Mount Hood. You could practically taste the pine-sharp chlorophyll on the ice-clean air. The birds were coming home to roost, the seven helicopters and three airplanes of her firefighting fleet.

The flesh-and-blood birds were also dancing in the last of the sunlight as they headed into their own nests among the towering Douglas fir trees on the north side of the runway. And if even one of them pooped on her helicopters, there'd be hell to pay.

By U.S. Forest Service contract requirements, right on the stroke of a half hour before sunset, all of the aircraft were out of the air and lined up on the grass. For the next dozen hours, the crews still fighting the fire on the ground would be on their own.

Emily and Jeannie were certified for nighttime firefighting, but that was awfully expensive and wasn't called for except on the very worst of fires. Also, if they flew at night, they still needed the mandatory eight-hour break out of every twenty-four.

Better to let them sleep and fly again at a half hour past sunrise than miss part of the morning.

Jeannie climbed out of Firehawk Oh-Two and waved at Denise. She treated her helicopter with the most respect of all the pilots. Emily in Firehawk Oh-One was so skilled after ten years in the Army that, while she didn't baby the firefighting Black Hawk, she never stressed the bird.

They were home safe now.

The two small MD500s for hitting spot fires were parked at the west end of the runway. A pair of the mid-sized Twin-212 Huey choppers were lined up next, then her three Firehawks parked neatly down the side of the grass strip field at midfield directly opposite the main camp buildings. The seven choppers looked so pristine and glossy in their black-and-flame paint jobs. All glossy, that is, except Firehawk Oh-Three with a dark smudge down the tail section from the scorched hydraulic fluid.

She sighed; she really shouldn't have harassed Vern. It wasn't his fault the line had cracked and sprayed the compartment with slimy silicone-based goo. At least it hadn't been the old hydraulic oil. That stuff would have burned rather than merely scorching and caused a major mess, if not an engine fire.

Denise was through the repair in ten minutes, and

about halfway through the cleanup when the dinner bell rang. Her hands would reek of the cleaner for hours despite the gloves. She hoped it was a knife-and-fork dinner tonight.

Betsy the camp cook had brought the bell back with her from when they'd been fighting fire Down Under in Australia over the winter. The old brass twelve-inch fire truck bell announced the exact moment of sunset, spooking aloft the last of the birds who were just settling into the trees. You think they'd get used to it—Betsy rang her new toy every night at this time. It echoed from one end of the airstrip to the other calling the helitack and smokies to come eat.

From her high perch atop the Firehawk helicopter, Denise had a clear view of the whole field. Malcolm and Brenna downed tools and checklists from the nightly inspection they performed on each aircraft and began wandering across the grass strip toward the cluster of picnic tables. Mark Henderson's twin-engine Beech King Air, the Incident Commander Air's aircraft, had landed without her noticing and was parked down by the DC-3s used for transporting the smokejumpers when they were needed.

Actually, some part of her brain had noticed.

She could recall that the engines had sounded clean, nothing to trigger her internal alarms to hurry over to inspect them immediately. Mark's landing had been as immaculate as you'd expect from a long-term Army pilot. Like his wife Emily, he flew smooth and clean every minute of every day. So no other warnings arose in her head and she knew it would be a normal nightly inspection.

All routine.

That was good. That's what it was supposed to be when she wasn't creating a failure like Oh-Three.

She set up a pair of worklights so they'd be ready after dinner when it was dark. She laid her flask of cleaner and her gloves across exactly the spot she'd left off so she'd be sure to start in the right place after dinner.

Today's fire had been a grassland range fire seventy miles to the southwest. Only the helicopter crews had been out today to help the local ground crews who'd been able to drive trucks to the fire. The MHA smokejumpers had the day off, so a lot of them were in town and the tables were less full than usual.

Most of the pilots, support crew, and ground personnel were already sitting around, reading or playing cards held in place by small stones against the light evening breeze that wandered lazily through camp. Thankfully, that same breeze washed away the bitter smells of cleaners and the sharp kerosene of Jet A fuel the pumper truck had dispensed down the row.

As Denise headed for the chow line, Emily and Jeannie came up to her. They were out of flight gear and looked casually pretty. Someday she'd like to find the nerve to ask how they made it look so effortless.

Of course, MHA's first two Firehawk pilots wanted to know what had gone wrong with the third craft.

"Damn!" Mickey, Vern's bunkmate and one of the twin-Huey chopper pilots, let out a low whistle of appreciation. "I've got to say… Da-amn!"

Vern glared at his poker hand a moment longer,

puzzled because his own cards certainly weren't worth any such statement. He saw that Bruce and Gordon were both still in the game, so he folded and tossed his cards into the pile, careful not to drop one between the boards of the battered wood of the picnic table. Then he glanced up and offered a low appreciative whistle of his own.

"Da-amn is right."

Denise, flanked by Emily and Jeannie, was strolling across the green grass airfield in the light of the setting sun. The sky was orange behind them and the lights above the chow line illuminated them like a Maxfield Parrish painting—kind light and impossibly beautiful women who belonged exactly where they were.

The image did strange things to his heart as if it had caught and stumbled on something it had never seen before. Or perhaps seen but not noticed.

Maybe his pulse was still stutter-stepping from that pressure alarm.

Bruce and Gordon turned to look over their shoulders and didn't turn back too quickly. Bruce was a very careful card player, except when women were involved, or even in the general vicinity. Vern saw enough to be glad he'd folded.

"Every time," Mickey whispered. "Every single time they come walking toward you side by side like that it takes your breath away. It's like you never get used to it. If Carly joins them, I could die a happy man."

Vern hadn't actually been commenting on the group; it was the diminutive mechanic who he would never tire of watching. He idly wondered if she'd ever been a dancer, or if she'd always walked as if she was floating just above the earth.

The trio moved into the chow line. Except when it was raining, Betsy always set up a long table outside. MHA ate buffet style, but their cook made sure it was the best quality.

The three looked so earnest that his ears were buzzing. He'd make a totally safe bet that they were discussing the smoky failure of Firehawk Oh-Three. Three beautiful women talking about him, but not. Yeah, that sounded about right.

Then Carly came out the door of the kitchen and joined the others. Mickey was right, they really did take your breath away. That they were hanging together was a common enough phenomenon at camp, but you still never got used to it. The noise level among the guys' conversation fell off by half across the entire chow area.

Emily Beale, with her toddler daughter riding on her hip, was the commanding cool blond—more than a little terrifying in her quiet control, if the truth be told. Carly, MHA's fire behavior analyst, was as tall and slender; her Nordic-light hair and pale skin aglow like a shining flame—the woman was also seriously intense. Jeannie was a sharp contrast with her dark hair, black leather jacket, and black jeans. She was as splendidly figured as the first two women were trim, and yet was as casual and easygoing as the other two were completely daunting.

But it was Denise who was really knocking him back tonight.

She was always around—she'd been with MHA for the last eighteen months of his four years here, but it was as if he was seeing her for the first time. She stood shorter than the others, as wonderfully built as Jeannie, with dusty blond hair that fell well past her shoulders and offset the softest imaginable tan that came from immensely fair skin but living most of the summer out of doors.

"Yep." Mickey sighed. "Seeing that much female beauty in one place is a burden that a man has to bear if he works at MHA. Now that's a serious perk."

Vern nodded. It was. Three were married, and Denise presented a bastion of pure steel to repel all boarders, but they were amazing to look at. Far be it from him to deny himself the pleasure of enjoying what millennia of species-based conditioning had trained, nay, bred him to appreciate.

There was something about Denise though.

He squinted, the way his mother had taught him when she'd started studying painting—he hadn't. The four women in line to get their fried chicken and mashed potatoes—he could smell it from here and it was making him really hungry because Betsy made killer fried chicken—looked the same, but he could now see them a little differently.

MHA's chief pilot, Emily Beale, was actually the one with the spine of steel, her military training made every motion appear both effortless and meticulously planned. Carly was the driving force brilliant spark and Jeannie the soft, steady one flustered by nothing.

But green-eyed Denise eluded him. As if she had a cloak of invisibility over her character.

"I'm hungry." He started to get up, but Mickey pulled him back down. It was probably just as well. His knees felt no steadier than after the landing when he'd had to lean against the chopper to remain upright. He'd lost three buddies to a mechanical failure back when he was in the Guard. Thankfully he hadn't remembered it was five years ago today until after he was on the ground.

Denise had laughed at him as his knees almost gave out when he walked away—not a sound he was used to hearing from her. But it had sounded like a kindly laugh not a cruel one. He'd been kinda pissed, but he didn't think there was a cruel bone in the woman. Maybe he'd missed some joke.

"Gotta finish this hand." The other guys turned back to the game at Mickey's prompting, but Vern had already folded. There was no money on the table anyway; they had been just killing time until dinner, not getting serious about poker—the only bets were who was buying the first round next time they went to the Doghouse Inn.

So he stayed put but still watched Denise as she moved through the line. She'd exchanged her work vest for one of soft leather. He watched how the ends of her hair curled down the back of the dark leather, mirroring the curves of her splendid behind that invited a man to dream of…

He shook his head. Who in the world was he kidding?

Getting the hots for Denise Conroy was about as useless as getting the hots for some movie star on the big screen. Sure, a guy could lust after Zoe Saldana, but that didn't get him on the bridge of the *Enterprise*.

No way it was ever going to happen with Denise Conroy. To make it even more unlikely, she'd been dating some townie for almost a year, which struck him as pretty damn serious. And her attractiveness level was off the charts. Vern usually did pretty well, occasionally very well though those occasions always surprised him, but Denise was up at a whole other level of amazing.

Vern turned back to the game. "Come on, you losers. My stomach is grumbling."

Mickey flashed his cards at Vern. Vern slapped his roommate on the back in a friendly way. It was a good thing that they were only playing for drinks. No matter what last card was turned up, Bruce was about to kick Mickey's ass.

And, boy, did he ever, getting a three-drink raise before driving the hammer down.

Damning himself for a fool, Vern swung wide as he and the guys threaded their way toward the chow line. The others bucked their way in the straightest line, weaving and dodging among the tables, occasionally goosing somebody as he was about to take a drink. You could easily follow the wake of turbulence they left behind them as they went.

Vern followed the line of least resistance, walking outside the perimeter of the clustered tables. A flight path that just happened to pass close by where three of the four women had settled.

Carly and Denise sat with their backs to him. Denise was half a head shorter than Carly, even sitting down. But the way her hair caught the last light of day and shimmered with each tiny shift of body position was a siren call.

He might have crashed right up on those rocks if Jeannie hadn't been facing him from across their table. She watched him, puzzled for only a moment, then offered him a knowing smile.

Shit!

The woman was too smart for his own good. Well, hopefully she'd have the common decency to keep her mouth shut, or he really would be crashing on the rocks.

He cut farther to the outside to get clear. That had him passing close to Mark, Emily, and their daughter. Tonight their island nation was slightly isolated to one side from the rest of the group.

He passed behind them just as Emily spoke softly to her husband.

"Honduras?"

Vern suppressed a shiver across his shoulders and paused at their table. "Honduras? If you're thinking of a vacation now that the fire season is almost over, you can do way better than Honduras."

Emily closed a folder that was sitting on the table before they both turned to look at him.

"You know Honduras?"

"I do."

Tessa sat at the end of the table beside Emily beating on a small bite of chicken with the back of her spoon and the enthusiasm of a two-year-old.

He circled around and sat next to her, started the airplane game with a small french fry to get her to eat it while he spoke to her parents. She was a bright, shining girl who looked much like her mother.

"In 2009, I was serving on the Coast Guard cutter *Bertholf*. We were coming out of San Diego as the Honduras coup d'état of that year was kicking into full gear. Five months of political train wreck."

He managed to land the french fry which Tessa began cheerfully chewing away on. He selected a bit of beaten chicken for the next flight.

"The Navy felt that they didn't have enough assets in the area, so they called us. Full steam south, mine was one of the two MH-65C Dolphin helicopters they had on board. I had search and rescue gear, but they had an airborne use-of-force package ready for me. We were on constant patrols, stuck offshore from June through September. Back a year later for flood relief following Hurricane Paula. Honduras sucks. Highest murder rate in the world there just as a bonus. Try Belize or Costa Rica. Much friendlier."

The flight of the chicken was a crash and burn. As soon as the bit of food in question finally made a soft landing on the plate, it was beaten once more with a spoon to ensure its complete suppression.

After they chatted for a few minutes and another successful french fry, he headed to the line for his own meal. Glancing back at the table, he saw that Emily had managed to fly some chicken in safe, but her attention wasn't on the task.

She and Mark had reopened the folder and were both studying its contents.

It was full dark outside as Denise sat in the pilot's seat of Firehawk Oh-Three and cycled down the hydraulic pumps. Everything checked out. As long as she was here, she turned on the Health and Usage Monitoring System and checked the readouts.

The HUMS tracked most of the problems and worked as a fair predictive tool for maintenance. It didn't like surprises though and it took her a few minutes to convince the computer that the line failure had been fixed. It was quite certain that the pressure drop and subsequent return to normal was a problem rather than external service done by a human it knew nothing about.

Then it convinced itself that due to the pressure loss, the rotor was on the verge of imminent failure even though they were sitting on the ground and the engines were off. She didn't start the twin turbine engines or even let them have any fuel, but she started the Auxiliary Power Unit and let the APU in turn cycle the engines once. That cleared its miniscule computer brain. She shut down the power. The HUMS, well, hummed at her, happily green across the entire screen. She shut it down as well.

The large LCD screens across the control panel went dark, and now the only light was the soft glow beside the few mechanical instruments that were there in case the electronics were blown. Beyond the windshield, night had fallen. There were still a few lights over at tables across the runway and small groups gathered about them.

Denise threw the last switch, the lights died, and now she sat alone in the dar—

"How's it going?"

She yelped. She didn't mean to, but she did. A totally girly sound of surprise.

"Sorry, sorry." Though she couldn't see him, Vern's voice was right outside the open pilot's door, not more than a foot from her elbow. For an instant he rested a steadying hand on her arm.

"Vern, you jerk. First you break my new helicopter, then you sneak up to scare the daylights out of me? What's up with that?"

"Sorry." His deep voice did sound really contrite. He was long, lean, and had a voice to soothe wild animals. The man should not be allowed to run around loose.

"You owe me!" He did. A new heart. Because her present one was still cranking at liftoff speed and might yet fly away without her at any moment.

His silhouette crossed in front of the camp lights outside the windscreen as he did that lazy-mosey thing that pilots did so well and circled around the chopper's nose to the copilot's seat.

She didn't leave, didn't gather her tablet computer with its checklists. She simply waited until he'd climbed aboard beside her and leaned back against the seat. The seats were comfortable enough—they had to be for the pilots to fly the hours they did every day—but they weren't loungers. They kept the pilot upright and facing forward.

Vern somehow managed to lounge in the seat anyway.

She became intensely aware that she was in his normal seat. Her toes could barely reach the rudder pedals because they were set for his long legs. She'd need to raise the seat several inches for a clear view over the top of the T-shaped console. The base of the T started on the deck between their two seats. After curving up until it was above their knees, it then branched to either side at the height of a car's dashboard. His hands would rest right on the controls that—

Denise jerked her hands into her lap milliseconds before she rested her hands over where his would normally be.

"Like we're at a drive-in movie." A hint of reflected light showed the joystick was moving. Vern must be nudging the cyclic around with gentle taps of his fingertips. The one rising between her legs brushed the inside of her knee.

She didn't move, but she did shiver. Curiously, her nerves insisted it was a good shiver, one that warmed rather chilled her skin.

The two controls were linked together so that either pilot could fly the craft at any moment. It was as if he were somehow sitting on her side of the cockpit as well. If she reached out and touched the cyclic, she'd feel his small motions...which was way too personal.

"I'm not your girl." She'd never been to a drive-in movie. She hadn't been...wasn't the sort of girl that boys took to "the movies."

"Seem to have noticed you weren't." His tone had a definite *Du-uh* quality to it. "How's Jasper?"

"Okay," she guessed. The relationship had fizzled out and finally died a quiet death a month ago, but she hadn't told anyone. She didn't like failure in any form, not even when it was mutual. Subject change. "I'm really sorry. I should never have certified this chopper for flight without—"

"What did you find?" With a wave of his hand that she could barely see in the dim light coming through the windshield, he brushed her apology aside as if hadn't been her fault.

She reached into her work vest pocket and offered him the six-inch piece of offending hose line about as big around as her thumb. She braced her eyes for the shock of a cabin light, but instead he held it out before him. He was holding it so that the camp lights across the runway would glance along the surface.

"That doesn't look right."

"Duh!" She felt pretty good about the casual sound. It came out correctly instead of her normal too-awkward-to-live sound when she tried such things. "There's a split blown right through the sidewall."

"Not that, this." He didn't hand it back to her. Instead he leaned over until their shoulders were almost brushing and she could smell the soap he'd used to shower. He held the hose out in front of her and twisted it back and forth slowly. She had to shift her position to get the distant camp lights to shine along the surface. A millimeter more and they'd be rubbing shoulders. It was so tempting to let herself take some comfort in—

"What's that nick?" And how had she missed it and a pilot caught it?

"This bird used to be Army before we picked it up used and converted it, right?"

"Sure, though it was the Sikorsky factory that converted it for us." She winced and clamped her mouth shut to stop herself. She was always correcting people to get things exactly correct, which she'd been told very clearly was one of her less charming habits.

Denise was torn between studying the hose and considering whether or not to lean against Vern and feel human contact for even a moment. She didn't miss Jasper.

Not at all.

Which was information she'd only just processed at this moment—a feeling supported by the fact that she'd thought in the general terms of their relationship ending a month ago rather than the twenty-seven days that had actually passed. Or was it twenty-eight? While she might not miss him, she did long for the casual intimacy of being with someone. She'd liked the human contact while it lasted and missed it.

But this was Vern Taylor, the handsomest flyboy in MHA and one of her coworkers—an absolute recipe for disaster. Men like him didn't notice women like her when they could have any cute girl passing through Hood River, Oregon, to windsurf the Columbia Gorge. What was she thinking? He always hooked up with the tall, loud, flashy ones who laughed brightly and easily. And probably gave the same way.

Personally, she'd never found sex to be the least bit easy. Occasionally good, but it complicated all matters and everything connected with them.

Like easing right on the cyclic to tip the rotor swash plate, she pulled away from Vern enough to create a small distance between them. But she didn't shift so far that she couldn't still see the hose…or sense the warmth of his closeness on her cheek.

"This Black Hawk." Denise actually had to swallow to clear the lonely taste her thoughts had left in her throat, as if the emotion was a bad flavor. "It served with the 101st Airborne, the Screaming Eagles. Three tours, I think."

Jasper had always been on her about how precise she was about everything. Four miles, not three miles to the nearest restaurant—rounded up from 3.85. "Sixty-five degrees outside," not "in the sixties." "It's seven thirty-eight," when asked the time. She wasn't being fussy, it was simply how she thought about things. She'd slowly been forced to append "I think" or "about" or "somewhere around" into most of her conversations until she stuttered like a mistuned radial engine.

Well, she was done with that.

"Three tours." She repeated definitively, then added the beginning and ending dates of service because she knew the history of every one of her birds from the moment they flew off the assembly line and to hell with any man who didn't like it.

Except for Firehawk Oh-Two. Something very strange had happened to that helicopter last winter, but she'd never been able to uncover what. And when she'd pushed, she'd not only been stonewalled. She'd been told flat out that questions were unwelcome and were a job-level "didn't need to know." Finally, when she still didn't back down, a security-level risk.

With no explanation and a maintenance record that displayed odd discrepancies, she didn't trust the craft. Without telling anyone else why, she'd had her team help strip the bird down and put it back together, but it was as flawless as any aircraft she'd ever seen. It still wasn't the bird she'd sent to Australia last year to fight bushfires.

She wondered if Vern knew what had happened, but she'd guess not. He hadn't traveled with the two Firehawks when they'd split off from the rest of the MHA team to fight a different bushfire.

Vern didn't comment about her elaborate precision and total command of Firehawk Oh-Three's service record. Instead he was once more inspecting the hose in the distant camp lights. She no longer had any excuse to remain leaning so close, so she sat back in the pilot's seat but could now feel his shape in the shapeless pilot's seat. How pathetic was she?

"That's a bullet crease."

"It's what?" She rapped his ribs hard with her elbow as she leaned back over to see.

"Easy there, Wrench. You could hurt a fella. See?" He held it out again.

"You're right. It looks like it cut through the first layer or two of the hose. How did you know?"

"Flying Coast Guard isn't only about pulling idiot tourists out of riptides."

Coast Guard? How had she not known that about him? If he'd been one of her choppers, she would have.

Denise tried to see Vern more clearly. His dim silhouette looked the same. Mr. Casual and Easygoing as a former U.S. Coast Guard helicopter pilot was pretty hard to reconcile.

Though it did make a certain kind of sense. He'd certainly been steady as a rock while his chopper had been trailing smoke. The sideslip to check his smoke trail and then his straightening out without ever breaking formation spoke of lots of practice with emergency situations.

Maybe there was more to Vern Taylor than just some charming flyboy with nothing but sex on his mind.

About the Author

M.L. Buchman has over 30 novels in print. His military romantic suspense books have been named Barnes & Noble and NPR "Top 5 of the Year" and *Booklist* "Top 10 of the Year." In addition to romance, he also writes thrillers, fantasy, and science fiction.

In among his career as a corporate project manager he has rebuilt and single-handed a fifty-foot sailboat, both flown and jumped out of airplanes, designed and built two houses, and bicycled solo around the world. He is now making his living as a full-time writer on the Oregon Coast with his beloved wife. He is constantly amazed at what you can do with a degree in geophysics. You may keep up with his writing by subscribing to his newsletter at www.mlbuchman.com.